Que
of Se
Star

BOOKS BY ANNA MCKERROW

Daughter of Light and Shadows
Crow Moon
Red Witch
Wild Fire

Queen
of Sea and
Stars

ANNA McKERROW

bookouture

Published by Bookouture in 2019

An imprint of StoryFire Ltd.

Carmelite House
50 Victoria Embankment
London EC4Y 0DZ

www.bookouture.com

ISBN: 978-1-78681-814-0
eBook ISBN: 978-1-78681-813-3

Prologue

'So you see, Faye Morgan, you have nothing to bargain with, and I will not allow you to leave the land of Faerie. Unless…' the Faerie Queen Glitonea looked appraisingly at Faye and held out her hand. 'There might be something. But you will not like it.'

The man slumped in Faye's arms; faerie soldiers pounded towards them.

'If this is the only way, then I'll do what has to be done,' Faye answered grimly. 'Will you help us get home? If I agree to your bargain?'

'Of course.' Glitonea's smile twinkled brightly.

'What is it? What do you want in return?' Faye took Glitonea's hand, and the queen waved her other hand at the soldiers; they slowed as if they were running in syrup.

'Something you can make but I cannot. A child.'

Faye frowned in disbelief.

'What? No! That's… inhuman.'

Glitonea laughed.

'I am not human,' she agreed.

'Why… a child?' Faye stammered.

'I would have a *sidhe-leth* heir of my own. I have observed you; the power you hold from both realms. It is full of potential, but it needs teaching from birth. Lyr has his by-blows, and they give him power. I would have the same.' Glitonea regarded Faye impassively. 'Or, I can wave my hand and they will take you. And they will put you and your lover in the darkest place in this castle and leave you to rot there. It is your choice,' she smiled icily. 'And believe me, *sidhe-leth*, the dungeons here are very dark, and filled with horrors you cannot comprehend.'

'It's no choice!' Faye cried. 'Please don't ask this of me.'

'Another plea. You humans are full of wants, and yet when your pleas are answered, you do not like the solutions,' Glitonea snapped. 'You are human. You can have other babies; as many as you wish. You will not miss one. And I assure you that it will be well taken care of. It will live as a Prince or Princess of Murias.' There was no compassion in Glitonea's eyes; no understanding that a baby was anything other than a possession or a pet. 'Choose. Quickly.'

I managed to get Rav away from Finn, Faye reasoned, *so I can make this right, too. For now, this is what has to be done.*

'Then the bargain is struck,' the faerie queen smiled.

Chapter 1

His breath was hot on her neck, and her skin was electric against his. *Faye, sidhe-leth, bruadarach, neach-gaoil*; his words were honey, his lips velvet on hers. Her pleasure came in spirals of golden light, deepening to red in a soft throb between her legs. She wrapped her legs around him, pulling him in deeper. *Finn, Finn*; she called out his name, kissing the golden skin of his sun-warmed chest. *Please, more.*

He called her *sidhe-leth*: half-fae. It was an identity she was still coming to terms with.

His body was so familiar. It fit with hers so well that Faye felt he'd been made for her; his muscular arms and strong, rangy torso with its tattoo of a kelpie, a Scottish water-horse, that reared from his waist to his neck. Kelpies were creatures from myth, yet Faye had first-hand experience of them now: she'd learnt that the faerie realms were as real – and as dangerous – as the ecstasy she enjoyed when she was with Finn Beatha, Faerie King of Murias. She'd fallen in love with him, once, but it was over now. Or, so she thought...

Rav rolled over and draped his arm over her, waking her from her erotic dream; it was so sudden that she didn't know where she was for a moment. Being jolted back into the ordinary world was painful; her heart yearned for Finn, and her body demanded its satisfaction.

'You were calling out something. A name,' Rav murmured sleepily. Her boyfriend. Rav, who was honest and decent and who loved her. She sighed and turned towards him, stroking his body, not wanting her pleasure to end so abruptly.

'Mmmm,' he said, still mostly asleep.

'Rav. Wake up.' Faye's hand caressed him, lower, lower, until she reached his pyjama bottoms. His eyes flickered open a little. 'Make love to me,' she whispered, kissing him, the heat from Finn's kisses radiating through her body.

Still half-enmeshed in the dream, she'd forgotten the shadowy nature of her faerie king's love. Faye's waking self knew that Finn Beatha was an amoral, selfish being, concerned only with his own pleasure, but her unconscious nature remembered only the delicious pleasure he'd enchanted her with; a lassitude of erotic delight he cast over her like a silk robe. A thousand of his kisses on her skin wasn't enough.

Halfway between dream and reality, Faye's desire for Rav merged with her desire for Finn, but perhaps most of all, the desire to forget. Faye craved the lulling effect of being in the faerie kingdom of Murias; she wanted the abandonment of knowing nothing but desire and its satisfaction. She didn't want to have to struggle with the two sides of herself: half-faerie and half human, light and shadow. She'd tried, and failed, to reconcile one to the other. How much easier it would be to forget everything, and be only breath and pleasure, *now, now, now.*

She made Rav lie under her, and straddled him in the light of early morning which was beginning to cast twisted shadows in the bedroom. He moaned softly when she took him inside her, and began to move rhythmically, pursuing her climax. Rav reached for her breasts; she leaned forward. The spiralling pleasure that had begun in the dream returned, and the need for satisfaction roared in her body. She closed her eyes, and Finn's perfect face appeared before her eyes; when her hands stroked Rav's chest, it was Finn's toned, well-muscled flesh they remembered.

Her pleasure grew and grew, and the erotic dream of faerie returned. Faye remembered the silk dresses she wore there, cut to the waist, exposing her breasts; she remembered the feel of the material on her skin. And she remembered the night of the masked ball, when, delirious from the faerie food and wine and from the desire that flowed in her veins, she and Finn had made love in front of an audience of fae creatures. At the time, it had seemed as though their pleasure fed their audience, and vice-versa.

As Faye felt her climax come, she was only half in the ordinary world. Half of her was in Murias, making love to Finn, who could exploit every feeling of pleasure in her – with his breath, with his tongue, with his fingers and with the ardour that seemed never to come to an end.

As Rav started to cry out in pleasure, her orgasm rocked her.

Yet it was Finn Beatha she cried out for in her mind, and had to bite her lip to stop herself screaming for; it was for Finn that she ground her hips as she came, hard and deep and hot. It was her faerie lover that was with her, his hot mouth on hers. Rav was just a body, a substitute, in that moment.

'You have not forgotten me.' Finn was there, behind her eyes; perhaps she'd conjured him in her lovemaking. The faerie king had forbidden her from ever returning to Murias, the faerie realm of water, because of her betrayal; because she chose a human lover over him. And yet, he was here, wanting her.

'No,' she breathed; the sheets became his skin, smooth against hers. Falling deeper by the second, she buried her head in them, seeking Finn's perfect body; his smell, which was of the sea.

'You are mine,' he breathed, as she came to him in dream, and as she reached for his lips with hers like a thirsty traveller at a well. 'You are mine, *sidhe-leth*; our bond is too deep to be denied.'

Chapter 2

'I know it's not the same as the one you lost. But… I dunno. It's something to remember your mum by.'

Rav pushed the small black velvet box carefully across the luxurious damask tablecloth to where Faye Morgan sat opposite him. Golden autumn sun streamed through the tall windows in the hotel where they had come for afternoon tea, making the silverware sparkle and the gold at the edge of Faye's plate catch her eye.

'What is it?' She frowned curiously at him, putting down the delicate bone china cup half-full of Assam tea. Next to her, a three-tiered cake stand held delicate confections in a variety of luxurious flavours: violet cream, chocolate tuille, mini lemon meringue cheesecakes. Along one wall, a collection of gold-edged vintage mirrors reflected the room, and Faye in it. It made her slightly uncomfortable, catching her own eye as she talked to Rav, who had his back to them.

'Just a little something. For you.' Rav smiled over the rim of his teacup at her, his dark brown eyes warm with amusement, though shadows lurked under them: he looked tired. 'Go on, open it.' He was dressed smartly: a dark blue shirt and black tailored trousers; his shirt had gold cufflinks.

'You don't need to buy me presents. You've already been so generous.' They had still only known each other less than a year, so she didn't *think* this was a proposal, but it struck her suddenly that it could be. They were at the fanciest hotel in London, which Rav had suggested they come to, seemingly, on the spur of the moment as they were meandering around the nearby exclusive shops. When she was getting dressed in the morning, she'd gone to put on her old jeans and a comfortable t-shirt, but he'd suggested she wear the full-skirted floral dress she'd brought down to London with her from Abercolme.

How would she feel if there was an engagement ring inside? Faye opened the little box, her heart hammering a little.

Inside the box, there was a gold ring, but it wasn't a diamond solitaire. Faye felt immediately relieved and, then, immediately guilty for it. But it was way too soon. Not that she didn't adore Rav; she did. But, this early in their relationship, it would have been awkward for him to propose now. There was still so much they had to learn about each other.

She took out the ring. It was a gold pentagram set in a circle, similar to the silver one she used to wear, that belonged to her mother, Modron Morgan, though she was always Moddie to Faye and everyone else. But Faye had lost the ring.

'Oh, Rav. It's so beautiful,' Faye breathed and slipped it onto the ring finger of her right hand, where she'd worn Moddie's for the eight years after her death. The indentation of Moddie's ring was still there. The new band was thicker than the old one, and slightly smaller, so it pinched a little. 'Thank you.'

She didn't know what else to say; emotion choked her throat. She still missed her mother terribly; to lose Moddie when Faye was eighteen, when she still needed her so much, had been awfully hard. And though she was older now, Faye still felt the emptiness in her life where Moddie should be: someone to tell her stories about her childhood, to know Faye's oldest hurts, and be there to comfort them.

'I know how much you miss her. So I had it made for you. I hope it's okay that it's gold and not silver.' He frowned, seeming worried that she wouldn't like it. 'I don't want it to be wrong. I mean, I don't know if silver's supposed to be special for, you know, witchy stuff...' He trailed off, anxiously.

Faye felt the tears well up and wiped her eyes with the back of her hand: she didn't want to cry, especially in such a grand place. She missed Moddie, but had her best friend Annie, and now she had Rav. It was such a relief to be able to have someone else to trust. And she was beginning to trust him: slowly, daily, she let a little more of him into her heart.

She was a witch, from a family of witches, as long as anyone could remember. Perhaps that was the reason why she had made so few friends and, though she'd had a few one-night stands, had no boyfriends before Rav. She was forever an outsider, a woman of power who had, herself, always been afraid of it.

But the main reason was that she didn't trust anyone with her heart; her father had left her and Moddie when she was a baby, and Moddie had died. She'd lost Grandmother before Moddie, at whose knee she'd spent so many hours, listening to her tales of faeries and the old Scottish legends: of winter hag goddesses up in the snow-covered mountains and of selkie women who married human men but returned to the cold, clear ocean as seals. She was afraid of love; of loving someone that would leave her, yet again.

And, after the Faerie King Finn Beatha, she was afraid of loving the wrong man; someone who would take what he wanted without any care for her.

She thought she could trust Rav. Her head knew it, but her heart was taking its time to let him in.

Faye got up, walked around the table and gave him a hug and a kiss. 'I love this. It's so kind of you, Rav. And, no, it's really no problem that it's gold.' She laughed a little, making herself be jolly, banishing the sadness as she was so used to doing: away in a little box, to be ignored or looked at later when she was alone. 'Believe me, I don't have a problem with being given expensive jewellery. Moddie couldn't ever afford anything other than silver, that's all.' She laid her forehead on his and closed her eyes for a moment. 'Thank you.'

'You're welcome.' Rav looked pleased, and returned the hug.

Her head against his, Faye opened her eyes to her reflection in the mirrors opposite. Some had the silvered appearance of old mirrors that had, perhaps, hung in decadent ballrooms or the powder rooms of grand houses. For a sudden moment, eyes that weren't hers stared back at her, and she blinked; a shadow passed over the silvered glass, and a faint voice called her name. *Faye Morgan, sidhe-leth. Faye, Faye.*

It was nothing. A trick of the light, she told herself. *Your imagination.*

She didn't want the faeries here; she wanted nothing more to do with them. She'd left her shop, Mistress of Magic, and come to London to get away from the memories. *You can't haunt me here.* Faye closed her eyes and murmured a protection spell. She slipped her hand into her pocket and rubbed the small mirror which she'd inscribed with a banishing sigil. *Be gone, be gone,* she thought fiercely.

'You've really been spoiling me, since we got here.' Faye took her seat again, cleared her throat and took a scone from the bottom tray of the cake stand, spreading it with jam and thick clotted cream. 'I could eat cakes and tea for every meal, I think.' She made herself enjoy its soft creaminess, seeking the grounding comfort of food. She knew that eating and drinking was one of the best ways to protect yourself against magic; to remind yourself, and the spirits that might choose to plague you, that you were blood and bone, heavy, resistant to their touch.

There had been other dreams, not only of Finn. Nightmares in which faeries dandled a baby she knew was hers in front of her, refusing her clutching hands.

'If you want to come here every afternoon for cakes and tea, I'll leave them my credit card details.' Rav smiled. 'They could reserve the Faye Morgan table for you. Near to the window and within earshot of the piano, but not too close,'

Faye was staring at the mirrors and hadn't been listening. 'I'm sorry. What was that?' She made herself return to the room.

'I was saying, you can come here any time you like. Are you okay, Faye?' Rav's gaze flickered to the mirrors and back at her.

'Of course. I could be a lady who lunches. No. A lady who teas. It wouldn't be very healthy, though, would it?' She made herself sound chatty, smiled reassuringly at him. She didn't want him thinking she was mad, or that she was tortured with nightmares of making a bargain with the faeries. In the old folk tales, mothers left their ailing babies out for the faeries to take. Sometimes they would leave a fae child for the human mother to raise while they took the human child to live happily in the fae realm. It was an old exchange, fae for human, a symbol of the once-close relationship between the two realms. No-one believed in it any more, of course. But in her nightmares, faeries stole a child she didn't yet have.

'Or affordable,' Rav added. She knew Rav owned his own company, and he didn't seem to be short of cash, but she wasn't sure just how well off he was. Her eyes flickered to the mirrors opposite, but there was nothing there. *See, nothing but your imagination*, she reassured herself, although her instinct knew better.

'If you ran for the bus after, it'd probably burn off the calories,' Rav deadpanned, his eyes twinkling.

'I get to come to the most exclusive hotel in London for afternoon tea every day, but I have to take the bus home?' Faye pretended shock; she'd become adept in masking her emotions over the years, but, more to the point, she wasn't going to tell Rav about the shadow of apprehension in the pit of her stomach. They were having a lovely time together, and she wasn't going to spoil it. 'I'm appalled.'

'We've got to budget for this champagne lifestyle somehow, Miss Morgan.' Rav raised an eyebrow archly at her, and she giggled.

'But we're not drinking champagne,' she mock-protested, reaching for the delicate white and gold china teapot and tilting it to pour herself another cup, but nothing came out. 'Oh. I need a top-up.'

Rav nodded to a waiter, who approached their table with a pleasant smile.

'Yes, sir?'

'My beautiful companion has just reminded me that we should be enjoying some champagne with our cakes, if you wouldn't mind?' Rav took a wine list from the waiter, trailed his finger down it and pointed to one of the champagne names written in flowing script; Faye's eyes widened as the waiter nodded and went off with Rav's order.

'I didn't mean… I was joking, Rav. Tea's fine,' she whispered when the waiter had gone. 'This is already lovely. You don't have to—'

'I know I don't have to. I want to.' He winked at her as the waiter reappeared with the champagne bottle in a silver ice bucket and two crystal champagne glasses. They were the wide, saucer-like ones that made Faye think of the roaring twenties. Rav took the bottle from the waiter. 'I'll pour; thanks a lot.'

Rav handed her a glass and raised his to meet hers.

'To us,' he said, meeting her eyes across the table. 'To Faye Morgan, who has enchanted this lowly creature.'

'To us. You're not a lowly creature, silly.' She tapped his glass lightly with hers, and sipped her drink; the bubbles fizzed pleasantly on her tongue and against her nose. 'You're lovely.' She felt her cheeks flush a little. 'You're my...' she searched for a silly phrase like his, but couldn't think of one. 'You're my knight in shining armour,' she replied, shyly, but meaning it. It was corny, but it was true.

Rav seemed touched, but looked away, embarrassed.

'I'm not perfect by any stretch of the imagination, but thank you.' He gave her a rueful smile. 'I'll do my best to... err, you know. Ride horses and... fight stuff for you? Now that I'm saying it, I don't really know what knights do.' He tapped his finger on his chin.

'Hmmm. Save princesses? Wear uncomfortable armour?' Faye laughed. 'Those metal face-grilles on the helmets do look quite difficult. You know, for daily wear.'

'I've heard they're being re-engineered for today's knight on the go. Mesh face-grilles. Breathable fabrics,' Rav replied, poker-faced.

'Kind of sounds like a balaclava, if I'm being honest.' Faye giggled. 'Are you planning to rob a bank?'

'I might have to if this continues.' He gestured to the gold arches that supported the Renaissance-style friezed ceiling in the room set aside for afternoon tea; the pianist, sitting at the white piano in the corner, launching into *Moonlight Sonata*. 'I'm joking, I'm joking. It's fine.'

'We have been... I mean, we've been to some very expensive places since we've been in London.' Faye felt the champagne warm her. 'Are you sure it's okay?' She couldn't help making the comparison to being in the faerie kingdom, which, when she was there, felt exactly like this: slightly soporific, slightly fuzzy, in a pleasant languor. But this was the ordinary world; this was real, and she was here with Rav. *Perhaps the ordinary world can feel like the faerie when you know how*, she thought. Yet she averted her eyes from the mirrors opposite; she didn't want to see what waited for her in them. Instead, she focused on Rav.

'Of course it is. You're in *my* world now. Let's enjoy it.' Rav took her hand across the table, and Faye let the happiness of the moment overwhelm her.

*

Later, the dream came again. She was back in Abercolme on Black Sands Beach, and the Faerie Queen of Murias, Glitonea, was asking her something, over and over again. In one hand, the faerie queen held decapitated human heads by their hair. With the other, she reached out for Faye's belly: Faye, in the dream, realised she was pregnant, and the beach behind her was on fire.

Faye understood that the faerie queen was demanding a bargain. Life for life, a child to save many human lives. In the dream, Faye knew that this had already happened; she'd already pledged a child to Glitonea in a bargain to save the people of Abercolme from a fire. She'd had no choice; she'd hoped that, somehow, the faerie queen wouldn't come to claim what had been agreed.

In the dream, Faye fell to her knees at the edge of the tide. *Please, please don't take my baby*, she begged, but Glitonea picked up Faye's palm, forced the fingers open and handed Faye the bloodied, twisted hair of the dead.

Now I will have what is mine, she cried, and Faye woke, crying.

Chapter 3

'Cut!'

A woman in black dungarees with crimson red hair in plaits pinned to her head walked out from behind one of the tall TV cameras which were pointed at the set.

From where Faye was standing, the set looked shabby and obviously artificial. It was supposed to be a witches' shop, but nothing like hers. Her shop was the converted downstairs of her family home; its white walls were uneven and bumpy in the way that old Scottish stone houses were. It sat in an old terrace on what was now Abercolme's high street; Muriel's bakery and a small supermarket were among the few independent businesses left in the small coastal village; many had been closed, driven out of business by a long recession and the bad luck that had plagued Abercolme for decades.

Her mother, Modron Morgan, had opened the shop in the psychedelic 70s, when the world was experiencing a wave of interest in the unseen and unusual. Grandmother had disapproved, saying that magic should be private, that no good would come of sharing the things that had been family traditions for hundreds of years. But Moddie, like every Morgan before her, was stubborn and saw the way that the world was opening up.

Mistress of Magic was glass-fronted and cheery; Faye often garlanded the window with seasonal flowers and plants, celebrating the year as it passed along. Inside, the old hearth was still there, and customers liked to settle themselves in one of the two flowery easy chairs beside it to read or, often, have a cup of tea with Faye and have their cards read. Faye made and sold her own loose incense and magical tea blends, packaged in shining jars; she sold tarot cards and crystal wands, books, home-made candles and other witchy supplies to locals and tourists.

The set for the TV show that her best friend, Annie, had left Abercolme for – the one she'd begged Faye to come and visit – was nothing like that. The walls were painted black, and reversed silver pentagrams shone dully from nails. From behind the camera, where an assistant had told her to sit until they'd finished the day's filming, Faye could see that the pentagrams were quite light and blew around in the lightest breeze; she thought they were probably made from plastic tubing, painted dull silver.

The set featured a shop counter, rather more baroque than her own, atop which various human and animal skulls sat. Faye wondered if they were real or fake. Animal skulls were easy enough to find if you knew where to look, especially in the countryside, though London was far too noisy and overpopulated for the quiet ways of the land. Faye had a goat skull in the shop, on top of the mantelpiece over the hearth, which had been there since her grandmother's day and perhaps before. The Morgans – she, her mother Moddie and her grandmother – had called it *an Gobhar*, sea goat. It had the long horns of the goats that ranged freely on the rocky shores of Arran, and all of the Morgans had rubbed it on the nose for good luck at some point in their lives. When Faye was a child she'd asked Moddie *why do we have a goat's skull on the mantelpiece, none of my friends at school have one*, and Moddie had said *more fool them*.

There were shelves of books on the set, but their spines were painted with bright white and gold symbols in the way that no real books were – no doubt, to make them look like ancient grimoires and recognisable as 'black magic' to the TV audience.

Faye allowed herself a smile. Her grandmother's grimoire was a green leather-bound notebook, foxed and aged, full of Grandmother's faded, spidery writing. No upside-down pentagrams there; indeed, as well as old spells and Grandmother's record of the success or otherwise of her spellwork, there were jam recipes and snippets of village gossip.

Annie had called the week before and asked her to visit her on the set of *Coven of Love*. It would have been difficult if Faye was still living in Abercolme, a small village on the Fife coast in Scotland where they had both grown up, but Faye had made the decision to close up the shop and move down to London with Rav for a while.

To get away. To make a fresh start.

Life in Abercolme had been very quiet since the night of the concert where eight people had disappeared in mysterious circumstances; Faye's friend and employee Aisha among them. Faye had reopened the shop for a while after she and Rav had recovered from the whole experience, but without Annie for support, and having lost Aisha, it wasn't easy; some days it was hard to summon up the will to get out of bed at all.

Rav was selling the house in Abercolme he'd so recently bought, and one day, in her herb garden at the back of the house, he'd suggested moving away. For a while. Just a while, to get some perspective. To live a normal life together.

Could she be normal? A part of her craved it: the normal, everyday life other children had had. Cheese sandwiches, the crusts cut off. Parents that worked at the post office or the bank and didn't give tarot readings at night to the other villagers; she'd yearned, sometimes, for a family that no-one looked at twice in the street.

Waving at Annie, Faye's fingers played with the ring Rav had given her. She'd never told Rav about the rose gold and opal ring that Finn Beatha had used to transport her to and from the world of faerie. He knew that Finn and Faye had been lovers, but that Faye had been under a faerie enchantment. *That's over now*, he'd said, that day in the garden, helping her prune the rose bushes. *Now we can move on with our lives.*

Faye had smiled in acquiescence and pushed her doubts away. Rav was a good man; a man with an ordinary life who loved her.

Yes, she'd said to Rav. *Let's try normal.* She'd meant it. And they had laughed, because nothing between them had been normal until then.

While Faye was catching up with Annie, Rav was spending some time at the London office with his business partner. *It'll do us good to have a change of scene,* he'd said, and Faye rationalised that he was right, *of course* he was right. Abercolme had meant nothing but destruction for both of them. So she choked down the part of her that didn't want to leave; the part of her that wanted to return to the faerie realm, even though Finn had betrayed her, and despite the fact that he'd made it impossible for her to return. And she choked away the part of her that wasn't *normal*; she silenced the voice of the child of the witch family, the child who knew how to draw protection sigils and brew mugwort tea from her grandmother's recipe; who knew the plants to heal a burn and which berries were poisonous, and which weren't.

'Sweetheart! Ach Faye, I'm so glad to see yer face!' Annie ran to her, picked her up and twirled her around before Faye had the opportunity to react. Faye held on to Annie and hugged her tight. Annie had always been her best friend, since the first day of school when she'd taken Faye's hand unobtrusively and guided her away from Bel McDougall, who had pointed and yelled *she's a witch, she's a witch*. Faye remembered the hollowness in her stomach, the shock at being singled out for something about herself she'd never known was different.

She hadn't thought Moddie understood – Moddie, who had recruited villagers to join her coven, who had taken out an ad in the village newsletter at Samhain – what was now called Halloween – that said *Support Your Local Witches*. Moddie, who refused to tell her who her real father was, saying she preferred being a single mother. Her mother had said, about Bel and the others like her *ignore it, they don't understand; and we don't need their understanding, Faye, they need ours*. Moddie had expected Faye to be a fearless cat, ready with her claws, but it wasn't in her daughter's nature – and the Bel McDougalls of the world knew it.

Yet, after that first week at school, Bel hardly seemed to notice Faye; her eyes slid over Faye's auburn plaits and blue eyes, seeking fresh bait. Faye had thanked the stars for Annie, who never tired of hand-clapping games, gathering wildflowers for Faye's homemade press, and making up stories in the dark when she slept at Faye's house. Annie, who did voices and accents, making up songs and spells as she and Faye traced careful circles and stars in the wet sand at Black Sands Beach and wished for the things that small girls wish for – treasures, riches, and friends that last forever.

Moddie had died in her early forties when Faye was twenty-two. There was something typical about Moddie's early passing; she'd grabbed death as she'd taken life, with a sureness of touch born of impatience. She'd refused to believe that she could be at risk, and when death came, she swung herself into its saddle with a kind of relentlessness. Moddie had ignored what didn't suit her, and hissed and clawed at the things that wouldn't be silenced by her turned head.

A year or so after Moddie's death, Faye was defrosting the freezer in the back room; the room had once been used for laundry in the days of mangles, tin baths and scrubbing boards. At the back of one of the freezer drawers, she found ten scraps of paper, folded into small squares. Some of them only emerged when the last of the ice had melted and disintegrated almost immediately between her fingers.

But there were some she could save. Inside the ones that could be unfolded, names were written in Moddie's slanted handwriting. Some names she didn't recognise, or dimly remembered as being adults when she was young who had moved away now or passed away from old age. But there was one name that she knew: Bel McDougall. Moddie had written her full name and, underneath, a tiny command that made tears spring to Faye's eyes. *To stop picking on Faye.* Moddie's pen had underlined this multiple times before she'd folded the paper up tight and buried it at the bottom of the freezer.

All those years, Bel's name had sat frozen along with, Faye presumed, others who had tried to single out the Morgans or make their lives unpleasant. Moddie's freezer spells were a more modern magic than Grandmother's, Faye guessed, though perhaps in Grandmother's day the same could have been done by leaving the paper outside in the freezing Scottish winter. Whichever way, the slips of paper had worked. But, the wet paper disintegrating in her hands as she stood there, Faye had cried. Because Moddie was as afraid as everyone else, and she'd been afraid like everyone else when death came for her, too.

'You look well,' Faye commented with a smile. Annie was in costume for her character in the show. Faye knew Annie was playing a witch, but she couldn't help laughing at the very low cut black velvet dress Annie was wearing; it was so different to her usual fashion-forward, asymmetric block printed dresses, vintage jewellery and statement designer pieces. 'Though I see the costume department seems to be stuck in medieval times.' Faye was keeping things jolly, but she'd missed Annie so much – Annie was the only one that understood her.

'Aye, shut up. It's dramatic, innit?' Annie rolled her eyes. She'd grown out her short hair which Faye was accustomed to seeing blue, orange or black, and it was now shoulder length and coloured a luxurious blonde. 'I had to wear a wig until they could make ma hair sufficiently glam. Gimme another hug, then.'

Annie bear-hugged Faye; Faye fought back tears. She'd been so lost; Annie had left Abercolme to come to London to work on this show just before everything had happened: before her faerie lover, Finn Beatha, had enchanted a whole audience at the Midsummer music festival. Before Faye had had to rescue Rav from certain death there. She shivered and pushed the memory away. That wasn't for now.

It was the first time she'd seen Annie since then; they had spoken on the phone and written, and Annie had poured out the whole story to her friend. Faye felt relieved that she didn't have to tell her the whole, strange story now, in the middle of a TV set. *Sometimes truth is stranger than fiction,* she thought, her eyes resting on the Coven of Love set.

'Well, you look good, anyway. London's suiting you, *innit.*' Faye extricated herself from Annie's fierce embrace and repeated the London slang on purpose to cover her awkwardness. 'Are you still staying with your ex? What's her name again?'

A peachy flush spread to Annie's cheeks. 'Susie. Aye.' Annie evaded Faye's gaze.

'What's up with you?' Faye asked, bemusedly. 'Why are you blushing…?' She frowned. Annie was never shy about anything. Then it dawned on her.

'You're back together, aren't you? Susie, I remember her now. Susie! Your one great love. The one that got away. *That* Susie.'

'Aye, that Susie,' Annie said with a grin. 'She offered her spare room and I needed somewhere to stay without much warnin'. I wasnae intendin' for us to get back together, but I guess the spell worked after all,' she snapped her fingers. 'Soon as I arrived, we more or less fell into bed and it's been like that ever since.'

'You think it was the spell?' Faye had cast a spell in the shop with Annie and Aisha. It had brought her two lovers: Finn Beatha and Rav Malik. Finn Beatha was a faerie king, a fact that Faye couldn't exactly mention in casual conversation: *oh, my ex, yeah, he's the king of the faerie realm of water.* Annie and Rav were the only ones that knew, and Rav didn't want to talk about it. He had asked her what she thought she should tell his friends, his family, about what had happened in Abercolme, and Faye had said, *tell the truth. It's all you can do.* As far as she knew, he hadn't. He was frightened and she didn't blame him.

But when it came to the realm of faerie, the truth was slippery, and thinking of Finn was like trying to catch a dream between her fingers; she knew how he made her feel – how she still felt, when she dreamed of him – but it was confusing. And there were some things Faye hadn't told Rav: the bargain with Glitonea, Faerie Queen of Murias, for her as yet unconceived baby, remained her painful secret.

'Aye. Think aboot it. I asked for a girl just like Susie. Fact is, I probably had her in mind when I asked for someone.' Annie sighed happily. 'Not exactly surprisin' that she's ma model for all other women.'

'I guess not,' Faye grinned. 'I haven't seen Susie for years.'

'So how long're you down?' Annie guided Faye over to some folding chairs that were set out by a table. She took two bottles of water and handed Faye one. 'I've got cutaways to do and then that's it, I think. We can get some lunch in aboot an hour.'

'Sure, and don't know exactly. We're staying at Rav's flat, so we can stay as long as we like.' Faye toyed with the label on the bottle. 'It's good to get away, if I'm honest. From Abercolme,'

'I know, sweetheart,' Annie shook her head. 'I'm so sorry I wasnae there to help ye.'

'You can't always be there.' Faye smiled as Annie reached for her hand and squeezed it. 'It's all right. I'm all right, really.'

Annie frowned and took a swig of water.

'I'll be the judge o' that. And you look thin and pale, Faye. Whatever happened, ye aren't yeself still.'

Faye shrugged. 'Maybe not. But I'll get there.'

'Hmmmm,' Annie answered, still frowning.

The woman with the bright red hair and dungarees who had ended the scene when Faye walked in tapped Annie on the shoulder.

'Sorry to interrupt, but we're starting again in five,' she said before smiling at Faye. 'Hi, are you a friend of Annie's?'

'Keely, this is the friend I was telling ye aboot. With the shop in Abercolme,' Annie interjected. 'Faye Morgan, this is Keely Milligan, she's the director of the show.'

'Nice to meet you.' Faye shook Keely's hand.

'Ah! The witch!' Keely smiled, and Faye laughed.

'So I'm told,'

'Great. What d'you think of our set?'

Faye tried to think of something complimentary to say. 'It's very... atmospheric,' she managed.

'She's bein' tactful.' Annie laughed.

Faye nudged Annie and gave her a stare, but Keely smiled.

'Annie's told me all about you. She said you'd have some good ideas about how we could improve the show. Representation of modern witches, regalia, equipment, that kind of thing. I'm not convinced we're really getting it right yet.' Keely had a penetrating gaze, and she gave Faye a long, appraising look. 'Look at you, for instance. You look quite normal.'

'Thanks,' Faye was a little affronted, but Keely blundered on.

'No, you know, I mean… how would I know you were a witch, by looking at you? But then there are a few little touches, here and there.' She pointed to Faye's index finger where she wore Rav's golden pentagram ring. 'That ring. Understated but noticeable. And your hair, that's very Celtic and beautiful.'

Faye felt like a prize cow being assessed by a cattle auctioneer.

'Hmm,' she said, noncommittally.

'The point is, how do witches dress nowadays? What do they look like? I don't know,' Keely rattled on. 'We've had some bad press about the first series. I'm trying to give it a bit of a revamp but I need some subject specialists. Annie suggested you.'

'Well, I doubt many witches are going about their days in a velvet evening gown, for a start,' Faye said, politely. 'You can't assume witches look a particular way. It's like saying all vegetarians look the same. And many witches don't advertise what they do. In the past, it was dangerous to be one.'

Especially for some. Faye thought of her ancestor Grainne Morgan who had been tried as a witch by the Scottish inquisitors. Unlike many killed as witches, Grainne actually was a wise and magical woman; most were average villagers that had inspired jealousy or lust. Any perceived wrongdoing on the part of another villager – or even a cow with the pox – could merit an accusation of witchcraft.

Grainne had kept her head down and her magic a secret, but not secret enough; she'd done her job as village wise woman and helped her friends, and she'd paid for it with her life. The Morgan women had always been the healers and helpers in their community: women in stays and bare feet and cloaks, black and red and brown hair flowing free in the strong winds that gusted in off the grey-green seas of Abercolme, their toes in the wet sand. They had summoned the wind for sailors; healed cuts, eased morning sickness, mopped feverish brows, repaired marriages and protected children with hagstone charms hung on plaited string. And they had done it happily, and passed down the knowledge of the old ways to each other.

'I suppose,' Keely nodded. 'The thing is, it all has to look dramatic. It has to be romantic, sexy, magical. That's what people want. That's what they're tuning in for. I'd just like it to have some kind of... I don't know. A modern relevance, I suppose. Would you be able to help with that? Answer a few questions?'

'Sure.' Faye smiled. 'I can help,'

'Excellent! Okay, Annie, I'm going to need you in makeup, and then ready for cutaways please.' Keely shook Faye's hand and hustled Annie away, who mouthed *I won't be long* over her shoulder as Faye turned to the refreshment table to make a cup of tea. Early autumn sun slanted in a gold shaft through the long black curtains surrounding the set. Faye held her hand up to it, watching the dust in the air illuminated gold: it was a sudden seeing of tiny hidden elements of her world, like the old tales about putting faerie ointment on your eyelids that would allow you to see the fae. Yet Faye didn't need any ointment or special enchantment. She was half-fae and, before she was banned from returning to Murias, she'd begun to learn about the power she could command.

Yet the power of faerie was destructive as well as beautiful: it was shadow and light, one unable to exist without the other. Murias felt a long way away from London. Perhaps here, she and Rav could make a new life for a while, away from the temptation of Finn Beatha.

But the secret she held in her heart, like a grenade or a bomb that could blow at any time, tugged at her conscience. In the light of day, she could persuade herself she didn't believe she could be under this kind of curse, this strange bargain for a baby with a faerie queen. Standing in the queue at the supermarket, posting a letter in the postbox, walking the London streets hand in hand with Rav, it seemed ridiculous. But at night, when she woke mid-dream and the worlds of faerie hung close, she believed it and terror choked her.

Faye stepped away from the sunlight that sliced through the black curtains and poured hot water into a mug, taking a biscuit to go with it. As she sat in the shadow and watched Annie pose on her mark in various postures and reactions, she felt regret cover her, and wished she could be free of it all: to walk out of the cavernous studio and find her way back to Black Sands Beach; to feel her toes in the wet sand and the night breeze blow against her naked arms and legs.

Chapter 4

Faye woke up with a start and stared at the unfamiliar ceiling, panic in her throat like a caught bird. The dream laid heavy on her, hot, even though she lay half out of the covers and a cool breeze played on her bare skin. *Finn.* She'd dreamt of him again, as before: the same lovemaking, caught in a place between the ordinary and faerie world. In the dreams, she wanted him; but when she woke, the thought filled her with horror.

She breathed in deeply and scrunched the white sheet under her hands against her palms, to remind herself where she was; to pull herself back to reality. It was just a dream, and dreams could be banished.

She sat up in bed and looked around her, reminding herself where she was. Rav's flat, Rav's bedroom: plain white walls, a framed black and white poster of The Damned on one side and a psychedelic one, something from a 90s rave, on the other. A large window looked out onto a private garden, shared with the other regency houses that backed onto it; most, if not all, had been made into flats now, with high ceilings, the rose moulding light fittings and fireplaces preserved by most owners.

Rav's wardrobe was messy, half-full of partially folded t-shirts, shirts on hangers hung on the wooden doors and jeans in a pile on the floor. The bottle of champagne they had drunk in bed the night before sat on a chest of drawers on her side of the bed; on the day they'd arrived, he'd emptied the drawer out for Faye to use. She'd tried not to look too closely at whatever he'd kept there, though she was curious. She and Rav were still so new to each other. She'd realised as she watched him working on his laptop on the train from Edinburgh that she knew very little about him.

She turned onto her right side and nestled into Rav's shoulder.

Faye and Rav had arrived in London two weeks ago. The first day had been fine: the train from Edinburgh had been quiet, and they'd travelled first class. They'd taken a taxi to Rav's flat in West Hampstead and when they got there, had ordered a takeaway and gone straight to bed.

After settling in and airing out the flat, they'd spent a couple of days pottering around West Hampstead, which was its own little village, looking at the upmarket shops and stopping for coffee and cake. Faye felt a weight lift from her on the third night as she and Rav walked back from dinner at an intimate Italian restaurant; the street was quieter than she would ever have expected a London street to be. She looked up at the crescent moon in the clear London sky and thought, *here, I can rebuild who I am. Perhaps here I can be me again.*

'Penny for them.' Rav had squeezed her hand as they walked along; the street was deserted, and lit with old, ornate black iron lamp-posts. Their yellow light was soft and gave the street a nostalgic air: it could have been London a hundred years ago.

'Oh, nothing. I'm just enjoying the quiet. It's not as busy here as I expected,' she'd replied.

'I know. Desirable neighbourhood because of that, and the chi-chi high street. Not like where I grew up, it has to be said.' Rav hummed a tune under his breath.

'Where was that again? I knew it was London, but I don't think you ever said where.'

'Further out west, near Heathrow airport. This is considerably more refined, darling,' he mimicked an affected voice, with a smile.

'What was it like?' Faye pointed to a city fox padding across the road ahead of them. 'Look! A fox!' The shaggy animal slid into an alley, disappearing into shadow. Rav nodded.

'Oh god, so many foxes. They come for the rubbish. I see way more of them than rats, which I'm guessing is a good thing. Pigeons, obviously,' he counted the animals off on his fingers. 'Better class of pigeon this neck of the woods, too. None of those pathetic one-legged ones you see in the West End... feathers missing, one-eyed...' Rav stood on one leg and made a pathetic-sounding cooing sound. 'Vermin. I hate pigeons.'

'First, thanks for the pigeon impression. I mean, that was... remarkable,' Faye said with a giggle. 'Second, you were going to tell me what it was like. Growing up.'

Rav continued hopping around on one leg, cooing and pecking at her with his lips, like a beak.

'You really shouldn't have had that last glass of wine,' she laughed, shooing him away. 'Hey! No more pigeon. I'm serious.'

Rav gave a sad coo then said, 'Pigeon doesn't miss the aeroplanes going over. So loud.' He shrugged. 'It was all right. But, you know I had my anxiety a lot when I was younger. That kind of ruined my teen years.'

'I'm sorry.'

He shrugged again. 'Doc says I self-medicate with the demon drink. I stopped taking the antidepressants a few years back and now I probably drink too much to compensate, but hey. No-one's perfect.

Anyway, I work in music, right? Everyone drinks.' He rubbed his head; Faye knew he was still suffering from the headaches that had started when he'd been taken unwillingly to Murias.

Faye hadn't really noticed that he drank a lot, but they had been eating out a lot since they'd got to London, and they usually shared a bottle of wine when they did, and Rav would usually have some aperitif, or a brandy afterwards. It didn't seem like a lot, but it made her think again still how little she knew him. She resolved to keep an eye on it.

'But you know. I had Mum and Dad at home. It was all very suburban. Guess it wasn't quite the same for you, being the village witches and everything.' He was deflecting, but she understood. She often did the same.

'Aye. Mixed bag.' Faye wasn't sure how much he wanted to know. Did he want to hear that sometimes, after she'd been sent to bed, men and women from the village – people she saw every day, delivering milk, hanging out their washing – would come to the house, wanting miracles? Faye would kneel up on her bed, watching them walk up the path, their body language fearful – slumped shoulders, light steps, like unsure cats on a narrow ledge.

Then there would be the murmur of voices: sometimes crying. There was never laughter at these evening visits: as she got older, Faye supposed that whatever brought the village folk through the Morgans' door, it was seldom a laughing matter. Now, as the one that opened the door, she knew what people wanted from her: their prophetess, sibyl, seer, wise woman. Spells to heal an unrequited love, curses, protection spells. Divination for debt, for arguments, cures for families fractured by long-simmered hurts.

Rav looked at her keenly.

'You can tell me. Didn't you miss… having a dad around?' he prompted gently, but she didn't want to talk about Abercolme. She wanted to be silly, to be light, to be just another person that lived here in London. And she certainly didn't want to talk about her absent father: Lyr of Falias, a faerie king she'd grown up for most of her life believing was some hippie who had bailed on Moddie at the first sign of responsibility. It didn't make things any easier that now she knew who he was; he'd abandoned them, abandoned Faye. There would always be a father-shaped hole in her heart: she'd accepted it.

'I don't really want to talk about that. Do you mind? It's nice just… being.' She took his hand and squeezed it. 'I will talk about it, I promise. But it feels as though we've spent so long in my world – and with all the strangeness…' she trailed off, not wanting to broach the subject of faeries or Murias. Especially not with the dreams of Finn Beatha she kept having; she couldn't stop them, and didn't know who to ask for help. Worse, the dreams where Glitonea offered her the bloody, blue-lipped heads in return for a baby. She felt as if she was going mad.

'Sure. But you know I'm here to listen.' They stopped at the end of Rav's street, the old street lamp casting a milky glow around them, like a protective circle. Newer, harsh white streetlights hadn't made it to this part of London, and Faye liked its little vintage details: the cast iron railings and lamp-posts, the black and white street signs with the postcode in the corner: even the new but retro-designed sleek, curved-edged red double-decker buses were a novelty.

'I know,' she said, gazing up at him. Someone who had never lost a parent – never mind both of them – could never understand the feeling of (after Moddie's death) having lost your childhood, or the deep, enduring lack, the space of a father in Faye's psyche. When Moddie died, there was no-one left to say to Faye, *when you were a baby, you used to do this*, or *remember your first day at school?* Or *when you were born, this happened*. All that was gone forever.

But what had never been there at all was a raft of other memories: a father to read her bedtime stories, to carry her on his shoulders, to argue with her as the headstrong teenager she might have become if she wasn't so frightened of being herself. All those things: a lifetime of support, of love, was lost. Instead, there was a compressed shadow that had turned brittle as she'd got older: a crystal, a splintered charcoal that took up space in her heart.

Rav wrapped his arms around her and drew her in for a long kiss. He smelt of a woody aftershave, and the taste of the late coffee they'd had at the restaurant was still on his tongue.

'I love you,' he murmured, kissing her forehead where her auburn hair tangled against her milky white skin.

'I love you too,' she replied, closing her eyes.

'You taste of coffee,' Faye murmured against his lips, in-between kisses. She was determined to forget herself in Rav, and he seemed to feel the same. They were both bruised: perhaps they could heal each other.

'We'll be up all night,' he murmured back; she could feel his smile against her lips.

'Will we?' she teased, as he led her by the hand to his front door. 'You seem very sure.'

'Eternally hopeful,' he grinned as he unlocked it. They fell into the dark flat, giggling.

For a brief moment, before Rav flicked on the lights, Finn Beatha stood in the darkness: Faye knew his outline, knew his body so well. It was him, or a shadow of him. Grandmother would have called it a sending, a brief impression, like spectres that warned of accidents on lonely roads. For a moment, she felt gold chains on her wrists, linking her to Finn with a strange, otherworldly fascination. His voice murmured in her mind, *Faye, Faye, sidhe-leth, my love...*

Fear flooded her; instinctively, she shook her wrists as if to cast away the chains that chafed against her skin. She closed her eyes to deny the vision: the dreams were preoccupying her, and maybe she'd projected an image of Finn outside of herself for a moment. It was possible. *No!* she cried out in her mind. *Be gone. You're not welcome here.* Heart pounding, she opened her eyes as Rav turned on the light.

The switch banished the dark and Finn's image with it.

You mean nothing to me. There's nothing here for you. She wanted to speak aloud into the room, to banish Finn and make sure he was under no illusion that she wanted him.

There *was* nothing keeping Faye connected to him, except the line of desire that pulsed in her: a trail of fire that called out to him, and a call of desire that she knew he could hear. Waking, she wanted an end to whatever hold he had over her. But in her dreams, everything was different.

'Faye. You look like you've seen a ghost.' Rav laid a casual kiss on her cheek and threw his coat on the couch. 'I'm putting the kettle on,' he called over his shoulder as Faye stood in the lounge, arms across her chest in a protective gesture. As soon as Rav was safely into the kitchen, Faye traced out all protective symbols and sigils in the air that she could think of. *Leave us alone!* she hissed; the kettle boiling in the kitchen would mask her words for Rav's ears. *Leave us alone. This isn't fair. I don't want you.*

But she knew it wasn't enough.

Chapter 5

'Faye, this is everybody; everybody, meet Faye Morgan.'

The restaurant was crowded and noisy, and Faye could feel herself contract against its busy-ness; the jostling, shouting and laughing stabbed at her: a cloud of pins. She'd never loved crowds, being used to quiet, coastal Abercolme, where the soft song of the sea lulled her dreams.

Still, Rav held her hand and she squeezed his wide palm affectionately. These were his friends; London was his city, where he'd grown up and worked all his life. His music promotion company had expanded to have an Edinburgh office to run festivals and band tours in Scotland, but she could see from the way his face glowed that he was happy to be home.

And who could blame him? Faye waved a shy hello at the men and women clustered around the long table, drinking, talking and laughing. Yet Rav still wasn't back to his usual self. He had refused to go to hospital after she'd rescued him from Murias, even though Faye had insisted that he should. The headaches had lessened, but she knew he still suffered from them, and the whole episode hadn't exactly helped his anxiety. Despite his obvious happiness at having Faye in London, she could detect some of the frayed seams under the smooth image he liked to present.

She was half-faerie; she could travel between the two realms. Even having a faerie king father and a human mother meant that when she'd been in Murias for long periods of time, she still needed to return to the ordinary world to eat and drink real food. Faerie food and drink didn't sustain her in the same way, though it filled her with magic, and every cup of the strange, herbal tasting, jewel-coloured wine made her forget a little more of the human world.

But Rav had been weakened by his short stay in faerie, violently abducted there by Finn Beatha, Faye's jealous faerie lover. Faye still had nightmares about the emaciated bodies that the faerie dancers trampled on in the castle of Murias. It was a slow, horrible death. Faye had managed to rescue Rav, but he had deep wounds that took months to heal.

Normal, she reminded herself as she smiled around her. Remember, this is *normal* life. *These people don't know anything about deadly faerie dances and wild kelpies.* As far as she knew, Rav hadn't told them the real story. And he certainly wouldn't want them to know about the bargain she'd made to save him and the others. She owed the faerie realm for his life, but it was her burden to carry, alone.

Rav introduced her to the people sitting around them: his tall, bearded business partner Roni and his wife, Sumi; a man with round John Lennon glasses and untidy blond hair, wearing a faded music t-shirt and a torn cardigan, called Jeremy, and next to him, a finely-featured woman with blonde hair to her waist dressed entirely in black, who Rav introduced as Mallory.

'It's so great to meet you, finally! I've heard such a lot about you!' Sumi grabbed Faye's hand across the table. She was deliciously full-figured, and her dress, a wrap-over in a green and blue palm leaf print against a pink background, caressed her curves. 'I'm so glad Rav's found someone. He's a workaholic. He needs a woman in his life.' Her smile was infectious and warm, and Faye liked her immediately.

'I'm glad I found him,' Faye said, smiling.

'So, tell us about this amazing shop of yours! Rav told us – and, by us, I mean he told Roni, and Roni told me.' She smiled affectionately at her husband, a tall, portly black man with a beard who was laughing with Rav. 'He told us you're a witch! And your place, it's been in the family for generations, I think?'

The table quieted and turned to stare at her; Faye would have preferred the noise to everyone looking at her.

'That's right. My shop's called Mistress of Magic. I sell candles, herb incense, crystals, tarot, books. That kind of thing,'

'Cool.' Jeremy, opposite her, raised his eyebrow. 'I do a bit of tarot myself sometimes,'

'Jer! You do not. You did it for me once and you just looked everything up in that book,' Sumi scoffed affectionately.

'Whatever. It takes practice,' he shrugged. 'I was going to do a course.'

'You should. There's bound to be some good teachers in London.' Faye nodded. 'I've taught people. It's not hard, really – it's a combination of practice, imagination – and some reading the book, too,' she concluded with a smile.

'Ooooh, teach me!' Sumi's eyes were wide. 'I'd LOVE that.'

'Sure, any time,' Faye laughed. She was increasingly aware that the woman dressed all in black to her right, who had smiled narrowly when they were introduced, was sitting silently, listening. 'What about you, Mallory? Ever had your cards read?' she asked the girl.

'A few times.' Mallory studied her nails critically and gave Faye a disinterested smile. 'I know someone who's really gifted. He's been reading for me for years, on and off.' The implication in Mallory's voice was that Faye was no comparison to Mallory's expert friend.

'Oh. That's... great,' Faye replied, not sure how to talk to this woman, who so obviously didn't want to talk to her. Mallory gave a tiny, brief upturn of her lips and turned away to talk to the person on her right. Sumi caught Faye's confused expression and leaned over the table.

'Don't worry about Mallory. She takes a while to open up, but she's a sweet girl really,' Sumi said in a low voice, just loud enough for Faye to catch over the talking and clinking of glasses. 'It took me three years to actually engage her in conversation. And that's me. I'd make a wall talk to me, right?! You'll get there.' Sumi gave a slight eyeroll, and Faye grinned, relieved it wasn't something she'd inadvertently said or done. 'Anyway. She's probably feeling a bit strange, given the situation...'

Faye leaned closer over the table.

'What situation?'

'Oh.' Sumi sat back in her chair and looked guilty for a minute. 'I thought he'd have told you.'

'Who would have told me what?' Faye felt a spectre of unease settle on her; among the revelry, she felt suddenly isolated once again. Rav reached for her hand, as if picking up on her body language, but he didn't stop talking to Roni.

Sumi got up and came round to Faye's side of the table and crouched down beside her chair.

'Mallory's Rav's ex,' Sumi whispered in Faye's ear. 'They split up about a year ago. Amicable. They started going out in university, same time we met.' She nodded to Roni.

'Who ended it?' Faye whispered, turning away from Mallory's back; she was talking to whoever it was on her other side, a black woman with pink and purple braids interspersed with her natural colour ones. Faye didn't think she could hear, but she wanted to be sure.

'Rav,' Sumi replied, looking at Faye speculatively. She held out her hand and said, louder, 'Come on, I'll show you where the ladies' is.'

Faye took Sumi's hand – she got the impression that people didn't often refuse Sumi – and followed her through the closely-packed black-lacquered tables in the restaurant. It was a purposefully debauched-looking place with cerise and black leather easy chairs, huge vases of exotic flower arrangements against luxurious gold wallpaper splashed with large roses, lilies and orchids in full bloom. Contrasted to the lavish, decadent décor, the menu was mostly vegan, and contained dishes with ingredients – oils, seeds, pastes – she'd never heard of.

The bathroom was plastered with 50s style magazine covers featuring women with rolled fringes and red lipstick. Round and square, ornate gilt mirrors reflected the sparkles from the black quartz sinks which contained slivers of gold.

'So. Look, I didn't want to talk about it in there, when she's right there. To save both of your feelings.' Sumi turned on a golden tap and ran her hands under the water.

'Okay.' Faye stared at her own face in the mirror. She looked pale and withdrawn.

'I think Rav's over her. He ended it, anyway. He told Roni they'd grown apart. I mean, that's only natural. When you get together at that age – you know, nineteen, twenty – you're not that likely to stay together. Roni and I have, but that's because, y'know, we're both terrified of change.' Sumi laughed merrily at her own joke.

Faye smiled. 'I'm sure it's more than that,' she said, generously, but her heart was pounding. That Rav was still friends with his beautiful ex-girlfriend wasn't exactly news that she was sure their new, vulnerable relationship could take.

Sumi wiped her hands with a thick white towel from a pile in the centre of a black quartz topped table and threw it into a wicker basket.

'Well, I love Roni. There's that. And he loves me. I think. Anyway. Not the point.' Sumi pumped some floral scented hand cream onto one palm and started rubbing it into her hands. 'Point is, I wanted to talk to you about what's going on with Rav. I mean, he gave us some kind of cock and bull story about you taking all these drugs together and *visiting fairyland*, when he was up in Scotland? And that's why he's like he is – I mean, he looks terrible. He's lost weight, he doesn't look like he's sleeping. Roni says he's drinking more than he usually would, and he seems edgy. I mean, I wanted to meet you... see if you were some kind of junkie he'd picked up with, you know, some weirdo. But now I see that you're...' Sumi trailed off.

'Normal?' Faye interjected.

'Well... yes, to be honest. You seem like a nice, normal girl. So, help me out here. I don't get what's going on. He wouldn't go on some drugs bender, and neither would you. I can tell. And I'm really worried about Rav. He's an old and very dear friend of both of ours.'

Sumi shook her head concernedly. 'I dunno... maybe he needs to see a psychiatrist? He's always had anxiety issues, but this seems different.' Sumi searched Faye's eyes; Faye considered lying. Considered agreeing that, yes, they'd taken drugs and had a consensual hallucination that Rav was abducted to Murias. That they'd been high as kites, and Rav was experiencing psychological trauma because of it...

Faye didn't know Sumi, but she wanted Sumi to like her. She wanted to fit into this loud, fashionable crowd that Rav was a part of. And she knew instinctively that while her witchiness gave her some novelty appeal, too much of it would make her strange. She remembered Bel McDougall shouting *she's a witch, she's a witch*, pointing, laughing; she wished Annie was with her.

But the desire to fit in wasn't as strong as the new power she was still coming to terms with; the new fae power that coursed in her veins, black and gold as the stone she trailed her fingertips across as she listened to Sumi.

'He might need counselling, you're right. But it did really happen – the fairyland thing. We weren't on drugs. I've never taken anything stronger than a glass of whisky,' she said, thinking, *unless you count faerie wine, which is a whole other thing*. 'I know it's hard to understand. But… Abercolme, where I'm from… we have a… close relationship to the old ways there. The realm of faerie is very close.'

Sumi frowned at her. Clearly, she'd been expecting Faye to be an ally in helping Rav with what she perceived as his delusional state.

'I don't understand. The realm of faerie. It's not real. I mean, outside books and songs and stuff. You can't just walk into it.'

'No, you can,' Faye insisted. 'I've been there many times. And Rav was taken there. I promise you that's what happened. But, yes, it's hard to explain to people that have a… more conventional world view, let's say.'

Sumi looked away and Faye felt the warm rapport that had extended between them loosen and cool.

'Well, maybe we'll have to agree to disagree,' Sumi said, carefully. 'Most importantly, we need to make sure Rav's getting the help he needs. Will you talk to him about seeing a therapist? He always used to go, but he stopped a few years ago. Roni says he stopped taking the meds too. To be honest, with all the stress of the business, I'm not surprised this happened. He had some kind of nervous breakdown.

Maybe the both of you did. It happens.' Sumi's expression was neutral; her previous friendliness was muted.

'But…' Faye trailed off, not knowing what to say. 'I'm not lying, okay?'

'I'm sure you believe you're telling the truth.' Sumi was trying to be kind, but she couldn't look Faye in the eye. 'But, please. For Rav's sake, don't encourage this fantasy. And we'd really appreciate it if you could help us talk him into seeing someone. You might need to, as well.'

Faye looked away. 'I care about him, you know.' Her voice was small; Sumi had prodded the guilt that lay close under Faye's surface. It was her fault, all of it: Rav was suffering because of her. *But you saved him too, don't forget that*, she reminded herself, and stood a little taller. *Sumi doesn't understand. Like Grandmother said, don't blame them because they don't know.*

'Of course I'll talk to him. About therapy. But you should know him well enough that you understand you can't make him do anything he doesn't want to do,' Faye added, meeting Sumi's eyes defiantly. Sumi was being a concerned friend, but Faye wouldn't say she was lying just to smooth things over between them or to assuage Sumi's ignorance on the matter.

'I know.' Sumi nodded. There was an uncomfortable silence. 'Well, we better get back, they'll wonder what happened to us.' Sumi fluffed her hair briefly in the long mirror and pushed the long, mirrored door. Faye followed her out of the bathroom with disappointment uncurling in her belly. A normal life seemed to elude her wherever she went.

When she got back to the table, Mallory was sitting in her seat, talking animatedly to Rav and Roni. Rav smiled affectionately at Faye when he saw her, and stood up to give her his seat.

'Faye, have you met Mallory?' Rav stood behind them both, like a matchmaker determined they would be friends.

'Oh, yes, Faye was just telling us all about her shop. It sounds amazing!' Mallory smiled a dazzling smile at Faye. Perhaps she'd read Mallory all wrong initially; there were all kinds of reasons why someone could be frosty on a first introduction. Faye knew that she wasn't always the most approachable person herself; and Sumi had explained that Mallory was difficult to get to know. Shy people could be like that.

So Faye returned the warm smile, which belied the tension that remained after her conversation with Sumi.

'You should come and visit sometime. I'd love to show you around,' she offered, and Mallory smiled glossily, running a black-fingernailed hand through her fringe.

'How lovely that would be,' she replied, though Faye noted that Mallory was looking up at Rav and not her when she replied. Still, Rav was the person Mallory knew best; people did that kind of thing when they weren't sure of others. Faye had trained herself to talk to strangers because of the shop, but everyone was different.

Perhaps Mallory stayed in a comfortable friend group because she didn't like meeting new people. Faye knew she couldn't judge anyone for any of those things; she'd only ever really had one close friend: Annie. Anyway, she was more upset about her conversation with Sumi than about Rav's ex-girlfriend. Was that how they all saw her? Some crazy woman who had encouraged Rav to have mad fantasies? Or, worse, who had turned him into some kind of drug addict? Faye scanned the faces of the group around her; no-one met her eyes. *You don't know what I did for him. What I sacrificed. What I risked*, she thought, angrily, but of course they would never understand. *You'd never have even known where he was, much less rescue him*, she fumed.

Rav topped up Mallory's wine glass and peered at the empty bottle.

'I'll get a new one when I go past the bar. Got to pop out for a minute and make a call.' He placed a kiss on Faye's forehead. 'Back in a minute.'

'Okay.' Faye didn't want him to go: he was her one island of safety. At least she and Mallory had broken the ice. Yet as soon as Rav was out of sight, Mallory gave Faye that same thin-lipped smile and turned her back again, leaving Faye with no-one to talk to.

The anxiety Faye had been fighting off since she followed Rav into the restaurant flooded back. She was worried about what Sumi and the rest thought of her, but there was an added environmental pressure: London sat outside the bar like a malign dog, growling at the door. Tonight, the clamour of the city felt oppressive.

This was the first night she'd come into the busier part of the city. It was a Friday night; the pavements teemed with people, and Faye found that, in places, she had to step into the road to get around them. The traffic was heavy and the air was full of food smells, underlying which was a grittier, smokier presence she was unused to. It put her on edge. She jumped when people nudged her, brushed past her or hurtled by unexpectedly.

Since being in the realm of faerie, she'd noticed something different about the way she related to the human world around her. She'd always felt connected to the natural world, and felt dissonant and lost if she didn't go outside every day, feel the earth under her feet and the air on her skin. But, after those first few times being in Murias, Faye felt more deeply connected to the trees, the grass and the sky, as if threads made of each element brushed her skin and tangled in her hair, held her, whispering their magic.

Coming out of the tube and into this chaos was more than dissonance: even in Hampstead she'd been able to feel some kind of connection to the natural world, but here, there was nothing. Faye felt turned upside down, as if all her usual compass points were missing. She was adrift. And being inside the bar, being ignored, made it worse. She felt panic rise up in her throat like acid and knew she had to get out of there.

She was angry now, too: furious that these trendy intellectuals dismissed her magic so quickly. To them, her witch shop and talk of tarot was an entertaining novelty, but they weren't able to understand anything deeper. They didn't have the language, the frame of reference, so they rejected her.

Faye got up, grabbed her coat from the back of the chair and made her way towards the exit, pushing past people queueing to be served by the glamorous bar staff. Outside, she gulped in the air, desperate for peace, but the air was grey and full of the heavy smell of fatty food. No, London wasn't a dog: it was something else, a fogged dragon, a thick cacophonous mire of other people's thoughts and energies that caught at her clothes, at her hair. That snaked through wet, echoing alleys and hazed the stars from the night sky with its orange breath.

'Hey. Faye! What's wrong?' Rav was on his phone, standing outside, but held out his hand for her. She knew she must look wild, like a cornered animal, because that was how she felt.

'Nothing. I… didn't feel well. Inside. I needed some air.' She tried breathing it in again and coughed.

'Not much air to be had out here. It's no Abercolme.' A haunted look flitted across Rav's face momentarily, then was gone; Sumi and the rest of them had seen this same look. Had seen the dark circles under his eyes.

'It isn't.' She wondered whether to tell him what Sumi had asked her. Whether to ask him if he wanted her to lie; to say that Murias had been a dream, a fantasy, a mutual high. Would that make it easier for him to recover?

Her instinct was to tell the truth: in that moment, she also wanted to tell Rav about the promise she'd made, to give a human baby – her future child, perhaps their future child together – to Glitonea, the faerie queen.

She wanted to go back into the bar with him, hand in hand, and tell his friends exactly what had happened in Abercolme. About Murias; tell them categorically, explain in detail once and for all what was real and what wasn't. Faye yearned for the release of that pressure; she didn't want to be the only one that knew what she knew any more. But she'd told the truth to Sumi, and Sumi hadn't believed her.

And Rav *would* believe her about the baby, because he had been in faerie and he knew the bargains they demanded; but he wouldn't want to hear it. And she was afraid he'd hate her for the choice she'd had to make to save him.

London was a beautiful city; its people were intelligent, cultured, varied and full of wisdom and wonder. But London had, for the most part, forgotten magic; it was too far from the remote places where it could still happen. The dragon was a forgetfulness. It was a confusion, a blanketing of disbelief, that Faye felt was hostile to her. She didn't belong here.

'Sorry it's so loud in there. Is it too much?' Rav was solicitous, as always. He frowned at her expression, which must have belied her anger and frustration. 'We can go somewhere else, or go home if you're not having a good time.'

'No, it's all right,' she lied, saving his feelings. 'I just… needed a moment, I suppose.'

'I wanted you to meet my friends. People from the business. So you could… I dunno. Know something else about me that wasn't being abducted by a jealous faerie king. You know? Although that is a pretty standard relationship milestone, obviously.' He half-smiled, looking away shyly. 'There's still so much we don't know about each other, Faye. I know I love you, but… dunno. You're a pretty closed book at times.'

'I know,' she said, feeling guilty.

'I know we need to talk more about… what happened. I know. But I'm not ready, okay? I'll tell you when I am. But I'm only just back on my feet, and…' he trailed off, closing his eyes and rubbing his forehead with his thumb and forefinger. 'God. I can't get rid of these bloody headaches, either,' he sighed.

'I don't expect you to talk about it until you're ready. I know how weird and scary it was, and I can only imagine…' She saw in his eyes that even this was too much for him, and so she trailed off and looked away at the bustling street. She knew he needed to heal. And, yet, there was a question in her mind that she didn't want to ask, and felt sure that she didn't want to hear the answer, so she pushed it away. What if Rav *never* wanted to talk about being kidnapped by Finn?

'Your friends think I'm lying. About Murias. They're worried about you. They think we're either both mad or we spent months high as kites together,' Faye blurted out. Perhaps she shouldn't betray Sumi's confidence, but the injustice of her accusations stung.

Rav looked away. 'I don't blame them. The more time I'm away from Abercolme, the more I wonder if I dreamt it all.'

'But you didn't dream it, Rav. You know you didn't, right?' Faye was aghast. What if, over time, Rav made himself forget that it had ever happened – or, pushed it so far down inside himself that it would be hidden, repressed, avoided – for the rest of his life? People performed conscious acts of forgetting for easier things. Could she live a life with someone who refused to acknowledge that trauma, which would also mean refusing to acknowledge a vital part of her, her faerie self? She'd run away to forget. That was true. But Faye knew in her heart that she couldn't deny that part of herself forever. Moreover, she didn't want to.

He smiled, but it didn't reach his eyes.

'I know. I know, okay? But... I don't want to talk about it. It's not the time.'

'Okay.'

There was an uncomfortable silence. Faye knew that she could never tell him about the baby. *Perhaps it will be all right. Perhaps it won't ever happen, it's a nightmare, a hallucination.* She tried desperately to reconcile it all in her mind, but she knew she was lying to herself. It had happened. She'd made the bargain. And she could never tell him.

'D'you want to go back in?' He reached for her hand. 'Promise I won't leave you alone with them again. They're a tough crowd, I guess, when you don't know them.' He smiled ruefully.

'You need to talk to them. To Sumi. Try and make her understand I'm not some kind of monster,' Faye insisted. 'Please, Rav. For me?'

'I'll talk to them. But not right now, okay?'

'Fine.'

Faye didn't want to go back in, but she acquiesced. Perhaps *normal* required a sacrifice. Especially from a witch.

She followed him back into the bar and let its darkness and chaos swallow her up.

She smiled, but it was a mask, and they both knew it.

Chapter 6

'What a bitch.' Annie poured a whole bottle of red wine into three enormous glasses and handed one to Susie and one to Faye.

'Which one?' Faye rolled her eyes and took her glass.

'Yeah, well. The friend, I guess ye could say she was only lookin' out for Rav. But the ex-girlfriend? She's obviously jealous. Probably still has feelings for the guy, the *sleekit* hussy,' Annie added before taking a large gulp.

'You've got to wait for it to breathe, you heathen.' Susie laughed and swirled her wine around her glass. 'Just as well I bought these big ones before you moved in,' she said, raising her eyebrow at Faye. 'You've probably gone teetotal without this one around, I expect,' she added, smiling. 'It's so good to see you again, Faye. It's been forever.'

'You too. I'm so glad you two found each other again. She never stopped going on about you, Susie.' Faye clinked her glass against theirs. 'To old friends and new love.'

An evening in Annie and Susie's quietly luxurious, comfortable flat was just the respite Faye needed after last week's night out with Rav's friends. They'd stayed out much later than she expected, going to another late bar and then out for food into the early hours. For the whole night, Faye had felt the foggy, malicious presence of London encircle her, nudging, licking at her unpleasantly.

She'd made herself smile and be pleasant, asked questions and laughed at jokes that she didn't think were funny and listened to long music business conversations that she didn't understand, but by the time they got back to Rav's flat at four in the morning she was so exhausted that she woke up the next morning with a pounding headache.

'Aye, shut up, Faye,' Annie blushed. 'I wasn't *always* talkin' aboot her. Ye make it sound like I was some lovesick hare, gazin' at the moon.'

'Near enough.' Faye grinned, taking a sip of the wine. It was lovely being with Annie again, and Susie was as adorable as Faye remembered; they'd been an item, years before, but the long distance hadn't worked out at the time. Susie was short, with a platinum blonde bob she wore straight for her work as a solicitor; tonight it was in slightly uneven pigtails. She was dressed in jeans and a t-shirt with an obscure computer game reference with a pink cardigan over the top and large gold hoop earrings with her name inside them in looping gold script.

Annie gave Faye an affectionate stare, pretending to be outraged.

'*Faye*,' Annie rolled her eyes at her best friend. 'Dinnae give away all my secrets, sweetheart. Or I'll be forced to tell the story of how ye wet yerself onstage at the school assembly.'

'What? That's not a story. Don't make things up to show off in front of your new girlfriend,' Faye chided. 'And I didn't wet myself!'

'Don't embarrass the girl.' Susie smiled knowingly at Faye. 'Luckily for Annie, I always held a bit of a candle for her too. Must have been divine providence that got her a job in London, that's all I can say. I thought I'd lost her to Abercolme forever.'

'Aye, well. *Coven of Love* made me an offer too good to refuse.' Annie stirred a pot of pasta on the hob and lifted the lid on a delicious-smelling sauce.

'It *was* good! You're a lead character. Though I have to say, that set *does* need some updating. I agree with the director there,' Faye said, frowning when she thought of the clichéd décor.

'She wants ye to come back in and give her some pointers.'

'Oh! I didn't think she was serious.' Faye was surprised.

'Aye. I told her she needed an expert opinion.' Annie held out the wooden spoon she'd stirred the pot with for Susie to taste. 'It's a good show, but some of the storylines are ridiculous.'

Faye raised an eyebrow, but said nothing – her real life had been pretty ridiculous of late, after all.

'More salt.' Susie reached past Annie to get something from the fridge, and Faye watched them with a sudden yearning. They seemed so happy together. Perhaps this was what she and Rav looked like from the outside, too; but Faye was aware that the comfortable delight that Annie and Susie took in these everyday parts of their life together – cooking, talking about their day at work, entertaining friends – eluded her and Rav. Both relationships were new – it wasn't a comparison of an established love to a new one. No, there was a closeness between Annie and Susie that was absent between she and Rav, despite their passion. Too much unresolved pain hung between them, and she didn't know how to help Rav and herself move on.

'You're quiet.' Annie spooned the pasta into the sauce, added some of the pasta's cooking water into the pan then spooned generous mounds onto three plates. Susie followed behind her, drizzling olive oil and grinding pepper onto each plate before bringing them to the table.

'Oh, it's nothing,' Faye lied, tasting the pasta, which was delicious. 'Mmmm! Annie, your cooking has definitely improved.'

'Hmmm,' Annie waved her fork at Faye as she ate. 'Nae bad. So is Rav still really sufferin'? From bein' in the faerie realm?' She shook her head. 'Ye wouldnae get me tae go there after what I know now, aye.'

'It's going to take a long time.' Faye sighed. 'And I understand that he wants to move on, forget about it, live a normal life, you know? I really do. But I'm not going to lie. What does that make me look like in front of his friends? And is forgetting really the best thing to do? I don't know if it is.'

'It's different for you. Ye're half a fae yerself. Remember that Rav isnae.' Annie reached for the cheese and grated some onto her meal.

'Exactly. It's half of me. It's part of who I am, right? So I can't forget it. And I don't *want* to. If he does, does it really make sense to be with me, a constant reminder of what happened to him?' she appealed to Annie, who shrugged. 'There's going to come a day where he doesn't want to be reminded of Murias any more. What happens to us then?'

Annie knew the whole story, but Faye hadn't told her about the bargain with Glitonea either. She'd merely said, *I managed to rescue Rav,* and *the faeries came when I needed them, the night of the concert.* She'd let Annie make her own conclusions after that. She'd never kept anything from Annie before, and she hated herself for it.

Why not tell Annie about the faerie bargain now? Faye steeled herself. She'd been afraid of a rebuke, of Annie's disapproval, but she knew her friend would help her. *You can tell her now. Just open your mouth and tell her, it'll be okay.*

She felt the words cluster in her throat, but rather than finding it easy to talk to Annie, to tell her anything as she always had done, they choked her. *No. You cannot tell,* Glitonea's voice echoed in her ear. *I forbade it as part of the bargain.*

Faye shook her head; it was just her imagination, surely. She tried again, suddenly anxious she *should* tell Annie, but the same thing happened: her throat felt like it closed up, and she started a coughing fit. The harder she tried to get the words out, the worse the coughing got; like faerie hands around her throat, she was being denied air. Or being drowned. Black spots swam in front of her eyes; Faye's eyelids fluttered closed, and she saw Glitonea's face with its strange, intense beauty; Faye watched her lips move. *You will keep your word as I kept mine.*

Leave me alone! Please! Faye screamed, inside her mind. She was far too disoriented to be able to use any witchcraft to defend herself from the faerie queen; the protection sigil she'd been keeping in her pocket was in her coat, thrown over the sofa in the next room.

Can I trust you, Faye Morgan? Glitonea's head tilted to one side as she watched Faye choking; her expression was dispassionate, calm. Faye gasped for breath.

You can trust me, I won't tell, please! Faye appealed in desperation as she started to lose consciousness. She was dimly aware of Annie slapping her on the back, of Susie saying something, *is she choking, what is it, should we call an ambulance?*

So be it. But I will be watching. Glitonea's face disappeared and the drowning sensation lessened immediately. Faye slumped onto the table, heaving in huge gusts of air. Gradually, she felt herself return to normal.

'What the hell was that? Are you all right, Faye?' Susie helped her sit up and handed her a glass of water. 'Here. Drink it carefully. Did you choke?'

Faye shook her head and heaved in a deep breath.

'I… I don't know what happened. Sorry.'

'Ye dinnae need tae apologise, daftie!' Annie laughed nervously. 'Ah thought ye were a goner for a second there.'

'I'm okay.' Faye cleared her throat. 'Something went down the wrong way, that's all.'

Annie gave her a searching look. She knew something was up, Faye could tell: they knew each other far too well. She avoided Annie's eyes.

'You'd tell me if somethin' was wrong, wouldn't ye, darlin'? No secrets between us, aye?' Annie stared at her with a strange expression on her face. It wasn't distrust, but something near to it.

'Leave her alone, Annie. She just choked, that's all.' Susie put a protective arm around Faye's shoulders. 'Faye wouldn't keep any secrets from you. You're like sisters. Let her get her breath back.'

'Aye, all right,' Annie agreed, but Faye still avoided her eyes.

Chapter 7

'Listen. About Rav…' Susie resumed the thread of their conversation as the three of them sat in front of the fire Annie had built in the blackened wood burner. 'You don't know what might or might not happen in the future, Faye. All you can do is be honest with him now.'

Honest. *If only it was that simple*, Faye thought. Her throat still hurt; she sipped the rich red wine which soothed it slightly.

'It'll work out. Maybe he needs to have some therapy, anyway. It's no bad thing,' Susie continued.

'What aboot this Mallory? She's got it in for ye, aye?' Annie interrupted. She was annoyed, Faye could tell. She could sense there was something Faye wasn't telling her, and she didn't like it.

'I don't know about that. She was just rude to me. But Sumi told me that they'd gone out. Her and Rav. And that she didn't think Mallory was over it.'

Susie rolled her eyes. 'The usual shenanigans. Does Rav still have feelings for her?'

'No. I don't think so, anyway.' Faye took a sip of wine and, then, another. 'But then, he wouldn't exactly say if he did.'

'Has he said he loves you?' Annie fired back. Faye felt suddenly under attack.

'Yes.' She knew she sounded defensive.

'Leave her alone, An,' Susie interrupted. 'It's early days for them.'

'Yeah, well, it's the same for us, sweetheart, but I don't like this Rav havin' his exes hangin' around,' Annie replied curtly.

'Are you angry with me, Annie? Why?'

'I'm not angry.' Annie stared down at her plate, but it was obvious that she was lying. Susie placed her palm on Annie's arm, like a steady hand to calm a wild horse, and smiled at Faye.

'Annie's been really worried about you, Faye. After all that's happened, are you really all right?' Susie's eyes were on Annie, intent and kind, but she spoke to Faye. 'And I think she feels responsible for you. She feels that she should have been there for you when everything went wrong at the festival. Annie likes to think it's her job to dive in and save everyone. Even when they don't need to be saved.'

'Is that true, Annie?' Faye was aghast. She'd never once thought that any of this might be her friend's fault. Everything that had happened – her journey to faerie, her affair with Finn, and what happened at the festival – it was Faye's fault, and hers alone. 'God, no. I missed you like crazy, that's a fact. But, Susie's right, it's not your job to protect me.'

'Nah, well,' Annie took a drink from her glass and looked away. 'Ye don' have to fling yerself into whatever this is with Rav just because ye had a bad experience with Finn.' She met Faye's eyes; Faye wondered if Annie thought that was what she was keeping a secret. That... what? She didn't really like Rav, but she thought she didn't have other options?

'It's not that,' Faye muttered. Annie raised an eyebrow and drank her wine, saying nothing.

I want to tell you, but I can't, Faye thought, furious, wishing Annie was telepathic. *Don't be angry with me. I'd tell you if I could.* She wasn't angry with Annie, but at herself and at Glitonea. And she was terrified, too. More than anything, she needed Annie. Annie always found a way to help: she could always think of a way around things.

'Look, Faye. Don't be so hard on yourself. You and Rav obviously like each other, but you had a really hard start. I mean, the guy was, like, literally tortured by a faerie king because of you. It's not a normal situation. So just relax, let it happen. Don't put any expectations on yourself. And anyway. Annie and I were already exes. We knew each other more than you and Rav do. Plus, we're lesbians. So, you know – two months in and we've bought matching burial plots.'

'Right,' Faye was grateful for Susie's gentle intervention; Annie said nothing.

'So. This Mallory,' Susie said. 'You need to make friends with her, I'd say.'

'I'd rather not have to,' Faye muttered.

'Well, it's going to be awkward if you don't. If she's in this social group, she's going to be around, whether you like it or not. Keep your enemies close and all that.' Susie raised her eyebrow and topped up their wine glasses. 'That's what I'd do.'

'Aye, but you're a Leo,' Annie snapped. 'Ye need everyone to love ye, even the ones ye hate.'

'I do *not*!' Susie looked offended; Annie's tone had been cutting. 'I'm just saying. It's the adult thing to do.'

'*Deil hae it*,' Annie muttered. 'I say we shut her nasty little mouth if she wants tae be a bitch to Faye. No' on my watch.'

'And how are we going to do that?' Susie shot back; Faye could see irritation growing between them. Annie knew something was out of kilter and it was bothering her; Susie obviously thought Annie was being difficult for no reason.

'Binding spell. Whatever.' Annie shrugged.

'Calm down, Annie. I met this girl for one evening and she was a bit off with me. And we know that she's got a reason for that. I'll do what Suze says. Be nice. Take the high ground. If she wants to join me there, great. If not, well, I'll have done the right thing.' Faye tried to smooth things over. *This really isn't the problem*, she wanted to say. But she knew she couldn't.

Annie shook her head.

'No, no, no. I'm tellin' ye both now, she's trouble, that one. Don't ask me how I know. I just do. Ex-girlfriends hangin' around, unfinished business, people still havin' feelins for other people. That way chaos lies, my poor deluded friends.'

'Annie. I'm not doing a spell to control a woman I've met once who has posed absolutely no problem for me,' Faye insisted. 'Let it go.'

'An, you're being way too protective of Faye. She's a big girl. She's got this.' Susie leaned over and kissed Annie on the cheek. 'Not that I don't love this fire and brimstone part of you. I'm glad you're on our side, is all I can say.'

'Aye, well.' Annie, mollified by the kiss, drained her wine glass. 'I care. That's all.'

'I know, but I think I can handle one ex-girlfriend,' Faye replied.

'Good.' Annie uncurled herself from her chair and wedged herself in next to Faye. 'I missed ye, Faye Morgan. That's all.'

'I missed you too.' Faye felt the tears coming. She buried her head in Annie's shoulder, and everything she'd been holding in came crashing out, wave upon wave of hurt and worry and grief. 'I'm sorry!' she sobbed, trying to stop herself, but Annie held her closer and rubbed her back.

'Never be sorry for ye tears, sweetheart,' Annie's voice burred through her chest; she hugged Faye tighter and Faye felt her kiss the top of her head. 'And never think I'm not here for you. Not even when we're apart.' Faye heard the crack in Annie's voice and knew she was crying too. It had been tougher than either of them thought to be away from each other. She resolved that she'd find a way to tell Annie everything. But at least, for now, her best friend was close to her again, and Faye could breathe a little easier.

Chapter 8

'The problem *is* that the powers-that-be –' Ruby, the wardrobe mistress, twirled her index finger around in a circle, as if to indicate a heavenly host floating above them, or perhaps someone on the floor above theirs – 'want drama. They want luxury, they want glamour. They don't want people wearing jeans and leggings.' She smiled apologetically at Faye, who was wearing black leggings under a green pinafore dress with a black vest underneath it. 'Don't get me wrong. I'm a witch, not that they'd ever take my advice,' she lowered her voice. 'It's quite a toxic workplace, if I'm honest. So I haven't mentioned it. You don't want to give them any ammunition. Surprise redundancies, that kind of thing.'

Faye liked Ruby immediately. She reminded Faye of Annie in the way she talked, though Ruby was dressed far less outrageously than Annie generally was, even though she worked in the costume department. She was short and curvy and was wearing black ballet pumps, skinny jeans and a baggy pink sweatshirt with GIRLS written on the front. Her black hair was short, shaved close to her head.

Keely, the director she'd met before, had asked Faye to come in to give Ruby 'some pointers about costume'.

'Oh,' Faye didn't know what to say. 'Sorry to hear that. So you can't... make sensible suggestions about what the characters might wear? Or do?'

'No. But you can, which is great. I've been dying for someone to come in and tell them this stuff. I mean, who in their right mind wears a velvet dress day in, day out? I mean, for a masked ball, fine. For a ritual, also fine. But popping to the supermarket or reading the gas meter? Velvet wouldn't be my choice.'

Faye laughed. 'Well, I guess there's a lot of fantasy about witches, isn't there? I mean, it's a romantic image.'

'I know, but doesn't it annoy you? Like, witches are real people. This show paints witches as, like, pre-Raphaelite tarts with magic wands. I mean, it doesn't have to be like that. That show in the US, *Spelled*? Those witches wear miniskirts, jeans, crop tops. They have normal day jobs. I wish it could be more like that.'

'Agreed.' Faye smiled.

'Oh, goddess,' Ruby smacked her palm on her forehead. '*Management*, babes. Always getting consultants in when they could have just asked their actual staff. No offence.'

'None taken.' Faye looked around her at the wardrobe room which was half filled with racks of costumes, boxes of accessories, and half with a couple of sewing machines and cutting tables. 'So you're a witch?'

'Wiccan. Since my teens. You?'

'Ummm. Always. My family were witches.'

'Oh, cool! Hereditary, then?'

'I guess so. Annie and I grew up in the same village. I own a shop there, Mistress of Magic. It's been in my family forever.' Though to many people, 'witch' might have meant one thing, Faye knew that there was a great deal of variety regarding how witches defined their own practice. Traditional witchcraft – an adherence to the native folk customs from whatever culture one had grown up in (Scottish folk magic, in Faye's case) shared many similarities with the modern witchcraft, or Wicca, but also many differences.

Wicca was a modern fusion of nineteenth century ritual and occult practice with the reverence of nature and worship of pagan gods and goddesses of other cultures: Greek, Egyptian, Mesopotamian, Celtic and many more. There was much of what Faye had learned from Grandmother that was recognisable in more modern practices – the seasonal festivals, knowledge of herbs, reverence of nature and the elemental faerie kingdoms – but Grandmother had rolled her eyes at the more modern witchcraft detailed in the books Moddie, and now Faye, sold in Mistress of Magic. *All that arm-wavin' an' long names. Ower ficherie a job, hen,* Faye remembered Grandmother tutting, confident in her older, simpler ways – *ower ficherie* meant fiddly and bothersome.

'That's amazing. I should introduce you to one of my coven. He runs one of the occult bookshops in London.'

'Oh! Well, that would be… that would be lovely, thank you.' Faye was somewhat taken aback at Ruby's free and easy attitude. Faye was used to there being a stigma about being a witch; was used to the old guard in the village with their tuts and raised eyebrows. But London was a big city. She wasn't the only witch in the village any more.

'Sure. We're meeting up on Hampstead Heath next week. You should come. It's a Mabon ritual.'

'Oh! … the Autumn equinox?' Faye realised that she knew very little about whatever 'scene' there was for witches in England – or even in Scotland, come to that. She knew of some groups around the Edinburgh area and a few further afield, as sometimes they came into the shop for supplies and to leave leaflets for events and courses they were running. But she'd always shied away from getting involved, for the same reasons that she kept a reasonably low profile in Abercolme. The fear that had resonated down the ancestral line from Grainne Morgan about being a witch; about having power when others resented you for it.

Fear about being a witch – and being punished for it – had been with her all her life. It had been there at every decision she'd made to stay home instead of go out, to read quietly and forage on the beach for shells and feathers, to walk on the other side of the street, away from the villagers that probably intended her no harm. It had shaped her life.

'Yeah. Falls on a Saturday this year. We run an open circle for the seasonal celebrations.'

'An open circle? So anyone can come?'

'Technically, though most times it's the same faces that show up. Anyone extra has to be personally recommended by a coven member.' Ruby smiled. 'High Priestess's rules.'

'Ah. Right.' Faye knew little of the arrangements of organised covens.

Ruby reached across the cutting table and peeled a clean piece of sketchpad paper from under some pages filled with rough drawings of costumes. She wrote something down and ripped it out, handing it to Faye. 'Here you go. We meet at this pub before we walk up to the Heath. You can walk up with us.' Faye had already walked up on Hampstead Heath with Rav; a forested, ancient, sprawling city park where dog walkers, joggers, families and lovers met.

'All right. Thanks.' Faye took the paper, on which Ruby had written the name of a pub, a tube stop and a date just over a week's time. 'What time?'

'Oh. Probably around eight? Then we can have the moon out for the ritual. Hope it's a clear night. So often we get, like, Hubble-telescope clarity two nights before a ritual but then, on the actual night, a no show. Not that it really matters, but, y'know.'

'Witch problems,' Faye said with a laugh.

'Right? You know. Where did you practice, in your village? Did you have an outside space you could use? Hampstead Heath's been used by London covens for a long time. We're lucky to have it. But there's still a fair amount of time we're in someone's front room.'

'Oh, right. Well. Abercolme is on the Fife coast. So I used one of the beaches there a lot. And the shop, out of hours. It used to be the front room of the house, so I like to think of all the past magic of my grandmothers, stuck in the corners, up in the webs and the dust on the ceiling. There's a reason witches' houses were depicted as full of cobwebs. Traps energy.' She smiled. 'That said, I like a good spring clean. And I think there's definitely a place for modern design.'

'Cool.' Ruby looked impressed. 'I'd love to do more sea magic. It's hard to do, here. I mean, some of us have done, like, day trips to the coast and hung out and done some stuff. But you have to wait for all the tourists to go home, and sometimes it's bloody freezing on those beaches at night by that time. If you live right by it, it must be so much easier.'

'It is, yes.' Faye felt a tug of homesickness for Black Sands Beach and for Abercolme, and swallowed it back like a bitter medicine. 'I miss it,' she added quietly.

'I bet. More reason for you to come out with us. Be with your own kind,' Ruby said kindly.

'Thanks. That will be really nice.' Faye smiled. She needed friends of her own here, and she missed her connection to the moon and the sea. A forest would be a good change of pace.

There was a knock on the door, and Keely poked her head around.

'Hey. Thought you'd like lunch, Faye, if you're done here?' She smiled and Ruby shook Faye's hand, a professional veneer sliding over her features.

'We've had a good discussion. Thanks for meeting with me, Faye,' she said, and Faye made sure she folded up the piece of paper and slipped it in her pocket. 'I'm sure I'll see you again. Around the set.'

'Always good to meet a kindred spirit,' Faye replied, smiling.

Chapter 9

They met at a pub at the edge of Hampstead Heath and walked up to the secluded grove on the Heath together in an unruly, chatty line. Faye was still getting to know her way around and by the time she'd found her way along the high street and into the residential streets to the Heath, she was late. By the time she'd found the pub (Ruby had texted *look for the one with all the hanging baskets*) the group was ready to go, and there was no time for a getting-to-know-you chat.

From what she could tell, the group varied widely in age, occupation and outlook. There were six women, including her and Ruby, and four men; one was white haired and bearded, and wore an aged leather jacket with his biker gang acronym on the sleeve, but the others were younger. One was shaven-headed with silver earrings to the top of his left ear, wearing black jeans and a hoodie. Another looked like he'd come to the pub straight from the office; he was middle aged, clean-cut, wearing a navy suit. He seemed quiet but well-liked in the group, who teased him about stocks and shares.

Faye smiled as they walked up the grassy hill under the slowly setting sun, listening. The girls were probably in their early twenties and both wearing jeans and flip flops; one had a dyed blonde short afro; silver bangles jangled on her wrists. The other girl had blonde hair in a long ponytail, a pink vest and a whole arm sleeve tattoo of pink and red roses that twined against her fair skin.

The last man in the group fell in step with Faye and Ruby.

'Aren't you going to introduce us, Ruby?' He smiled a little wolfishly, but his voice was low, courteous and well-spoken. 'I demand that I be made known to this delightful woman of power you've brought to our most august gathering.' He had a twinkle in his eye that indicated his formality was more for fun than his usual way of speaking.

Faye found herself smiling back. 'Faye Morgan. And you are?'

He took her hand and bowed a little.

'Gabriel Black. A pleasure to meet you.'

'Faye's the one who has the shop in the Scottish village. You two have a lot in common.' Ruby took a drink of water from the bottle she was holding and looked confusedly at her other hand for a minute. 'Oh, damn. I've left my scarf in the pub.' She ran back down the hill, waving. 'I'll be back in a minute! I'll find you.'

Faye watched Ruby run off, feeling a shadow of anxiety settle in her stomach. She didn't know any of the rest of them.

'Blessings of Mabon.' Gabriel nodded politely.

'Blessings to you,' Faye replied.

Tonight, Annie was working and both of them were away from Abercolme. It felt strange to be distanced from their tradition: when they could, they celebrated the solstices and the equinoxes on Black Sands Beach, so when Ruby had followed up with more details about her group's Mabon ritual, Faye was glad to have somewhere to go. She'd considered staying at home and doing some kind of ritual in Rav's flat, but when she mentioned it to him cautiously, the look of confusion on his face made her change her mind. Clearly, a seasonal ritual didn't fall within his definition of their new life together in London.

'So, tell me about your shop.' Gabriel adjusted a backpack on his shoulder and slid on a pair of expensive-looking black sunglasses, even though the night was already well on its way. He was probably in his late thirties, Faye thought, with jet black hair and deep brown eyes; the black shadow of a beard covered his jaw, but his skin was pale. He wore a white, fitted dress shirt with a subtle pleat on the middle section of the chest, with the sleeves rolled up to the elbows and dark-dye black jeans that fit his slim frame.

He was a little taller than her but not much, but there was something about him – an aura, a feeling of power. Faye was, by now, accustomed to sensing power in others; she could tell that Gabriel wasn't faerie, like Finn Beatha, but she felt a velvety blackness about him that was warm and wicked.

They walked on, past a blue-painted bandstand in the middle of the open Heath, which looked over London. Faye saw two other women in the group, older women who she assumed were the coven leaders, walk along a path along the edge of the woodland. Dense forest lay at the edge of the long grass of the open field, where people still sat with drinks and picnics, or walked their dogs, enjoying the summer evening.

'My shop? Well, it's called Mistress of Magic. It's my family home; has belonged to the Morgans for generations.' Faye repeated what she'd told Ruby about the shop; what it sold, what Abercolme was like. Gabriel listened attentively.

'Sounds divine,' he said, lowering his sunglasses and looking over the top of them at her. 'I imagine you have a lot of contact with the water elementals, being that close to the sea up there?' His gaze was penetrating but friendly; like Rav, his eyelashes were long and dark.

'Yes, I… that's right,' Faye stammered and looked away. It was still a new experience for a stranger to mention magical things in conversation with her, as if they were talking about what they'd had for lunch or exchanging polite accounts of their summer holidays.

'I'd like to hear more about that sometime,' he said, his voice low and charming. 'You'll have to come and visit my place, see how it compares. I sell books only, though. Antiquarian, modern and second-hand. We're the oldest occult specialist book shop in London.'

'I will,' she smiled. 'What's it called?'

'Fortune's. My father and grandfather owned it. Before that, it belonged to one of the most notorious magicians in the country.'

They had reached the dirt path that led into the woods now, and Faye heard running footsteps behind them, which were the only sound in a stillness that seemed to emanate from the woods.

'Gods, that hill's steeper than it looks,' Ruby panted.

'Last, but by no means the least, dear Ruby,' Gabriel purred, taking her hand, and then Faye's. 'Let us enter our sacred space; I'm honoured to escort two such delicious creatures…'

'That sounded sooo creepy, Gabriel.' Ruby rolled her eyes. 'You're not about to eat us.'

'No gentleman would dream of such a thing,' he agreed, and they made their way through the trees to the secret clearing.

Chapter 10

The circle stretched across the clearing under the oak trees. They were ten in all; idly, Faye wondered if there was any truth in the tradition that a coven should comprise thirteen. Her experience of witchcraft was either working alone, learning from her mother Moddie and her grandmother when they had still been alive, or with Annie. Just once, she and Annie had become a group of three when they and Aisha had cast their love spell. But the result of that working had been tempestuous, to say the least.

It had been a hot summer, and the end of September was pleasantly cool. The two women who had been at the front of the group had already set up much of the circle when Faye arrived with Ruby and Gabriel. One was plump, middle-aged, with long, wavy henna-red hair and wore a greyish, once-white t-shirt that stretched over her chest, bearing the anti-nuclear sign on it in rainbow colours and a thick padded jacket over the top; on the bottom, she wore a long, full patchwork skirt. The other woman, who was setting out four hefty storm lamps at the cardinal points of the circle, was older, with short, white hair in a bob. She wore cargo trousers and a lilac fleece jacket.

Faye smiled to herself and thought that if Ruby could only bring the rest of the creative team from *Coven of Love* along to this, they'd be extremely disappointed that no-one was dressed in a floor-length velvet gown.

In the centre of the clearing there was a convenient tree stump on which the red-headed woman was setting out some basic equipment: a wooden wand, an earthenware cup – which the white-haired women filled with red wine from a screw-topped bottle – a pentagram made of slim sticks, tied together with string and a Moroccan-style silver metal censer.

Ruby took Faye over to the white-haired woman, who was rummaging in her bag for something and looked up warily as they approached.

'Lighter! Wouldn't get very far without that,' she muttered, putting it down on the stump.

'Sylvia – this is Faye Morgan, the one I told you about.' Ruby was strangely formal, all of a sudden, almost bowing to the older woman. 'Faye, this is Sylvia. She's our High Priestess. Thank you, Priestess, for allowing me to bring Faye to the group.'

'Welcome, Faye.' Sylvia looked at first glance like someone running a cake stall at a village fete, but when she spoke she was abrupt, in the manner of a powerful woman who hadn't had to be polite for a long time. She maintained a slightly aggressive eye contact with Faye, almost like a stare, unblinking.

'Thanks for letting me come to your ritual,' Faye replied, politely.

'I open the seasonal festivals to small numbers of approved visitors, but don't be under the misapprehension that attending the festivals is a way into the coven. There are stringent initiation requirements.' Faye felt as though she was being told off in the Headmistress's office all of a sudden.

'I'm not looking for a coven to join. I just thought it would be nice to mark the season with a like-minded group.' Faye held Sylvia's gaze; if the older woman was trying to intimidate her, it wasn't going to work. Sylvia looked away first.

'It's not to say that the coven is closed to you, of course, but you'd need to show a sustained commitment to the group over a long period of time before you were considered. I'm sure you understand how careful I have to be, as the guardian of the group. Their safety lies in my hands. We tread, after all, a path of shadows, when we dance with the old ones.'

Faye raised an eyebrow.

'I understand that more than you might think.' She wasn't going to be lectured about the perils of witchcraft by someone she'd just met, regardless of what title she had given herself. *When you've danced on corpses in the faerie reel, come and talk to me about treading the shadow path,* Faye thought. Perhaps Sylvia picked up on the thought, or felt Faye's lack of fear of her, because she nodded briskly.

'As long as everyone knows where they stand. I understand that you come from a hereditary background, Faye?' She busied herself with laying out the altar, and Faye exchanged glances with Ruby, who gave her the thumbs up.

'That's right. My ancestors have been witches a long way back, in Abercolme,' Faye replied.

'And they taught you the old ways?'

'Yes. I suppose it's what you'd call a mix of folk magic and traditional witchcraft,' Faye replied. 'But my mum taught me some Wicca too, so a mix, I suppose.' She wasn't ready to talk about the darker magic she knew; the power of the element of water that Glitonea had taught her in the realm of Murias.

'And what deity did you work with? The Cailleach? The Morrigan?' Sylvia named two Celtic goddesses, standing up; it was a challenge, in some way. Sylvia was testing her.

'No. I know of them; I know people who honour Callie Beara.' Faye gave the familiar name of The Cailleach, a Scottish winter goddess of mountains, snow and rain. 'We…' Faye shivered unexpectedly, thinking of Finn. She didn't want to think about him; not here. It was too complicated. 'We honoured the fae.'

'I see.' Sylvia's expression was impenetrable. 'One of this group's matron goddesses is Morgan Le Fay, Mistress of Magic. We'll be calling to her tonight.'

'Morgana Le Fay?' Faye used the faerie name – Morgana rather than Morgan, not that it mattered. Morgana was the Queen of the Crystal Castle at the centre of the four elemental fae kingdoms. As far as Faye knew, one had to journey to one of the faerie realms and then walk a perilous crystal bridge to reach her.

Faye didn't think that Morgana – a High Queen of Magick and much more powerful than even Finn Beatha or his faerie queen sister Glitonea – could easily be summoned from her realm. There was a certain comfort in that. She didn't want to be confronted with anything belonging to the faerie realm. A quiet, respectful Mabon ceremony in nature would be just fine.

'Your namesake?' Sylvia raised an eyebrow. 'Are you familiar with Morgan Le Fay? I assume you must be, if your worship has been with the elemental realms.' The others were watching her keenly; assessing, perhaps, whether she was all she claimed to be.

'Oh… yes, I'm familiar with Her.' Faye was noncommittal.

'Really?' Sylvia looked Faye up and down, critically. 'Welcome, then. We'll be starting in a moment; it might not be exactly what you're used to, but the main elements will be similar, I'm sure.' Her tone was brisk again; if Faye had thought that all powerful women had Grandmother's warmth, then she was evidently wrong.

Faye felt a tremor of nerves in her stomach, partly pleasurable: she could already feel the weft of the natural magic of nature under her feet.

'This is Penny,' Sylvia beckoned to the red-haired woman who was talking to Gabriel. 'She's my second-in-command; High Priestess in training, if you will. Penny, this is Faye.'

Penny shook Faye's hand.

'Merry meet,' she murmured, and Faye repeated the greeting.

'Do you need any help, setting up?' she asked, but Penny demurred.

'Minimal setup, otherwise we'd be lugging tons of stuff up the hill. We'll get going in a minute.' She nodded and turned away to finish her preparations.

Ruby squeezed Faye's hand as they walked back to join the circle.

'Good going. I think she liked you,' Ruby whispered.

'Liked me? What would she have been like if she hated me?' Faye hissed back.

'She's kind of a badass, but she's just being... you know. Protective,' Ruby replied, under her breath. 'She's got our backs. I like that.'

Faye didn't reply; she respected Sylvia, but she didn't like power games, and that was what it had felt like was going on. Sylvia might be the leader of the group, but she wasn't responsible for protecting Ruby, Gabriel and the rest from their own experiences. To see herself as a mother of grown adults seemed like a strange kind of ego trip.

The rest of the circle had begun singing softly. Faye put her misgivings about Sylvia to one side; she was here to celebrate Mabon, that was all. She joined her voice to the group's and felt the energy around her; from the circle, from the trees around her, interspersed with the special energy of the autumn equinox. It had a feeling all of its own; the perfect balance between light and dark, when the days and nights were of equal length and in perfect equilibrium – dark and light, masculine and feminine. But, Faye remembered, the equinox was the cusp of a transition: from now on, the year began to wane. From this moment, darkness began to defeat the light.

Faye shivered in anticipation of the coming darkness, even though she knew there was nothing to be afraid of. Dark was natural; dark was night and death and sleep. But she still couldn't make peace with the darkness in herself.

Fighting her instincts, Faye caught the simple melody of the song, and raised her voice as the bright moonlight filtered through the canopy of branches above.

Chapter 11

They stood in a circle an arm's length from each other, able to touch hands when they needed to. Faye stood between Gabriel and Ruby and watched as Penny called in the elements, just as Faye had so many times, in her herb garden at the back of the shop or on Black Sands Beach. Just as many times, she'd stood on the worn hearthstones inside Mistress of Magic, in front of the fireplace where generations of Morgan women had opened their arms to the moon and asked for its blessing.

They had sung the simple song, about the growing and the cutting of the grain, over and over until Sylvia had beckoned them to stand in the circle, drawing it outside them with wand, lit censer, cup and by sprinkling earth around them to create a protected space.

'I call to the watchtowers of the spirits of the North; of earth, be with us in our rite!' Sylvia's voice rang out clear and confident in the night; her face was lit by candlelight as she moved from one quarter of the circle to the next, calling in the elements as power to the circle. As she did so, Faye felt the hairs on the back of her neck prickle, and a chill went up her spine. She felt the raw elemental energy coming; earth from the north, air from the east, fire from the south and water from the west, their power rushing in to the circle and melding, merging into something new. The circle held their energies; the men and women around the edge were part of the circle. Everything of them was part of the circle, and the circle was part of them. Even though that elemental energy was the energy of faerie, there was no getting away from it, and Faye would never want to. The energies of nature were one thing: dangerous faerie kings and queens were quite another.

Faye half-closed her eyes, watching the energies shift and dance in the circle. She could see the air sprites, the sylphs, dancing like dust motes in the shafts of moonlight that sliced into the clearing. She watched the fire elementals, writhing like snakes, salamanders, changeable as their native element, and the earth energy, slower and fuller and richer, like stones building into cairns, combining to spiral up in the space between them all.

Her heart beat faster for a moment as she felt the energy of water rush into the circle, recognising its familiar lull. Did those in Murias – Finn and Glitonea – know she was here if the water spirit was here? She assumed not; these beings – a swirl of a tail here, a disembodied gill there, the overall sense of flowing, crashing, changing – they weren't the faeries of Finn's grand court who had been shaped by human imagination over the years into separate characters; who walked in the human world as they wished, enchanting and cursing if they wanted to. The sprites that entered the circle were pure element, pure force: the dense material of natural world.

Sylvia stood with her arms outstretched and called out loudly.

'Blessed Morgan Le Fay, goddess of magic, witch, independent woman, be with us at this time when light and dark are in perfect balance; bless us with your wisdom this Equinox! Enchantress, we implore thee, lend us your power to see clearly in the coming dark! Keeper of wisdom, teacher of the crescent moon, healer of the sick! Goddess of magic, we beckon you, protect us in the darkness, and open its mysteries to us. We implore you, grant us your sight this Mabon night.'

The circle joined hands as Sylvia continued to call out raptly to Morgan and started to pace. Faye was aware of the many gods and goddesses that other witches worked with; she'd called to some of them herself before now, but it was the Fair Ones that her family was connected to, for good or ill. She was still surprised that Ruby's London coven honoured Morgana Le Fay, a faerie queen.

In Abercolme, it was the fae kingdoms they were closest to: in the sea, in the wind, in the ground under them. Perhaps the faerie kingdoms were closer in those rural places; in cities, she'd supposed that people found it harder to connect to the nature elementals. But, she reminded herself, Morgan's influence in books and films was considerable. She remained the iconic witch: misunderstood and misrepresented, perhaps, but a symbol of power nonetheless.

Faye heard Ruby and Gabriel chanting *Morgan Le Fay, Lady of Magic! Morgan Le Fay, Enchantress of the Moon!* and followed suit; the circle's pacing turned into something faster and more unruly; still, their hands stayed clasped together. *Morgan Le Fay, Lady of Magic! Morgan Le Fay, Enchantress of the Moon!* Faye heard her voice rasping, starting to lose her breath, as the volume of the chanting increased. She still didn't believe Morgana would appear; the High Queen of Magick didn't need to leave the Crystal Castle; she was the emanation of all magic in the human and faerie worlds. It would take more than chanting to bring her through.

Faye was sweating from the wild skipping and chanting. She closed her eyes and saw the circle as if from above, the flickering candlelight, the moonlight on their faces. In her mind's eye, Faye saw two dirt paths run from one side of the clearing to the other, crossing each other at the centre of the circle. And at the point where they crossed, a gate made of the same pink-white crystal she remembered from the seven-pointed castle opened in the ground, and Morgana Le Fay appeared.

Faye opened her eyes, startled; as if they had seen the same thing, the circle stopped dancing. She narrowed her eyes; there was a shimmer of non-colour at the centre of the circle, and the candles inside the lamps guttered, making exaggerated shadows in the trees, but otherwise nothing.

It can't be. Faye stared at the ground, aghast. *She wouldn't be summoned so easily.*

Faye closed her eyes again; the Queen stood there again. Tall, silver-white haired and black skinned, she wore long silver robes and a silver circlet on her head, with a crescent moon that pointed to the sky. Her face wasn't human, but a shifting mass of light. She bowed her head to Faye; Faye bowed, eyes closed, in response. Her heart was pounding with the shock of Morgana's presence; *how had this happened?* She'd been so sure that she was safe. She'd clearly underestimated the power of the coven.

'I bless your circle; I am Morgana, the one you seek; I am Morgana Le Fay, goddess of witches and Mistress of Magic. Speak thy wishes,' the faerie queen intoned.

'She is here!' Sylvia cried, exultant, her head thrown back.

Faye opened her eyes; she caught Gabriel staring at her.

'You see the goddess?' he whispered.

'Not clearly in the circle. With my eyes closed, yes,' Faye stammered.

'I see you're accustomed to using magical imagination,' Gabriel smiled, closing his eyes. 'Not everyone sees Her. That's why Sylvia is… translating, shall we say.'

'Oh.' Faye couldn't express what she was really feeling, which was a mixture of fear and anticipation; she'd been resisting the call of the fae ever since she'd been in London. But at the same time, her soul was alight: she was half-fae, however much she tried to deny it.

'I come with a message for one among you.' Morgana's voice hung in the air between them all and sounded inside their heads at the same time. 'Faye Morgan, *sidhe-leth*, step forward.'

Faye's heart beat faster, and she released Gabriel's hand.

'I'm… I'm here.' She tried to get her voice under control, but her nerves showed.

'Faye. There is something important you must know about the war between the faerie kingdoms,' Morgana's voice sang with the splash of oars in a still lake and the vibrant hum of the pink-white crystal of her castle. 'I come to speak to you, and you only. I have been trying to communicate with you for some time.'

Faye thought of all the shadows, the dreams, the smoky fingers of the fae that had reached out to her since she'd come to London. She'd ignored them all.

'Why?' she asked. 'Please. I wanted to start a new life here. Can't you leave me alone?'

'No!' Morgana's voice echoed in her ears. 'There is a prophecy that drives this war. The rifts between the elemental kingdoms are deepening because of it, and you lie at its centre.'

'A prophecy? What prophecy?' Faye demanded.

'Your involvement with Finn Beatha has begun a series of events that can only end in—'

But there was an interference, suddenly, like an electrical storm, or the irritating black and white snow on the TV set when a storm knocked out the aerial, back at home in Abercolme where Faye's TV was the same ancient one she'd grown up with.

The goddess's outline flickered; Faye stretched her hand out, as if she could touch Morgana, but her fingers closed around air as the goddess faded.

'They will not let me through,' Morgana's voice faded away. 'Do not trust them!'

Faye opened her eyes, but the goddess was gone. Yet, not everything was normal. A different forest appeared around the circle, slipping against the oaks of the Heath like a blurred negative. Faye looked around her, but the rest of the coven seemed to be caught in a moment of stillness; frozen in time.

'Can only end in what?' Faye screamed, but there was no answer.

Instead of the familiar, thick trunks of the oaks, with Hampstead Heath beyond them, a new, golden-green forest stretched out around her. Immediately, she knew she was in the faerie realm.

To her right flowed a merry stream, with a bridge over it. The bridge was in the shape of a woman's body, with her toes and fingertips the points where soft grass met the banks of the stream. The bridge was carved from wood and varnished in a golden brown, gleaming in the strange light.

The walkway over her back was unsupported by a rail, and the bridge was narrow. No bridge in the fae worlds, it seemed, was an easy one to cross, and all of them required fearlessness. Faye's breath caught in her throat. Was this the way to the faerie forest, the entry to Falias, the Faerie Kingdom of Earth? Had this place, somehow, interceded on Morgana Le Fay's power? Its presence had banished her from the circle: someone hadn't wanted her to deliver her message to Faye. What had the faerie queen been trying to tell Faye? She felt rattled by the experience, her heart beating with panic.

Beyond the bridge, Faye saw a tall, golden gate leading into the forest; again, the gate itself was formed of the carvings of two women embracing, made of the same gold varnished wood. The hinges of the gate were at the heels, bottoms and elbows of the figures, whose bodies were entwined in an eternal kiss. As she watched, the door swung open, as if to show Faye what lay beyond.

Her panic quieting, Faye walked over the bridge and to the gate. She stood at the entrance to the deeper forest and stared in, but roots and vines wrapped themselves around her feet and ankles, and she could go no further. She could see the exposed black roots of the trees beyond, and the black soil that glowed with jewels: amber, citrine, jet and emerald sparkled in the ground like pebbles on a beach, and huge unpolished chunks sat like menhirs among the densely packed trees. The air smelt of lemons, but underneath there was the taint of copper: of blood and earth. *Stop, traveller. Only one pure in her desire may enter the Queendom of Moronoe, Mistress of Earthly Delights* a chorus of voices sang out. *Have knowledge of where you tread. Know thyself and admit thy deepest desires.*

Faye's awareness flickered back to the circle, but she was only vaguely conscious of the rest of them. She tried to return to the ordinary world, tried switching her awareness completely, but the faerie forest was too strong. She could hear soft laughter: the cries of delight attracted her, drew her in, lighting a flame of desire in her belly. *I want... I want...* she tried to say what she felt, but she was too confused. *Stop this, I don't want it. Return Morgana Le Fay to me. She had a message for me.*

The laughter seemed to come from the lumps of crystal; from the deep black hollow slits in the trees. *Many would like the pleasure of your company* came the answer. *We await you.*

Faye realised she was stamping her feet as if to free them from the roots. There was a flash of golden light and a deep voice rumbled through the trees; like a persistent echo in a mountain range, like the sound of the earth shifting under their feet. A different voice than the laughing one; the husky woman's voice that had called her into something dark, somewhere she desired to go but didn't know why.

Daughter.

The scene changed and Faye was standing back in the circle, but the faerie one that overlapped the ordinary world. She could see the Hampstead Heath oak grove, but she stood within another circle, one with gold-green trees ringed with light.

Daughter. The call came again and a splintered shard of loss in Faye's heart twisted uncomfortably; it had been there ever since she'd been old enough to know what a father was, and know that she lacked one. The other children in Abercolme had fathers. Cheerful ones that cracked jokes, quiet fathers that helped them with difficult homework, fathers that shouted, fat ones, thin ones, fathers that smelt of whisky. She was left out; she'd experienced none of those things. Being called *daughter*, suddenly, by someone she didn't know, was more hurtful than she expected.

This voice was a man's, loud and deep.

A figure strode through the trees, a gold light pooling around him in the night.

For a brief second Faye thought it was Finn, and she recoiled, her awareness returning to the ordinary world. He was tall and graceful in the same way as Finn was, and his outline was similar: strong shoulders, a regal bearing.

Yet when Faye saw his face, it wasn't one she'd seen before. This man was dark where Finn was blonde and blue-eyed; his hair was black, his skin was brown like sun-baked soil, he wore a short, shaggy beard. His features were as perfect as Finn's, but his jaw under the beard was squarer, his face broader.

He was dressed in a black tunic, pinned at the shoulder with a yellow-gold stone brooch, and black trousers underneath; he wore sandals of dull copper leather, and a belt of the same, which featured a seven-pointed star on the buckle.

Lyr of the Faerie Kingdom of Falias stepped into the circle and the glow around him, like an aura of gold, lit up the whole clearing. He bowed his head respectfully to Faye.

'I come for my daughter, on this night of equal power between our realms of earth and magic, light and dark, day and night,' he said, his voice as deep as the earth. He held out his hand. 'Come. We have much to say to each other.'

Chapter 12

Faye stayed where she was and kept her hands at her sides.

'I did not call you,' she replied as coolly as she could, although her heart was racing. 'You're not welcome here.'

'I am the High King of Falias, Faerie Kingdom of Earth. When you call on the elements for power in your circle, you call me,' he replied. 'I am welcome anywhere on Earth. This is my realm.'

One night, when she was eight or so, and after she'd been told to go to bed, Faye had sneaked out onto the landing and crouched at the top of the stairs leading up from the shop. Moddie had been talking to one of her friends and their voices echoed up from where they sat in front of the old hearth.

Faye wasn't sleepy, and knew that she'd been sent to bed so that the adults could talk in private. There was laughing and murmuring: Faye couldn't make out any of it, really. The friend had asked something – Faye could tell from the tone in her voice, which lilted up at the end. Moddie's voice replied, a murmur without inflection. They were gossiping about the other villagers, no doubt. Faye had rested her head against the wall and closed her eyes. She didn't like being in her room if she couldn't sleep: large shadows crept across the ceiling, snatched at her face, whispered in her ear.

Moddie said it was probably her imagination, but she'd put a crystal under Faye's pillow anyway. Faye knew it was meant as protection from nightmares, but the shadows weren't nightmares, because she was awake.

Moddie's voice became louder and Faye had realised her mother was walking towards the door that led up the stairs; eight-year-old Faye had scuttled out of sight. Moddie might have been on the hippy side, but she had a sharp tongue when she wanted to. Moddie's friend sounded as though she asked a question.

'No. Haven't seen him since Faye was born. Ran off,' Moddie replied. Faye knew instantly she was talking about her father, because it was what she always said when anyone asked her. There was another murmur that came from the friend which Faye couldn't make out.

'No. Almost killed me, I...' Moddie had closed the door before Faye had a chance to hear the rest.

Almost killed me. It had stayed with Faye; she'd never asked Moddie what she meant by the phrase, because it seemed obvious enough. Faye's absent father had tried to kill Moddie before he ran off; that was what she'd always thought, until the Faerie Queen Glitonea had told her that she was half-faerie, and that Lyr was her father.

Faye was angry. He wasn't the hopeless hippy she'd once imagined he was, but he was still the one that had hurt her mother and abandoned her.

'I have nothing to say to you, Lyr of Falias. And you weren't called – we called on Morgana Le Fay, who had a message for me,' Faye snapped. She was aware that the circle had returned to life and were staring at her; she glanced briefly at Gabriel, who, like the rest of them, looked as though he'd been awakened from sleep.

'I am family, Faye. And I have much I would tell you.' His hand remained outstretched. She stared at it in shock. Finally, after all these years, he was here. She wanted to slap his hand away and scream *why now?*

Instead, she left her hands by her sides and stared defiantly into his eyes.

'No. Where were you when I needed a father? My entire childhood, I heard nothing from you. I'm a woman now. I'm grown. I don't want you, or need you,' Faye held her arms out in front of her and then crossed them over her chest, which Moddie had taught her was the stance of banishing. 'I banish you, Lyr of Falias, back to your realm.'

'You cannot banish me,' he said, simply.

The rest of the circle was dead quiet, watching in disbelief. Could they see Lyr or, to them, did it look as though she was a madwoman, shouting into thin air? Gabriel's face was composed, but Ruby and Victoria's expressions were somewhere between terror and disbelief. Lyr took a step forward, towards Faye, and Gabriel took an instinctive step backwards. So, they could see him: Lyr could choose to be seen if he wanted to.

It was as though the realm of faerie wouldn't let her go, and she hated it. And she was embarrassed, too; this was a group of new friends, potentially; people she could have shared magic with. And now that was probably ruined.

'You're not welcome here,' she repeated. 'And how dare you interrupt this ritual? These people didn't ask you here. I didn't ask you here. Be gone!' Faye shouted as loudly as she could and removed the banishing sigil from her pocket: she had it on her at all times except when she was asleep, and that was only because she slept naked; if she'd suddenly started wearing pyjamas or something with a pocket, Rav would have thought it was odd. She held it up in front of Lyr's face, but he smiled, took it from her fingers and placed it gently back in her pocket.

'You do not need protection from me. I have told you, I am your father,' he repeated. 'Don't you want to know why I am here, daughter?'

He stepped forward to take her hand. 'Aren't you at all curious about me, after all this time?'

'No. Leave me alone.'

It wasn't just the shock of being confronted with her long-lost father that had floored her so deeply. She'd just begun a new life; a new start, with Rav, in a different city, far away from Abercolme. Away from Finn Beatha and the horrors of Murias.

Lyr regarded her dispassionately.

'I'm not your child, and I'm not part of the faerie realm any more,' she cried. 'Please, just leave me in peace!'

'As you wish, daughter.' Lyr stepped away from her. 'But know that Falias is your home as much as this world is, and that it awaits you. As I do.'

He nodded to the circle, and walked away into the trees, his golden light dimming until blackness replaced it, and Faye felt she was blind.

Chapter 13

Mallory had her feet up on the brown leather footstool and was flicking through the TV channels with the remote control from the sofa when Faye got back to the flat. She looked up, laughing; Faye could hear Rav crashing around in the adjoining kitchen.

'Oh, it's you, Faye. I was hoping the pizza delivery boy had let himself in,' she drawled. 'Have you just finished your witching now? It's late.'

'Yes, it is,' Faye said pointedly, but in truth she was taken aback. Why was Mallory here, at eleven o'clock on a Saturday night? In Rav's flat, the two of them apparently enjoying a few drinks? Rav definitely hadn't mentioned Mallory being invited over; if she'd known, Faye wondered whether she would have wanted to go out and leave them together. Although, a night in Mallory's company wasn't exactly something to savour...

Mallory eyed Faye coldly, picked up a beer bottle and drank from it, not bothering to get up. Rav came in, also holding a beer, and stopped when he saw Faye. For a brief moment, she saw surprise and panic in his eyes; clearly, he wasn't expecting her home yet, or had lost track of time.

'Oh! You're back.' Rav enveloped her in a huge hug. 'How was it? Fun?'

She could smell the beer on his breath. Over his shoulder, Faye could see six or seven empty bottles littered the coffee table; one had rolled on its side and a small pool of sticky beer was soaking into a pile of music magazines. He was drinking more and more often at home and it had begun to worry her.

'Interesting more than fun.' She disentangled herself from his hug and walked into the kitchen to get a cloth for the spill, but also to have an excuse to gather herself a little. She was upset as it was; Lyr appearing at the ritual had thrown her completely and, on the train home, changing from one confusing underground line to another, she'd been holding on to the thought that she'd get home to Rav, who would listen and understand. She was also worried about what the rest of Ruby's coven thought of her. After Lyr had disappeared, Faye could tell that Penny and Sylvia weren't happy; they'd closed the circle swiftly, making sure that all the quarters – the four elemental powers that had been drawn into the circle – were banished. They had wanted her to stay and talk about what had happened, but she'd made a shaky excuse and run away. She hadn't known – didn't know – how to deal with it.

She needed Rav. But Rav was drunk and his ex-girlfriend was draped over the couch like she owned it. Faye took a deep, wavering breath, fought the tears back and walked out into the lounge.

Mallory watched her wipe up the beer without any acknowledgement.

'Hey, Faye. You okay?' it didn't take a genius to work out that Faye wasn't exactly thrilled, and Rav was picking up her mood, despite the beer.

'Fine. I'm going to bed.' She didn't bother saying anything to Mallory. Rav followed her to the bedroom.

'You're not all right. What is it? Mallory? We're just friends.' He looked guilty though, and it irritated Faye even more.

'She's your ex-girlfriend and she's here drinking beer with you while I'm out,' Faye snapped. 'You didn't even tell me she was coming over. And you're acting guilty about it.'

'She called around. I was working, fancied a break. That's all.'

'How convenient,' she muttered, getting undressed.

'Come on, Faye – you really aren't one to talk. It's not like *I'm* two-timing you with some faerie queen. It's just a beer.' The words were out of his mouth like they had been sitting there on his tongue, waiting to be said for months.

'*Excuse me?*' Faye stopped unbuttoning her jeans and stared at Rav; he looked away, uncomfortably.

'I didn't mean that,' he muttered, but the words were lodged in the air between them, each letter like a brick, making a wall, and it was too late to take them back.

'I didn't two-time you. You know I didn't,' Faye said in a low voice, conscious that Mallory was in the lounge – it wasn't a huge flat and she could probably hear everything they were saying. Faye jabbed her finger in the direction of the lounge. 'She still has feelings for you. Sumi told me. You shouldn't be encouraging her.'

'I'm not. She came to see me! It's not fair,' Rav protested.

'Who cares about being fair to Mallory! What about me? It's not fair to *me*. It's not okay that you guys are here getting drunk together without even telling me, Rav.' Faye sat on the bed in her bra and jeans half-undone and felt the tears coming again. 'Especially not after what happened tonight.'

'Wait, what happened tonight? Did someone hurt you?' Rav sat next to her, cautiously. 'If anyone laid a finger on you, I'll end them,' he muttered. Faye rolled her eyes.

'Spare me the macho crap, Rav. It's not like you'd ever do anything.'

She thought guiltily of Finn. Being a faerie king's lover had once given her protected, special status: Finn had almost killed Rav for pursuing Faye. She knew it wasn't fair to compare them: Finn was a spoilt, sulky and tempestuous faerie king, compared to Rav, a man that loved her, who made her laugh, who listened to her and wanted a life with her. But everything felt shaky right now; everything was off balance. Right now she needed to feel safe and Rav, who had been the stability she needed these last months, was suddenly showing himself to be… what? Unreliable? A liar? Her throat tightened and the feeling of drowning returned.

'Thanks a lot.' He got up and walked out; in the lounge, she heard voices, then the front door opening and closing again. Faye finished undressing and put on her bathrobe before following him into the lounge.

'She's gone. Said she didn't feel comfortable staying since we were obviously having a row. Happy now?' He drained his bottle of beer.

Yes, actually, she thought, but didn't say it. *She hates me.* 'No.'

'Seems there's a lot you're not happy about,' he said, turning off the TV and facing her.

Faye sat on the edge of the sofa, her head in her hands. 'My father turned up in the circle. Lyr, High King of Falias,' she said, not meeting his gaze. 'It was an intense kind of night.'

'Your father?'

'That's right. Remember, I told you? When you were recovering. About Moddie falling for him. She never saw him again after I was born. Apparently, he's famous for it. Siring half-human babies.' *Half-human babies.* She wanted to tell him what she'd promised Glitonea, but even thinking about it caused her throat to close up again, threatening to choke her. She coughed hard until the sensation passed. What would happen if she ever did fall pregnant? If she and Rav had a child together, how would it be, knowing that it could be taken from her at any time? And what would he say, how horrified would he be if that happened and he found out she'd known it would? That she was unable to stop it? Faye felt sick.

'I do remember, it's just that… it's all a bit fuzzy, you know? Sometimes I think I imagined the whole thing.'

Faye peered through her fingers at Rav's expression; it was one she saw all too much of: a haunted blankness she'd tried to erase with kindness. He didn't want to remember; he was trying to bury what had happened to him.

He wanted a normal life and so did she. Sadness welled up in her. She didn't want to argue, and she didn't want to see that expression on his face.

Faye reached for Rav's hand.

'I'm sorry. It's just been…. quite a night,' she said, squeezing his fingers. 'I know you weren't doing anything wrong. I was just… jealous, I guess.'

'You don't need to be jealous. Ever.' Rav squeezed her hand back, and his eyes were full of tears. 'I'd never do anything to hurt you, Faye. I love you.'

'I love you too,' she replied, but there was also a sadness in her that she closed away beyond a door, along with everything she'd wanted to tell Rav: about her fear of who she was; the power that she felt within her, and the curse that had been cast on her. He didn't want to be told – and she couldn't tell him – so she stayed quiet.

But in doing so, a part of her was lost, just like when she'd been in the faerie realm too long. Yet this was a part of her that was lost to the mundane human world: it was another little sacrifice, a shallow cut that she sliced from herself as an offering to the normal life that Rav wanted. And it hurt.

Chapter 14

Regent's Park was striped by the golden morning sun like a tiger's back; the trees threw frosty shadows onto the grass where the sun hadn't yet managed to warm the ground. As Faye walked, the sun and chill alternated on her skin and she pulled her thick tartan shawl around her shoulders.

She'd left the flat with Rav and said goodbye at the tube station; Rav was going to the office, and she needed to get out. In Abercolme, Faye had walked in the fields or along the coast path most days, either before opening the shop or after closing. She wasn't used to the city, and that day she'd woken up needing to feel her feet on grass or sand. It was a deep, physical need: to feel the power that coursed through the earth, to draw it up into herself, to renew herself in sunlight and rain and under the quiet solace of ancient trees. The argument with Rav wouldn't stop going around and around in her mind. *We came here for a fresh start. I don't want this in my life.* Faye felt betrayed, cut loose on a roiling sea with no anchor.

She hated the tube, but she'd taken the bus for a few stops until Regent's Park came into view. As she walked in, she caught her breath: it was far more beautiful than she'd expected. Hampstead Heath was wonderful, but it was wild and unkempt compared to the manicured lawns, carved fountains and exotic trees that drew her steps here.

It was still early, but, like anywhere in London, there were people about. West End workers power-walked to their offices, carrying takeaway coffees and frowning at their phones. Faye passed a group of elderly, coiffed and manicured ladies in velour tracksuits who were walking equally manicured dogs on jewelled leads. An early group of Japanese tourists photographed swans on a tranquil pond.

However, as Faye followed the paths further into the park, she left them behind. Pushing last night's argument to the back of her mind, she took off her ballet pumps and held them in one hand, walking on the close-cut grass instead of the delicately gravelled pathway. She half-closed her eyes and attuned herself to the energy of the place. It had an old majesty about it, a queenly, regal feeling, like the gold-bedecked hotel where she and Rav had enjoyed afternoon tea. And yet, as well as that, the park had a different, less genteel energy. Faye breathed in the power of the earth through her bare feet as she walked, meditatively, seeing its green and black and gold power twisting up through the ground, through her soles, into her legs and coiling into her sacrum like a serpent. She'd a sudden vision of the faerie forest as she'd seen it at the Mabon ceremony; thick, green-black pines that grew out of a shining black crystal ground.

Connecting with the spirit of the place in this way, she knew, intuitively, that this was ancient forest land and always had been, even though it was now a playground for the rich. Faye had a sense of the land before a city had ever been here; of deep forest stretching up to the river; of a people that lived under the trees and worshipped the muddy Thames as life-giving goddess. So many years, so many layers of city that had been built over that faraway London. But the bones of those ancient people lay somewhere under her feet, as did the echoes and shadows of the tree roots that once grew wild around her. It gave

Faye a sense of belonging, even though Abercolme was her land; there was a connection to the past here, and it was good to make it. It gave her something to hang onto in a city that felt alien: at last, below the surface, there was a London that spoke to her.

She walked further, breathing in the quiet, feeling it echo and fill her body with a peace she longed for. Magpies flitted from tree to tree, calling to each other, breaking the quiet with their throaty cackles. Faye smiled, and thought of the old rhyme. *One for sorrow, two for joy; three for a girl, four for a boy.* There was more than one, so there would be no sorrow for her today, and she was grateful for it.

She walked on, past a coffee stall, then, putting her shoes back on, thought better of it and went back.

'Lovely morning.' The girl inside the powder-blue painted refreshment shack looked up from her magazine. Faye nodded and asked for a mocha.

'What's the best bit of the park? I don't want to miss anything I should definitely see.' Faye looked around her; the sun was getting stronger now and reaching into the corners it hadn't earlier.

'Rose garden?' The girl wrapped a napkin around the paper cup and handed it to Faye. 'Past its best, this time of year, but there are still some in flower. I love it in there, anyway. Follow the path when it forks to the right, you can't miss it.'

'Thanks.' Faye sipped her drink and walked on, delighting in the peace in the park and the sweetness of the chocolate mixed with the strong coffee in her veins. She breathed out a sigh of happiness; finally, she was feeling like herself, probably for the first time since being in London. And, after the Mabon ritual, she needed some peace. She needed some time to return to herself, to evaluate and sit with what had happened. Seeing a long-lost father for the first time, unexpectedly, was difficult. Your long-lost faerie king father appearing to you during a ritual with virtual strangers – and disappearing back into his faerie realm – took it to the next level.

There was no-one else in the circular rose garden when Faye stepped into the first of its concentric circles and took a sharp gasp of surprise. For a moment, she saw a vision of it in full bloom: thick, velvet-petalled yellow roses, blowsy with their rich summer scent; small, perfect blood-red rosebuds atop stiff, thorny stalks; perfect pink roses with their outer petals a little browned by the heat. Yet, as she blinked again, it returned to the way it was – there were few roses left apart from some late-blooming white ones that shone against the glossy dark green leaves of the bushes.

Faye walked the outer circle and followed it inwards, reminiscent of the spiral walk she sometimes did as part of ritual; a spiral inwards to raise and focus the power, a spiral outwards to let it go. She could still smell roses on the air, but when she sniffed the white flower, it had little perfume. She shivered involuntarily. *It's my imagination*, she told herself. *Nothing more*. The roses were gone for the autumn, and their blooms would wait until next summer to return.

No, it's a faerie place, she suddenly realised with a degree of shock. Not that all nature wasn't part of the realms of faerie – Grandmother had taught her that the four elemental faerie kingdoms were the high thrones of power for the four elements of the ordinary world – air, fire, earth and water. But the rose garden itself had the same sense of enchantment that she'd felt before. The rose perfume returned, intensified, and Faye closed her eyes, starting to be pulled under by its scent. With her eyes closed, she could see a rich golden light rising upwards from the rose bushes, like rain in reverse, and heard faerie voices singing sweetly. Faye stood at the centre of the circles of rose bushes and spread out her arms, turning her face up to the sun with pleasure. The suffuse, sweet scent of roses bathed her senses in its luxury and she breathed it in.

Something like fur brushed her hand and something sank its teeth into her palm.

She screamed and opened her eyes, but she was alone in the garden.

'Leave me alone!' she cried, and ran out of the circled rose bushes, their thorns catching at her skirts like fingers.

Chapter 15

Faye ran out of the park and onto the road that bordered it, weaving her way through the businesspeople, mothers in running gear, pushing their babies in sports buggies and the ever-present packs of wandering tourists. *Leave me alone, no, no!* she thought, not knowing if she was muttering under her breath, and not caring.

Eventually, her run slowed to a walk and she began to feel more normal again. The crowds were a balm of ordinariness she lost herself in, and instead of seeking the side streets, she let herself be swept along the wide, busy pavement alongside shops and cafés, next to the slow-moving traffic. *Why can't it leave me alone?* she thought. *I don't want faerie. Not now.*

She walked and walked, not intending to go anywhere in particular, just following the crowds. Dully, she looked at the shop windows; some of the department stores featured Halloween displays with grinning orange pumpkins, pillowy ghosts and cartoon witches with green faces. The sight made her angry. She was a witch: was she a green-faced caricature? Was she a cartoon, a stock image, something that was an equivalent of a ghoul or a vampire? Faye would readily admit that she had a sense of humour failure about caricatured representations of witches like these. It was as if everyone had forgotten that the warty old women on the Halloween face masks represented real women that had once been tortured and killed for having a small degree of wisdom. How was it still all right for shops and books and magazines and TV adverts to roll out this same stereotype about a group of people that had been murdered en masse in actual history? How had the world not moved past this hatred of women? And why did the world believe that witches – real witches, people who made it their life's work to reconnect to their own natural power – were as fictional as monsters?

She had wanted to reconnect to nature and now, here she was, trudging along the grimy London roads, breathing in car exhaust and being deafened by people: their shouting, laughing, catcalling; the discordant sounds of street buskers and unidentifiable music blaring from shops.

Instinctively, Faye turned off the busy street and followed a side street that led into a Georgian terrace bordering a quiet green square. She drew in a deep breath and exhaled loudly a few times, letting her anger and dismay go. It wasn't the Halloween witches as much as the strange experience in the rose garden that had put her on edge. Wasn't it possible for her to connect to the land in the slightest way without an echo, a touch from faerie reminding her of her parentage, and of her half-faerie nature? Lyr was still trying to make contact with her, she knew. But she wasn't ready to face the father that had abandoned her. Not yet. She worried again about the impression she must have made at the ritual. The others – what had they thought of her? That she was mad, possessed, damaged in some way? Her stomach clenched with anxiety. She wanted to explain, but she wouldn't know where to start. Even for witches, Faye's story seemed unbelievable.

Faye walked across the quiet square. Three casually-dressed young men came out of one of the smart blue-painted doors to her right; they passed her, carrying folders of documents, talking about something she couldn't catch. Faye noticed the name of a well-known book publisher on the brass plaque next to the door, whose books she stocked in her shop.

She followed the men, taking the recognition of the publisher as a sign. She didn't know where she was, and the street names meant nothing to her. Faye didn't feel particularly lost, as such, because she knew she could hail a cab to take her home at any time. It was more that she had a feeling that her day's exploring wasn't over, and that there was still something she was supposed to do.

The young men walked around a corner onto a busy, narrow street, and a huge building, colonnaded by pillars, appeared in front of her. Awed by its size, Faye followed the line of people snaking through the black gate in the cast iron railings and found herself in a wide courtyard.

Facing the building, she gazed up, through the eight central pillars to branded posters featuring a new exhibition: The Celts. She smiled, thinking *I'm a Celt, here I am, home.* This was the British Museum; she remembered leafing through a book about Egyptian mythology Annie had got out of the village library, sitting at the kitchen table at Annie's house. Annie's mother had wrinkled her nose in distaste at the mummified bodies and the canopic jars, where Egyptian embalmers had stored the organs of the dead king or queen, ready for their voyage to the underworld. But Faye and Annie had been rapt, reading out their favourite bits of the text to each other.

Faye wandered in to the vast museum. She knew better than to think chance had led her here; this was a magical place and the home of so many cultures' magical items: their gods, their goddesses and holy treasures lived here. She gazed up in wonder at the high glass roof inside, glazed in a geometric pattern that seemed to elevate the museum into the clouds. At least, if the coven wasn't going to invite her back, she'd found a place she could come to feel connected to magic. It was a different kind of magic, in some ways, to the traditions Grandmother had taught her. But it was a page in the same book, and Faye was grateful for that.

Faye followed the signs to the Celts exhibition: it was housed in a long, wide gallery and at first she marvelled at the gold and silver torcs, jewellery that had belonged to queens and warrior chieftains. She herself had worn something similar in Murias; instinctively, she put her hand to her throat, but the choking sensation didn't come.

Faye walked reverently among the exhibits, noticing a group of people surrounding one area in particular. She waited for the crowd to abate a little and stepped forward.

On a raised dais behind strengthened glass sat a wide, deep silver cauldron, over half a metre wide and a couple of feet deep. Faye gasped as her eyes took in its detail: the bulls, stags, dogs and snakes engraved on the fine silver on a number of panels, depicting Celtic gods and goddesses driving chariots and soldiers fighting ancient wars. It was deeply beautiful, intricate work, and it reminded her of the golden cup of Murias she'd often seen in her dreams; a cup big enough to stand inside.

Faye's vision blurred for a moment, and it was as if she half-dreamed the cauldron in front of her at the centre of a great hall, where a queen stood with it at her feet in the midst of a great ceremony. Hundreds of men and women lined the hall, singing; there was a burst of light and smoke, and a great cheer.

Faye blinked open her eyes, returning to normal awareness. She took a deep breath and felt the smile fill her face. Somehow, this artefact had connected her to her ancestors for a brief moment. Again, she had the sense of familiarity, of home, that she'd lacked since arriving in the city. Standing near to this ancient cauldron felt right, felt like something which was hers. The power of the silver cauldron soaked the gallery in its magic. Faye closed her eyes and let the energy fill her, bowing her head in reverence.

Lend me your strength and grace, glorious ancestors, Faye prayed. *Protect me in this city. I'm thankful to have found you.*

Someone stood next to her; she opened her eyes and glanced to one side.

Gabriel Black cleared his throat politely.

'I'm so sorry; I didn't want to interrupt your communion,' he said, holding out his arm formally; as before, he was dressed impeccably in a well-cut black suit and crisp white shirt undone at the neck. 'But when you're finished, I wonder if you'd like to come to my shop for a cup of tea?'

Chapter 16

Fortune's was down a narrow street opposite the museum, with a pub at the end of the road and a small café opposite. Next door to the shop there was another bookshop with statuettes of Egyptian gods in the window among many leather volumes. On the main street outside, regency terraces lined the road with black cast iron railings, smart against white walls that featured a blue plaque here and there, remembering the great men and women that once occupied their high ceilings and graceful reception rooms.

'Come in, come in!' Gabriel swung the shop door open and ushered her inside. 'I'm so happy that I ran into you. Providence,' he said, smiling over his shoulder. 'Or something magical at work, more likely. Don't worry about wiping your feet.'

After she'd run away from the coven at Mabon, Faye was pleasantly surprised at Gabriel's friendly invitation to his shop. She'd convinced herself that all of the group would think she was a lunatic.

Faye knew that Gabriel's shop sold new and old occult books; he'd told her at the ritual. She glanced at shelves heaving with a mix of garish occult novels, old hardbacks with cracked spines and new, luxurious slipcases adorned with mysterious symbols in gold foiling. Her feet squeaked on the dark floorboards; the high-ceilinged shop was lit cosily by a Lalique-style pastel-green glass lamp which stood on a mahogany desk that was slightly bowed in the middle. Two dusty crystal chandeliers hung from the plastered ceiling, adding their milky luminescence to the atmosphere. An ornate incense holder, like a small silver minaret, scented the shop with the meditative, churchy aroma of frankincense.

'Everything from ritual magic to druidry, crystal grids to spiritual healing, Atlantis to grimoires of the damned and famous.' Gabriel smiled as she scanned the shelves. 'Open eighty years and they haven't closed us down yet. Do you know this area? I don't suppose you do.'

'No, not at all. I read a book about the museum years ago, so I recognised it when I...' she frowned. 'It was the oddest thing. I just... happened upon it.'

Gabriel smiled and offered her a teal leather armchair with bronze studs around the edges. Faye sat in it gingerly; it looked ancient, but as she relaxed into it, it tilted backwards slightly and seemed to hug her in an unexpectedly comfortable posture.

'Bloomsbury's chock full of magic, dearest Faye. Secret societies, covens, antiquarian bookshops, magicians, strange antique dealers.... It's no wonder you found your way here. It's like a gigantic occult magnet to anyone with even the slightest inclination for the distinctly un-mundane.'

'It's lovely.' Faye smiled. 'I stock some books, but only a few shelves' worth. This is such a wonderful collection.' She looked around the shelves and saw a shelf marked *Scottish Myths and Legends*: she peered at the spines.

'That was some introduction to the coven the other night. Talk about making an impression.' He took out a brown hardback from the Scottish Legends shelf and handed it to her. 'Here. This'll be useful, I'd say. A gift from me.'

Faye took the book, surprised and pleased.

'You don't have to…' she stammered, touched by the act of generosity. She looked at the spine: *Faeries in Their Elements*, by Reverend R W Smith.

'It's my pleasure. I didn't know if I was going to see you again, after the ritual – you ran out of there like a scared rabbit as soon as the circle was closed.' Gabriel placed his slim, long-fingered hand over hers as she held the book.

'Was Sylvia angry? I got the feeling she was.' Faye felt embarrassed.

'Maybe a little. We all wanted to talk to you about it, more than anything. Make sure you were all right. I'm glad you're here,' he said quietly, looking into her eyes. Embarrassed at his intimate scrutiny, she looked away. She didn't quite know what to make of Gabriel Black just yet.

'I doubt I'll be allowed back after that performance,' she said, expecting him to agree, albeit kindly. She'd disrupted the whole ritual; granted, it wasn't something she'd planned but, again, Faye's faerie half had threatened her normal life, and any illusion she had about being able to control it was ruined. Her eyes strayed to a glass-fronted mahogany cabinet opposite, inside which a number of crystal balls sat on a velvety, mustard-coloured shelf. The shelf below held a variety of crystal skulls – large and small, and carved from black, clear and even pink stones. Faye got the impression that, if she asked, Gabriel would be able to show her some far more unusual magical artefacts and tools.

'Of course you will!' Gabriel reassured her.

Fortune's reeked of old, occult magic in a way that was very different to her own cosy shop in Abercolme. Mistress of Magic was a place of dried herbs by the hearth, herbal soaps, wands and spell kits. It was a place where anyone could be assured of a warm welcome, advice if they asked for it, their fortune told and their worries assuaged.

Fortune's was different, though Faye still liked it immensely: she could feel the long, complicated rituals that had been performed here, the invocations to old gods, the strange incenses burned and spirits summoned.

'We told Ruby she had to ask you back. I mean, we were all a bit freaked out, sure…'

Gabriel was being kind, she knew. 'Come on. More than freaked out. I saw their faces. They were terrified. So was I.' Faye traced her fingertips around the brass buttons that held the turquoise-blue leather of her chair in place.

'Well, it was… errr… remarkable. I'll say that. But don't worry about it.' Gabriel pulled up a straight-backed black leather easy chair from behind the shop counter and sat next to Faye. 'Come on. No-one who stands up to a faerie king like you did should be apologising to a measly bookseller. I mean, you're… half-faerie? Am I right in saying that?'

Faye nodded. 'Unfortunately.'

'Then you should be firing arrows of flame from your fingertips at minions, in a castle somewhere,' he consoled her. 'We should thank you. *I* should thank you, anyway. I've never seen a faerie king before. It was… yeah. Wow.'

'The arrows have gone in for their annual service,' Faye joked, but she still felt mortified. She hugged the book to her. 'And you're not measly.'

'No, well. Not glamorous, anyway. Sometimes days pass and no-one comes in here. All dressed for the ball and no-one to waltz with.' He stretched out his arms and pulled at the deep cuffs of his tailored shirt; Faye noticed he wore monogrammed cufflinks.

'You're very… do you dress this smartly every day?' She changed the subject, smiling at his well-cut clothes and precise black hair.

'You never know when a faerie queen will drop by.' He gave her that inscrutable smile again, and she looked away, not sure what to say. 'Don't change the subject. You can't invoke the Elemental King of Earth and not explain yourself.'

'Ugh. Where to start…?' She sighed. Did she really want to tell Gabriel the whole story? He was a stranger, and Faye was used to keeping her business to herself. A life in Abercolme had left her with few other options, outside of Annie.

But if she was to have a life here, she'd have to open up sometime. And, she admitted to herself, she needed a friend. Especially one that didn't think she was crazy if she talked about magic. Not that she could tell him everything; her hand went to her throat again, fearful of the choking sensation.

Faye chose her words carefully. 'Rav and I moved down – to London – because some bad things happened, back in Abercolme. In the faerie realms, and in the village. He… he was badly injured.' She met Gabriel's gaze, expecting to see ridicule or disbelief there, but his black-brown eyes showed only interest. 'He wants us to… I don't know. Have a normal life here. Be normal people. But I'm…' she trailed off, aware that she sounded crazy.

'But you're not normal,' Gabriel finished for her. 'You're half-faerie, and Lyr's daughter.'

'Yes,' she said, and it was both a relief and a kind of dread to hear someone else say it. Her faerie half was like a dirty secret; it was the shadowy side of her; in faerie, she'd done things she would never do in her normal, ordinary life. And yet, now that she'd opened herself up to the shadow, she missed it.

Gabriel stared at her with a dark intensity.

'He's right. You're not normal, and you never will be,' he continued, his eyes never leaving hers. 'You're more magical than most people will ever be, Faye. If he can't stand in your light, then he deserves to live in the dark. And you deserve someone who knows how to walk in the shadows with you.'

Chapter 17

Gabriel leaned towards her. His eyes were intense, staring at her, but not in an unpleasant way.

Close up, he smelt of sandalwood and frankincense; a subtle, woody scent that went alongside something else, something that was just him: under his slightly foppish ways, there was a quiet, strong masculinity.

'So… this Lyr thing. Aren't you in the least bit curious about what he wants with you?'

Faye saw the fascination in Gabriel's upturned face and allowed herself to imagine how he saw her. Her auburn-red hair was tied in a long ponytail and she wore a short, bright blue knitted dress with her ballet pumps; she'd taken off her black belted mac as she sat down. She was taller than average and, perhaps, there was a magical glamour of some kind about her that came from her faerie blood. She had the high cheekbones of the fae, and their clear, sharp bone structure. She knew she could enchant Gabriel if she tried: perhaps she already had.

'Yes,' she replied. 'But the faerie realms are dangerous. I don't want to… I promised Rav I wouldn't…' she trailed off. Here and now, Rav seemed far away; surrounded by so many magical books, she remembered how it had felt, being in Murias. How sweet and charged, and how full of power it was – how powerful *she* could be. Imagining that she'd never feel that again filled her with sadness.

'Rav wouldn't ask that of you if he loved you,' Gabriel said. 'I mean, I don't know him. I'm sure he's great and everything. But you know I'm right. If you're half-faerie, what, you're supposed to deny a whole half of yourself because he's not comfortable with it? First rule of magic: know thyself. Faye, you can't be a witch, or a faerie queen for that matter, without being at peace with who you really are.'

'It's easy for you to say. You don't know the history,' she muttered.

'Then tell me.' His eyes challenged hers. 'All of it.'

*

'So your friend's still there? In Murias?' Gabriel hadn't moved throughout Faye's whole story – of discovering Murias from the faerie road that bisected Rav's beachfront house, of going through the labyrinth to Finn's castle; of her own enchantment there, and her eventual disillusionment. Last, haltingly, Faye told him about the concert in Abercolme: when Dal Riada, Finn's band, had whipped the crowd into a state of vicious, sexual fervour, and had disappeared, taking eight humans into the faerie realm, including Aisha. Her friend. The only thing she couldn't explain was the bargain with Glitonea.

Faye looked down at her hands that twisted together with anxiety. 'Yes.'

Faye continually asked herself if she'd run away from her responsibilities towards Aisha. And if she had, could anyone blame her? She went around and around with the thought, starting at guilt and ending in a kind of dejected defiance. No-one *would* blame her, because almost no-one believed the true version of what had happened. The story taken up by the papers was that Finn Beatha's band, Dal Riada, had disappeared with several concert attendees in tow after their concert at the summer solstice; the first solstice celebration in Abercolme for hundreds of years. There had been a fire and general panic, in which many were injured.

The papers seemed to suggest that the band were a kind of cult that had run away with locals they'd convinced to follow them.

Yet, the villagers knew, or suspected. Some of them – the ones that remembered the fae from the old lore their grandparents and great-grandparents had shared with them when they were bairns – they knew what Faye had done to try to save them, and knew where Aisha and the others had gone. And, perhaps, they were the only ones that had made their peace with the likelihood that the missing would be unlikely to return.

'And you're... what's the word? *Excluded* from Murias now? You can't go back?' Gabriel's voice brought her back from her worries.

'No. I've tried. It's cut off to me now, unless I go back to Finn. But I can't. I don't want to.'

Gabriel eyed her coolly. 'Don't want to, or are afraid to? Sounds like Finn had quite an effect on you.'

Faye breathed out a long sigh, got up and started pacing the small confines of the shop. The smell of old leather from the antique books was comforting; she leaned her head gently against a high shelf with her back to Gabriel. How could she explain what Finn had done to her? It wasn't normal. He wasn't human; all the usual frames of reference for relationships – he was controlling, he was emotionally unavailable, it was just a sex thing – were invalid. He *was* controlling and unavailable, and the sex was incredible. But it was so much more than that: Finn was a faerie king; his power was all-encompassing. He was faerie, who didn't live by the same rules of love and compassion as humans.

'It's hard to explain. The fae... Finn is...' she stopped for a moment, trying to think of the best way to describe the faerie king.

'I've read the legends. I know they're irresistible when they want to be,' Gabriel added.

'But it's so dangerous there. For humans, that is. I'm half-fae. The effects of being in the faerie realm weren't as strong for me, and I was… Finn's consort, so I had special treatment, I suppose. But the humans that go there, to be lovers or to bear the half-fae children, they don't survive. One way or the other.' Faye shivered as she remembered the human bones littering the floor of the faerie ballroom; of the emaciated bodies there that weren't quite dead, but too weak to move. She herself had danced on them without knowing, lost in her own enchantment. The thought still made her sick.

'I read that sometimes they take women who have just given birth to breastfeed their faerie babies. Human wet-nurses,' Gabriel added.

'It wouldn't surprise me, but I didn't see any. But the castle's huge. I only saw the areas Finn wanted me to. Or his sister Glitonea's chambers.'

'The High Queen? What was she like? They say that the faerie queens are too beautiful to be described.' Gabriel's eyes were wide, like a child's. Faye remembered the rapt and dreamy eyes of Glitonea's faerie lover as he danced in her arms, and the tortured gaze of the Frog Queen's partner through his mask. *She'd take everything from you*, she thought, looking at him; *she'd dance and kiss and love every ounce of your moon-cowed, human adoration and leave you to die when she'd drunk her fill. And you'd let her do it, because dying would be so sweet.*

'She is a beauty. Golden-haired, tall, strong; her eyes are the same as Finn's. Like the ocean,' she answered. Gabriel didn't have to know about the horror of loving a faerie queen, and Faye didn't talk about why she'd been in the faerie queen's chambers in the first place: the magic she'd learnt there, or the bargain she'd struck with Glitonea to escape. 'They're both beautiful beyond description. But they're also remorseless. Cold. Selfish. They're only concerned with fulfilling their own desires.'

'The Charge of the Goddess says *I am what is attained at the end of desire*.' Gabriel was talking about a part of Wiccan ceremony that Faye knew had become ubiquitous; a call to the goddess, the symbol of feminine power in the universe. 'Desire isn't a bad thing. It's the condition of being human.'

'Of course not. They're fae. They are doing what's natural for them, like cats hunt mice. It's not our job to place human morality on them. But it's sensible for a mouse to know a cat will toy with it, and kill it when it gets bored; the mouse knows to avoid the cat if it wants to live.'

'To be a faerie queen's lover, though,' Gabriel sighed wistfully. 'What a way to go.'

'You're serious, aren't you?' Faye frowned at him. 'It's not something worth wishing for. Really. Believe me.'

Gabriel made a dismissive sound. 'Men like me – magicians, or ones that fancy themselves as something like it – have been obsessed with other worlds, and the delights we might find there, for hundreds of years. Come on, Faye.' Gabriel picked up a dusty grimoire and waved it at her. 'What is there for me here? Old books? If the opportunity arose, I'd take it. What's a life worth unless you live it?'

'But that's just it, Gabriel! You'd die there,' Faye exclaimed. 'The fae are savage, amoral creatures. If you'd seen what I have…' she shuddered. Gabriel was so naïve; she wished she could tell him exactly what Glitonea had forced her to agree to. Faerie queens might become a lot less desirable for him.

'But I haven't, Faye. That's the point.' He put the book back on the desk and sighed. 'Anyway. If you need to get Aisha back – and the rest of them, I suppose?' Faye nodded. 'Finn *will* let you back in. You just have to be his lover again.'

'That's not a choice. It would ruin my relationship with Rav; I'm not going to be unfaithful to him. Plus, he doesn't want me to be involved at all with the faerie realm. He wants to leave that all behind us.' Faye sighed.

'But you can't leave it behind. It's who you are.' Gabriel frowned.

'I know, I know.' Faye began pacing again.

'As we speak, Aisha's been there, how long? Hasn't Rav been helping you think of ways you could get her back? I mean, I know he's not a witch, but maybe he has some ideas?'

'No.' Faye looked out of the plate glass panels at the front of the shop, through the backwards lettering; the simple, traditional font that spelled out *Fortune's* in gold letters. It was raining and the strip of grey sky she could glimpse above, between the close terraces on either side of the small street, framed her mood.

No. Rav wanted to forget it all – his abduction, his imprisonment in the faerie ball. Daily, Faye knew that he willed himself to forget the pain he'd suffered at Finn's hands in Murias. Rav knew Aisha was there, still, but in the way that humans could think two opposite things at once, Faye knew that he'd also almost convinced himself that the whole thing was a kind of communal fantasy, a shared hallucination. Roni and Sumi and the rest believed that and perhaps, because of their influence, he did too.

Aisha was gone, but Rav hadn't once commented on her absence. Perhaps, in his mind, she'd gone on a long holiday somewhere. Or, perhaps, he believed that Aisha had gone of her own free will, and that it would be all right for her in Murias; a place of magic and wonder.

But Rav *had* been to Murias, and he knew that even if Aisha had been enchanted well enough to jump willingly with the rest of them, that consent wasn't freely given. She'd been under Finn's spell, and Finn had manipulated her to get what he wanted. Rav had danced in the faerie reel, and he knew as well as Faye how brutal it really was. Yet, his own self-preservation was more important.

'Okay, then. Couldn't Lyr help you in some way? I mean, he *is* a faerie king too. He's as powerful as Finn, right?' Gabriel asked.

Faye sighed and paced along the far wall of the shop. 'In the realm of earth, though. I don't see how he could help in Murias.'

'But he's trying to make contact with you.' Gabriel raised an eyebrow.

'I didn't ask him to,' Faye muttered, knowing she sounded like a child. 'He doesn't care about me. The fae don't have feelings like us. He wants something from me.'

'Don't you think you should at least find out what that is, though? You make a bargain with him. You give something, you get something.'

'Meaning… he gives me access to Murias?' Faye sat down and rustled a biscuit out of a packet on Gabriel's desk.

'Worth a try, right? At least that way you're not…' he blushed and looked away. 'You know.'

Forced to become Finn Beatha's lover again. Faye filled in the rest of the sentence in her head. *Would she do it to save Aisha?* Yes, she would, because saving a life was more important than saving a relationship. But it was a last resort. If there was any other way, that would be vastly preferable.

'You're right… we should at least ask Lyr if he can help.' She pushed her doubt to one side; there was fear there, too, but she ignored it. She, at least, was half-faerie. She had some knowledge already, and she was able to resist the weakening of the faerie realm. Aisha had no such power. 'Can you help me? I think I know a place we can use.'

Chapter 18

'We could have invited the group, you know. Safety in numbers, and all that,' Gabriel hissed as he held out a hand for Faye, perched precariously at the top of the black iron railings that surrounded Regent's Park.

Faye reached for Gabriel's slim, silver-ringed hand and hoisted herself up so that she could reach her foot to the top.

'I'm okay. Jump down,' she whispered back; she heard a thump as Gabriel fell into a bush on the other side of the railings. More daintily, Faye engineered herself to the top and lowered herself down the other side.

'I can't believe you're making me break into one of the royal parks,' Gabriel tutted, dusting himself down. Seemingly not possessing any casual clothes, he'd done his best to be anonymous in black trousers, a black polo neck and a black overcoat.

'You look like a French detective,' Faye whispered. 'It's not my fault the park closes so early at this time of year. Anyway, it's good. It means we won't be disturbed.'

'There's nothing wrong with being stylish, dear Faye. We're like magic detectives, anyway.' Gabriel helped her onto the gravelled pathway; Faye pointed to where she remembered the garden. 'Imagine me as a Wiccan Hercule Poirot.'

Faye rolled her eyes at him.

They had waited for a full moon, almost a week after Faye had visited Gabriel's shop. Full moons were a time of heightened power, and the moonlight lit the park in its blue-white brightness. Unusual shadows suggested themselves at the edges of Faye's vision; the moon's reflected light wasn't enough to cast the sharp shadows she'd walked through before, but its oddly stark glow cast an eerie almost-there lens over everything.

'It's this way.' Faye led Gabriel the way she remembered, keeping to the edges of the pathways in case anyone was patrolling the park. They walked quietly under the close trees, the fallen leaves under their feet. In the dark, with no-one else there, the energy of the park was completely different. Gone was the pleasant drone of activity, gone was the busy human story that evolved there every day. Instead, there was a watchfulness, a humming pause in a low, mournful tone. It wasn't a threat, but something waited for them. Something was alive in the dark.

They reached the concentric circles of rosebushes. With the moonlight on them the leaves looked waxy and artificial; the white flowers Faye had seen previously were petals on the ground, trodden into the mud. But, tonight, Faye didn't even have to close her eyes to detect the fae magic, because the mini labyrinth, such as it was, was alive with faeries.

Faye glanced at Gabriel.

'Are you seeing this?' she whispered, but the expression on his face was enough to tell her that he was. Gabriel's eyes were wide with wonder; he met Faye's eyes with an incredulous grin.

'I can't believe it. But yes, I am.'

The rose faeries danced an organised reel somewhat similar to a country dance or an old English dance from something like Tudor times, though it was difficult to completely characterise it. In the circular footpaths, orderly lines of faeries circled and twirled in perfect unison, dipping and bowing in a courtly way to each other. They were the size of small children, but had androgynous human features at the top half of their bodies and rose petal garments that swept to the ground on their lower halves. Their skins were varying hues of yellow, red, white and pink, like roses themselves, and the perfume Faye had smelt before – an intense scent of roses, sweet and earthy – filled the air. As they danced, the faeries sang a simple melody which was surprisingly mournful; in a strange way, it fitted the measured gravity of their dance. It wasn't sad, but serious and regal.

Like before, the gold dust-light appeared to rise from the rosebushes and float upwards, like bubbles underwater or an upside-down sleet. Gabriel reached out his hand for it, but Faye pulled him back and shook her head.

They stood completely still, watching the faerie dance, knowing that if they moved even slightly, they might frighten the faeries away. Yet when the dance ended, two of the faeries turned to them and held out their hands.

'We shouldn't,' Faye warned, though the sudden wave of temptation that hit her when the fae's attention diverted to them was difficult to ignore. 'They're dangerous. I don't know where this leads, Gabriel. We might take their hand now and come back in fifty years. Or not at all.'

'What do you suggest, then?' Gabriel spoke out of the corner of his mouth. 'We came here to summon Lyr. We can't do it now they're here.'

'Why not?' Faye turned to him, thinking fast. 'These are his creatures. This is the earth realm. They can help us. Lend us their power, like we would ask in calling in the quarters. These fae are partly who we're calling on every time we do that.'

She crouched down and undid her backpack, taking out Grandmother's grimoire.

'I brought this. It's got a ritual for summoning faerie kings and queens in it. We can do it here.'

Gabriel looked at the rose faeries.

'It seems a bit… rude, to ask them to stop their dancing so we can use their space,' he whispered doubtfully.

'It's not rude,' Faye whispered back with more confidence than she felt. Yet, she had power, and she could feel it rising up in her already. It was half the electric power of the fae and half her training as a witch; every time she worked magic, now, she felt it growing, an unwieldy, explosive something that coiled in her belly, gold and ready to rise up in her like wings of fire.

'We could… I don't know… do the summoning somewhere else?' Gabriel looked around.

'Gabriel. Are you scared?' Faye took his hand for a moment and searched his eyes. 'There's no need to be,' she lied, but she thought she was probably good enough to convince him. Gabriel wanted to be convinced, anyway, she could tell.

'Look. What point would there be doing it somewhere else when we made all this effort to break into the park? Just look at this, for goodness' sake.' She gestured to the golden light falling upwards, and to the rose-skirted fae creatures that had resumed their solemn dancing. 'This is a place of power. We need somewhere like this if it's just the two of us; we need the power. On the Heath we had a whole coven. It might not work if we summoned him in some random back garden. So this is the place of power we're going to use. And this is where we find Lyr again. Okay?'

He nodded. It was strange to see him without his usual affectations and camp swagger.

'Okay,' he breathed. Faye squeezed his hand.

'It's going to work. I promise.' She gave him a brighter smile than she really felt.

'That's what I'm afraid of, Faye Morgan.' Gabriel smiled uncertainly.

Chapter 19

Grandmother's ritual had been to summon the different Queens of the four faerie realms – Murias, Falias, Gorias and Finias – to learn magic from them. The summoning had to be done at in-between places: tidelines, forests, in storms and with ritual fires – places where faerie and human could meet halfway between their worlds. Faye hoped that the spell would work for Lyr, and that the rose garden was a good enough place. It wasn't the enchanted faerie forest, but this place seemed so dense with fae energy that she hoped it would be good enough.

> *To summon Her from her home element, you must create a ritual space of high vibration. Ideally, conduct the summoning as close to the right element as possible.*
>
> *Dance or pace out the circle clockwise and then pace into the centre of the circle as if in a spiral. When at the centre of the circle, call out her full name three times. Your calling should be urgent and passionate, from the heart. Repeat this process, walking the spiral in and out and calling the name, three times.*

'Lyr, High King of Falias, Faerie Kingdom of Earth; Master of Stone, Emperor of gnome and dryad kingdoms, come to me!' she called at the centre of the circle; Gabriel echoed her, his low voice vibrant in the night air. They repeated the process once and then twice.

When you have called their name three times, entreat them to be with you Grandmother's book had instructed. Faye stood at the centre of the rose garden, drawing power up from the earth and into her body in a meshed haze of rose petal and earth, feeling it fill her, ground her into the earth.

Beloved of the Fae, King of your Element
I seek communion with you; I seek knowledge of you and your realm
Bestow your magic upon me, I am fain to know your secrets
I am open; fill me with your blessings. Lyr, Father, I call on you
Father, I beseech you, enter the space I have prepared for you
Father, I would love you with my mind, my heart and my body
Lyr, I summon you from your Kingdom
I offer something of mine that I can give freely; this is the exchange
This is the promise between faerie and human
So mote it be

Faye raised her voice and called out the words with as much strength and passion as she could muster; every time she said *father*, unease twisted in her. Her feelings about her father were a mass of confusion: she needed him now, but she still hated him. But this was for Aisha, *Aisha*, she reminded herself as she felt the power in her. She was doing what she must.

'Hail and appear, Lyr of Falias!' Faye cried, her arms outstretched, coming to the last line of the invocation the book detailed. The same kind of heat shimmer Faye had seen at the Mabon ritual appeared in the middle of the room; that time, it was Morgana Le Fay that had been summoned to the circle. 'Hail and appear!' she shouted, louder, feeling power zinging through her arms, her fingers, from the hot core of her body.

Gabriel took her hands in his; together they formed a kind of battery. That part wasn't mentioned by Grandmother, but when Gabriel touched her, she felt that same explosion of energy as before: closing her eyes, she saw two poles of energy between them, positive and negative, joining together to create a kind of magical circuit. Only, Gabriel was the negative and she was the positive pole. Faye hadn't worked magic with a man before, but she'd read about this: that in magical working, the woman was the originator of power, and the man was the receiver. Faye didn't so much think it was odd – these were modern times, after all – as much as being pleasantly surprised to feel it in action.

Together, they called to Lyr: *we command you, Lyr of Falias; we desire your presence. Honour us!* repeating the phrase, over and over, Faye felt alive with the energy that flowed between her and Gabriel. She threw back her head, laughing in delight with the sheer power that they generated; it felt enough to light up the whole park. Dimly, she worried that it would alert a night watchman.

Lyr towered over them both; he appeared taller than when he'd come to them on the Heath. He bowed regally to them.

'Daughter. You called for me and I came.' Like before, he was extremely civil.

Faye studied her father. This time he wore a plain golden circlet on his long black hair and two-inch wide plain gold cuffs at his wrists. Instead of black, he wore a green robe belted with something that looked like plaited reeds or leaves; his feet were bare.

'Thank you for coming. I was…' she faltered, but Gabriel's hands in hers gave her strength. 'I was hasty to dismiss you at the ceremony.

I… would like to know you, and the realm of Falias. And… ask for your help.'

Lyr laughed a deep, rumbling laugh. 'You are my daughter, truly, then. You desire a boon.'

'Yes.' Faye stood her ground and looked the faerie king in the eye. Unlike Finn's, his eyes were the brown-black of the fertile earth, but they regarded her with the same dispassionate regard as Finn and Glitonea's shifting, cold ocean eyes.

'You are much like your mother,' Lyr said, smiling. 'You have her spirit. Ask, then. What is it you desire?'

Faye wanted to say, *don't talk to me about Moddie. You deserted her when she needed you.* But she pinched herself on the inside of her wrist and made her expression neutral.

'A friend of mine has been taken to Murias. I wish to take her back.'

'Murias is not my realm, daughter,' Lyr rumbled. 'Ask Finn Beatha to have her back, though I doubt he would concede a lover merely at your request.' He smiled.

'I can't ask Finn. He has banished me from Murias,' Faye replied. 'I need you to help me get back in without his permission.'

'Finn Beatha can be persuaded, child.' Lyr smiled and arched his eyebrow. 'I do not need to tell you how.'

'I don't want to be his lover again,' Faye retorted. 'I've chosen a human man and I intend to stay loyal to him. There must be another way.'

Lyr regarded Gabriel dispassionately.

'This is the object of your stubborn desire?' A derisive smile lifted the corner of his mouth. 'Foolish daughter, to choose a human man over a faerie king. Humans are so fragile; they ruin so easily. You will come to regret that choice.'

Faye felt a shadow of truth in Lyr's words, but she pushed it away. 'No… Gabriel is just… a friend.' She shot an awkward look at Gabriel, who gave her a rueful smile.

'An interesting choice, then, that your chosen one is not the one you picked to help summon me.' Lyr raised an eyebrow.

'You can find it interesting all you like. But it's my choice,' she argued back. She stood with her feet planted firmly. She hadn't trembled in front of Finn Beatha, and she wouldn't in front of Lyr either.

The faerie king regarded her for a moment; Faye was aware of Gabriel's hands in hers, and the power that still radiated from them both, looping between them in lazy arcs. It might have been awkward for a moment, but that didn't disrupt the power flowing between them.

Lyr held out his hand to her. 'Come with me to Falias and we will discuss this further, child. For I have a boon I would ask of you in return.'

'Are you saying yes? You can help me?' Faye asked, breathing hard now. She exchanged glances with Gabriel.

'I can consider it. If we strike a bargain,' he replied.

'Go,' Gabriel said under his breath. 'You won't have a better opportunity.'

'What about you?' she whispered, confused. 'I'm not sure if I should.'

'Go,' Gabriel repeated. 'I'll be here when you get back.'

Faye reached out, and Lyr's hand enveloped hers.

Chapter 20

A swirling mist surrounded Faye, and she had the sensation of falling. Flashes of green, yellow and brown surrounded her, as if she flew in a storm of earth and pollen; all the while, she felt Lyr's hand in hers.

In the next moment, she felt her feet touch earth, and she held out her other arm to steady herself, shaking her head to clear it and look around.

She stood on a bridge of rock between two mountains that stretched high into the clouds. Lyr stood next to her and caught the wonder in her eyes as she surveyed her new surroundings.

'Welcome to the entrance to Falias. Is it not the most wondrous of the realms?' he boomed, and pointed with their clasped hands to a golden gateway at one end of the bridge, which led into the mountain. Faye leaned forward just a little; the chasm under the bridge loomed up to greet her. She couldn't see the bottom; it was wreathed in mist. She swallowed nervously and leaned back.

'It is beautiful,' she agreed; clearly, in Falias, danger was woven with beauty just like Murias. The bridge itself was carved from rock, and intricate patterns twisted below her feet and at the edges of it where a waist-high barrier sat between them and the vertiginous drop. Looking down, she could see the swirling mists through the twists and loops of the pattern; Faye wondered how many years it had taken to carve.

She thought suddenly of Glitonea and froze. This wasn't Murias, so Glitonea should have no power over her here. But the way that she'd been able to reach through into the ordinary world and manipulate Faye into keeping quiet about the curse made her wary.

'Am I safe here?' she called out to Lyr; he turned and held out his hand for hers, frowning.

'Of course. No being will harm you here,' he replied, but Faye kept her hands at her sides.

'Not even… other faerie queens? Kings?' she wanted to be sure; perhaps her being in the faerie realms at all would alert or anger Glitonea or Finn Beatha.

'This is my realm. Not theirs. You are free from them here,' he repeated, and she nodded and followed him.

'You called me father before. Was that just for the summoning, or did you mean it?' he asked, suddenly, as he walked in front of her, his cloak flowing out behind him. He didn't look at her, and his question hung in the air between them, words made in mist that she didn't know how to answer.

Faye concentrated on putting one foot in front of the other over the thin stone bridge, but unease enveloped her, and she was very aware of the drop that fell away under her feet.

'No.' Faye took a deep breath and focused on her feet as much as she could. 'You abandoned us. You hurt Moddie. I'm here because I need you, yes. But don't think we can start playing happy families just yet.' She was sarcastic, but she couldn't help it. *What did he think was going to happen?*

Lyr stopped dead, ahead of her.

'Your rudeness will not help you,' Lyr snapped, turning to her. The bridge was very narrow; Faye tried not to look down. She wanted to get to the other side, to get away from the precipice, but he grabbed her by the shoulders. 'You wanted me. You called to me. Do not refuse me now.'

He shook her, not hard, but it was enough to make her grab at him in panic.

'Don't shake me. Not on this bridge,' she panted.

He released her shoulders and gave her an analytical stare.

'Threatening my life won't help me trust you,' she repeated his words back to him in the same tone, and was relieved to see regret in his eyes.

'You're right. I'm sorry.' He turned away and walked on.

Faye knew so little about him that it was hard to tell if he was sincere, but for now she just wanted to get off the bridge. Lyr was fae, so he was changeable and untrustworthy, but she'd genuinely detected a regretful sadness in his eyes.

Be sad, then, she thought. *A little sadness won't do you any harm: you've inflicted enough sadness on other people.*

'This way.' Lyr led her towards the golden gate. Looking over her shoulder, Faye saw a similar gate at the other end of the bridge, though that one was black where this one was golden, and the gate was closed, with tall black doors bolted shut.

'What's that way?' she asked.

'Nothing.' He dismissed it with a flick of his hand.

'Tell me what that is. The black gates at the other side of the bridge,' Faye repeated, pointing behind her. 'If you want us to have a relationship, you can at least talk to me. Answer my questions.'

Lyr turned to look behind them and frowned, shaking his head.

'That way leads to my sister's quarters, the Queendom of Moronoe, as she insists on calling it. We are not on speaking terms,' he said, huffily, and led Faye into the dark recess of the mountain beyond the golden gate. 'But this is my realm; the *Kingdom* of Falias.' His tone inferred that his realm was the correct one, though Faye could detect an irritation in his voice, and wondered why Falias was divided in this way. She remembered, the night of the Mabon ritual, that she had heard laughing faerie voices beckoning her to Moronoe.

'My aunt, then?' Faye stared back at the forbidding gates and wondered what lay beyond them.

'She is your blood kin, yes. But I doubt you would see much of yourself in her,' his tone was flat.

'Why aren't you speaking to each other?' Faye asked.

'It is not something I wish to discuss,' he shot back, and swept forward. *Spare me*, she thought. *He's treating me like a teenager.*

She followed Lyr through a long, dark stone passage; unexpectedly, the rock was dry and, as she reached out for it, somehow warm. In the distance, she could hear music, but of a different kind to Murias's faerie reel, played by fiddlers and drummers. This was a song of women's voices, laying notes in harmony over each other in ever more radiant harmonies. Forgetting her confusing feelings for Lyr for a moment, Faye felt a deep accord in her belly, in her soul, for the music. She'd never heard it before, but it was familiar nonetheless.

They emerged into a mellow, gold-green light, and Faye blinked her eyes after the darkness of the tunnel. She supposed that they must still be inside the mountain somewhere, because the land she looked on sat inside tall walls of stone, as if it had been hollowed out of the mountain; however, she could see stars above her; even more strangely, sunlight dappled the glade before them.

'Come.' Lyr led her down a long staircase cut into the rock; Faye was reminded of the great ballroom Finn had led her into in Murias, his hand in hers, her gauzy skirts billowing deliciously against her skin.

Below them was a kind of village or settlement, a little like the diagrams produced of Stone Age or Viking villages by archaeologists. Perhaps twenty little reed-thatched houses were scattered through an open glen, bordered by deep woodland; smoke curled through chimneys and fae children raced around, playing games and calling happily to each other. To the left, fields of golden wheat, yellow seed and purple lavender swayed happily in the strange green-gold light.

'Oh!' Faye breathed, taken aback. She'd expected – what? She couldn't say, but perhaps something more similar to Murias's golden castle and luxurious rooms draped with silk. This was altogether more bucolic and… she searched for the word. *Honest*. It was earthy, honest, rural.

'Many human women have been entranced by the realm of earth,' Lyr rumbled, his voice companionable.

'I'm not fully human,' she replied archly, noticing how different she felt here in Falias. Murias – and Finn, whether in his realm or out of it – was spellbinding, like drowning in pleasure. In Murias, she'd been plunged into a delicious lassitude it was almost impossible to resist. But here, she felt aware and grounded. She could keep her head; she could stay focused.

Lyr raised his eyebrows, but he was pleased with with her reaction, she could tell. Yes, it was beautiful here, but Faye couldn't forget that. She wouldn't ever forget it. Let Lyr think what he liked, that she'd be his daughter, that she could love him. She couldn't love him; in fact, she refused to. She was only here to find some way to rescue Aisha from dying in Murias.

They reached the end of the stairs and Lyr guided her through the village. The fae came out of their houses to bow as he walked past, and smiled and bowed at Faye, too. Compared to the variety of fae at the ball and in the market at Murias, the faeries here were far more similar to each other, and all of them had the look of the earthy realm: their skin was brown in varying hues, like Lyr's, and their clothes were simple, homespun materials in greens and yellow tones, embroidered with leaves, twig and flower designs. Faye noticed that many of them had a central tattoo or mark on their forehead: a square containing the seven-pointed faerie star.

Lyr led her towards a grand dwelling in the centre of the village; it was larger than the rest, though made of the same thatched reed material. Its wide doors were made of burnished copper, and as they approached, Lyr raised his hand for them to open.

They swung apart, and Faye followed Lyr inside.

'Sit, daughter,' he motioned to a couch piled with soft grey, white and black furs. Four tall bronze lamps shone a warm light around the hut, which was more like a grand hall or lodge; numerous finely carved wooden cabinets stood against the walls; one displayed items made of bone and antler made into shapes Faye didn't recognise. She sat, feeling him calling her *daughter* like a barb. *I'm here for Aisha*, she reminded herself. *This isn't my home.* Looking at the luxury of Lyr's dwelling, though, she felt a pang of sadness. She could have had this. The comfortable opulence, the status of being the King's daughter. She and Moddie could have lived here. They could have been happy; Faye could have had a father.

Faeries don't make good fathers, her instinct whispered. *It's just a fantasy. You had a family. You were happy.*

But Faye felt the old, clutched-at longings of the fatherless child resurfacing. The hunger for a father, to be like the rest of the children. To have family holidays and in-jokes and memories, afternoons playing board games and catch at the beach. Not to feel that loss, that sadness, that sense that Moddie and Grandmother were doing their best to replace a shadow, a father that wasn't there, but was noticeable by his absence. Being all the more jolly to compensate for the father-shaped hole in her life; to pretend it wasn't there.

Perhaps Moddie wouldn't have died, if we had been here. If he hadn't left us. The thought rose up, unexpected and hurtful, from that same bruised, child-memory, but she pushed it away. There was no way she could know that, and it wasn't true, anyway. Moddie had had a stroke; sudden, unusual at her young age, but not unheard of. Like being struck by lightning. Yet that same voice nagged at Faye. *She died of a broken heart. How many more years could she have had if it had never been broken in the first place?*

She felt tears threatening, and pinched herself again, hard. In her childhood stories, characters had often pinched themselves to see if the wondrous places they visited in their adventures were real; Faye dug her nails into her own skin for the pain that would eat her sadness. She remembered doing it as a child, with other habits that she now recognised as self-harming: pulling and biting the skin around her fingers until it was sore and bled; scratching her legs until she created sores; biting the insides of her mouth. There was a satisfaction in all these things. Wounds were distractions.

To the back of the lodge she could see an ornate glass-walled room, like an orangery or a summerhouse; in it, plants and herbs were garlanded from the roof, and a low circle of hedge was arranged in the centre, with what looked like an altar at the centre. On it Faye could see three large pillars of smoky quartz, each easily a foot high, surrounded by smaller tiger's eye, clear quartz and what could have been black obsidian crystals. She'd seen crystal grids like this before, though never with crystals that big; she could feel the power coming from them like a huge battery, even from the next room. In her shop, she sold books that told people how to set up crystal grids – laying small, pocket-sized crystals in patterns and energising them with a particular aim in mind. She wondered if this was the same thing but on a much grander scale.

A hammered bronze table with a large copper bowl filled with unfamiliar fruits on top of it was placed in the middle of the room, within Faye's reach. Lyr clapped his hands and a small, bearded faerie man wearing a brown apron knotted around his waist appeared.

'Wine for my guest,' Lyr ordered, and the faerie – was he a gnome, Faye wondered? – chose a tall black glass decanter, from which he poured a rich red liquid into an elegant copper goblet and offered it to her. Faye hesitated – she wanted to keep a clear head here. But she needed to manage Lyr; to hide her feelings from him to get what she wanted from him: a favour, an intercession in another faerie realm, perhaps. If being in Falias was bringing back some powerful and confusing childhood emotions, they were nothing compared to the pain Aisha was suffering now. So, she took it with good grace and raised the cup to her lips.

'To you,' Lyr raised his goblet and drank deeply; Faye followed suit. The wine was rich and sweet, like berries bursting in her mouth. It was powerful, but drinking it made her feel more focused: the opposite to the faerie food and drink in Murias. She was grateful for it and drank again. Her anxiety receded a little.

'Thank you. Why is it that the wine here – and the place itself – why doesn't it make me giddy and confused, as in Murias? I was enchanted there.' She took another sip, more daringly now.

'This is your home. Earth is your natural element, both as my daughter and as a human woman. If you were not half-fae, this place would still enchant you, like it does our other human visitors. But this place represents everything you are. Murias is the realm of water, and its power is strong; for humans, it is impossible to withstand the current and the weight of water. The depths that crush a human body are no place to swim, even though you may splash safely enough in the shallows. You survived, as I would. But it is not my realm, and it is not yours.'

'So, of all the faerie kingdoms, Falias is the... the least dangerous for humans?' Faye asked, setting her goblet down on the table. A perfumed smoke wafted the smell of orange and something else – was it geranium? – through the lodge.

'In a sense.' Lyr smiled. 'They find a welcome here. Some choose to stay, but as in all of the faerie kingdoms, there is a price. The sacrifice is different in Murias than it is here, but there is always a price.'

'What is it, then? Here?' Faye asked. Lyr set his goblet down and stretched.

'The question is, Faye Morgan, what you would offer in return for the help you ask of me?' He stared at her keenly. 'You ask something very dangerous from me. We are at war with Murias. Even if we were not, I cannot defy the judgement of another faerie king or queen in their own realm. If Finn Beatha has banished you from Murias, I cannot go against his wishes... without very good motivation.'

'When you say you're at war, you mean...?' Faye narrowed her eyes at Lyr.

'I mean, a war. There is fighting. Fae warrior against fae warrior. All four faerie kingdoms are involved, and there are two sides. Falias stands with the Fire kingdom, Finias, against Murias and the Air kingdom, Gorias. There have always been conflicts, but this is the war to end all wars.' He put down his cup and leaned back in his chair, his gaze never leaving hers.

'Why are you fighting each other?' Faye asked.

'The four elemental kingdoms are as old as time itself. At the creation of the world, we were given our own kingdoms, our territories, our creatures to govern. As the long ages passed, ice covered the world, then water, then earth rose; this world began as fire, as liquid metal and rock in a furnace as hot as the sun. Over time, the elemental realms settled into a harmonious agreement. We needed each other to flourish: the forests need rivers and sunlight and oxygen to grow, after all. For many ages, the natural world was at peace.'

Lyr rose and went to one of the cabinets against the walls. He picked something up and weighed it thoughtfully in his hands before returning to sit opposite Faye.

'At the centre of the four faerie kingdoms sits the Crystal Castle of the Moon.' He held out the piece of opaque pink-white crystal he was holding to her. 'Take it. This is from there. You will feel the magic of the place by holding it.' Faye took it, and took in a deep breath as its strange and familiar power flowed through her palms and into her heart.

'The Crystal Castle sits apart from the elemental kingdoms, but is their heart. It is the home of Morgana Le Fay, Mistress of Magick. She cannot exist without us, but we cannot exist without her. She is the centre of all our power, but she is also the beacon that shines between the worlds. She connects the human world and our world together.'

'Yes.' Faye nodded and turned the crystal over in her hands.

'In the human world, Morgana is the Moon. Her power is night power. Human imagination and magic is governed by her. She is the mistress of your realm of dreams, and humans can journey to us, to her castle, even, and learn magic because of this connection.

But as the years pass, humans are less and less connected to our realms. They have poisoned and polluted the natural world and hurt us. They have stopped honouring us and strengthening us by melding their bodies and souls with ours. Thus the faerie kingdoms have lost power, and our harmony has been disrupted. We fight for the power that remains.'

'But why turn against each other?' Faye frowned. Lyr held his hand out for the crystal; she was reluctant to give it back.

'You don't need to understand the deep meanings, Faye.' Lyr was dismissive again, like the father he had no right to be, and it put her on edge. 'I'm just trying to explain to you why it will be very difficult for me to... intercede on your behalf with Finn Beatha.'

'But you can do it?' Faye demanded. 'My friend is dying there. I need to help her.'

'First, you must tell me the promises you have made to them and I will tell you what I require,' he said, picking up a yellow fruit that could have been a pear from the bowl on the table, and taking a bite. The juice rolled down his chin into his beard, and he wiped it away.

'The Faerie Queen Glitonea is who I owe favours to,' Faye said. 'She helped me escape Murias and bring my human lover back with me. Finn had kidnapped him in jealousy. I promised her...' she stopped, expecting the horrible drowning sensation; dread filled her. 'I can't tell you.'

'What did you promise, daughter?' Lyr finished the fruit, stalk and seeds included. 'I can assure you that a promise made to Glitonea is a very serious matter indeed.'

It was the terrible, jagged secret that had sat inside her heart like a grenade all these months; Faye was terrified of it, lest her admission caused her to choke to death. Yet she longed to be free of its weight, the worry that choked her. Tears filled her eyes.

'You don't understand. I can't tell you. She's... cursed me, or something. If I try and tell you, it's like I'm drowning.'

Lyr grimaced, and he sat forward, staring at Faye.

'If she has cursed you, I can remove it.' He leaned forward and drew a number of shapes under her chin and grunted. As soon as he did so, Faye had the strangest sensation: as if she'd been wearing a tightly collared shirt all this time, and it had been unbuttoned. 'Hmm. That should do it.' He sat back slightly, though he kept his eyes on her face steadily. 'Now. Tell me.'

'You've... I can tell you? I'm not sure,' she traced a finger anxiously inside the neckline of her dress.

'It's gone. Trust me,' he said. 'You should have told me this; I could have loosed the curse before now. Now, speak.'

'A baby. My... future child,' Faye stammered, expecting her throat to close, for the hands to reappear around her neck. But nothing happened, and when she heard herself say it out loud, it sounded surreal. Faye laughed to hide her anxiety. 'I mean, I said yes. I had to. But she can't possibly make it happen... make me... pregnant. I mean, maybe if I was in Murias, but even then... what would she want with a baby?'

Lyr slammed his goblet down on the low table, jumped to his feet and turned his back on her. He exhaled slowly, as if he was trying to control his voice.

'You offered her your child? For a human lover?' His voice was low.

'Yes. But I don't have one. I might never even have a baby. And anyway, if I do, she can't exactly come and take it. It's stupid. I think she wanted to ... I don't know. See how far I would go, or something.' Faye appealed. Her heart was pounding, her face was flushed.

Lyr strode over to her and slapped her face. Faye reeled with the impact, and shock brought tears to her eyes. Like the pinches and tears she made in her own skin, the slap was also a relief. The spiked metal bomb she'd been holding had gone off, and she was still alive.

'Stupid girl! You made a bargain with the High Queen of Murias and offered her my blood! It is my blood she wants. If she has even a drop of it, she can destroy me, just as Moronoe could destroy Finn or Glitonea with a little of the blood that runs in their veins. Your child will have my blood, just as you do. It matters not what happens to the child after she gets what she wants.'

Faye held her cheek, trying not to cry. She'd thought all these weeks and months that it was Rav that willed himself to forget what had happened in Murias, but she was the one that had been protecting herself from this horrific secret.

'I'm sorry. I was desperate, and it seemed… I don't know. So unlikely.' She watched Lyr warily as he paced in front of her.

'It is entirely likely that you will be with child one day, and when that day comes, they will destroy me,' Lyr fumed, and punched the wall as he walked past it. Faye jumped; just like in Murias, the beauty of Falias had distracted her, and she was reminded that she should always be on her guard in the faerie realms.

'What will she do with the baby?' Faye asked, askance. It was a theoretical, future child, but terror stabbed at her heart.

'I do not care about the fate of the child that does not yet exist. I care about my own self-preservation, and the preservation of my realm!' Lyr shouted, and paced the lodge. He came back to the table, poured another goblet of wine and drained it, then stared suspiciously at Faye. 'She made no other bargain with you? Glitonea is a Mistress of Magic. I sense that if you were close to her power, it may have been irresistible for you. Yes,' he looked deeper into Faye's eyes; she wondered about lying for a moment, then knew it would be impossible to lie to Lyr.

'She did offer you something else. You bargained for more than your rescue. What was it? Speak, child!'

Faye looked at her feet, distressed. She wanted to go home and forget all of this: in that moment, she thought of Rav. She'd been wrong to judge him for wanting to forget. For wanting a normal life.

'I didn't know you. You were… a distant concept. A father I had never known,' she protested.

'What did she offer you, and what did you agree to give her?' Lyr insisted, and Faye gulped. He seemed to have grown larger, and towered over her in the lodge.

'She said I could help them. To be a weapon against you when the time came, in the war. It wouldn't hurt me. I agreed to that.'

Lyr swore under his breath and kicked the table over. 'And what did she give you in return?' he growled. 'The life of some other worthless human lover?'

Not worthless. The man I love, Faye thought. The same protective urge that had taken her back into Murias to rescue Rav reawakened, and made her angry. How dare this faerie king lecture her, when he'd done precisely nothing to help her know any better about surviving in the faerie realms? She'd been desperate there: under threats she'd little way of countering. Lyr could have known her when she was a child. He could have taught her the power that she sought now, belatedly – the power that was her birthright.

'She taught me the magic of Murias.' Faye met Lyr's stare and refused to drop it. 'I refused to be Finn Beatha's whore. I wanted to go back and forth in the faerie realm as I wished, so she gave me some of her wisdom. And, yes. I promised what she wanted. I would do it again to save the man I love, and save myself,' she heard her voice grow louder, like his. 'I don't owe you anything, Lyr of Falias. I don't expect you to be a father to me now; it's too late. But you owe me the respect you should give one of your family, at the very least,'

She turned to go, but he gripped her arm.

'Stay,' he commanded, but she pulled her arm free.

'You can't command me,' she spat, and strode out of the lodge and into the village.

Chapter 21

Lyr had brought Faye to Falias, and she had no idea how to get home. Still, she stalked through the village, scowling. Lyr had treated her like an errant daughter, and it rankled. Yes, he was technically her father, but he hadn't been a father in any of the important ways. He hadn't helped her with her homework, or read her bedtime stories, or taken her to the park. He wasn't there when she was ill, and he wasn't there when Moddie died, leaving Faye to run the shop on her own. Last, he'd denied her faerie heritage. Lyr was a father in blood only and, clearly, blood was all he cared about.

She heard him behind her and increased her pace, but she was no match for him. Lyr strode past her easily and stopped her with one hand on her shoulder. She shook it off.

'Leave me alone,' she muttered.

'No, Faye. I apologise for my anger. We do not know each other and it was inappropriate,' he rumbled. 'Please. Come back and we will talk. I was angry, I did not expect it… to have gone this far. I can get you into Murias to find your friend. I have no love for Finn and Glitonea, so it will be my pleasure to deny them a human follower. And…' he broke off, and looked away. 'There is much magic to be learnt here, too, child. As a daughter of Falias it is your birthright.'

'Maybe I don't want to learn your magic,' she scoffed, but she was lying. Being back in the fae realm – even one as different as this to Murias – was intoxicating. The power of the fae ran in her veins, and and this place shone with an immanent glow of power. The faerie part of her felt at home here; the faerie part of her wanted to know it intimately. Perhaps he'd read her mind just now. Perhaps he felt the sorrow she did when she thought about everything he could have taught her: all the power he could have helped her to gain, without her having to resort to dangerous bargains with the Queen of Murias.

'That is your choice,' Lyr said quietly. Faye shrugged.

'You haven't told me what you want from me yet.' She spoke clearly into the strange air, watching three fae children play a game, dropping sticks into a gurgling stream that wound between the houses. It could have been her; perhaps she could have lived half her life here, in Falias, learning the crafts of the fae; listening to Lyr's deep rumble as he laughed, as he showed her which crystals could be found where in the faerie forest. Half here, and half in Abercolme, like a true *sidhe-leth*.

But that had been denied her, by Lyr as well as Moddie and Grandmother, in their way.

'Come back to the dwelling and I will tell you what I require,' Lyr answered, testily.

'No. Tell me now,' she insisted, and stood her ground. The faerie king glared at her. 'I told you my secret. Now you know. You know everything. Tell me.'

'And I rid you of the curse, do not forget.' He breathed out testily and gave her a searching look. 'Fine. Then, what I require as your side of the bargain is a human woman to bear my child. You will know of someone, I'm sure. Fear not, they will not be mistreated, and I am a generous king to those who please me. In times past, I would go into your world and find my own lovers; find strong women to bear my children. But now, with the war, I am tired.'

'No!' Faye exclaimed; she was horrified. How could Lyr ask her to deceive another woman, to assign her to the same fate as Faye?

'You asked what my side of the bargain was. That is it.'

'It's intolerable. I won't do it,' she spat. 'I can't believe you'd ask me.'

'It is what I want,' he repeated.

'I've heard you have many half-fae children,' she retorted. 'Why do you need another?'

'There is a purpose for this child, but that is not your concern,' Lyr dismissed her question. 'Just bring me the woman, and I will do the rest.'

'No. Until you tell me the fate that awaits the child, I'll do no such thing,' Faye replied; she felt exhausted; it was all too much. Her feelings about Lyr. Her childhood memories. The exhaustion of the curse. She hadn't known Glitonea's twisted intentions for her baby-yet-to-be when she'd made their bargain: she wouldn't be sucked into such an agreement again. 'And, anyway, whatever you want a baby for, it's unconscionable for me to agree. You can't spirit babies away to your realms, away from their mothers. It's just not right.'

'The child will be treated with every care and luxury my realm allows.' Lyr shook his head. 'I would never hurt a child, human, half-human or otherwise. Of all the realms, mine is the one most intimately associated with your kind, and I am fond of humans beyond all the other faerie Kings and Queens.' Lyr stepped aside to let the children run past, whooping and shouting excitedly in their game.

'You have to tell me what you want the child for,' Faye insisted.

'As you wish,' he sighed. 'I have an heir, my full-blood faerie son, Luathas. He will soon command my faerie legions in battle. But it is too risky to have him in the field, so I would have a half-fae child, a boy, who I could substitute for him. If he is half human, he will have the physical endurance and strength of a human as well as his fae abilities. He just needs to be dark, like Luathas and me.'

'No!' Faye cried. 'It's just not right.' She was disappointed – in Lyr and all of them. None of them had an honest reason for wanting any contact with humans; every time, it was to get something they wanted. And they seemed to have no conscience about it at all.

'Then I cannot help you rescue your friend from Murias.' Lyr frowned. 'And you have seen what happens to the lovers of the fae there.'

'Then I'll find another way.' Faye wanted to go home. To pull the duvet over her head and sleep for a thousand years.

'You will do what you will, Faye Morgan,' Lyr replied wearily. 'Remember my offer. It is the only way you can return without acquiescing to Finn Beatha, and undoing everything you have done so far.' Lyr took a wooden wand from his leather belt and drew a circle on the dry earth floor. Inside it, he scratched a symbol, something Faye didn't recognise. 'Lest you forget your friend,' he said, and blew on the dust.

The dirt made way for something else; for a moment, a hole tunnelled down through the earth; Faye glimpsed roots and stone, and strata of old earth. Immediately, it was replaced with something like a mirror or a glass, though it seemed to grow within the space like a translucent mushroom. In it, it was hard to make out what she saw; the picture was distorted, as if she looked through a magnifying glass or circus mirror.

The room she was looking into was dark, the edge of the picture faded and rounded into blackness. Dim yellow light flickered against shapes in the shadow.

'Aisha?' Faye squatted down and peered into the magic mirror, if that was what it was. 'Is that Aisha? Where is she? It's dark. I can't see anything.'

'Look closer.' Lyr's voice was dispassionate; like Finn and his sister, the Faerie Queen Glitonea, her faerie king father claimed to have great fondness for humans, but he was immune to their cares and sufferings as much as his cousins. Nonetheless, she squinted to make out what she was seeing.

Whatever the room was, she hadn't seen anything like it when she'd been in Murias. Gone were the golden balustrades and luxurious, heavy tapestries; in this room, there were no faerie musicians playing a merry jig.

Four figures slumped against rough stone walls; a small fireplace of sorts in the corner illuminated rusty chains that shackled their wrists to the rock with a dim orange glow. At the moment that Faye looked, one figure turned its face up, as if reaching for light or oxygen, and Faye recognised her friend's face.

'Oh, my god.'

Horror choked Faye. She wanted to look away but couldn't: Aisha's skin stretched tight over her cheekbones, and her usually bright, intelligent eyes were dull. The skin around one eye was bruised, and her shiny black hair was matted and dirty.

'Where is she? Why… Finn took her to be his lover.' Faye looked aghast at Lyr, who kicked dirt onto the strange mirror and traced a different symbol in the dirt; as soon as it had appeared, it faded back into mud again. Faye fell to her knees and scratched at the ground, but Lyr put a warm hand on her shoulder.

'It is gone, daughter. Earth magic, no more, no less.'

'But… what I saw? That was real?'

'Yes.' Lyr tried to take her hand, but she shook it free. 'I merely showed you the truth, Faye. It is not my doing.'

'But she's… Aisha, she's… trapped there. Suffering.'

'You knew she was in Murias. This cannot come as a surprise.'

'I know, but…' Faye felt shocked tears run down her cheeks. 'I… I thought at least she… he… I thought he wanted her. And she went willingly.'

'You of all people know that Finn Beatha's lovers enjoy his favour at his whim.' Lyr's tone was neutral; he didn't seem to judge the other faerie king, but recount it as fact. 'You escaped the extremes of Murias, as you are half-faerie. But you know that the human loves of the fae of Murias are not so lucky.'

Faye had no response; she knew Lyr was right, and she also knew she'd been denying the truth to herself. She had known. She'd seen the faerie reel, seen the broken bodies under it. She'd known that was Aisha's fate sooner or later.

'I suppose I… I didn't want to believe it.' Faye's heart felt like lead. It was all her fault; her fault from the day that she, Annie and Aisha did that love spell on the floor of her shop; it had worked – too well. In less than a year, reality had spun on its axis. Everything had changed. Annie had found love with Suze and Faye with Rav. But Aisha had walked willingly into faerie, and now she was dying there for a fascination she mistook for love.

'How… how long will she survive there? If I… before I get to her?' Faye stammered. She was in shock; she wanted to go back through that glassy surface, to grab Aisha and pull her through, but she knew she couldn't.

'In human time? It is hard to say. A few months, perhaps. Half a year at the most.'

Faye's heart was a stone falling into a still, black loch.

'My offer still stands.' Lyr's voice was low and soft, but Faye heard the steel under it. 'Find me a human woman to bear my child and I will help you bring your friend home.'

'I want to go home.' Faye needed time to think; *though time is one thing that Aisha doesn't have*, she reminded herself. *You think you have the luxury of time, but Aisha is dying. Because of you.*

'Then go,' Lyr sighed, and held something out in his hand. 'Take this. A gift, from me to you.' He handed her a black crystal wand, very like those she'd seen on the table, making up the powerful grids. Was this the same, or something different?

'What is it?' She took it and turned it over in her hand; as soon as her skin made contact, the crystal vibrated, thrumming with warmth. She let out a surprised cry. It was heavy and smooth as glass, but it felt alive.

'It is made of obsidian – volcanic glass: a magic of fire and earth combined. A part of my realm, daughter. Something of your home, to be with you. Should you need me, or need the power of Falias, use it, hold it to make you feel connected to the earth; it will keep you safe.'

Faye held it to her heart, and felt a strange reassurance emanating from it.

'I will be here, daughter.' Lyr waved his hand and the mists swirled around her again: gold and green and brown. She felt the same dissonance of being and not-being, all at once.

'Remember your heritage, Faye. Remember who you are. You are the daughter of Lyr of Falias,' his voice echoed in her mind as she closed her eyes. 'And remember my offer, daughter. While you rail against what you know must be done, your friend grows weaker.'

In her heart, she knew that the horror she'd seen was true, not an illusion created by Lyr for his own ends – him showing her the vision was manipulation enough. But some truths were too hard to face dead on, and her mind sought madly for ways to rationalise it, ways to mask it and make it reasonable. Yet there were none.

No… no…no… Faye ran into the mist, away from Lyr. All she wanted was to forget; the guilt was too great, and she wanted oblivion like a drug. She wanted comfort. She wanted Rav and the cosy flat, all the mundane human things.

She hated herself for her fickleness, in that moment. Why couldn't she just decide, either way, who she was? Why couldn't she just submit to the fae and their amoral ways, or forget faerie altogether and be happy in London with Rav? Human or fae? Light or shadow?

As the mists took her, she was full of despair. She knew she was as much a part of the chains that lashed Aisha to the wall as the smiths of Murias that had forged them. But as she felt the solidity of the ordinary world form under her feet, and as the shadows thinned, Faye was too exhausted to think of a way to break them.

Chapter 22

'You didn't call or text. Nothing from you for over twenty-four hours! Where were you?' Rav paced the lounge in his flat, furious. Faye stood in the corner of the room, watching his bare feet on the faded red and cream Oriental rug. Lyr had transported her back to the rose garden after her time in Falias; Gabriel had waited patiently for the hours that had passed until she returned.

'I stayed at Annie's. I forgot to text.' She felt like a naughty schoolgirl being told off by her father, or, how she imagined that felt, having never experienced it. 'I'm fine. As you can see.' It was a lie, but if she told him the truth, she might lose him.

'Faye, I was worried sick!' Rav yelled. She understood why he was annoyed, but bristled at his tone.

'You're not my dad. I do have a life of my own, you know.' The trauma of her time with Lyr hit her suddenly, like a rough shove; perhaps it was also the tiredness that came from visiting the faerie realms. Her head pounded and she sat down heavily on the sofa. It was too much, too real, all of a sudden. *Did I really expect anything else from my faerie father?* she thought angrily as she closed her eyes and massaged her temples with her fingers. *He doesn't want me. He wants what I can give him. He's as heartless as the rest of them.*

'I know that. I was worried something had happened. Surely you can understand that, given our recent history?' Rav's tone softened, and she felt bad for lying about where she'd been.

'I know,' she breathed, trying not to exacerbate her headache. She should tell him, even if it caused an argument, or worse. She sighed. 'I… I was…'

She opened her eyes carefully, blinking at the light, thinking that she'd tell Rav, but the expression in his eyes halted her. His voice might have been soft, but his eyes were watchful. There was no trust there; she swallowed the words she'd been about to say.

Instead, Faye looked around the room; a half-eaten takeaway sat on the coffee table along with a few empty beer cans. 'You kept yourself busy, I guess. Dinner for one… or two?' It was a pointed question, but she was angry and confused; and she hadn't forgotten – or forgiven – coming home to Rav and Mallory's cosy night in together.

'What does that mean?' Rav shot back.

'You know what it means,' she snapped back, her throat tense with the words she could have said. But would it have made this better or worse? She didn't know, and the moment had gone.

'I can't believe you're still going on about that.' He stormed out of the room and into the kitchen. He came back, holding a bouquet of flowers: blue iris and white chrysanthemums, and threw them at her feet. 'Mallory actually felt so bad about that night she dropped these around for you earlier. There's a note.' He shook his head, watching as she bent to pick the flowers up. 'She wants to be your friend, Faye. Shame you don't want to do the grown-up thing and just get on with her.'

I've had quite the day, Faye thought wearily, *so excuse me if I'm too tired for another argument.* Nevertheless, she opened the white envelope;

inside, there was a tasteful card featuring a detail from a painting she didn't recognise. She read Mallory's spiky, slanted handwriting:

Dear Faye,

I'm so sorry that you thought I was being inappropriate by visiting Rav the other night. Maybe I was – I'm used to him being there for me when I feel low; yes, we were a couple once, but now we are really 'just good friends' as the saying goes. However, I recognise that it's not okay for me to just come around and pour out all my troubles to him any more; he's got you now. I would like us to be friends, even though maybe I haven't made the best start. I hope you like the flowers; maybe we can go out for a coffee sometime, just the two of us? But if you don't want to, that's totally okay and I will understand.

All the best,

Mallory

Faye's first instinct was to distrust the letter. Was this some kind of manipulation on Mallory's part? If so, she was trying pretty hard to get Faye on side. Maybe Mallory really did want to be friends, in which case, Faye had totally misread her.

'Oh.' She didn't know what else to say.

'*Oh* is right. Maybe you should give her a call and say thank you.' Rav held out his phone.

'Give me her number, I'll text,' she replied tersely. Rav called it out to her, looking at his screen. Faye hesitated.

'You going to say thank you?' He stared pointedly at her phone.

'God, can I get in the door first? I'll do it later.' She went to the bathroom to splash water on her face, avoiding his gaze. She knew she was being unreasonable, but she also knew Rav wouldn't want to hear about what had happened with Lyr. To him, a polite reply to someone she hardly knew about a bunch of flowers was more important than the real reason she'd been gone for so long.

Faye sat on the toilet lid and unlocked her phone. *Might as well get it over with.*

Thanks for the flowers and card, Mallory. Faye x she typed. It was noncommittal but pleasant. She didn't expect a reply; she very much suspected that the flowers were intended as a public relations exercise to raise Mallory's profile with Rav, rather than sent with any particular care for her feelings. But Mallory replied almost immediately. *So glad you like them. Coffee?*

Faye was surprised. She didn't really want to meet up with Mallory, but what if the girl was genuine?

She tapped out a quick reply. *Sure, let me know where and when.* She washed her hands and put the phone in her pocket, seeing that Mallory had suggested a coffee shop somewhere in the west end to meet up in a couple of days' time. She was definitely keen to be friendly all of a sudden, but why?

Rav was watching TV when she walked back into the lounge. She gave him a bright smile. *Paper over the cracks, be happy!* She felt like a 1950s wife. *Don't bring your husband your worries! He's had a busy day. Put a ribbon in your hair and make sure the children play quietly.*

'We're meeting for coffee this week,' she said. He smiled, looking relieved.

'Ah. That's great.' He patted the cushion on the sofa next to him. 'Sorry if I was a bit… you know. I really was worried about you.' He kissed her cheek as she sat next to him; it was a chaste kiss, almost brotherly.

'I'm sorry too,' she made herself say it, even though she didn't feel it. 'I'll text next time.'

'Just tell me next time so I don't worry,' he smiled, but his eyes evaded hers. She felt awful for the lie.

They watched a TV documentary in silence, but Faye wasn't paying attention to it at all; she was thinking about Lyr and Falias, and the bargain he'd offered her. It was a choice that was no choice: she couldn't swap one human life for another in the faerie realms. What could she do? There had to be a way.

She curled up next to Rav and nestled her head onto his chest. He rested his arm on her shoulder and stroked her hair with his wide palm: his were practical, reassuring hands. *I have to fix this. I can't leave Aisha in Murias. I just can't.* But – what? Trap another woman in her place, force her to bear Lyr's child? Trading an innocent woman for Aisha wasn't any kind of solution. There had to be something else. She imagined the problem to be a black, twisted labyrinth. Every way she turned in it was a dead end; with every avenue, sharp thorns tore at her skin and drew blood. *There must be a way out. There must be*, she thought, closing her eyes. But she was tired, and the frustration and grief built in her, like a small girl running down a long corridor of doors, banging at every one of them with her fists, wanting one to open: just one. *Come on, Faye*, she goaded herself. *There must be something you're missing here. There has to be a door. There has to be a way to get to Aisha.*

A single tear rolled from under her eyelid and down her cheek; she wiped it away surreptitiously, the pressure of frustration building in her throat.

'Faye?' Rav tilted her head up to meet his eyes, a concerned expression in his face. 'Faye, what is it? Please don't cry.' He held her face in his hands. She pulled away, not wanting him to see her cry. But the tears wouldn't stop as Faye remembered Aisha, her beautiful face starved, the skin so tight over her bones. And frustration filled her that she was sitting here, on the sofa with Rav, not doing anything about it.

'It's Aisha, Rav. We have to do something about her, I can't pretend it hasn't happened any more. You've got to help me, please, please help me find Aisha.' The words tumbled out of her; she couldn't help it. Rav held her to his chest, stroking her hair, saying nothing. 'You know where she is. Don't pretend that you don't.' She tried to regain her composure, sitting up, wiping her eyes. 'Please, Rav. I know you want us to have a normal life here. But I can't. Not while I know she's suffering.'

'She might not be. Suffering,' he said, in a quiet voice. 'She went willingly, you said?'

At least I've got him to acknowledge what actually happened, Faye thought.

'You know what happens there. No-one goes willingly. They're enchanted, and used, and when they can't be used any more...' Faye broke off, sorrow wrenching her heart. 'You of all people know.'

Rav sat up and leaned forward, his head in his hands. 'Faye. Look, I don't know if this is connected to where you were tonight... what you were doing. But, if I'm totally honest, I don't want to know. You know I'm trying to forget what happened. I can't. I just... can't go back there. Or even think about it. Please understand. I know she was your friend. She was a nice girl. But...' he sighed deeply.

'But *what*? There is no *but*, Rav. Aisha is lost in Murias. She's dying there.' Faye raised her voice; it was instinctive, as if she could get him to hear her that way. He flinched at the word, but didn't sit back down.

'I can't, Faye. Please understand. This is all I have. I'm doing everything I can to forget, to get my life back on track. You know how bad it's been, the anxiety. I can't... I just can't engage in this kind of communal fantasy with you any more. It's too destructive. I thought you… I thought you wanted to forget it, too.'

'I can't!' she cried. 'It's in me, Rav. This is who I am. And it's not a fantasy. You know that. And you know I can't just leave Aisha there. I'm responsible for her. I rescued you.'

'I didn't ask to be sucked into your weird world!' he shouted suddenly, standing up. 'I didn't ask for… that! I have nightmares about it every night. I'm paranoid every minute of the day that some –' he waved his fingers in the air, as if conjuring up the fae – 'some supernatural entity that's obsessed with you decides he wants to kill me. D'you know what that's like, Faye? D'you have any fucking idea how scary that is? I hate it. I hate that it makes me sound completely insane if I try and talk to my friends about it. And I hate it that I fell in love with you.'

As soon as he'd blurted it out, Rav looked mortified.

Faye took a step backwards, shocked.

'I'm sorry. I didn't mean it.' He reached for her hands, but she wrenched them away. 'Faye! Please. I love you. I… that came out wrong, okay?'

'Did it? I don't have the luxury of forgetting Murias.' Faye stood up, facing him; when she met his eyes, he looked away. 'This is who I am, Rav. You knew that when you said you wanted to be with me. Be honest with yourself. Don't you think that at least some of your attraction to me is because I'm half-faerie? You could have chosen anyone else, but you chose me.'

'I know. I didn't mean it. I do love you. I just… you know I find that part of you… what happened… difficult. Come on, Faye. You have to understand that.' He balled up his fists and slowly relaxed his hands, trying to control his emotions.

'I don't understand much right now. But this is who I am. There are… things about me being half-faerie that will never go away. I'll never completely lose that part of myself.' She thought suddenly of the bargain she'd made with Glitonea for a baby, and her stomach lurched; knowing that it would be the final nail in the coffin for her relationship with Rav, if she told him, even if she never became pregnant. 'I… I'm still working it out. But I want us to work,' she said it because it was true; she loved Rav, but she was angry at him, too. 'I have to do something about Aisha. Okay? I can't pretend that's not happening. I can be your girlfriend, we can be together, we can have the happy life you want… that *I* want. But I have a responsibility towards her, and I'm not going to leave her there.'

And as far as the baby curse goes, we can deal with that if and when it happens, she thought. Perhaps it was a cavalier attitude, but it was a practical one. She could only fix one traumatic situation at once. And perhaps, by growing in power as a witch, she'd be able to fight the power of faerie when it tried to ruin her life. Perhaps.

'I know. I… I guess all we can do is be honest with each other,' Rav sighed, and a knife twisted in Faye's heart; Lyr had made it possible for her to talk about the curse now, but it felt impossible to bring it up. 'You know how I feel. I know how you feel. There's got to be a way we can work past this… I mean, couples have faced worse together and stayed standing, right?'

She made herself smile. 'Sure.'

Faye could make it right, but it would be something she'd do on her own.

Rav hugged her hard; she could feel the desperation in his embrace. He held on to her as if she was a life raft in a stormy sea. *But I'm the storm, not the raft*, she thought, sadly. *You'd be better off without me.* Yet she didn't want to lose him, so she hugged him back just as fiercely.

Chapter 23

She dreamed of Finn Beatha again.

In the dream, they weren't in Murias. She was banned from the faerie kingdom of water; instead, Finn took her to an in-between-place under the waves; perhaps it existed only as a place in the dream world, where anything was possible. As she fell under the spell of his hot, sweet touch, she found herself with him in a golden four-poster bed with ripped, gauzy white curtains that rippled in the warm current under a turquoise sea.

As it was a dream, she could breathe underwater, just as she had on the kelpie's back on the way back from the Crystal Castle. The usual rules, such as they were with a faerie king, didn't apply.

The bed sat atop a grey-green hunk of rock on the sea bed; beyond them, the white sand of the sea floor stretched away to the underwater horizon. Time had no meaning here; though her dreams may have passed in minutes, she spent hours with Finn, making love in every way possible. She surrendered herself to him completely: on her knees, on her back, she took everything he had to give her, and wanted him more for it.

In the daytime, when Faye thought of Finn, she hated herself for doing so. But tonight, the defences of her rational brain were released, and her instincts could take over. Tonight, she welcomed his ethereal kisses; she welcomed him as he took her down under the waves.

'Be my lover, Faye,' Finn breathed against the nape of her neck. 'I miss you.'

Her body was addicted to the rush of Finn; when she was with him, she forgot everything else, even herself. Yet, though it was a dream, she steeled herself not to answer. She wanted to say yes; he was like a drug, and she'd do anything to continue the high of being in his golden light. She knew from experience that dreams were more real than they seemed, when Finn was concerned. He could reach her there, as he could in all the between-places, like the seashore at Abercolme.

But even though her flesh craved him, and her mind craved the languorous high of one too many glasses of champagne that being with Finn brought, she shook her head.

'Faye, my love. No mortal woman is one such as you,' he breathed against her skin, and roses bloomed from the nape of her neck to the delicate arches of her feet. Kissing her breasts, then her stomach, his lips trailed to her hip, where he lingered, brushing his fingers softly against her clit.

In her sleep, she sighed deeply and rolled over; the contact with Rav's back brought her back to reality a little.

'Faye, *sidhe-leth*, come to me. Be my lover, my courtesan, my one most desired,' he breathed. As Faye's eyes fluttered open, the dream fell into soft shards; closing her eyes for one moment more, she watched as the tide-torn silk curtains of the bed scattered themselves like confetti over both of them. *The water makes us a wedding* Finn's voice teased her ear: *celebrations for the lovers.*

But there will never be a wedding, and you will never treat me as anything other than your whore. As it was a dream, Faye wasn't sure whether she'd said it or not, but if she had, Finn showed no sign of having heard her. Instead, he dipped his head, watching her with devilment in his eyes, and kissed her slowly, tortuously, making her writhe in the sheets.

'Don't forget me.' He smiled, looking up at her, denying her pleasure now. 'The King of Murias awaits you at your pleasure, Faye Morgan. If you desire Murias, it desires you: only by admitting your desire for me will you find your way back here.'

She opened her eyes, feeling the heat in her body and the wild beating of her heart as the magic of Murias resonated in her bones and thrummed electric under her skin. Desire was the way back, but she'd made her choice.

As London's grey morning light infused her cells and readjusted them back to mundanity, she felt shame that she hadn't thought of Aisha once in the dream. Aisha was still trapped in Murias – a flash of memory showed Faye the dungeon again, and Aisha's starved and beaten countenance – and Lyr had offered her a way to rescue her. Yet, Lyr's way was as cold as his seduction and abandonment of Moddie: Faye wouldn't subject another woman to that, and especially not the innocent child that she'd be required to donate to faerie, to fight in a war, as a decoy, as meat, to be sacrificed for another more favoured child.

That was no fate for anyone.

Chapter 24

It was a Saturday and the street market was full of people, jostling, laughing, tasting cheese and olives, artisan bread, cured meats and all manner of other delicacies.

'This is amazing!' Faye's eyes were aglow, taking in the different stalls with their striped awnings, shining glass counters and cabinets groaning with colourful food and drink. Rav looked pleased at her reaction.

'I'm so glad you like it. It's one of my favourite places in London.' He took her arm and guided her through the walkway between stalls that thronged with people. 'What shall we look at first?'

'Coffee first. Then I want to… hmm. Taste things. Cheese! Bread. Oh, look at that vegetable stall!' Faye exclaimed, sighting row upon row of glossy purple aubergines, green courgettes and huge plump red tomatoes.

'Okay, okay!' Rav laughed. 'First things first.' He steered Faye towards an organic drinks stall and ordered two coffees, handing her one. 'It'll keep your hands warm.' He smiled over the top of his paper cup as he took a sip.

'Thanks.' Faye blew on hers; it was a bright autumn day, but still chilly in the mornings. 'I'm glad you made me get up so early now.'

'Thank god. You're *not* a morning person, can I just say.' Rav rolled his eyes.

'Shut up,' Faye bantered back. 'I came, didn't I?'

'Only because I bribed you.'

'Speaking of that. I seem to recall cake was mentioned in said bribe.' Faye raised an eyebrow, archly.

'I thought you wanted to look at those vegetables first? Cheese?'

'Yes, yes. All of that. Cake mustn't be forgotten, though.' Faye wagged her finger at Rav.

'I wouldn't dream of forgetting, Mistress,' Rav tugged at an imaginary cap. 'What cake dost thou desire?'

'I'm accepting all suggestions.' Faye shrugged. 'As long as they're big and have lots of icing or cream.'

'Top five cakes of all time?' Rav swapped his coffee to his other hand and linked his arm with hers.

'Oh, gods, now you've asked… I mean, I'm going to have to give that some serious thought.'

'Really? Surely everyone knows what their top five are.' Rav pretended amazement. 'I have to say, I'm staggered by the fact that you don't know right away.'

'Well, there's no need to get so excited about it,' Faye said with a grin. 'I can definitely think of five!'

Rav sighed. 'I'm not angry, Faye, I'm just disappointed.'

She laughed. 'What's yours then?'

'Easy. Victoria sponge. Carrot cake. Chocolate fudge cake. Red velvet. Aaaaannd…' he gave a dramatic pause 'Black forest.'

'Wow. Straight from the 80s.'

'Nothing wrong with that. Chocolate, cherries and cream. Killer combination.'

They stopped at a stall selling French cheeses, and the stallholder offered them both a taste of a soft blue cheese that had an extraordinarily delicious sweet yet salty flavour.

'Now that, I could eat all day long.' Faye half-closed her eyes, an expression of sultry delight on her face. 'Let's get some.'

'For that face,' Rav shook his head 'I would buy you all the cheese in France and possibly beyond.'

Faye reached for another piece and popped it in Rav's mouth.

'You mean…Belgium?' She widened her eyes in mock amazement.

'Let's not go mad.' Rav grinned and kissed her fingertip. 'Anyway, isn't Belgium famous for chocolate and beer, not cheese?'

'That works for me too,' Faye licked her fingers. 'Come on. We haven't bought any exotic breads yet. To go with this cheese.'

*

The lights from Greenwich's bustling bars, restaurants and shops on the opposite side of the Thames river made a pattern of stars on its surface. After the market, they'd wandered down to the river and walked along, leaving the busy stalls behind them as the sun started to set. They were headed to a quiet restaurant Rav knew of, but though Faye was peckish – they'd eaten at the market, tasting and nibbling as they walked around – she wasn't starving, and anyway, she was enjoying an autumn walk, holding hands with a handsome man that made her laugh.

'Beautiful, isn't it?' Rav cuddled up against Faye as they stood at the river wall, looking out onto the river at night.

'It really is,' Faye agreed, watching a solitary boat make its way along the black water. Lights flashing, they could hear the music coming from on board.

'Party boat.' Rav rolled his eyes. 'Can't think of anything worse. Nowhere to go if you're having a crappy time.'

'You could swim for it if you were *really* desperate,' Faye mused theatrically.

'In the Thames? Not likely.' Rav took her hand and they walked along the quiet river path. Faye peered over the chest-high wall and looked at the river water, scummy at the edges.

'It's not very clean, is it?' she agreed. 'Not really up to my standards.'

She stopped herself, thinking that she shouldn't have mentioned Abercolme, but Rav just smiled.

'I bet you miss it,' he said softly. Surprised, Faye met his eyes.

'Yes, I do. But…' she looked out onto the Thames. 'I like it here, too. With you.' It wasn't a lie; it had been a happy day.

'I think… if you give it a chance, you can be happy here,' Rav said quietly, not meeting her eyes. 'This is how I want it to be, between us. Having fun, as a couple, free of… worries.' She met his gaze and her throat caught at the hope in his expression. A normal, happy life was so little to want.

'I want that too,' she replied softly. And there, standing on the edge of the river with Rav, with his arms around her, she believed she could have it.

Chapter 25

Faye looked up from her book about spirit possession to see Ruby closing the shop door of Fortune's behind her.

'Ruby! Hi!' For a moment Faye wasn't sure how to be around the other girl – she hadn't seen her since the night of the Mabon ritual – but Ruby gave her a bright smile.

'Faye, long time no see! We were beginning to think you'd disappeared into the faerie mists or something.' Ruby dropped into the teal leather chair next to Faye's worn black easy chair and put her feet up on a grubby leather footstool. Gabriel, standing on a small ladder, tutted from where he balanced, dusting books.

Faye had come back to the shop to research the faerie realms at Gabriel's suggestion. They'd been texting back and forth, a mix of sending silly internet clips and a continuing conversation about how Faye could get back to Murias and find Aisha. *Books is what I can offer*, he'd texted. *If you've got the time. Probably a solution to everything, somewhere in Fortune's.*

Faye had thought it was a pretty good idea. Gabriel was right: the shop was packed tight with arcane knowledge: there must be something useful here, if they could find it. She'd arrived just after Gabriel opened the shop at half past nine, and he'd directed her to some likely tomes while he tidied the shop. Faye had asked if she could help – she felt a little guilty, reading, when Gabriel was dusting, polishing and hoovering, but he'd refused, saying it did the shop good to have someone reading in it.

'Make yourself at home, why don't you?!' Gabriel greeted Ruby.

'I will, thanks. Cup of tea going?'

Gabriel sighed theatrically and climbed down the steps, feather duster in hand.

'As Madam demands.' He flicked the switch on the white plastic kettle next to some mugs on the desk that held the old-fashioned shop till – Gabriel refused to buy a modern, computerised system – next to pots of pens and chewed pencils and receipts and paperwork strewn around the wooden surface of the desk, or speared on a metal hook that looked like a reshaped coat-hanger.

'You could do with tidying that desk,' Ruby observed as Gabriel opened a mini fridge under it, took out some milk and splashed it into three mugs.

'It's on my list.' Gabriel tapped his temple and made the tea. 'So, Faye. Any joy yet?' he asked as he handed her and Ruby a mug each. Faye took hers with the sleeves of her cardigan wrapped around her hands to protect them from the heat.

'Not yet.' She didn't want Ruby to know what she was researching, exactly: Gabriel was the only one that knew all the details about Aisha and Murias, and Faye wasn't sure she was ready to tell anyone else. She glanced subtly at Gabriel and knew he understood, because he changed the subject.

'So, what brings you here, Ruby? Always delighted to see you, of course.' He sipped his tea, leaning against Faye's chair. 'Oh, I've got that book you wanted. *Modern Witches.*' Gabriel rummaged in a deep drawer under the desk and pulled out a glossy, modern paperback. 'Here you are.' He handed it to her.

'Great, thanks. Can I pay next week? I'm broke until payday.' Ruby flicked through the pages: Faye could see it was a collection of photo portraits of modern witches, young and old, men and women from different cultures and traditions, accompanied by profiles.

'I'll put it on your tab.' Gabriel sat on the edge of the counter.

Ruby passed the book to Faye. 'Thought this would be useful for work. You know, they liked meeting you and everything, but that whole message about the reality of people's lives as witches seems to be taking a while to sink in at *Coven of Love*. I'll show them this as inspiration.' Ruby sighed. 'Still. Probably too late; the show's airing, so it's not like we can make any major artistic changes now. Styling's done. Annie's doomed to a life of corsets, I'm afraid. As am I, in the costume department. Unless I find a new show to work on.'

Faye took the book and leafed through it. 'I'm sure she'll cope.' She smiled. 'D'you think you'll leave? Work on something else?'

Ruby shrugged.

'Dunno. Maybe. We'll see how it goes. It's not a bad show.'

'Right,' Faye looked at the pages and pages of modern witches, wondering if any of them had experienced what she had. Or, maybe not exactly the same, but something similar. An encounter with an elemental being of some kind.

'So, what've you been up to? We missed you at the coven. Thought you were going to come along on the regular.' Ruby slurped her tea. 'Gabriel, have you got any biscuits?'

Gabriel rolled his eyes and got up again to rummage in the capacious drawer under the desk; Faye wondered what he *didn't* have in there.

'Oh, you know. Settling in, getting used to London,' Faye said, intentionally vague. Ruby raised her eyebrow.

'Nothing else to say? We were all there at the ritual, Faye. It was weird. It's not like that's an everyday occurrence for anyone.' She took a biscuit from the packet Gabriel offered.

'No, no, it's my pleasure,' he grumbled, waving them under Faye's nose. She took one, mostly to have something that meant she couldn't respond too quickly to Ruby's question.

'Yes, that was odd,' Faye agreed, and smiled. 'Look, Ruby… it's a complicated situation, okay? I kind of…' She broke off, not knowing what to say. She wanted to confide in Ruby, but she was scared of letting anyone else in to her secret.

'It's okay, Faye. You can tell me. It won't go any further.' Ruby leaned forward, holding her tea. 'If it makes you feel any better, before I joined this coven I saw some pretty weird shit. I was in this other group, and they were…' Ruby shook her head, eyes wide. 'I mean, they were crazy times. I left because that didn't feel like magic to me, what they were doing. Not the kind of magic I wanted to do, anyway. So don't feel like I'm not gonna believe you, babes. Believe me, after that experience, I believe anything's possible.' She shook her head again at the memory.

Faye sighed.

'It's complicated. But okay.'

*

'You weren't kidding.' Ruby's tea was cold by the time Faye had finished her story; Gabriel sat quietly, listening, as Faye talked. No-one had come into the shop whilst they'd been talking. Telling everything again felt strangely good, a relief: perhaps the more she talked about it, the more likely she'd be to find a solution.

'No,' Faye laughed, despite herself.

'So, you're…' Ruby picked up the book Faye had been reading when she came in. 'Researching? For…?'

'Something to help me get back into Murias. I don't know. Anything would be a help at this point,' Faye sighed.

'Well, we better get reading, then.' Ruby started leafing through *Modern Witches*. 'I'll start with this one – you carry on with spirit possession, Gabriel can make a start on the medieval grimoires, and we'll meet in Enlightenment sorcery. Deal?'

'Deal.' Gabriel hugged Ruby where she sat. 'Thanks, Ruby. We could do with an extra pair of eyes.'

'These extra eyes need tea,' Ruby said, not looking up from the book.

'Of course they do,' Gabriel sighed theatrically.

Chapter 26

Faye could hear the music from two streets away, and almost turned back more than once before reaching the club where the London covens were holding their annual Samhain party.

It was pronounced *sow-in*, the old Celtic name for what was now Halloween. In the old pagan days, it was the festival announcing the onset of winter, and traditionally the time when the division between the ordinary world and the otherworlds – the elemental lands of faerie, the spiritual origin of nature and the lands of the dead – was easiest to transgress. Samhain was the night witches remembered loved ones that were in spirit, and, traditionally, it was a night for divination and all kinds of mediumship, being that it was so much easier than usual to talk to the ones in the next world.

At home, Faye always set a place for Grandmother and Moddie at the dinner table, sharing stories and memories of them with Annie. Then they would usually read each other's cards for the year ahead and walk down to Black Sands Beach to dance under the moon, perform a ritual they had planned out in advance, or just sit companionably and watch the waves.

Yet, tonight, as the city's children dressed as ghouls and wizards and collected sweets door-to-door, Faye found herself standing outside the wide steel doors of a club on the south side of the river, uncomfortable in a pair of black stiletto-heeled boots and a short black dress that she was glad her coat hid. As it was Samhain, she'd made her makeup darker and more dramatic than usual, and curled her reddish auburn hair into long ringlets. Tonight, Rav was going to some work drinks again – he'd asked her if she wanted to come. *It's Halloween! Your thing, right?* he'd asked, but she'd explained she had a Samhain celebration to attend. He'd looked disappointed, but not enough to persuade her not to go.

As she stood there, Faye gazed up at the stars. The night was dark, velvet, magical: the deep layers of the past spread out in black-gold layers; each star, each tree, each leaf a door to another life, another time. Samhain always gave her this special feeling; it was a time of magic, when anything could happen, when the otherworlds were close, and slippage could occur.

Faye was waiting for Annie and Susie. Annie had suggested they invite the cast of *Coven of Love* 'for research' but in actuality the guest list was too exclusive: only members of London covens or their approved friends and contacts were permitted, and no-one without one of the ornately foiled tickets got past the two tall, tattooed men on the door.

She tried not to stare at the people filing into the club, but in some cases it was hard not to look twice. Not everyone was hiding their eveningwear under a long coat, and, in fact, if anyone apart from Ruby at the *Coven of Love* set had attended, their preconceptions would only have been confirmed: tonight, there were plenty of floor-length gowns, velvet and otherwise. Faye was reminded of the faerie ball in Murias, as some attendees wore faerie wings and elaborate fae costumes with leather leaves and flower crowns; some wore gothic outfits that fitted the stereotype of the witch or wizard, with black cloaks and pentagrams hanging from their necks.

Yet, also, there were a number of other amazing looks and outfits, from prom dresses with delicate fascinators to a man with a pink

Mohican who, Faye could see as he removed his jacket to enter, was stripped to the waist and wearing only a pair of sequinned shorts. The variety of London's witches was staggering.

'Wondered if I'd see you here.' Faye felt a hand on the small of her back and turned to see Gabriel Black, who was dressed in his trademark black tailored suit and white shirt, but this evening with the addition of a black bowler hat and red pocket handkerchief. 'May I escort you into the ball, Miss Morgan?'

'Hi, Gabriel. Looking sharp.' Faye gave him a shy kiss on the cheek.

'Ah, well. One must do what one can,' he demurred. 'Are you waiting for someone?'

'My friend Annie and her girlfriend. You can wait with me, though.'

'I'd be delighted.' He took the pocket handkerchief out, re-folded it and replaced it in its pocket. 'How are you?'

'Okay,' she sighed. 'You?'

'I think we've gone past the social niceties by now,' Gabriel replied, nodding and smiling at some people going in. 'Customers,' he said, by way of explanation. 'How are you, really?' Gabriel laid a gentle hand on her arm, and Faye held it in hers.

'I'm okay. Just... frustrated that I... we...' she smiled, acknowledging Gabriel and Ruby's efforts on her behalf at the shop 'That we didn't find anything. Nothing that seemed like a way to get into Murias. And all the time, Aisha's trapped there.'

'Most of the coven will be here tonight. I know you told Ruby, but are you going to mention your adventures in Falias to them, or...?'

Am I going to tell the coven about Lyr and Falias? Or keep it a secret? Faye finished Gabriel's question in her mind. So much of her life was secret. Was that a good thing? Sometimes she felt choked with secrets.

'If you don't mind, I'd like to keep it between us. For now, at least. It's personal.' She frowned, wondering if she should tell the rest of the coven. But she wasn't a real member and, she rationalised, she didn't owe them anything.

'Of course.' Gabriel nodded, and there was a not-uncomfortable silence between them until a moment later when Annie got out of a taxi with Susie, yelling at Faye from across the street. 'Your friends, I assume?' He tipped his hat to them as they crossed the street.

'That's them.' Faye felt a rush of happiness as Annie, dressed in a skintight black PVC catsuit and black biker boots, danced over to them and planted a kiss on Faye's cheek. Even though she had to keep her hair long and blonde for *Coven of Love*, she'd curled up the ends into a sixties style.

'Howaya, sweetheart?' Annie took a double take at Gabriel. 'Who's this, aye? I didnae tell ye I was goin' to be Emma Peel tonight, but look, ye've found ma John Steed for me.'

'Annie, this is Gabriel Black. Gabriel, this is my best friend Annie and her girlfriend, Susie.'

'Delighted to find a fellow fan of vintage British espionage.' Gabriel shook Annie's hand, laughing. 'And I assure you, it's a happy accident. I'm afraid I usually look this way, though the bowler isn't an everyday thing.'

'Charmed. Hi, Faye.' Susie kissed Faye on her other cheek; Faye suspected that she now had red lipstick on one side of her mouth and pink on the other. Annie's girlfriend was dressed in trousers, a gold waistcoat under a nicely cut jacket and her hair was arranged in a sleek blonde bob.

'She's Emma Peel, I'm Pussy Galore,' Susie explained. 'Formidable women of British cinema.'

'Right,' Faye laughed. 'Bewitching, both of you.'

It was good to be completely herself with the people she liked and trusted most. *If Rav was here, would it be the same?* she wondered, and suspected that it wouldn't.

Chapter 27

Inside the club, it was busy. Annie and Susie immediately lost themselves on the dancefloor and Faye followed Gabriel to the bar. The floor was sticky and the music was excessively loud, but Faye felt at home immediately, though she wasn't much of a club person. There was something to be said for being among her own kind.

Onstage, a rock band were playing; Faye had no idea who they were, but she danced a little on the spot, listening to them. Gabriel handed her a bottle of beer and she tapped the top of hers against his.

'Cheers!' he shouted. 'You look beautiful this evening.' Faye felt her cheeks flush, and looked away. 'But you always do,' he shouted again, smiling. Faye didn't know what to say.

'Thank you,' she shouted back, awkwardly. She would never usually wear a dress this short, but when she'd looked at her wardrobe, it was the only thing that seemed appropriate. Ruby had invited her by text; when Faye texted back to ask what kind of event it was, Ruby had sent a smiley face and written *drinks, dancing, costumes – anything goes.*

She didn't have a costume, and she would never have worn one; fancy dress was for the adventurous. But when she'd zipped up the short dress – one she'd bought on a whim when shopping in the West End – she'd felt sexy, so she'd worn it. It had a scoop neck and long sleeves, and she'd left her legs bare. Surprisingly, they were more tanned from the hot summer than she'd have expected, but she and Rav had spent a lot of time walking around London's parks – eating ice-creams, talking, or reclining by the ponds and rivers that ran through the city's green spaces, lazily reading the papers or just lying in each other's arms.

'Hey! This party is awesome!' Annie and Susie reappeared and Gabriel handed them both a beer each. Annie grinned and took a long drink. 'Faye. I love this guy.'

Faye smiled, and tipped her beer bottle into her mouth. Gabriel took her hand.

'Dance?' he asked, and she nodded, leaving her drink on a nearby table and following him to the dancefloor.

Gabriel was a good dancer. Faye felt herself relax in the sea of bodies, all of whom were enjoying themselves, and none of them watching her. She felt the music take her over, and she moved to it, within it, enjoying the waves of music that took her from elation to energy and a sense of togetherness with the crowd. Gabriel took her hand and twirled her around. She laughed, and twirled him back. It was good to feel this carefree: she'd never usually allow herself to be so... she searched for the word. *Liberated.*

As they danced, she wondered momentarily if Gabriel had feelings for her, but she hoped that he didn't: she valued him as a friend, and she had precious few friends, especially ones that understood about magic. There was a part of her that wanted to ask him. Then, if he'd confessed that, yes, he felt something more than friendship, she'd have the opportunity to explain how, to her, it was so much more important to have him as a steady light in her life.

But it wasn't the moment, not now.

She felt free, dancing with Gabriel and with Annie and Susie there. Yet she'd been enchanted by dance before now: in Murias, in Finn

Beatha's kingdom, he'd danced with her in the faerie ball, and she'd lost herself in it. Had taken pleasure in losing herself to everything but him and the powerful desire that beat between them.

It was still in her: the unsatisfied craving for Finn. Even though she knew it was wrong; that she'd been enchanted and unable to see the truth of what lay under her feet as she danced. And though she knew the darkness at Finn's core, she still wanted him.

Outside the club she'd observed the amazing variety of costumes of the attendees, but as she looked at Gabriel, Faye realised that some of the bodies she saw in the corner of her gaze, dancing, jostling and kissing, were different to the rest of the coven members there. It wasn't that their costumes or dress was strange, but the bodies themselves were less… real. She frowned and focused her gaze on them. Surely it was a trick of the dim light?

Yet, there was a translucence to some of the figures that danced and jumped, tapped and twirled. And it was a look that she recognised.

She shouted in Gabriel's ear.

'There are faerie folk here. Elementals. They're not human!' she yelled, hoping to be heard over the band, but Gabriel winced, shook his head and pointed at his ear. 'Elemental beings. They're here, dancing in the crowd!' she repeated, and watched as understanding filtered across his expression.

'Are you sure?' he mouthed at her, and she nodded impatiently.

They stopped dancing, suddenly still in the sea of movement around them. Faye pointed into the crowd.

'Look. There! And there!' She pointed at the vague, hazy figures that glittered at the edge of perception. Perhaps, because she was so accustomed to being in the faerie worlds now, she could see them more easily. Or perhaps it was her half-fae nature. But as soon as she pointed at them, they disappeared and Gabriel shook his head. He couldn't see any of them.

Faye heard laughing behind her and spun around, but there was no-one behind her except dancers, headbanging intently and definitely not laughing.

'Did you hear that?' she shouted, but Gabriel shook his head again and looked at her doubtfully.

'Faye, maybe we should get some air,' he shouted, and took her elbow, aiming to steer her off the dancefloor, but she pulled away.

'I saw them! I'm not going mad!' she shouted back as the song slowed.

The opening bars of the next song started; a ballad that held the crowd in a sweet lull of expectation.

She felt a strong hand in the small of her back and looked around, confused. Who else but Gabriel was trying to get her attention?

But it was Finn Beatha who leaned in and kissed her cheek, smiling that pouty-lipped smile that she could never resist.

Chapter 28

'No!' Faye screamed, and stepped away from the faerie king in shock. She'd seen him in her dreams, but she hadn't expected to ever see Finn Beatha in person, in the ordinary world, ever again. Her heartbeat accelerated until it seemed to thrum in her chest with the frantic rhythm of a bird's. She realised that she was sweating; her forehead, her chest, behind her knees.

His physical presence was overwhelming. He was tall and rangy, muscular without being bulky; he was fair, though his hair was a dirty blonde when he appeared in the ordinary world, she noticed, and more golden when he was in his own realm. Tonight, when of all nights he could have worn his faerie robes without attracting any more notice than a very attractive man might, he wore a black tuxedo with a sharp white shirt underneath, like Gabriel's. Yet, while Gabriel managed to look like a reasonably attractive civil servant in his smart clothes, Finn Beatha had the effortless and otherworldly beauty of a film star. His longish dark-blonde hair was tied up, Faye noticed, in the kind of bun that hipster boys in London favoured, and he was clean shaven.

Finn was always overwhelming to Faye because of his sheer beauty, but also because of the bond they had. It began, as always, when her eyes met his dark blue gaze: she felt the energy of their connection overcome her immediately, as if they were the only two people in the room. Finn's gaze never left hers, and everything else – the club, the dancers, the band – melted away. In fact, as she fought to break their eye contact, she looked around her and noticed that they stood still in the club, but apart from it. They stood as if beyond a hazy sepia screen. Everything moved around them, but slowly, as if on pause, and only she and Finn were real and in colour. Everything else was the colour of a vintage photograph; momentarily unreal, already a memory, already a dream.

'What have you done?' she demanded, although she knew; Finn could move between Murias and the ordinary world as he chose to, and he could manipulate time in the human world. She remembered that it was Samhain, the night when the veil between the worlds was thinnest. Tonight it was easier than ever for him to cross over. And, she supposed, it was the same for the other fae creatures she'd glimpsed.

'I wanted to dance with my *sidhe-leth*. Surely that is no crime.' He smiled and kissed her cheek again. Despite herself, she felt the heat in his lips and yearned for more; she fought the rising tide of desire he always prompted in her. 'For old times' sake,' he added, a twinkle in his eye.

'You told me I would never see you again,' she challenged him.

'I was angry.' He batted his eyelids at Faye, playful now. 'But I cannot stay angry for long. It's boring,' he sighed and placed both his long-fingered hands on her waist, one on each side. 'This dress is very appealing, I must say, Faye. You look as wicked as I remember you in Murias.' He brushed aside her hair and stroked her neck softly, and Faye felt herself melt under his touch. *No, no!* she tried to tell herself not to give in to the pleasure that blanketed them both in its soft spell.

'So... you just thought you could... reclaim me? Just like that?' Faye mustered her self-control and removed his hands from her waist.

'Haven't I?' he murmured against her ear, taking her hand and placing it on his heart. 'You feel it, Faye, as I do. I love you. I miss you. In my heart. Not just my bed.'

She felt the tears well in her eyes as he said it, and wiped them away furiously.

'You don't love me,' she shot back. 'You don't love anyone or anything. Your heart is as cold as the ocean, Finn Beatha. And I won't be your lover.'

'I know you love me, Faye. And I know you will come to me again before too long,' he said, drawing her to him. He kissed her, then, deeply, and she lost all ability to rail against him. It was a kind of return to her deepest self when she was in his kiss; as if he was a river she had forgotten she belonged to, a part of the tide that rushed against the stone bank. Desire for him erupted in her, and she felt herself grow wet with desire for him and everything she knew he could give her.

'See, you would have me now,' he whispered, and Faye knew that she'd be lost unless she acted fast. Reaching into the cross-body bag she was wearing, her fingers found the obsidian crystal Lyr had given her: she'd kept it with her ever since. As she grasped it, she felt the crystal's dual earth-and-fire energy fight the power of Finn's element of water, and she found that she could break away from him.

'I would not,' she replied, and held the crystal up to him. He frowned at it and stepped away from her.

'I see that you have met your father,' he said, dryly. 'Do not think just because he has given you a trinket that you can forget the bond that exists between us, *sidhe-leth*. You are mine, and you will come back to me. I have foreseen it,' he said, taking a step backward, and then another. 'Tell your father that I look forward to seeing him and his ill-begotten son Luathas on the battlefield.' He smiled and now

Faye could see the sulk on his lips, like a child that has been refused its favourite treat.

'Tell him yourself,' she retorted, and held the crystal up in the room. Black, green and gold light emanated from it like a lamp, dispelling the sepia light in the club, banishing it like mist.

'So be it.' Finn held up his hand in a sign of surrender. 'But I tell you, I have foreseen it. We will be lovers again, Faye. Don't deny your own desire.'

Faye held the crystal higher and kicked off her high heels, standing firmly on the sticky floor of the club in her bare feet. She summoned up tendrils of flickering emerald, black and gold earth energy from the ground and breathed it up into her body.

'Be gone! I banish you, back to your kingdom!' she shouted. Colour and animation started to bleed back into the hazy sepia effect around her; life began to return to the ball.

Finn melted away, out of the crowd, along with the flickering figures of the other visiting fae.

I know you. I know you will come to me. His voice was in her mind, and she shook her head, as if she could get rid of his influence like shaking water from her ear after swimming.

'No.' She said it out loud, firmly. She could resist Finn; she wasn't the bewildered girl he could bewitch whenever he wanted, any more.

'What just happened?' Gabriel was standing next to her, blinking, and she replaced the crystal in her bag.

'Maybe we do need to get some air,' she said, and grabbed for his arm before her legs gave out from under her.

Chapter 29

Faye had already drunk half her coffee by the time Mallory walked into the coffee shop, shaking the rain from a plain black umbrella. She wore a long black and grey houndstooth check coat that reminded Faye of a cape, and tall black boots underneath. She was as slight as Faye remembered, yet she made her way imperiously through the café.

'Hi.' Faye smiled openly, feeling that her own outfit of blue jeans and a cream knitted jumper was somehow less cool, less elegant, less London than Mallory's seemingly effortless style. Today Faye had plaited her long, auburn hair, which hung over one shoulder; she wished she'd perhaps curled it and left it long, and worn something less homely. Mallory's hair was as luxuriously long and blonde as she remembered, and when she took off the long coat, she was wearing a plain, fitted black t-shirt and tight black jeans that showed off her petite figure.

'Ugh, terrible weather out there.' Mallory threw her coat onto the leather booth seat facing Faye; she didn't apologise for being late and called her coffee order across at a waitress. 'Flat white. Extra shot.'

'I don't mind it. Reminds me of home, a little,' Faye smiled, aware that she was being artificially jolly. It was a lie; London didn't remind of her of Abercolme at all, but she was making conversation, smoothing out the jagged peaks of Mallory. Annie, with her actressy dislike of social faux pas and bad manners, would have said something like '*Get it up ye, bessie, at least say hullo*'. Faye wished Annie was with her; she also knew that Mallory most likely wouldn't know that *bessie* was an insult. She tried again. 'Thanks for your card. And the flowers. That was kind.'

'S'ok. I work next to a florist, so it's no hassle. They give me a massive discount, I'm in there so much.'

'Ah.' The waitress brought Mallory's drink and asked Faye if she wanted another; she shook her head hurriedly. If this was how it was going to go, she didn't want to be stuck here with Mallory.

'So. Tell me about the coven.' Mallory leaned back against the blue leather booth and sipped her coffee, watching Faye intently. 'When I saw you at Rav's, that's where you'd been, right?'

'The coven?' Faye hadn't expected Mallory to ask her about that; when they'd met, at the bar, she'd been distinctly uninterested in talking about tarot. Except, Faye remembered, that Mallory *had* said she was familiar with it; it was just her tone and manner that implied she wasn't interested in talking about it with Faye. She'd forgotten that.

'Rav said it's a London-based group. I'm quite keen to find one, so I wanted to know what you thought.'

'What I thought?' Faye knew she was repeating Mallory's words like a simpleton, but she was having trouble getting to grips with the surprising turn the conversation had taken.

'Yeah. You know. What are they like? What did you do? I mean, I don't want to join just any group.'

Faye took a drink of her coffee to disguise the laugh that had jumped to her throat, and coughed instead. Mallory obviously thought that joining a coven was like choosing a bikini waxer.

'Well, they do run open rituals at the seasonal festivals, but you have to be a friend of someone to go. You can't just say you want to join and they'll have you.' Faye remembered Sylvia going out of her way to make it clear that she was welcome at Mabon, as long as she knew her place. *If they've got any sense, they wouldn't take you in a blue moon, anyway* Faye thought to herself. 'Why do you want to join a coven?'

Mallory shrugged. 'Seems like the right thing to do, y'know? Look at me – I always dress in black. I listen to a lot of Fields of the Nephilim. I dunno, it's obvious… I'm such a witch.'

Faye raised her eyebrow and said nothing; a favourite colour was hardly a prerequisite for witchcraft. She'd always chosen to work alone or with Annie, but, because of the shop, she knew plenty of local Scottish covens and less formal groups – groups of people that ran regular specialised workshops or retreats, dedicated to particular goddesses or gods, or focused on a range of techniques from seership and clairvoyancy to herbalism and healing, incense-making and traditional crafts to shamanic soul retrieval and breathwork, and everything in between. Everyone who ran those groups, or attended them, was serious about their craft; no-one was in it for the image, and indeed many of them tended not to talk about their work much with those who weren't in the know.

'Dunno. Like, I did this love spell when I was twenty or so. Just made it up. And the guy ended up being my boyfriend for, like, years.'

'Uh-huh.' Faye raised her eyebrow; not that she'd had much experience, but usually having enough sex with a smitten young man was enough to manage them becoming your boyfriend, never mind spells. Though, she checked herself; she, Annie and Aisha had done a love spell, and it had definitely worked, in a way that couldn't have been predicted.

'Yeah. I've tried some stuff for myself. Crystals and tarot. I just feel like it's something I want to look into more, so when Rav said that's where you were, I thought I'd ask you.'

Clearly, Mallory didn't remember Faye mentioning that she owned one of Scotland's most well-respected witchcraft shops, or that she was a hereditary witch; she'd had the opportunity to ask Faye as much as she wanted about her experiences, about Moddie and Grandmother and Black Sands Beach, when they'd sat next to each other at the bar. But she hadn't been interested then. Faye also noted that this coffee date definitely wasn't an opportunity for Mallory to apologise, which was the impression she'd given Faye in her text. Probably she knew that Faye wouldn't have come along otherwise.

Still, Faye gave her the benefit of the doubt. Mallory might be woefully socially inept, and just because she hadn't expressed any meaningful reason for making the huge commitment that being a member of a coven was – or, a reason for why she was interested in magic herself, or any sign that she really understood what she was letting herself in for – didn't mean that maybe this wasn't the right thing for her on her path. She'd definitely learn a thing or two by training to be a witch, even if it wasn't what she expected.

Mallory reached over the table and took Faye's hand.

'I'd really appreciate it if you introduced me, Faye. I know I can be a bit of a bitch. I could have been more welcoming, whatever. It's not me, being all super-friendly, y'know? But at least for Rav's sake, we should be friends. He's a good guy.'

Faye was bewildered by Mallory's sudden direct contact, and had the strange experience of hearing herself reply without being aware that she'd made the decision to.

'Well, I can put you in touch with Ruby, and she can tell you when the next open ceremony is.' Faye found herself offering and regretted it immediately. She'd enjoyed getting to know Ruby recently and she felt a little protective of her new friends. She didn't have many, and she didn't want to lose them to. Plus, having Mallory there would be a huge pain; she could feel it.

'Great, thanks.' Mallory signalled to the waitress for the bill. *What just happened?* Faye wondered. Clearly, now Mallory had got what she wanted, there was no more reason for her to be here. 'So, text me? Or give me her number.'

'I'll let you know,' Faye said, noncommittally.

Mallory nodded and got up, putting her coat on; they'd been in the coffee shop for twenty minutes at maximum, and that included Mallory being late.

'Cool. Sorry, I've got to run.' Mallory picked up her umbrella.

'What do you do, again?' Faye asked; all of Rav's friends worked in the music business in some way, but she couldn't remember knowing what Mallory did.

'Music PR. Mostly modern acoustic folk acts, singer-songwriter vocalists, that kind of thing. I get to be artificially cheerful and upbeat all day long.' Mallory flashed Faye an intentionally false shark-like smile. 'Like this. Okay Faye, take care, speak soon, yeah?'

Without waiting for any kind of response, Mallory left, swishing her way through the café again. Faye watched her go, feeling ill at ease.

Chapter 30

Annie crammed a forkful of fries into her mouth and shook her head. 'Fuckin' cheek, aye. Ah've not met the lassie but if I did I wouldnae like her one bit. Pass me the sauce.'

Faye squirmed in the uncomfortable seat on what used to be a bus and had now been turned into an on-set catering van for the cast and crew of *Coven of Love*. She sighed and picked at her curry; she'd lost her appetite.

'I just don't know how it happened. She held my hand, and I was so surprised that I said she could come along. I don't want her to, though. I don't like her.' She passed Annie the bottle of ketchup and watched her squeeze it all over her dinner. 'That doesn't look very healthy,' she added. 'Aren't you and Suze on a healthy eating regime?'

'Aye. But I get so hungry,' Annie looked guilty. 'Don't tell Suze. She's doin' so well. It's alright for her. She likes all that – quinoa and lentils.' She shuddered and made a face. 'It's like eatin' rabbit food.'

Faye pulled an imaginary zip from one side of her mouth to the other. 'My lips are sealed. What should I do about Mallory, though?'

'Ignore her.' Annie shrugged. 'It's not hard, aye.'

'But what about when I see her?'

'See if ye can avoid talking to her, and if ye cannae, just give her the brush off. Say you haven't heard from Ruby.'

Faye sighed.

'Thing is, Rav really seems to want us to be friends. For me to be nice to her. I don't know how he can't see how self-centred she is.'

'Men don't tend to notice stuff like that, especially if they want to sleep with a woman.' Annie raised her eyebrow.

'They *have* slept together, remember? They were in a relationship and they broke up. He broke it off.'

'Hmmm. Well, maybe he's still got a soft spot for her, aye.'

'Thanks, that's a huge comfort.'

Annie held up her palms in defence. 'Hey, now! I'm just sayin'.'

'Well, don't *just say*,' Faye snapped, and immediately felt bad for it. 'Sorry. It's just…' she wasn't sure whether to mention anything about Lyr and the faerie realm to Annie; not here, anyway.

'What?' Annie asked, mid-chew.

Faye leaned across the table. 'Faerie realm stuff,' she whispered.

Annie leaned in conspiratorially; the bus wasn't full, and the tables behind both of them were empty, so it was unlikely they'd be heard anyway.

'Faerie realm? As in… Finn?'

Faye blushed at the mention of his name. 'Kind of. I've… dreamt of him. A couple of times,' she said, evasively, not wanting to go into details, though that was stupid, now that she'd brought it up. She hadn't told Annie or Susie what had happened at the club, but she'd told Gabriel. She'd had to – he was right there when Finn appeared, and he knew something was up, even though Finn had frozen him out just like everyone else. She felt odd, somehow, for telling Annie.

'When ye say *dream*, ye mean…' Annie raised her eyebrows suggestively. '*That* kindae dream?'

'Yes.' Faye looked at the table, feeling her cheeks flush.

'D'you think he was… really there? That's what he does, aye? He can come to ye in dreams.'

'I think so, yes,' Faye admitted.

'But—' Annie began, but Faye cut her off.

'I know!' Faye hissed. 'God. Don't you think I know? He tried to kill Rav.'

'What aboot what he did to Aisha? Faye, really, sweetheart,' Annie put her fork down; her expression was concerned. 'Ye cannae start all that again.'

'I know, and I'm not going to! Give me some credit,' Faye whispered acidly. 'It's not that. That, I can handle. It's something else. When I was at the ceremony, with Ruby's group? At Mabon?' She was lying to herself about being able to handle her erotic dreams about Finn, but that was beside the point for now.

'Yeah,' Annie was frowning, leaning forward. 'What happened?'

'My father. Lyr, the Faerie King of Falias. That's the realm of earth, like Murias is water. He appeared to me in the circle. Totally freaked everyone out.'

'No shit!' Annie's eyes were wide in fascination. 'What happened?'

'Well, not much that time. We were doing this ritual, speaking to ancestors; I told him to go, and he disappeared. But then I… we – me and Gabriel, that is – we summoned Lyr. In the rose garden at Regents Park, actually.'

Annie's eyes widened.

'Ye didnae!'

'Yeah. Well, it worked. Lyr appeared. Took me to Falias and he showed me Aisha. An, she's stuck in some kind of terrible dungeon.

She looks like she hasn't got much longer. She looks terrible. And he said…' Faye felt the tears blocking her throat; she hated it that she cried when she was upset or angry. Why couldn't she just get the words out? 'He said he could help me rescue her, but in return he wants me to give him a human woman to have his child, to use as a sacrifice in this war they're having.'

'Wow.' Annie blew out a long breath. 'Not exactly ethical.'

'Yeah. Well, I refused, of course. But I keep thinking about Aisha. Every day that passes, she's getting thinner and weaker. And I thought…' Faye took a deep breath. 'I thought maybe, if I pretend to want to be Finn's lover again, he'll let me back in to Murias. It's the only way. And when I'm there, I can bring her home.'

Annie shook her head.

'Faye. Are ye mad? Ye can't stay sober while you're there; he has this effect on ye, like, he makes ye a sex zombie. The whole place, it's one giant lust palace, aye? Ye can't control yerself there, sweetheart. And there's no way they'll let you near her. That faerie queen, what was her name? I dinnae like the sound of her at all.'

'There must be a way. Last time I was there, I was learning their magic. That was always my intention, to learn to be able to be there without being under Finn's spell.'

'But ye never got to that part, aye?' Annie shrugged. 'So yer back to square one,'

'I've got to try, An. She's dying.'

Neither of them said anything; Faye felt the tears rolling down her cheeks.

'Have ye talked to Rav aboot all this?' Annie asked, gently, leaning over the table and wiping away Faye's tears with the cuff of the fleece she'd no doubt borrowed from someone on set to wear over her costume, which was another floor-length crushed velvet dress of the kind that Ruby and Faye had laughed about, weeks before. Annie didn't own any clothing as pedestrian as a fleece jacket; everything she wore was usually a mix of vintage and designer wear in bright colour combinations.

'He doesn't want me involved in all of that. He wants to pretend it never happened,' Faye admitted with a sigh. 'I mean, I understand. He's sympathetic, but when he was there, that was a really terrifying experience. He doesn't want to go back or have anything to do with the faerie realm. I get it, I really do. But…' she trailed off, not knowing how else to explain.

'But he knew Aisha. He must have some sympathy.' Annie slid out of her chair and into Faye's, putting her arm around her. Faye buried her head in her friend's shoulder.

'I think he's almost convinced himself … all the faerie stuff… even the time he spent there… it was all a hallucination or something. Temporary madness.'

'Oh.' Annie hugged Faye, and handed her a paper napkin from the table. 'Well, I'm here. Okay? And we're goin' to make it right. I promise, okay, sweetheart?'

Faye blew her nose noisily, not caring now if people were watching. They could think what they liked; even in their wildest dreams they'd never guess what she and Annie were talking about, anyway.

'Okay, well. Why don't ye talk to this Gabriel? If he had something that helped ye summon Lyr before, then he might be of some use again, aye?'

'I have. He's been really helpful, and Ruby? She's the wardrobe mistress here? They've both been very supportive.'

'Good. Look, I'm due back on set now, but let's talk later, okay?'

'Okay.' Faye wiped her eyes as best she could without all the makeup coming off. Annie made a face.

'Ye might want to fix your face before you go.' Annie planted a kiss on Faye's forehead and wriggled out of the long bus seat. 'Ah love ye, ye daftie.'

'Love you too.' Faye watched her friend go, unhappily.

Chapter 31

It was a Saturday and Faye had invited Gabriel, Annie, Susie and Ruby around for dinner at Rav's flat. After she'd picked up the food she needed for dinner in the morning – some fresh salmon from the fishmonger on the high street, wine from the friendly traditional vintner on the corner who let her take her time choosing the perfect wine to accompany it, and some delicious smelling granary bread from the bakery – she got on the tube, heading to the West End so she could walk to Fortune's to meet Ruby and Gabriel. From her seat on the train, Faye watched her fellow passengers and realised she felt like a local for the first time. She remembered that night when she and Rav had gone to that bar: how crowded it had felt, how choked she'd been by the traffic fumes outside. Now, she'd grown used to London, and liked the anonymity that cloaked her when she rode the train or walked around; she kept the black obsidian crystal on her, usually, when she was out and about, which made her feel protected from the chaos of the city.

Perhaps because of the crystal or perhaps because that's just how it was in London, no-one paid her any attention, no-one cared what she looked like or who she was. In their strange, polite way, she found Londoners generally far more quietly tolerant than the villagers in tiny Abercolme, who noticed and remarked on everything. Here, she felt a new kind of freedom. She felt that she could have run through the streets shouting that she was half-faerie, or a witch, and absolutely no-one would react. Unlike Abercolme, there were so many different cultures, occupations, languages and identities in the city that Faye being a witch and faerie just blended into the mix.

When she reached Fortune's, Ruby and Gabriel were standing outside, waiting for her. Ruby was swathed in a shocking pink pashmina over the top of her tailored navy blue coat which was cinched at the waist with a wide navy leather belt; she wore knee-length beige leather boots underneath. Gabriel wore his black suit and white shirt underneath, as usual, with a black overcoat on top. Faye kissed them both on the cheek.

'You both look gorgeous.' She felt happy at the day ahead: an afternoon with Ruby and Gabriel who were becoming good friends, and dinner with Annie and Susie joining them later. It was more than that: she felt like a normal person, having fun. Life could be fun, and she'd forgotten.

'You always do. We're always playing catch-up.' Ruby gave her a hug and took her arm. 'Okay, so: Star Herbs for necessary witch shopping. Then, cake. Then back to yours.'

'Sounds perfect.'

Star Herbs sat on the corner of a little courtyard off a similar small cobbled street to Fortune's, hidden from view. An apothecary-style herbalist, it boasted an oversized old-fashioned wooden castle door, studded with metal in the shape of stars. Faye traced their irregular bumps with her fingertips as she followed Gabriel inside.

'They also sell amazing home-made candles, incenses and oils,' Ruby said as they entered, the pungent smell of frankincense billowing around them.

Inside, the shop was an L-shape with a flickering, tiled fireplace under rows of bookshelves to Faye's left. Along the walls, many-drawered antique apothecary cabinets boasted a combination of original Latin calligraphy labels and more modern additions in marker pen: *Passiflora Incarnata, Achillea Millefolium, Gingko Biloba*. To Faye's right, the long glass-topped shop counter stood in front of a wall of labelled jars selling herbs by the ounce like old-fashioned sweets. The jars were arranged for practicality over beauty, but the mix of oversized plastic sweet jars with their generic white tops, green and blue glass jars with wide-necked glass stoppers and the occasional Mason jar with peeling-off, yellowed sticky tape around the label appealed to Faye. She took in a deep breath.

'This is amazing,' she breathed. Immediately she compared it to Mistress of Magic, her own shop, taking in the vintage décor, the candle on the counter that burned in a wine bottle almost entirely covered with the multi-coloured drippings of old wax. To the right of the counter, on the other side of the L-shape, tall and short candles in all the colours Faye could image were stacked in careful triangle-shaped piles.

It was different to her shop, yes, but Mistress of Magic had its own character. Hers had been a family home: generations of Morgan women had warmed themselves by the hearth, told fortunes, dispensed remedies. Faye felt a sudden tug of homesickness: a vision of Mistress of Magic, closed to customers, its display windows getting streaked and dirty from the rain, struck her. When was she going back?

'Hey.' Ruby nudged her as Faye stared at the candles, not seeing them, thinking of the shop. She and Rav had never put a time limit on her being in London: she'd been reluctant to, and Rav had been desperate to leave Abercolme. His house, the modern glass mansion on Black Sands Beach, was still up for sale. Faye doubted it would sell anytime soon. Had magic – her spell, specifically – summoned Rav to Abercolme? There had to be a reason that he'd bought a house that had otherwise lain empty for almost as long as she could remember. The house lay on a road to the faerie realm, and the faeries would discourage any new owners, she was sure. But her shop was in Abercolme, and she couldn't leave it forever. Soon, she'd have to go back, or find a more permanent solution.

'Hey.' Faye blinked, coming out of her daze.

'So?' Ruby was already carrying two brown glass bottles of herbal tincture and a tall white candle labelled 'Peace'. She grinned at Faye. 'You like it?'

Faye smiled. 'I love it. Thanks for bringing me here.'

'You're welcome, witch.' Ruby nodded at the candles. 'Deciding what to get?'

'Oh… no, I was just thinking about my shop, Mistress of Magic.' Faye turned around and looked at some goddess sculptures on the wall behind her. 'It's been closed a while now. I… at some point, I have to decide what to do with it.'

'You'd sell it?' Ruby's eyes widened.

'No. No, I'd never do that.' Faye was caught off guard by the rush of sorrow and homesickness that overcame her at the thought. She swallowed, embarrassed by the tears that suddenly choked her throat. 'Sorry. I… I don't know what's come over me. I was fine a minute ago.'

'Oh, darling. Come on, let's go outside for a minute.' Ruby set her treasures down on the shop counter before leading Faye outside the shop and to a green cast iron love seat in the little courtyard outside. Tall palms in wide pots helped obscure the shop from the idle passer-by.

'It's amazing they get any custom, the shop's so hidden away,' Faye observed.

'People that need it, find it,' Ruby replied. 'It's an institution. So, come on. What's going on?'

Faye sighed. 'It's kind of a long story. But basically, my shop's closed up, in Abercolme, and I haven't made any long term plans about what to do with it. And I realised that's because I don't really know what's happening with me and Rav. I don't want to sell the shop. That's my family's heritage.' Faye felt the tears filling her eyes again and wiped them away impatiently.

'Sure,' Ruby nodded, 'I wouldn't want to either.'

'But what I do with the shop's a barometer for my commitment to Rav, don't you think? I don't have a plan for either. That worries me.' Faye looked into the distance.

'It's not ideal, babes.' Ruby took out her vape and turned it on. A cloud of raspberry-scented vapour surrounded Faye. 'I don't know what to suggest. I mean, it's okay not to know, that's the first thing. You don't have to be definite about the guy until you are, one way or another.'

'I know, but... the shop is an added pressure.'

'You should speak to him about it, then. If you can see this is going to become an issue. He knows it's your business, I mean, he owns his own business, right?'

Faye nodded.

'Okay, well, stands to reason that he's going to understand all the practicalities. I mean, maybe you can get a manager in temporarily? Or go back yourself for a while?'

'I can't really open it here and there. You have to be reliable for customers.' Faye thought of her mix of locals and the witches that often made Mistress of Magic a particular stop on their holiday. 'But, yeah. I need to talk to Rav about it. You're right.' She didn't know what the outcome would be, but she had to make a decision at some point.

'It'll be okay, sweets.' Ruby kissed her on the cheek, surprising Faye. 'Ha. You didn't know we were at the cheek-kissing stage, did you?'

'No, but it's fine.' Faye smiled, her heart warmed by Ruby's obvious care.

'Look. Gabriel's a good listener.' Ruby nodded and squeezed Faye's arm. 'Gods know he's listened to my woes enough times. But I am too, okay? It's been nice getting to know you, Faye. I don't have that many witchy girly friends.'

'Me neither.' Faye gave Ruby an unexpected hug.

'Come on, then.' Ruby turned off her vape and put it back in her bag. 'Let's shop. And then, cake, definitely.' She rearranged the fluffy fuchsia pashmina around her shoulders; Faye rubbed her hands together. It was getting cold in the days now; she needed new gloves.

Gabriel poked his head out of the shop door and gave both of them an enquiring look. 'Ladies. All okay out here? You're missing out on some serious retail therapy.'

'We're fine. I needed a vape.' Ruby waved dismissively at Gabriel. 'We're coming back in now.'

Gabriel ignored Ruby's wave and came to join them; he pulled a wooden garden chair to sit next to Faye's side of the love seat.

'What's going on?'

'It's okay. I was thinking about my shop, that's all.' Faye smiled.

'Ah,' Gabriel frowned.

'What?' Faye prompted.

'No, it's just… I was wondering if this was about Aisha.'

'Oh god. No, I wasn't thinking about that.' A new wave of despair overtook Faye.

'Sorry. I shouldn't have said anything.' He looked uncomfortable. 'It's just that we were talking about it before. I know it's on your mind.'

'Gabes, don't upset her.' Ruby looked concernedly at Faye.

'He's not,' Faye sighed. 'The thing is, I could get into Murias. There is one obvious way. But…' she met Gabriel's eyes. 'You know what I mean. What do you think?'

'You mean…' he frowned again. 'You said that was a definite no.'

'*What* was a definite no?' Ruby looked back and forth at them both. 'Can someone please remind me know what we're talking about?'

'Aisha. There is one way I know I can get back to Murias, and rescue her. Maybe.' Faye exchanged a glance with Gabriel. 'But it would mean being his lover again. The faerie king.'

'Riiiight,' Ruby took a long drag on her vape. 'And you'd do that?'

'I don't know. What do you think?'

'I think it'd be really bad for your home life with Rav.' Ruby exhaled the smoke, eyebrow raised. 'As a massive understatement. But… I dunno. Maybe it's more a question of making Finn believe you would, rather than "going all the way"?' She made quote marks in the air with both index fingers.

'Ruby, darling. That's a little oversimplifying,' Gabriel chided her. 'I don't know, Faye. It would be hugely dangerous. For you, for Rav – even for Aisha. What if it made things worse for her – if Finn found out what you were doing, and punished her for it? Have you thought of that?'

'Of course I've thought of that!' Faye snapped. 'But time's moving on, you know? Even if it moves differently in Murias. She's still there. It's still my responsibility to save her.' Faye took in a long breath. 'What I want to know is, do you think it would work?'

Gabriel looked away, thinking.

'It might. I mean, I don't have the same knowledge of the faerie realm as you do. And, as you know, I *am* fascinated by the idea of having faerie lovers.'

'It's not what you think it is,' Faye argued back, but Gabriel's indication that it might be possible – that she might somehow be able to pretend with Finn long enough to get to Aisha – was seductive in ways that she didn't want to admit to herself.

'Maybe. But if it's something you decide to do, I'll help you, if you need it.' Gabriel stuck his hands into his pockets. 'You know I'm kind of… obsessed with the fae. Like a fanboy.'

'You really shouldn't be,' Faye warned.

'Maybe. But you know better than anyone how addictive they are,' he replied, and Faye knew she had no reasonable response except to agree.

Chapter 32

Ruby, Gabriel and Faye had already opened the wine and were chattering merrily in the kitchen when Rav got home. Faye was making a salsa verde to go with the poached salmon and Gabriel was laying the long scrubbed pine dining table; Ruby sat on the kitchen counter with a glass of wine, finishing the end of an outlandish story she claimed was true, about her experiences with her first coven.

'So, he was laid out cold for *hours*, I'm not even joking, and when he came around, he said he'd been talking to his ancestors and they foretold the Royal Wedding. *A prince will marry a commoner*. After all that prep, that's the message he got.'

Rav walked in, smiling. 'Party's already started, I see.' He kissed Faye and shook Gabriel's hand. 'Hey, I'm Rav.'

'Gabriel Black. Delighted,' he answered with a friendly, Gabriel-esque nod; sometimes Faye thought Gabriel must have walked out of the 1940s, he could be so quintessentially English.

'And you must be Ruby.' Rav kissed Ruby on both cheeks. 'So! What have I missed?'

Faye handed Rav a glass of the white wine they were almost at the bottom of already.

'Ruby was just telling us about her first coven,' she explained. 'Tell Rav what you used to get up to!' she laughed, going back to the worktop and pouring the salsa verde into a bowl. She was trying not to think about what she, Ruby and Gabriel had talked about earlier; that, while Gabriel had warned her of the dangers of going back to Murias, the fact that neither of them had absolutely said that she *shouldn't* bothered her more than it should. She almost wished they had both told her uncategorically that it was a terrible, unworkable plan, destined to failure.

Ruby blushed.

'Oh, it was nothing really,' she insisted, looking uncharacteristically embarrassed. 'We were young then. So, tell us about yourself, Rav?' Ruby had changed the subject adeptly, and Faye wondered if she was uncomfortable talking about witchcraft in front of a non-witch. If Rav noticed her slight discomfiture, he didn't show it. 'You run your own music company, don't you? Faye was telling us earlier.' Rav sat down at the table as the doorbell rang.

'Yeah, it's been running, what ten, twelve years now? We've been fairly successful. Promote tours and festivals, that kind of thing. That's how I met Faye.' He shot Faye an affectionate smile, and she swallowed a little of the nervousness she had about the evening. Rav hadn't spent a lot of time with her friends, and this meant a lot to her.

'I'll get it. It'll be Annie and Suze.' Faye wiped her hands on a dishtowel and welcomed the couple in. Annie gave her a bear hug.

'How are you, Faye?' Susie handed her a bag from the wine shop on the corner.

'That guy in the wine shop's a talker, aye? Couldnae get a word in.' Annie took off her coat and threw it on the sofa; Susie picked it up wordlessly and looked at Faye.

'I think what Annie meant was, where should we hang our coats?' she said, brightly. Faye took them, laughing. 'Everyone's in the kitchen. Go on in, I'll be right there.'

She opened a door to the utility cupboard, a little alcove with the boiler in and the place Rav stashed his shoes and various random golf clubs, magazines and tote bags with his company's logo on them, and hung up the coats. When she turned back into the lounge, she was surprised to find Annie still standing behind her.

'Gods, you frightened me.' Faye put her hand over her heart.

'How are things?' Annie whispered, nodding in the direction of the kitchen. 'I wanted tae ask before we do the social chitchat.'

'Between me and Rav? They're okay. Good.'

'Ye sure, sweetheart?' Annie had always been able to see into her soul.

'Okay, okay. Same as before, then,' Faye hissed.

'Ye havenae talked to him yet?'

'Not yet. But I will.' It seemed that there was a lot Faye needed to talk to Rav about; she could feel herself resisting it, though. She didn't want to upset their fragile balance. 'Come on, come in and say hi to everyone.' Faye led Annie into the kitchen, where Rav and Ruby were laughing about something; Gabriel was standing next to them, smiling politely. He grinned as Annie walked in, spun an imaginary walking cane and made a bow.

'Emma Peel! As I live and breathe!' he trilled, making Faye laugh.

'Oh, jolly good, it's my loyal companion John Steed!' Annie, being an actress, could change accents at lightning speed, and when she wanted to, her Queen's English was clipped and aristocratic. They laughed and Gabriel hugged her and Susie. Obviously, they'd all made quite an impression on each other when they'd met at the witches' ball; kindred spirits.

'Okay, time to eat! Everyone, sit down.' Faye directed everyone to where they should sit, placing Rav between Ruby and Susie, and Gabriel between her and Annie on the other side of the table.

'Darling, this looks delicious.' Rav raised his wine glass to her. 'To Faye, chef extraordinaire.'

They all toasted her and Faye felt her worries recede temporarily in a mist of good cheer.

The conversation and the wine flowed – Faye put a second and then third bottle on the table as the six of them laughed and talked. She was feeling tipsy, but hadn't had too much. It was making her feel nauseous, so after the first glass she switched to water.

The conversation had turned to Annie's TV show, *Coven of Love*, and Annie and Ruby were regaling the table with funny stories about other members of the cast.

'And of course there's the *Coven of Love* ghost,' Ruby said, deadpan, holding up her index finger for quiet. 'Seriously. He's called Cyril and he brushes against you sometimes in one particular dressing room. And you can hear shuffling footsteps going up and down the hallway outside, and sometimes he coughs.'

'He sounds like a strangely underwhelming ghost for a witchy TV show,' Susie commented. 'I'd expect… I dunno. Some wailing or something.'

'Most spirits are those mundane ones.' Gabriel helped himself to a spoon more of the salsa verde. 'It's just films that make people think it's going to be, like, Henry VIII appearing at the end of your bed holding Anne Boleyn's head or whatever.'

'Yeah. He's nice, anyway, Cyril. Been there years apparently.'

'How do you know that?' Rav asked.

'Maintenance man told me. He's worked there most of his life, he's heard Cyril shuffling about loads of times.'

Rav raised his eyebrow. 'And you believe him?'

Ruby blinked. 'Why wouldn't I?'

Rav shook his head. 'I don't believe in ghosts,' he stated. Gabriel smiled, but didn't say anything.

'Oh. Well, lots of people don't. It happens a lot more than you think, though. People pass on and get lost, get trapped in this realm.'

Rav smiled politely and nodded, but Faye thought they all could see on his face what he really thought.

'So. Rav. Tell us aboot yourself.' Annie sat back and took a sip from her glass, smiling neutrally. Faye knew Annie well enough to know that this was the smile she reserved for people she was assessing. 'I know we met in Abercolme, but I don't feel I know ye. Tell us some fascinatin' facts about the man that is Rav Malik, aye.'

Susie elbowed Annie. 'Don't be so nosy!' she chided, but Rav smiled; Faye thought he was probably glad that Annie had changed the subject.

'S'ok. Fair question. Right, fascinating facts… hmmm…' He reached for some bread and tore it apart as he was thinking. 'Okay. The first album I ever bought was *Bat Out of Hell 2: Back into Hell*.'

'Classy,' Susie said with a grin.

'Yup. Ummm, what else. I'm scared of moths?'

'I'd expect more from a Meatloaf fan,' Annie laughed as she drank from her glass.

'What was yours, then?' Rav topped up his glass and offered the bottle to Ruby next to him, who shook her head. 'You going to claim it was something ridiculously cool? People always do that, but they always like the cheesiest things in secret.' He rolled his eyes.

'New Kids on the Block. It's a 90s classic.' Annie shrugged. 'I'm proud of eight year old me. Better than Meatloaf anyway!'

'Fair enough. Someone had to like that manufactured teeny crap.' Rav met Annie's eyes and Faye saw a challenge there. 'What did Faye like?'

Faye felt angry. Rav was being a little rude. She'd always been nothing but polite to his friends, even though they apparently thought she was a liar. She'd swallowed it down for him – why couldn't he do the same?

'Why don't you ask her?' Annie shot back. Faye could see Ruby exchanging a glance with Gabriel. She didn't want this to be awkward; she just wanted everyone to get along. But there were tensions under the surface, and they were showing. Was Rav anxious about what Faye had told her friends about him? Or was he uncomfortable because he stood outside their group – even Susie, though not a witch, was knowledgeable about it and supported Annie's interest. Frankly, she didn't care. There was no excuse for rudeness.

'Oh, I forgot. Faye's not really into music,' Rav continued. 'I doubt she's ever bought an album, much less had a favourite.'

'Not true. And please don't talk about me like I'm not here,' Faye snapped.

'I rather thought Faye enjoyed that Scottish band. Dal Riada?' Gabriel interjected, his eyebrow raised. 'I'd applaud her for her taste, myself.'

A silence filled the room.

'Excuse me?' Rav lowered his wine glass and looked straight at Gabriel.

'I was just saying. I know that Faye particularly enjoyed Dal Riada's music,' Gabriel replied coolly, meeting Rav's eyes. 'I wouldn't underestimate her if I were you.'

'Gabriel. That's enough,' Faye ordered, glaring at him. *What had got into him?* She could see from his body language that he disliked Rav, and it was mutual. Rav was staring at Gabriel with undisguised contempt.

'Don't tell me what I know about my girlfriend, mate, okay?' Rav's tone was conversational, but everyone could hear the anger under it.

Gabriel nodded politely.

'Of course. I didn't mean any offence.' He smiled, his face a mask of politeness that everyone knew was false, and took a long drink from his wine glass. Faye glared at them both. She wanted to say *thanks for ruining my dinner party, both of you*, but she stewed in silence instead.

There was another uncomfortable pause.

'This salmon is great, Faye,' Ruby broke it after a long minute. Annie and Susie agreed enthusiastically, filling the quiet.

'Yeah, really tasty. Love this green stuff,' Annie added.

'The bread's really good. Is it from a local bakery?' Ruby added.

Faye smiled and nodded. What she really wanted to do was shout at Rav for being so inhospitable to her friends, but she didn't want to make a scene, so she got up and started clearing the plates instead.

Rav got up and disappeared into the lounge; Faye heard him going into the bathroom.

'Sorry.' Gabriel carried the bread plate into the kitchen and placed it next to the empty wine bottles. 'I shouldn't have said that.'

'No, you bloody shouldn't!' Faye hissed. 'That was unnecessary. I know he was being an idiot, but even so.'

'I know. He just... I don't know. It annoyed me that he was belittling you.'

'I can fight my own battles,' Faye muttered. She had the obsidian crystal in the pocket of her dress and found that she was squeezing it for reassurance.

'I'm sorry. Really.'

'I know. I'm not angry with you,' she sighed. 'We drank too much. That was probably to blame.'

'You didn't drink.' Susie frowned at Faye. 'You all right?'

'I'm fine. Just didn't fancy it tonight.'

'It was a shame. It was a lovely dinner.' Ruby handed Faye some used napkins from the table. 'It was nice hanging out with you guys.'

'It was,' Annie agreed. 'Next time, come to ours, aye? Suze can cook.'

'Or come to dinner above the shop,' Gabriel offered. 'It's the least I can do.'

'Can *you* cook?' Faye gave Gabriel a gentle smile.

'I'm a veritable maestro in the kitchen, Faye,' Gabriel said with a low bow.

'Literally no-one here believes that,' Ruby remarked.

'Words can hurt, Ruby,' Gabriel shot back, grinning, but his expression changed to wary as Rav walked back in, came over to the sink and gave Faye a hug.

'Hey. I'll do clean-up. You guys go and relax in the lounge.' He smiled at Susie and Annie, and held his hand out to Gabriel. 'Hey, man. Sorry if I was out of order.'

Gabriel shook Rav's outstretched hand. 'My fault. Sometimes my mouth runs ahead of my brain.'

Rav nodded.

'I find all of the… magical stuff… kind of difficult. Probably had too much wine.'

'We did drink –' Ruby looked at the empty bottles lined up for the recycling – 'five bottles. Between six of us. And Faye only had, like, one glass.'

'That would explain why I feel so pooped.' Susie made a face. 'Seriously. I think we should probably head off,' she said, giving Annie a meaningful look. 'It was a lovely dinner, Faye. Thanks so much for inviting us,'

'You don't have to go!' Faye knew Susie was being polite, sensing that she and Rav needed to talk.

'No, really.' Susie hugged Faye tightly. 'It's time to leave.'

Annie squeezed Faye fiercely.

'Management's orders, I'm goin', I'm goin',' she muttered. 'It was lovely seein' ye, sweetheart.'

'You too.' Faye pressed Annie's palm in hers.

'I'm here. Day or night. Just call,' Annie whispered as Faye stood back; she nodded in response.

Ruby followed suit and dragged Gabriel out, getting their coats on the way.

'Honestly, Faye, I don't know if I can walk straight,' she mumbled, hugging her on the way out. 'And I've got to make sure Gabriel gets home safely too.'

'I'll be fine,' Gabriel huffed, but allowed himself to be pushed out of the door. 'Thank you Faye. It was a marvellous day.'

'Talk to Rav about your shop in Abercolme. You have to make a decision sooner or later,' Ruby whispered.

Faye waved them all off, then closed the door behind her.

'Something I said?' Rav looked up from stacking the dishwasher, then saw Faye's expression. 'Hey. I'm joking, I didn't mean it.'

'Rav. We need to talk. About the shop.' She sat down at the table. 'I have to make a decision. And I need you to help me.'

Chapter 33

'I can't just let it sit there, closed until further notice.' Faye held Rav's hand across the dinner table. 'You understand that, right?'

'Of course I do,' Rav sighed. 'I suppose I just hoped… you wouldn't have to go back so soon.'

'I didn't say I was going back. I just need a plan, and I need to know…' Faye trailed off. 'I need to know where we are first.'

'We're here.' Rav smiled at her. 'Faye, I've had a lot to drink. Can we talk about this another time?'

'But when? You've been working late a lot. You don't want to talk when you get in. Can we just talk about it now?' Faye argued; nausea sat at the bottom of her stomach like a low, yellow tide.

'Fine. Where are we, then?'

Faye took a deep breath to quell her irritation.

'I think things are going okay, but there are… tensions between us. You know that.'

'We talked about that, Faye. You know how I feel. I want a clean break from all that faerie stuff.' Rav put his head in his hands. 'Do we *really* need to talk about this now? I'm so tired. I need to crash.'

'Yes, we do,' she sighed. She'd talked about the possibility of becoming Finn's lover to get to Aisha with Ruby and Gabriel. But it was one thing discussing it as a theory with her friends and another even thinking about it now. There was no way she could do that and expect to maintain a relationship with Rav – it would be wrong, and it would haunt her if she did it. *Why am I even considering it?* she berated herself. 'How would you feel if I did go back? Temporarily, at least?'

'I'd miss you. But I know it's your business, your home. I wouldn't stop you, of course. If you need to sell it, rent it out, I dunno. Find a manager for the shop.'

'What if...' she trailed off, not knowing how to say it. Rav was assuming that she was going to stay in London, but she wasn't sure of that. *What if I want to go back? Permanently?* she thought.

'What?' His head was still on the table and his words were muffled.

'The shop doesn't make enough for me to pay a manager,' she replied. 'And the rental market's not exactly buoyant in Abercolme.'

'Dunno what to suggest then. Sell it?' He lifted his head off the table and looked at her blearily; he was drunk. She shouldn't have brought it up now; he was right.

Faye stared at him, wondering what he would remember of this conversation the next day. The thought occurred to her that she could tell him everything, right now, right here. Her thoughts about rescuing Aisha. Her time in Falias, Lyr, the rose garden in Regents Park with Gabriel. She opened her mouth, heart beating wildly. Even if he didn't remember it, there would be a comfort in having told him. In being heard.

Rav snored. He had fallen asleep.

Faye sat opposite him, staring at the top of his head. Was this really the man she'd give up Mistress of Magic for? Her home, her heritage? Her heart?

She sat there for a long time, listening to his steady snores. She knew, in her heart, which she'd choose.

Chapter 34

The party was being held in what had been a warehouse in the once-poor docklands area of East London, now a haven for banks, luxury apartments and exclusive bars. Faye imagined that it would be bustling and vibrant in the summer, but in November, the concrete walkways and steps were slicked black with rain, and the glass skyscrapers only reflected the depths of the charcoal night onto the flat river Thames that lay alongside them.

Rav helped her out of the taxi; Faye had chosen a full-length evening dress as Rav had assured her it was a dressy affair; he was handsome in a black dinner jacket and sharp white shirt underneath. Faye's dress was black also: an off the shoulder gown that clung to her breasts and hips, skimming over her flat stomach. The silk folds of the skirt had pooled around her feet until she'd put her heels on at the flat; now, as she picked her way carefully over wet cobbles to the door, she wondered how she was going to stand on the vertiginous heels all night. They were celebrating the success of some album or another that Rav's company had been doing the promotion for; it had just gone over a million sold worldwide.

Faye followed Rav into the shady interior of the converted warehouse, giving her coat to a young man in a small cloakroom as they entered. She ran a hand nervously over her hair, which she'd braided around her head like a Greek goddess. Its auburn had become a little lighter in the summer, and it still had dark blonde flecks among the reddish brown. She wore a pair of earrings that Rav had given her: long droplets of rose quartz set in gold.

'Wow. You really look beautiful tonight,' Rav murmured, and kissed the edge of her mouth.

'Thank you,' Faye kissed him back, and expected him to pull away, mindful of the people ahead of them and behind them. But Rav encircled her with his arms and pulled her in for a deep, passionate kiss, and Faye submitted to it, feeling her body become soft and responsive to his touch. Recently, they hadn't been as physical as they were at the beginning, but Rav seemed to have forgotten their recent quarrels and misgivings as his hands caressed her back. 'Mmmm. Do we have to go in?' he whispered into her ear. She laughed, quietly, prodding him in his side.

'I think you'd be missed,' she replied, smiling.

Rav took her hand as they walked into the main room.

The warehouse had once belonged to an importer of tea, it seemed, according to the remaining signage that had been painstakingly preserved inside; however, the rest of the interior had been converted into an industrial-chic steel and glass bar with a ballroom space, in which Rav's employees milled around a number of tables and chairs set for dinner on one side, the other side having been freed for dancing. Faye didn't know much about DJ equipment, but she guessed, looking at what was set up at the side of the room – and, being that this was a staff party for an organisation that set up and promoted gigs and festivals, after all – that they were in for a good set or three later on.

Rav led her to a table at the centre of the room, where she recognised Sumi, and Rav's business partner, Roni. Sumi wore a short, low cut, shocking pink cocktail dress that displayed all her curves with pride and glowed against her light brown skin; Roni, as heavily bearded as before, wore a safari suit with a loud orange-and-green Hawaiian shirt underneath and a black bolo tie.

'Faye! So good to see you again!' Sumi cried, enveloping Faye in a fierce hug, even though her head only came up to Faye's shoulder, with the heels on. 'Wow. You look *stunning*! Roni. *Roni!* Doesn't Faye look stunning?' She nudged her husband, who smiled broadly.

'Faye, you look stunning, I don't know if anyone's told you,' Roni admitted with a grin.

'Good to see you dressed up, man.' Rav clapped Roni on the back. 'Feel like I overdid it with the dinner jacket now,' he added, sarcastically.

'Dude. Safari never goes out of style.' Roni handed them a flute of champagne each and held his up for a toast. 'To Malik & Marquez, Impresarios of the Great and Good.'

Rav clinked his glass against Faye's, and held her gaze as he drank.

'To us,' he added. Faye smiled, and sipped her champagne. They *could* be happy, she told herself. It was all there for the taking.

'So, how's all the magic going, sweets? I still need you to read my cards.' Faye hadn't seen Sumi since that first time at the bar, but if Sumi still thought Faye was a bad influence on Rav, she wasn't showing it. It was a party; she was being polite.

'Oh, whenever you like,' Faye replied, knowing it would never happen. 'But since I've been in London, I've been so busy with other things,' she lied.

'What about your shop? Is someone running it for you, now you're not there?' Sumi asked, apparently concerned, though Faye thought she could detect another message. *Why don't you go back there and run it and leave him alone.* 'From what Rav said, I doubt you'd want to be away from it for long?'

Faye smiled with a brightness she didn't feel.

'It's fine. I've closed it temporarily. We'll see, I guess,' she replied, and took a longer drink from her champagne glass. Mistress of Magic was who she was. Her mother had worked hard to build the shop as part of the pagan community in Scotland, and within the village too. She'd run evening healing circles, taught spell-casting, read fortunes and made herbal salves and draughts for the villagers. Leaving the shop empty was taking a toll on business but it was also breaking down all the good work Moddie had done for all those years. After her one-sided conversation with Rav – he'd woken up with the mother of all hangovers the next day, and had spent the day in bed – she still hadn't made a decision about the shop, but she was considering going back for at least a couple of weeks to check in and make sure everything was okay.

Mistress of Magic was Faye's home, just like it had been home to all the Morgans before her. The house itself – its thick stone walls, the worn flagstones of the shop floor that had once been where the family gathered around the hearth – was part of her. She drew her strength from Abercolme – from Black Sands Beach, from the sea and the sand and the rough scrubland around the shore – but most of all, the stone house and its little garden, packed with roses and herbs, were her mainstay. As she stood in the crowd, in the hubbub of people talking and laughing, Faye suddenly felt terribly alone and lost, untethered from where she should be. Nausea roiled in her stomach, and she set down her champagne glass on a nearby table; it was nerves. She knew what Rav's friends thought of her. It was uncomfortable being there.

The dinner passed without any further difficulty; Faye sat between Rav and Roni who, together, were a double act, entertaining everyone else at the table. Rav played the straight man to Roni's surreal, deadpan humour. Faye remained nauseous but made herself drink, using the alcohol as a shield to hide her shyness.

'Oh, it's Mallory! Hi, sweetie. You look gorge.' They had finished their main courses, and people were starting to mill around between tables as the desserts arrived. Sumi stood up to kiss Mallory; instinctively, Faye looked at Rav to gauge his reaction, but he only glanced at Mallory, meeting Faye's eyes instead.

'Did I tell you how glad I was that you two met for that coffee?' he said, reaching for Faye's hand. 'You'll be okay if I have to do the friendly boss bit for a while? Got to go and say hi to everyone.'

'Sure, okay,' Faye smiled brightly again, not wanting him to go. Reluctantly, she turned to Mallory.

'Hi, Mallory,' she said, as amicably as she could.

'Oh, hi, Faye,' Mallory replied in the same falsely jolly tone. 'Don't you look… severe, this evening.'

It's like she has literally no social skills, Faye thought. *Where was Mallory when girls were taught to be nice to each other at school?*

'Thanks.' She didn't bother to exchange a compliment, genuine or otherwise. 'Excuse me. Going to the ladies.'

Faye made her way to the toilets, found a cubicle free, went in and leant against its wall, closing the door behind her. Her head was spinning from the champagne. She had absolutely no desire to talk to Mallory and was keen to avoid her nagging about attending Ruby's coven meetings; hopefully, when she got back from the toilet, the other girl would be gone.

She rarely drank this much and she hated feeling sick, but she could feel it coming…

With much of her stomach's contents gone, she felt a little clearer and closed the toilet lid, sitting down and wiping her mouth.

As she did so, Faye heard the door to the bathroom open and voices spill into the white-tiled room.

'She's some kind of witch, I heard,' one said, over the sound of a cubicle door opening and closing.

'Scottish,' another voice confirmed. So, she was being talked about.

'She's really pretty,' the first voice commented. 'They met up at that Scottish festival last summer. The one that was in the papers?'

'I heard about that. Weird goings-on,' the other one called out from the cubicle.

'Mallory says she's, like, enchanted him or something,' the other voice, out by the sinks, ventured.

'What, like, cast a spell on him? That's stupid,' the other girl said. Faye heard her ripping off toilet paper from the dispenser. 'Mallory's jealous, that's all.'

'I don't think she is. Just concerned, like. That's what she told me.' Faye smelt perfume being applied. 'Have you got any lipstick on you? I forgot mine and it's come off already.'

The cubicle door clicked again and Faye heard the girl rejoin her friend.

'Don't believe it for a second. *Concerned.* Like she doesn't want Rav back, big time. It's so obvious. Always hanging around him, staying back after meetings. Calling into his office. It's not like she has a reason to, not as much as she does. I've heard them in there, laughing, joking around. They're not working. Took some files in the other week and she was sitting on the edge of his desk, leaning over in this low-cut top. I swear they'd just kissed or something 'cos they both looked really guilty when I came in.'

'What? *Really?!*' The excitement in the other girl's voice was in a directly inverse proportion to Faye's dread, which roiled her stomach.

The nausea had returned; absently, Faye wondered if perhaps that she'd eaten something that disagreed with her.

'Definitely. I'm telling you!' the first girl's voice was smug, thick with triumph at her secret. 'Don't tell anyone I told you, obviously. Rav made out they were looking at some spreadsheet or something, but she left right away and he was really embarrassed. I could tell something was going on.'

The door opened and closed, and their voices trailed away, leaving Faye alone. Carefully, she opened the cubicle door, stepped into the communal space and stared at herself in the mirror.

A few weeks ago. About the same time that she'd come home to find Mallory in the flat. They'd likely kissed. Mallory and Rav. And he'd lied about it.

He'd had the nerve to make *her* feel guilty. And the even greater nerve to send her off for coffee with his… whatever Mallory was, to make nice. To make friends, presumably so that he and Mallory could carry on their affair behind her back, without her suspecting anything.

She couldn't go back to the table and pretend everything was okay. She wouldn't be able to keep up any pretence that she hadn't heard what she'd heard.

Faye pushed the door to the ladies' bathroom open and stepped out, back into the main room, keeping to the wall. While she'd been in the bathroom, a DJ had started a set, and a lot of people were dancing already. She watched their drunk, jerky movements, looking for Rav. He wasn't much of a dancer, so she wasn't surprised not to see him there, though Roni had joined the fray and was flailing around flamboyantly in his shirt and trousers, having taken his jacket off.

Faye kept to the wall and walked along it, scanning the crowd. She didn't want to talk to Rav; she was too angry, but she needed her coat and bag. She was leaving, and she didn't want him trying to persuade her to stay, or, worse, to have a huge argument in front of everyone.

He wasn't anywhere near the table, so she made her way quickly to where she'd left her bag and picked it up, avoiding the glances of the people standing around it, talking. Sumi waved at her from the bar, beckoning her over, but Faye only smiled and pointed off into the room as if she was needed elsewhere.

It was then that she saw them. Mallory had her hand in his, half-dragging him to the dancefloor; Rav was protesting, but the crowd of friends around them were pushing him towards the other bodies, laughing; he was laughing, too. He wasn't looking for Faye and he wasn't refusing Mallory: his hand stayed in her grip.

Faye watched as Rav and Mallory joined the writhing bodies, jumping and moving to the heavy beats that filled the warehouse like a pulse. Her own heart pounded along with it, but it was anger and sadness that fuelled it.

Faye turned her back on the scene; the shadows from the dancers were too similar to the ones of the enchanted crowd at Abercolme, before some of them had been abducted into faerie. She wondered, then, if Rav had now forgotten everything that had happened; or, if he too sought the same kind of wilful oblivion that she had, when she'd accepted the kiss of Finn Beatha, High King of Murias. Finn Beatha, who was her drug; who was the tribal beat in her blood, lulling her into soft submission to all of her darkest fantasies.

She couldn't do this: couldn't stay here and watch them, whatever was going on. And if Rav truly wanted to forget the faerie kingdom, then he'd be better off with Mallory and not her. Faye had tried so hard to iron down, reduce and minimise her faerie half for his benefit, but none of it had worked. She'd always feel out of place with his friends, no matter how nice they might try to be. That part of her, the velvety shadow that knew the faerie realms still wanted them; they were as much her home as the human world. Like a mermaid, to restrict herself to this world would be like cutting out her tongue and walking on knives. She couldn't go on with someone who didn't want all of her.

Without thinking, she picked up a white napkin from the table and wrote a note to Rav.

I'm going to stay at Annie's for a while. I don't know if anything's going on with you and Mallory, but if it is, maybe it's better for you than this. I can't be what you want me to be. I need some space.
  Faye

Blundering out of the door, she wiped tears from her eyes.

She needed to think clearly and sat down on the empty bench under a nearby bus stop. Thinking of the faerie reel had made her think of Aisha again; if she no longer had to consider Rav's feelings, she knew how she could get back to Murias to find her friend. She'd always known; Finn had dominated her dreams, leading her back there. *Be my lover, love me, sidhe-leth.* She'd discussed it with Gabriel and Ruby, but rejected the idea because of Rav.

Finn had told her that he'd foreseen her being his lover again. Did that mean it definitely would happen? She didn't know, but what if she could resist the overwhelming power of Murias? If she could resist Finn's seduction, keep strong and fight the lassitude and forgetfulness that always enshrined her when she was with him, then she could find Aisha. She could bring her home.

Faye's heart leapt with the thought. It would be dangerous, but she quelled the fear that rose up within her.

Could she lie to Finn? Could she resist him? Being in Murias was overpowering, but Lyr's crystal had helped her banish Finn from the Samhain ball. Perhaps it could help her remain detached from his power just enough if she went to Murias again. If she pretended to love him again, and waited for an opportunity to rescue Aisha.

Faye pushed her heartbreak to one side. Aisha was what mattered; all this time, she'd been trying to balance too many plates: she'd been concentrating on her relationship with Rav, but it could never be right between them. She'd been trying to fit in, to be normal, and it hadn't worked. She was half-fae, and there was no denying it.

And while she was trying to play normal with Rav, Aisha was dying.

Faye's heart convulsed with the guilt; denying her identity had put Aisha in even more danger. She should have had the strength to refuse to be anything other than she was, but she'd believed a lie: that she could be happy if she denied her faerie half. She should have gone to Murias earlier.

She got out her phone and composed a message to Gabriel. *If there's ever anything I can help with, let me know.* He'd said it when they sat talking outside Star Herbs. She hoped he meant it.

Hey. I need your help, are you around?

She pressed *send* and watched the screen as the message was delivered and then read. Almost immediately, Gabriel replied:

Of course, silly question. Always available. What, where and when?

I'll text a list of stuff, can you bring it and meet me? I'll meet you outside the Greenwich foot tunnel. Island Gardens side, she messaged Gabriel. *Need you for impromptu ritual. I know what I have to do.*

A car's headlights washed over her as it drove up the empty street; Faye pulled her coat around her. She still wasn't that used to the city and being out alone at night in this strangely quiet part of it was unnerving. She took a deep breath, made sure she kept her phone in her hand in her pocket if she needed it, and started walking to the meeting place. She'd get there first, but there was a tube station nearby and at least that was a better place for her to wait for Gabriel.

Okay. Be with you in half an hour, he replied.

Faye fired off a list in a separate text as she walked: lamps or candles – it would be dark out at the riverside at night, especially somewhere quiet, which was what she needed – incense in some kind of portable censer, a cup. The rest, they could make do with what there was when they got there.

She didn't know for sure if something was going on between Rav and Mallory, but the fact that there was enough of a rumour going around that the girls in the toilets earlier were discussing it openly made Faye's stomach tense with anxious sadness. She was angry, too – she hadn't liked seeing Rav dance with Mallory, no matter how innocent it may have been. If he'd kissed Mallory, could she forgive him?

She searched her feelings. A kiss might be an accident, a fleeting moment. More than that would be harder to forgive – something planned, something continuous. But regardless of whether she could forgive him, and regardless of what had actually happened, it didn't matter. She didn't have any right at all to be jealous of Rav and Mallory when her relationship with Finn Beatha was as complicated as it was – and when she was about to make it much more entangled.

She got to the tube station, lit up like a welcome beacon, and stood slightly inside to avoid any unwanted attention. Across the river, Greenwich twinkled its lights onto the Thames, but on her side, only a new block of flats in development overlooked her. A gang of drunk kids in their early twenties, boys and girls, wandered along the opposite side of the road and she watched them warily, but they passed the station.

She paced up and down, waiting for Gabriel. When he arrived, twenty minutes later, wearing a black trenchcoat and fedora and carrying a Fortune's tote bag, she gave him a fierce hug. He hugged her back, surprised.

'What's this all about, Faye? Are you okay?' Gabriel untangled himself from the hug and peered concernedly into her eyes, the fluorescent light of the tube station throwing harsh shadows on her pale cheeks. 'You've been crying.'

She felt the tears well up in her eyes again, but wiped them away. A car's headlights swept the street outside, and disappeared again, leaving the orange-tinted lights to punctuate the dark.

'I'm okay. Thanks for coming.'

'I told you I'd help if you needed it. I'm your friend.' Gabriel tipped his hat to Faye and handed her the tote bag. 'All as requested. The lamps are battery powered, small but surprisingly bright. Don't worry, I put a lighter and some real candles in there as well.'

'Thanks, Gabriel. I appreciate it,' Faye replied quietly. 'Come on. Let's walk along a bit. There's a sheltered part of the beach just around the corner; the wall means if anyone comes along, which I doubt, we won't be seen.'

'Right you are.' He linked his arm in hers, and they crossed the road into the shadows.

Chapter 35

'I assume you've checked the tide times.' Gabriel fell into step with her as they walked along the deserted river; in the distance, London droned its industrial hum. 'Nothing worse than starting a ritual and being flooded out halfway through. Many a city witch has soaked their shoes or worse, all for not checking basic information.'

'I'm not a city witch,' Faye reminded him, smiling. 'So, you not up to anything else tonight?'

'Just hanging with my harem of sexy vampires, but when I got your text, I sent them back to their crypt.'

'That's good of you.' Faye grinned, despite her mood.

'I'm honoured to be called out,' he replied, seriously. 'So. What's this all about?'

They turned the corner; the wall between the pathway and the short, muddy London beach below was exactly as Faye remembered it from when she and Rav had walked this way before. It was structured in such a way that it afforded a few metres of privacy for anyone behind it, facing the river. Until she saw it again, it hadn't occurred to her that the space might also be ideal for other people looking to avoid being noticed in the middle of the night, but it was deserted.

'Nice spot to get out of reality for a while,' Gabriel commented, as if he was reading her thoughts. 'Drugs or magic. Your choice.'

'Hmmm,' Faye was distracted, looking up at the moon, which was a slim crescent in the winter sky; though it was dry now, the rain clouds were massing again. 'Not sure how much time we've got until it tips it down again.'

'Right. And this is where you tell me what's going on before I have to ask you for the sixtieth time.' Gabriel raised his eyebrow questioningly. 'Come on, Faye. This isn't normal, even for witches. You ask me to meet you in a dodgy part of East London in the middle of the night at late notice. You're on your own and you've been crying. What's up?'

'I'm going to summon Finn Beatha. I'm going to tell him that I want to be his lover again, and let him take me to Murias. And when I get there, I'm going to find Aisha and rescue her,' Faye replied.

She watched his face for incredulousness, but Gabriel held her eyes with only a frank curiosity.

'Right.'

'You're not… shocked?'

'Faye, I'm the owner of a magic bookshop. Ritual magic, summoning demons, past life regression… it's literally my daily bread. No, I respect your decision. But when we spoke about this before, you didn't see it as an option. Because of Rav.' Gabriel buried his chin into his scarf for warmth.

Faye looked away. 'That's… not an issue any more,' she said, not wanting to talk about it.

'What does that mean?' he asked.

'It means I've split up with Rav,' she shot back.

'Whoa. No need to be angry at me.' Gabriel held out his hands as if for protection.

Faye sighed. 'Sorry. It's just been… quite a night.'

'What did he do? Do you need me to... I don't know. Rough him up?' Gabriel was frowning in concern at her; despite herself, she laughed.

'*Rough him up?* Really?'

Gabriel made a face. 'Look. Just because I'm a snappy dresser doesn't mean I can't bring the heat when I need to.' He grimaced theatrically at Faye.

'Wow. Was that your war face? I think I'll be okay, but thanks.' She shook her head, smiling for a moment. 'Listen,' she continued. 'I could do with someone in my corner. But not about Rav. I mean... if the ritual... goes wrong.'

'Goes wrong? In what way?'

'If I can't get out. If his power is too strong. Finn could make me forget everything – you, Aisha, this world, everything. It's a risk.'

'What do you want me to do if it does? Go wrong, I mean,' Gabriel asked.

'Find a way to call me back. Get the coven together if you have to. But don't, whatever you do, come after me,' Faye said, grimly.

*

First, create the environment for the Queen of your chosen element. Faye had committed Grandmother's words to memory: a ritual written at the back of her personal book of magic, what modern witches called a Book of Shadows. However, Moddie and Faye had always referred to it as Grandmother's grimoire; a handwritten book of charms and spells passed down from one generation of Morgan women to the next.

To summon Her from her home element, you must create a ritual space of high vibration. Ideally, conduct the summoning as close to the right element as possible.

She knelt down, putting the bag on the mud and taking the tools from it. She set the four battery lamps in a circle, north, east, south and west, and flicked them on. Their soft yellow glow lit the shoreline around them and cast an oily glitter on the dirty Thames water. *Oh well*, Faye thought; *it's water. I hope it's enough.* Water was Finn's element, no matter how polluted. And, she reminded herself, the Thames might not be as romantic a stretch of water as the sea at Black Sands Beach at Abercolme, or elsewhere on the stark, rugged Scottish coastline, but it was ancient. In fact, one of its old names was the Isis, named for the Egyptian goddess of magic.

She handed a blackened abalone shell to Gabriel, who placed a charcoal disc inside it and lit it so that the disc flamed with a red line of fire, permeating it with a bright heat. From a bag he sprinkled some loose incense on the smoking disc; immediately, the smell of frankincense and copal filled the night. Taking a cup from the bag, he went to the river's edge and scooped some water into it, bringing it back and placing it carefully by their feet. She still felt sick, but she ignored it.

'Cast the circle.' Faye indicated that Gabriel should take the incense around the circle and charge it with the power of air. Following him, she lit a candle inside a small storm-lamp and blessed the circle with the power of fire. Without being told, Gabriel took the cup of river water and sprinkled it around the circle; Faye followed, tracing a line in the muddy sand for earth.

Dance or pace out the circle clockwise and then pace into the centre of the circle as if in a spiral. When at the centre of the circle, call out their full name three times. Your calling should be urgent and passionate, from the heart. Repeat this process, walking the spiral in and out and calling the name, three times.

'Call in the elements?' Gabriel asked, but she shook her head.

'Only water. That's what we want, the High King of Murias, faerie realm of water. We put all our focus on him,' Faye replied, remembering Grandmother's spidery writing. 'Remember, same as before. We walk inwards in a spiral, call out his name at the centre, and then spiral out again. Three times. Then I'm going to call him.' Gabriel nodded.

She swallowed nervously. Was she ready to see Finn again? Was she ready for his power; the power that he held over her? She wasn't sure, but it was too late now. She had to save Aisha.

Faye held onto the anger she'd felt just earlier; anger would help her navigate Finn and Murias. If she held onto its sharp clarity, it would help her. She had Lyr's crystal in her bag; she got it out and stuffed it inside her bra, hoping it would be protection enough against his enchantment.

'All right. I remember what to do.' Gabriel nodded. Faye took a deep breath and focused her thoughts on Finn Beatha. *Finn, hear me. Come to me,* she thought, and started pacing the circle.

'Finn Beatha, High King of Murias, Faerie Kingdom of Water; Master of the Cup, Emperor of undine, nixie, sprite, kelpie, frog, fish and water-serpent, come to me!' Faye called out the words that felt right at the centre of the circle; Gabriel echoed her, his low voice vibrant in the night air. They repeated the process once and then once more.

Overhead, the clouds rolled across the moon; rain was coming. Faye stood at the centre of the circle, drawing power up from the earth and into her body in a line of gold filament, feeling it fill her, ground her into the earth. At the same time, she closed her eyes and imagined the strange, alien silver magic of the stars streaming into her.

Finn Beatha, I beseech you, enter the space I have prepared for you
Finn Beatha, I would love you with my mind, my heart and my body
Finn Beatha, I summon you from your Kingdom
I offer something of mine that I can give freely; this is the exchange
This is the promise between faerie and human
So mote it be

Faye raised her voice and called out the words with as much strength and passion as she could muster; anger and concentration shaped her words and sent them to cut the air. *You will come to me*, she thought, *you arrogant, controlling bastard. I will have what I want from you.*

Droplets of rain landed on Faye's hair, but Finn Beatha didn't appear.

'Call him again,' Gabriel said, looking up at the charcoal clouds that massed over their heads. 'It's going to rain.'

'More water can only help us,' Faye observed, and pulled the hood of her black cape-like swing coat over her head. *Now I really look the part*, she thought. She called out the invocation again, but nothing happened.

'Am I doing something wrong?' Faye appealed to Gabriel. 'I'm doing what I did before, in Abercolme and in the rose garden. It worked then…'

'I don't know. I guess with these things, it's always about the intention, isn't it? All the rest's window dressing, mood-setting, to some extent. You're supposed to be calling out with a kind of intense passion.' He gave Faye a half-critical look. 'If I'm honest, I don't hear it in your voice. The passion. I'm guessing that when you summoned

Lyr, you really wanted to see him. Tonight, I don't know. You want to see Finn, but you don't want to at the same time.'

'I can't let myself be taken over by it like I have before. He wins if I do.' Faye exhaled in frustration. 'I've got to keep my focus,' she muttered.

'But—' Gabriel started to argue, and she felt the anger rise up in her again.

'No! I have to stay in control. You don't know what it's like! He's like… it's…' she wanted to scream at her own sudden lack of eloquence. 'I lose myself. I… forget. Everything except him. It's…' How could she explain that the pleasure of Finn and of being in Murias made everything else pale by comparison? That when she was in his arms, she'd sacrifice everything else to stay there, wrapped in the dark ecstasy of his touch? And how could she tell Gabriel how much that loss of control lured and terrified her in equal measure?

'Faye,' Gabriel held out his hands for hers and clasped them in his, 'from everything you've told me about your connection with Finn, it's… deeply passionate. Right? It's desire that links you.'

'Yes, but—' she tried to explain, but he shook his head.

'Faye. You have to open yourself up to that desire. Don't judge it. It's part of you; you might think it's a dark part, something in the shadows. But the things in the shadows are what give us power. That's what magic teaches us, right?'

She nodded: he was right, but knowing something and having the courage to feel it were very different things.

'You've got to let go,' Gabriel said, softly. 'Call him with all the desire you have for him. I know it's in you. And he knows, too.'

'But what if I get lost there again?' Faye felt as if she was standing on the edge of a cliff. She knew she had to jump; she knew that she *would* jump. But the thought of the fall rising up to meet her still made her stomach lurch and her head spin.

'Then you get lost,' Gabriel replied, completely serious. 'Maybe that's what you were supposed to do all along.'

So she began again, letting the desire for Finn overwhelm her, and when the wave came, she surrendered herself to it. Dimly, she was aware that the wave on which the faerie king arrived, riding a black kelpie – half-faerie horse, half serpent's tail – submerged the whole of the empty, muddy Thames shore. But she was already under Finn's influence, and couldn't know whether Gabriel had got out of its way in time.

Finn swung her onto the back of the kelpie, and she clung to his waist as the creature dove back under the water.

Chapter 36

'I knew you would come.'

Finn Beatha, High King of the realm of Murias, removed her cowl-like hooded coat and threw it to one side of the palatial bedroom. This time, they hadn't even had to travel through the marketplace and the court of the Castle of Murias in which he resided; Faye had passed out underwater and awoken, strangely dry, in the room she remembered so well.

She didn't trust herself to reply, and so remained silent.

'You called out to me in desire. You called me to be your lover again, *sidhe-leth*.' He stood behind her and kissed her collarbone, his hands cupping her breasts. 'What took you so long?'

His warm hands smoothed the black silk of the dress she wore; already it seemed impossible that just an hour ago she'd been at the party, and moments ago at the muddy tideline of the Thames. Already, her memory of the ordinary world was fading and Finn was filling her senses. She leaned back against him, remembering how his muscled torso fit perfectly against her back; remembering how sure his hands were, how he knew exactly how she wanted to be touched.

'Are you no longer the human man's lover?' Finn breathed against her neck; for a brief second, the mention of Rav made Faye freeze, but she controlled herself with her breath.

'No.' She said no more, but it seemed that was enough for Finn.

Faye knew that she had to stay lucid if she wanted to return Aisha to the ordinary world, and she felt within herself for the anger that had made her summon Finn in the first place. It was still there, a fire that burned in a rich velvet blackness that threatened to snuff it out. *No*, she reminded herself. *Tend the fire; use it to burn your way out of here if you must.* Yet, at the same time, she had to submit to her desire for her plan to work. And so she turned to Finn and wrapped her arms around his neck, pulling him down to her. There was no reason not to, now. She'd ended it with Rav.

Lyr's crystal was stuffed into her bra. She panicked about what to do with it if he undressed her.

'I've missed you,' she said, and it wasn't a lie: none of it was, as her lips found his and drank his kisses as if they were wine.

The fire of his touch on her skin made its way to the flame of rage that smouldered deep inside her, and when it made contact, acted as a current. The anger flowed into her body and wove itself into her desire for Finn; *this, this*, her body told her, as her instinct combined kiss with bite, and sweetness with a hunger to consume him she'd never felt before. Faye dragged him to the bed, her nails digging into his perfect, golden skin. She'd drawn blood where she'd bitten his lip and she ran her tongue over it, measuring him with her eyes.

Surprise flashed briefly in Finn's ocean-blue eyes, but a hungry smile turned up one corner of his mouth.

'I see that my *sidhe-leth* has grown claws,' he murmured as she pushed him onto the wide, deep bed; it occurred to her that the golden posts at each corner of the bed were very like the ones of the bed she'd met him at in her dreams; the place underwater, a bed on a rock where they had made love. Dreams she'd awoken from, hungry for satisfaction. 'I am your willing subject, tigress.'

She tore off her dress; underneath, she wore only a brief black lace thong and her black strapless bra, which she kept on, hoping he wouldn't tear it off. He reached for her, but she pulled away quickly, knowing she had to take control. Ripping her dress in half, she took both stretches of the black silk and tied his wrists to the golden bars that linked the bedposts. Finn craned his neck, wanting to kiss her, but she straddled him and sat up, away from his head and shook her head, smiling.

The fiery desire that filled her now was something different to before. She wanted Finn just as much as she had before, lost in a whirlwind of lust. She wanted him inside her, wanted his mouth on every part of her; she wanted to hear him call out her name when he came, urgent and hot. But unlike before, where she'd felt pulled under the waves, unable to do anything but submit to her most shadowy erotic pleasures, now she wanted to render Finn powerless to resist her actions.

Slowly, she caressed him until he was crying out to be inside her, but she refused; instead, she leant forward to kiss him again; to tease him maddeningly, taking her pleasure from him and refusing his; repeating the pattern until he was on the edge of climax.

Last, she made him beg.

'I want to hear you tell me how wrong you were. To ever refuse me entry to Murias,' she murmured in his ear as she positioned herself over him. She definitely felt more in control of herself than she had before in Murias. Her desire for Finn was the same, but the fuzzy-headedness was no longer there. Briefly, she placed her hand on the outside of her bra, making sure the crystal was safe.

'I was wrong. I was wrong, *sidhe-leth*,' he moaned, desperate for release. 'Please…'

'Acknowledge that I am your mistress,' she lowered herself slowly, taking him inside her.

'You are my mistress. I adore you,' he moaned. 'Oh, oh…' he closed his eyes as the sensation overtook him.

'You would do anything for me. Allow me anything. *Say it.*'

'I allow you anything I can grant. Any boon or pleasure that is in my …' he groaned, and Faye felt her own pleasure build as his cock slid inside her. She leaned forward and buried her face in his neck, moving forward and back, finding the speed and angle that felt right.

'That is?' she murmured, as the soft, sweet tightness grew in her thighs and belly.

'…that is in my power to give, you may have it,' he murmured; finding his lips, she kissed him deeply.

'Give me something, then, so I know you're not lying,' she whispered in his ear as she moved back and forward, her pleasure growing.

'What?' he gasped. She was in control, and Finn Beatha had lost his. 'Faye, please, I want to…'

If he managed to orgasm, she'd have lost the opportunity. She slowed down.

'I want to know…' she couldn't just come straight out and ask for Aisha. *What could she ask?* 'I want to know who has been in your bed since I've been gone.' Perhaps approaching the subject this way would give her a clue; he'd taken Aisha as his lover, so if he named her, it would give Faye a road to other questions.

'Many have graced my bed,' he panted, wild with desire. 'But none like you, *sidhe-leth*,'

'What about Aisha? The girl you stole at the concert?'

Faye brushed her lips against his chest and he moaned in pleasure. 'She was here,' he murmured.

'And now? Does she rival me for your affection?' Faye watched his face closely for a reaction: Finn grimaced, but she couldn't tell if it was in pleasure or not. 'Pledge yourself to me. I am your mistress, the queen of your desire.'

'No, no, Faye, there is no-one but you. I have banished them... all, on your arrival.' He was breathing fast and his eyes were half-closed. Faye felt her own orgasm near; even though she was concentrating on extracting information from him, it was impossible not to be aroused by Finn.

'Banished them? Where?' she panted. She laid on top of him now, her skin against his, hot and slick with sweat. It would only be moments now.

'Don't worry, Faye. You will not be troubled by her now,' Finn muttered, and she could feel her and his climax coming, unstoppable, like a wave. 'She is deep... deep, oh, oh, Faye...'

'Deep where?' Faye held on to sobriety for one last second before allowing herself to be lost in the pleasure that would cover them both.

'The lower dungeon!' he cried out.

'Finn... Finn!' she cried, meeting his blue-black eyes with hers; his were the dark of the deepest ocean, the deepest places that held mysteries, that were alien lands in their own right. She ground against him: once, twice, *more, more*, her body cried out, and she gave it what it hungered for.

Her climax came, then, like a wave that crested higher and higher; she rode him, lost in her pleasure, as the ecstasy broke over her and through her abdomen, up to her heart, through her belly and back. It drummed deep inside her; a primal blackness that resonated red on her closed eyelids. She threw her head back and cried out, a long guttural cry.

'Yes, yes, I swear it, you have my word, oh, oh…' Finn's mouth gasped open, and his body bucked with the force of his orgasm in response to hers. Faye kept riding him as the echoes of her orgasm transmitted themselves through her body, out to her fingertips, her ears, her scalp, coming to a slow stop as peace filled her soul and she relaxed against his prone body.

Tenderly, she kissed his lips, his chin, and his chest, before slowly extricating herself from him and crawling to the head of the bed where she undid his wrists from their binds.

Finn enveloped her in his arms and kissed her, long and slow. Faye felt a dreamy languor of him draw her in, but it wasn't enchantment, just the aftermath of lovemaking, and she didn't resist it. She'd changed the polarity between them in the act of lovemaking, and the faerie king had accepted it. She was Finn Beatha's lover again, but she need not submit only to his desire; he would submit to hers, and in so doing, she'd persuade him to give her Aisha. No-one could control a faerie king, but in his wildest moments, she might ask things of him that he would never usually allow, if she was his mistress. Or, so she thought.

Chapter 37

The moon outside the castle windows hung heavy; Faye sat up in the palatial bed strewn with unconscious fae creatures and reached for the emerald-green faerie wine that heightened her senses and energised her when she reached exhaustion. Drinking deeply, she looked around her. Finn reigned over a court of servants, courtiers and assorted fae folk that fought for his shifting, tidal favours.

She didn't know how many days she'd been here. There were no clearly recognisable days or nights, as the light in Murias was always a kind of moonlit dusk or dawn. She slept at no particular time, and was roused by the onset of Finn's – or another's – touch. She'd barely left Finn's rooms, as a parade of strange and eerie fae visitors paid their respects to the King and his most revered mistress at all hours.

Before she'd passed out, she and Finn had been entertaining a trio of river sprites; slender, delicate faerie women who inhabited rivers and helped or hindered humans that came their way, depending on their inclination. Their bodies were long and malleable, cold and slightly blue-skinned; their algae-green hair retained its wetness even out of the water, and Faye recalled its cold kiss on her skin along with their brackish lips. Now, they slept, sprawled on the velvety blue covers of the bed, their flowing limbs contorted like disjointed dolls.

Unlike before, she'd been fully aware of what she was doing. But while she enjoyed the pleasure that was offered her, she waited for an opportunity to elude Finn. Now that she knew Aisha was in the lower dungeon, wherever that was, she just had to find a way of getting there, and getting Aisha back to the human world. Neither would be easy.

Faye had known that returning to Murias as Finn's lover was a risk, but she'd done it anyway. She knew that she, at least, could withstand the deterioration wreaked by Murias on her body and mind better than one who was fully human. And yet, as she delved deep into the shadow side of her faerie self, it was harder and harder to retain focus on the reason for coming here at all. She told herself that she was building Finn's trust in her, and that he'd promised to allow him anything; she'd made him promise again and again when she took control of their lovemaking, and he'd agreed, fiercely, as she allowed him his orgasm.

But she'd done nothing to help Aisha, and every moment that she'd been in Murias, Aisha grew weaker. Lyr had told her that Aisha would survive only a few months in Murias before it killed her. How long had she been here? Faye counted the months since midsummer: in the human world, it had been five months. It was too long.

Faye got up carefully and slipped on a blue robe and soft leather boots that lay at the end of the bed; the servant fae had laid out clothes for her again as they had every time she'd visited. As silently as she could, she slipped out of the heavy door and tiptoed into the corridor outside.

Faye knew that there were dungeons in the castle at Murias, but she had no idea where they were, apart from downwards; she took the first stairway she could find and followed it, and then, when that one came to an end, she walked to the other end of the hallway it had taken her to, and went down the next stairs, and the next. The walls seemed to close in, and the air grew less clear and more and more dank, but as far down as she went, there was no sign of anything apart from empty rooms.

Dizziness overtook her and she sat down on the stone floor for a moment to regain her senses. She had no idea of how long she'd been intoxicated. The faerie wine, the faerie food, and Finn's lulling, dreamy influence on her had taken its toll, and she felt nausea overcome her. How had she thought that she could walk out of Finn's bedroom and happen upon Aisha so easily? There was magic here, in the castle; Finn's prisoners would be closely guarded.

She felt the gorge rise in her throat, and her head spun. Faye rested her head on the stone wall behind her, and panic overwhelmed her for the first time since she'd returned to Murias. *What was she doing here? How had she thought that she could find Aisha and bring her home when she knew the power of Murias and its effect on her?*

Had she really forgotten the horrors she'd seen here before? Her terror at the piles of human bones under the feet of the faeries as they danced, and, worse, the emaciated bodies of the men and women who were still alive, being slowly trampled to death? Had she really forgotten how hard it had been to save Rav from that fate?

Perhaps she had. Among the distractions of the ordinary world, she'd forgotten. She closed her eyes. She knew that she'd been here too long; like before, when she'd overstayed, her body was beginning to reject the excesses of Murias.

Yet when she opened her eyes, she found the High Queen, Glitonea, standing in front of her.

'Faye Morgan. I had heard that you had returned, but thought that surely it couldn't be true. You would not return without what you promised me.'

The faerie queen was beautiful in the same way that Finn was: they were of the same blood, or whatever else coursed in their veins – brackish river water, or the clear tide that gathered in rockpools, perhaps. Her hair was the same dark gold as his, and her face as finely featured. Yet her eyes were a darker blue, and she had no tattoos on her flawless skin.

Glitonea's tone was icy as she towered over Faye; she crouched down on the cobbles of the stone corridor so that she could meet Faye's eyes levelly.

'Answer me. We made a bargain, and you have not come to me to deliver what was agreed,' the faerie queen hissed. Up close, Faye noticed that the material of her diaphanous robe seemed to be made of fish scales, gleaming in the dim lamplight; it was transparent, and underneath it, Glitonea was naked.

'I… there hasn't been enough time,' Faye lied; she had absolutely no intention of either getting pregnant or of giving that baby to the faerie queen. Yet, rationality seemed a distant comfort in that moment.

'My assistance can be withdrawn as it was given,' Glitonea regarded Faye's face, tracing one fingertip over her pale, sweaty forehead. 'Though you are unwell, it seems.' Her expression became watchful, and without warning, the faerie queen grasped at Faye's stomach, through the silky dress, holding her hand on Faye's abdomen. 'Aha. Perhaps you have not betrayed my trust after all, *sidhe-leth*,' Glitonea smiled wolfishly, and Faye's hand went instinctively to her belly in protection.

'What?'

Glitonea smiled even wider. 'I believe that, with your kind, being with child gives you the nausea you currently find yourself with,' she arched an imperious eyebrow. 'Indeed, I doubted your fealty, *sidhe-leth*. It would seem that I had no need to question it.'

'But I'm not...' Faye began, and trailed off, not knowing what to say. She wasn't pregnant, was she? Surely this was the same faerie hangover as she'd had before. She would know, surely... Her mind raced. If Glitonea wanted to believe that she was pregnant, she wouldn't disagree: in fact, it could work to her advantage if the faerie queen thought she was with child.

'What has brought you to this part of the castle? Did you seek me? To tell me about the child?' Glitonea held out a hand and pulled Faye upright. Her head spun and she felt the sickness rise again, but swallowed and took a deep breath to steady herself.

'Y-yes, my queen. Though I also sought another. A friend that Finn holds prisoner in the dungeons here.' Faye thought quickly. The bargain of a child, her child, was a considerable one; if Glitonea believed that she truly would get what she'd asked Faye for, then she'd probably be willing to help her again. Yet Glitonea was watching her closely, and Faye knew that she was trying to tell if she was lying. She couldn't slip up.

'A friend?' A secretive expression crossed Glitonea's face; her eyes darted away from Faye's.

'A woman, Aisha. Finn took her, with the others, from the concert at Abercolme. I've seen her in dreams, and I know she's dying here.' Faye allowed the emotion to flood her voice, and reached for Glitonea's hand. 'Please, dear queen. Please help me once more. I have acted on my part of the bargain.' She made herself lie and hoped she was doing it convincingly.

'I have already fulfilled my side of the bargain.' Glitonea pulled her hand away. 'You are the one who is in my debt and not the other way around. Go back to my brother for as long as you desire to be his whore, Faye Morgan, but never think that you can ask anything else from me.' Her voice was cold, like the sea at Abercolme in winter, where a couple of minutes of swimming would induce hypothermia. Faye shivered and wrapped her arms around herself.

'Please, Glitonea. For the child,' Faye appealed to the faerie queen, but Glitonea's mouth stayed pursed in a line.

'I do not owe you anything,' she repeated, and turned away, opening a door opposite. 'Look after the child for me, Faye Morgan. When it is time, I will help you in your labours. That, I *will* do for you,' she sneered, and opened the door wider. 'I have paid the price for interfering in my brother's affairs of the heart and have promised him I will do so no more. For you see, I have my own human lover, and I would not want my brother to take this one away from me.'

The heavy wooden door swung back on its hinges as Faye stumbled forward to look inside what she realised must be Glitonea's personal chamber. She saw inside for just a moment before Glitonea slammed the door in her face, but it was enough time for horror to soak Faye's heart with its dread dark.

Inside, chained to the opposite wall, hung the unconscious, naked body of Gabriel Black.

Chapter 38

Faye didn't remember being carried back to Finn's quarters or laid out on his bed; all she saw in her feverish dreams was Gabriel's body, striped with lines of blood, and bruising at his wrists where they were cuffed to the wall.

Yet in her dreams, Gabriel's eyes met hers with a mixture of pain and desire as Glitonea knelt, naked, in front of him and took his engorged cock into her mouth, and his words, back in the shop, echoed in Faye's confused memory: *what life is this, here with these dusty old books, better a life lived* and Faye, in her dream, tried to reach out for him, to release him from his bonds, but he turned his head away. *No, no. I am hers.*

Faye was dimly aware that light faerie hands raised her body up and trickled faerie wine down her throat; that they washed her and dressed her, but she had no awareness of time passing. She was lost in a dream, walking the corridors of the castle of Murias, searching for Aisha and Gabriel, calling their names. Yet every doorway in the corridor she opened, in her twilight consciousness, opened onto a cliff edge with a drop that yawned under her, or a wall of black water in which large, indistinct shapes moved – shadows within a darkness that made fear flick its tail in her belly.

She could feel consciousness tugging at her; in her dream, light suffused one end of the corridor, and she walked towards it.

Yet, just before she walked into the light, her perception changed, and she saw the castle for a moment as if it was made of glass. She could see everything; the levels indexed like cards in a box, the contents of each room; the secrets of the castle laid bare. And in that moment, she saw the dungeon that she was searching for, closer than she'd expected.

She awoke with Aisha's name on her lips, and found Finn sitting next to her on the bed. Seeing her open her eyes, he placed his warm hand on her brow.

'You're cooling down. That's good.' He propped her up on pillows and lifted a cup to her lips. 'Here. Drink this.'

Expecting it to be the faerie wine, Faye turned her head away, but Finn tipped it up to her lips, making her drink. 'It's just water. Drink it.'

She drank, and felt herself slowly return to her body.

'It is the human part of you that is suffering,' he breathed, kissing her cheek softly. 'You have been here too long, enjoying our pleasures, *sidhe-leth*. Perhaps it is time for you to return home for a time. To recover fully.'

Faye closed her eyes and sipped at the water again. There was nothing more she wanted than to return to the ordinary world, but she'd awoken with the knowledge of where Aisha was. She couldn't return to the ordinary world and leave her here. Or Gabriel.

'I… I'll be all right. I want to stay,' she lied, although every fibre of her being cried out for home. She reached for him and kissed him, though her stomach lurched when she did so. 'I would miss you too much.'

Finn returned her kiss, and she felt him respond to her immediately; Finn's ardour knew no end, like the waves on the ocean that rolled continually. She found it galling that he should think nothing of trying to make love to her when she was so obviously unwell, and pulled away from his touch. He looked annoyed and the sullen snarl she remembered returned to his full-lipped mouth.

'Clearly not enough,' he remarked pointedly.

'Let me recover, my love.' Faye laid back against the pillows and took a deep breath. She didn't know if she had it in her to try and get to Aisha one more time, but she had to try; both she and Gabriel were in terrible danger.

'Fine.' Finn stood up and paced the room. 'What would you have me do while I wait for your recovery?' He was like a child; spoilt and sulky. Faye smiled so that her face wouldn't show her disdain for his immaturity. She thought fast. There was one way, perhaps, to ensure that Murias could be distracted enough for her to try to get to Aisha and Gabriel.

'Perhaps a ball would cheer me up, my love?' she suggested, injecting all the warmth she could into her voice. 'In a few hours I should have recovered sufficiently to dance.'

Faye doubted that she'd feel up to dancing later, but if Finn was deep into the crowd and she sat out for a dance or two, then perhaps she could sneak away to find Aisha and Gabriel. She'd seen it, the place where Aisha was kept; if her vision had been correct, then Aisha was being held in a room not that far from Glitonea's quarters. She'd been closer than she knew when Glitonea had found her; if she hadn't been so sick, perhaps she would have found Aisha.

What is this sickness? A voice in her mind needled at her. *Is it the effect of Murias, or was Glitonea right? Am I pregnant?* But Faye refused to believe it. She'd been feverish; pregnancy didn't give you a fever. Murias made her like this if she stayed too long; she could be here for longer than ordinary humans, being half-fae, but it still took a toll on her. Glitonea was wrong. *She was playing you for some reason*, she told herself, though she couldn't think of a reason why Glitonea would lie. *Faeries lie.* Perhaps there was no reason; it was just their nature.

Finn obviously didn't pick up on her duplicity; perhaps it was his pleasure in the idea of a ball that distracted him, but in any event, Faye was grateful when he smiled, and the spoilt child disappeared.

'A ball. Yes! An excellent idea,' Finn cried, and clapped his hands. Five faerie servants appeared, and he fired instructions at them. *A fine gown and jewels for my lady. My grandest attire. Food, drink, music! You know what to do*, he ordered as Faye felt herself slipping under the cover of sleep again. She felt him come to the bed again, when they had gone, and caress her breast. Yet, to Faye's surprise, he pulled back the bedcovers and picked her up gently, carrying her to the bathroom where the palatial sunken bath was already full of rose and neroli-scented water; rose petals floated on the surface of the water. Even more gently, Finn lowered her into the warm water, making sure she was comfortable, took up a sea sponge and began washing her with slow, hypnotic movements.

Faye made herself lie back against Finn's strong arm. She couldn't show any sign of her duplicity.

'We must make you presentable for the ball,' Finn murmured as he wrung the sponge over Faye's head, soaking her auburn hair and rendering it wetly black. Faye gasped in surprise, but Finn merely smiled and repeated the soaking. 'I like you drenched.' He smiled again, his ocean-blue eyes dancing in amusement.

Finn's warm, wide hand circled the sponge over Faye's breasts and shoulders, caressing them gently; she fought the responsive warmth in her abdomen at his touch. As if knowing her arousal, he continued his slow circling. Finn wore the soft blue trousers and robe he often did, and, taking his arm away from her for a moment, he pulled off the robe so that he was bare-chested.

The oil-scented water glimmered in the light of hundreds of white candles that unseen hands had lit before Finn carried her into the room.

'Now, where was I?' He smiled knowingly as he took a bottle from the side of the bath and poured something from inside it into his wide, cupped hand. Faye smelt rose with an underlying tang of bitterness as Finn stroked the oil over her shoulders and breasts. 'Close your eyes,' he ordered, and when she did, Faye felt Finn's oiled fingers massaging gentle circles on her cheeks, temples and forehead. Finn's fingers made their way onto her scalp, massaging the oil into her hair and her head.

'Does that feel good?' His voice caressed her as gently as his hands. She nodded, fighting to retain her composure. Lyr's crystal was hidden in one of her slippers under Finn's expansive bed, and without it, she could feel herself slipping back under Finn's spell. *No, No!* she closed her eyes and steeled her will against his—

'More?' his tone was gently teasing, but she opened her eyes and pulled away from his touch.

'I'm a little tired,' she said, not meeting his eyes. 'Perhaps you shouldn't tire me further ahead of the ball.'

Finn sat back on his heels and regarded her coolly for a moment, but then got up from his knees.

'As you wish, mistress. I forget you are half human. Even a *sidhe-leth* cannot keep up with the desires of a faerie king.' He smiled somewhat smugly, obviously proud of his powers of endurance. 'I forget myself.'

Faye kept the smile fixed on her face until he'd left, when her expression became watchful. She knew what she had to do, but she was afraid.

Chapter 39

Faye fought the giddiness that summoned an acid sourness in her mouth as Finn twirled her around and around the ballroom.

As before, the dress that had been laid out for her by the unseen faerie hands fitted her perfectly, but was even more revealing than it had been at the last dance. This gown was split into two sides; one side black and one side a coral pink, with gold stitching that held them together, breast to thigh. The pink half of the dress had a long, flowing skirt and a loose, flowing top part that draped sensuously over the top of Faye's arm.

The black side of the dress wasn't even really a dress, by any description, but a series of black bands of silk no more than a few inches thick that wrapped themselves around the apex of her right breast, waist and hip, and only vaguely covered the triangle between her legs. One black shoulder strap held the entire right side up. For jewels, Finn had presented her with a choker and tiara of black opals, with matching earrings that were so long, they trailed on her shoulders. Faye was wary of any jewels given from the faerie king, because of the way he'd used an opal ring in the past as a tool to to summon her. But Finn had insisted that she wear these. When he wasn't looking, she'd reached for Lyr's crystal in the slipper hidden under the bed and torn a hole in the narrow doubled-over band of pink silk that made up the waistband of one side of the dress, easing the crystal inside it.

The nausea hadn't left Faye; in fact, it had grown worse, but she was holding on to her composure as best she could until she could reasonably insist that she sat down for a while and wait for Finn to disappear into the throng. Faye thought that she knew where she would need to go and planned out her route in her mind as she danced with Finn. It might be tight, but she'd have to try.

The music was as wild as it had been before; onstage at the centre of the dance that revolved around them, three gnome-like faerie fiddlers played a fast reel along with two female ogre drummers and a delicate, reptilian flute player whose webbed blue fingers were almost a blur. The crowd were as uproarious and extravagant as she remembered, too; bare-breasted nixies danced with fish-headed faeries, winged creatures twirled beautiful and courtly members of the royal house – Faye guessed they were minor royals – and radiant, ephemeral figures that were almost made of pure water or light, dipped and wove through the crowd.

Faye didn't know whether it was the enchantment she was under by being with Finn or whether the floor of the ballroom had changed its state, but the bones and bodies she remembered from before were gone, and she and the rest of the dancers pounded their rhythm on what looked to be a glass-topped water tank. She'd only glimpsed flashes of it as she and Finn danced, but it looked as though the whole of the ballroom now sat on top of the sea, somehow, and shapes and shadows moved under them: sea serpents, strange gilled creatures, mermaids, the black shadow of a whale. Faye craned her head to try and see it better, but it was no use; all she saw was the odd intriguing flash of something, and then the legs and feet above.

'Faye Morgan. How well you look this evening. You have such a glow about you.'

Glitonea's voice snapped her back to attention. The faerie queen was dancing next to her and Finn; Finn nodded graciously to his sister. The comment was meant to imply Faye was pregnant, of course, but Faye didn't think that had entered Finn's mind… and anyway, Glitonea was wrong about that. *Is she wrong?* The voice in Faye's mind questioned again as her gorge rose and she fought the impulse to be sick. She ignored it.

'I'm quite well, thank you,' she lied, avoiding Glitonea's gaze.

'Indeed.' The faerie queen raised an eyebrow in disbelief. 'I believe you know my dance partner,' she added and smiled radiantly at the human man with her, whose eyes never left her face. Faye hadn't seen him until now – Glitonea's body had concealed him – but now her eyes widened as she recognised Gabriel's dark eyes and pale skin.

'Gabriel!' she cried, and reached out for him, but Glitonea laughed and danced him away before Faye could touch him. Never stoutly built, Gabriel was already gaunt, and the clothes he'd been given hung off his frame. Faye remembered the first time they'd met: remembered the smart dinner jacket and white shirt he'd worn underneath at the shop, slightly foppish, with a kind of magical beauty about him. He would certainly die here if she didn't help him.

'Oh dear. I do feel a little bit weak, actually.' Faye staged a stumble in Finn's arms and affected a faint kind of look. The faerie king frowned, irritated: she'd learnt that he'd little patience for weakness. 'I think I need to sit out for a little while.'

Finn laughed and picked her up, twirling her around to the frantic beat of the music.

'Nobody stops the dance, *sidhe-leth*,' he taunted.

'Finn! I want to get out. Now!' she cried helplessly, but he wouldn't let her go and danced her around, faster and faster.

'This was your request, Faye. A ball in your honour,' he shouted above the din. 'You are the king's most lovely consort. The fae thrive on your beauty and our desire.'

She pushed him away, angry, but he held her to him.

'You cannot stop dancing,' he cried, holding onto her waist tightly; the dancers seemed to become even more frenzied around them. Faye had to duck a few times to avoid being struck by flailing limbs. 'If you do, it is a great insult to my faerie court.'

'They are not *my* faerie court,' she shouted back, and, with a great effort, wrenched herself away from his grip. The dance held him and flowed away from her like a wave. She fell and landed painfully on her hands and knees on the thick glass floor.

Through the glass, she could see corpses floating in the water. One of them was Aisha.

Chapter 40

Faye stood between Simon and Manu as Sylvia and Penny opened the circle. It was December and the secluded oak grove on Hampstead Heath where Faye had come before smoked with incense made of pine and frankincense. Candlelight flickered on the rough bark of the sentinel trees that guarded their privacy.

Faye was deep in the shock of mourning. She felt blank, as if she was mummified in layers and layers of bandages; when she spoke, she heard herself talking as if it was someone else. Her thoughts were slow and cold, and her eyes were red with crying. She felt dissociated from everything around her, floating, muffled, even with the kind, grounding influence of white-bearded Simon next to her in his worn leather waistcoat covered in motorcycle gang patches, or the firm grip of Manu's hand in hers on the other.

The coven thought that they could call Gabriel back from Murias, and Faye had promised to help – she could hardly refuse. It was Faye Gabriel had followed into Murias, despite her warning; perhaps he'd intended to all along, or perhaps he'd been swept up with the wave that Finn used to draw her in to his faerie realm. Either way, it was her fault, just as it had been her fault that Aisha had been ensnared by Finn Beatha. And Aisha was dead.

Faye was adding her presence and power to the coven's calling Gabriel back, but she was the only one that knew Murias, and Faye knew that Gabriel was too deep in Glitonea's enchantment to want to leave. In any case, it was immaterial if he wanted to leave or not. Glitonea would never let him go.

When she'd woken up in Rav's bed, returned from Murias, she had no idea how she'd got there. A flu-like malaise laid her out for two weeks after that: she knew it was her body rejecting Murias, like going cold turkey. Each time she stayed too long it was the same.

When the fever had abated and she was left weak as the tea that stayed untouched on the bedside table, Rav had carefully asked her where she'd been; she'd disappeared after the party and been gone for three days. To Faye it felt like weeks.

'You came stumbling into the flat in the middle of the night.' Rav's voice maintained a careful line between accusation and concern. 'I found that note you left me; I was out of my mind with worry. You were gone for three days. *Three days*, Faye. I thought you'd been at Annie's, but she said she hadn't seen you.' He clearly suspected that she'd been in the realms of faerie, but he needed to hear it from her. She was too tired to lie, and had told him all of it.

He had asked her to leave; she'd broken it off with him anyway, hadn't she?

She'd wanted to ask him about Mallory – *had there been something between them?* – but it wasn't the right time. Perhaps there would never be a right time now. It had been her choice and it was the right one. But it still hurt.

Aisha and Gabriel's faces were imprinted on her mind. Wracked with pain, emaciated, dead. Faye stared at one of the oak trees in the grove, looking at the pattern of its bark. How could trees still stand and the sun still rise every day when Aisha was dead, and Gabriel gone? Her eyes sought a comfort in the pattern of the bark. She thought, if she concentrated on it hard enough, she could forget everything else.

'We are here tonight on a mission of mercy,' Sylvia intoned to the group as they stood in the cold night air. Faye, used to being out on Black Sands Beach in the winter, was still chilled to the bone, but she hardly felt it, muffled in her grief. She didn't care if she froze. It was a penance.

Sylvia and Penny had visited Faye while she was convalescing at Annie's, bringing her herbal remedies for regaining strength and giving her energy healing and aromatherapy massage. *We look after our own.* Penny had nodded briskly when Faye had thanked her.

Faye told them about her time in Murias, and how Gabriel must have been carried in with her when they summoned Finn Beatha at the edge of the Thames.

'He was a seeker. Is a seeker,' Sylvia had corrected herself as she massaged Faye's feet with citrus-smelling oils. 'He was fascinated with the fae worlds, but he'd never had an experience with faerie outside the circle. He must have been beside himself when you turned up.'

'He was very enthusiastic, but that was nice.' Faye coughed, and Penny slapped her on the back. 'It was good to have someone like that in my life. Who believed me. Who…' she trailed off, thinking of Rav. 'Who understood who I was. Fae and human halves.'

'Your boyfriend wasn't as understanding,' Penny said. 'I've been there. Not many non-witches, or, you know, non-mystics of some kind really get what this life is about. They can't accept what they can't see.'

Annie had sat down next to Faye and handed her a glass of wine.

'It wasnae like he hadn't seen it for himself, ye know. Tha's what I dinnae understand.' She'd leaned over and kissed Faye on the tip of her nose.

And Faye had cried again, because she couldn't stop: the grief ran deep in her, like the sap in the old oak she stared at, standing in the circle. Annie had ushered Sylvia and Penny out. *It's too soon, she just needs rest.*

Sylvia and Penny had told her that while Faye had been gone, Mallory had become part of the circle. Not part of the full coven, she'd nonetheless apparently come to some pub meet-ups and a couple of workshops; now, she stood in the circle opposite Faye, cowled in a long, dark coat that could, to all intents and purposes, be a cloak. Faye could feel the girl's disruptive energy emanating across the air at her like a knife-edged cloud of resentment and superiority. Faye hadn't spoken to her at all since arriving. What could she say? It didn't matter now. None of it mattered. Faye was too deep in her grief to be able to respond to Mallory. *If you wanted him, then he's yours now,* Faye thought, still staring at the tree.

'One of our own, Gabriel Black, is lost in the realm of Murias. He has become enchanted by the Faerie Queen Glitonea, and we understand that his situation is perilous. Though he may not want to leave, he must be forcibly removed, and so we will entreat any powers willing to help us call him back to us,' Sylvia intoned.

The coven members exchanged glances and a murmur of disbelief went around the circle.

'We need your undivided attention, friends,' Penny continued. 'Work with us now. After I call in the elements and draw the boundary, we will raise the power as greatly as we can. And we will ask for guidance from the gods and the faerie powers,' she added, looking at Faye. 'Faye already has experience in this regard.'

Faye blinked, struggling awake. She willed herself to be tethered to the earth, to take strength from something. She clutched at the obsidian crystal in her pocket. What had Penny just said? *The faerie powers.* Her instinct rose up, hot in the cold stone of her heart.

'No,' Faye's voice wavered. 'Don't call on them.'

'What?' Penny's voice cut through the lamplit circle.

'The elementals. Don't call on them. Other gods, spirits. Call them instead. Leave the fae alone.'

'Why? Why on earth wouldn't we ask for their help when that's where Gabriel is? I think the shock's affecting your judgement, dear. Don't worry. Let us lead this.' Sylvia was kind, but there was a thread of steel in her words.

'No. You don't understand. They'll offer a bargain, but you can never take it. But it'll sound like the only way. They're persuasive. Please. I… I feel it.' Faye knew she sounded foggy, wavering; she wasn't herself. But at the same time, she knew in her bones that calling on the fae would lead to more loss, more heartbreak. 'Please listen. I…'

Manu, next to her, squeezed her hand.

'It's going to be all right, Faye. I promise. Okay? And Simon promises. Don't you, Simon?'

The silver-bearded man next to her gave her a reassuring smile.

'I promise I won't let anything bad happen. To you or anyone else.' He was jolly, but Faye wanted to hit him. She pulled her hands away from both of them.

'You can't control the fae. You have no power over them. You can't protect me, or yourselves!' she cried, going to Penny and grabbing her by the shoulders. 'Penny! You can't. You don't understand.'

Faye was sweating, although the temperature was barely above freezing and her head pounded with the headache she hadn't been able to shift since coming back from Murias. The pain added to her overall sense of dissociation; perhaps, this time, some part of her spirit or soul had become permanently stuck in the faerie realm. Faye swayed on her feet, feeling like she was going to pass out.

'Sit down, Faye. Calm down. Here. Take some water.' Penny made her drink from a water bottle. 'I didn't think you should have come. It's too soon for you.'

'But I wanted to. For Gabriel.' Faye felt the tears coming again, and hugged her knees to her chest. 'I want to help. Please... I just...' she couldn't explain it to them. None of them could know the horrors of Murias. Faye had finally seen them for herself, and they were more terrible than she could have dreamed.

'I know. It's all right,' Penny soothed her. Manu and Simon rejoined hands without her; now, Faye sat inside the circle. She couldn't stop crying; her body was racked with sobs, her throat ached with remorse. She was still nauseous; she couldn't shift the feeling, and refused to think about what Glitonea had told her. That she was pregnant. It was unthinkable.

Penny drew the circle around them in earth, air, fire and water and walked from one quarter of the circle to another, calling in the elemental powers from north, east, south and west, Despite being so upset, as soon as Penny called in the elements, Faye felt the power of earth rise strongly around her.

Faye closed her eyes as she felt all four elements swirl into the circle; as the coven started to circle clockwise, she felt the four powers wrap her in a golden light, combined of earth, air, fire and water, as if she was being wound in a ribbon, over and over. Her psychic body as well as her physical one drank up the earth, fire and air hungrily. Slowly, her headache started to ebb away and her focus started to return. *Gabriel. Gabriel. Please. Any powers that are listening. Bring him back safely to us* she implored, sending her wishes into the centre of the cone of power they were building.

The magic circle was in itself an inbetween-place; a created space where beings from other worlds could be invited to tread.

The feeling of being bandaged, frozen, was strange. Usually, magic was like slipping into a natural rhythm, as natural as breathing. Tonight, she couldn't relax and let it flow through her. Her heart was that stone in the cold loch still: falling, untethered and full of fear. The grief made her magic waver and fade.

'Powers of the elements; gods of the old ways, spirit guardians. We request your help. One of our own is lost in the kingdom of Murias; we desire your strength to help us call him home,' Sylvia called, standing at the centre of the circle now, holding the power between her hands in a ball of golden light. She threw her head back, holding the ball of light up. 'Powers, gods, guardians! Help us!' she called, and Faye opened her eyes.

Lyr, Faerie King of the Realm of Falias appeared at the centre of the circle and bowed.

'I am at your service, Priestess,' he rumbled.

*

'We ask respectfully for your assistance, King of Falias.' Sylvia bowed her head. 'And thank you for attending our rite.'

'No!' Faye cried out, but Lyr only smiled.

'My help comes at a price, as my daughter knows.' Lyr nodded courteously; Faye refused to meet his eyes, but her hands clutched at the crystal. Holding it made her more certain of her feet on the ground, and she felt the power of the earth flowing up through the mud and rock, through the trampled grass and into her feet, ankles, legs. *No, no, no.*

Find me a human woman to bear my child and I will help you bring your friend home. Faye knew what Lyr's bargain was: in return for a suitable woman to bear his half-faerie child, he'd return Gabriel to them. But the price was too high, like it always was. She had warned them.

'We are willing to make offerings to you; tell us what you require in return for your help in this matter,' Sylvia continued, her voice strong and steady.

'Don't listen to him. He wants what they all want. A human sacrifice! Can't you see?' Faye cried, appealing at them, turning around the circle to make them understand. But the rest of the coven stared at Lyr raptly; Faye guessed that he'd enchanted them already. Perhaps they couldn't hear or see her any more; perhaps Lyr was inside their minds, distracting them with their inmost desires. Sylvia was the only one whose attention remained on Faye and Lyr. Perhaps she was the only one strong enough to be able to resist his magic, or perhaps there was a reason that Lyr wanted her awake.

Lyr turned to Faye.

'You know the bargain, daughter. It still stands.' He was refusing to answer Sylvia.

'What is the bargain?' Sylvia demanded. 'I'm in charge here. Your daughter is a part of the circle that brought you here. I'm the one you will bargain with.'

Lyr laughed softly. 'I bear you no disrespect, Priestess, but I came here because of Faye and Faye only. We have an unfinished business, and she knows it. Think of it as a test of your loyalty to your fae family, daughter.' His smile could be wolfish, and it was now.

'Never.' Faye turned her head away.

'Come now.' Lyr stood behind her now, his large hand on her shoulder. 'What other reason is there for her to be here? You know who it is. And you have no love for her.'

Faye's gaze darted across the circle at Mallory and then at the others; they were all frozen and unmoving.

'What have you done to them?' she demanded.

'Nothing permanent. They are quite well.' Lyr shook his head. 'So. You tried your own way in Murias, and you failed,' he said, matter-of-factly. 'Are you ready for another of your friends to die?'

'No,' she muttered. 'But I refuse to let you take Mallory. She might not be my favourite person, but she's not a whore for the taking.'

'I am appalled that you should think I would want her as one. She will be cherished as the mother of my child,' he rebuked her.

'The mother of a half-human sacrifice, you mean,' Faye shouted suddenly, tears thick in her throat, furious at the way the fae treated her and other humans. Grief for Aisha struck her bones; she ached with the loss. 'We are *people*! We have our own lives. We're not here for your amusement or to be used as baby-making machines.' Instinctively, her hand went to her belly.

'Then I wish you luck in extricating your friend from Glitonea's clutches.' Lyr shrugged, and turned to walk out of the circle. 'He is fully human. How long do you think he can withstand the force of her adoration?' Lyr raised an eyebrow. 'The faerie queens love far more savagely than the kings, so they say.'

The force of her adoration. Faye remembered the bloody whip lines that crisscrossed Gabriel's slumped body, chained to the wall where she kept him; yet, she also remembered the look in his eyes as Glitonea danced with him at the ball. *You'd die there, because dying would be so sweet,* she remembered thinking when they had been at Fortune's. She wondered if it would have made any difference if she'd told Gabriel then what she'd seen before; if she'd told him about the human lover she'd first seen Glitonea with. But she knew it wouldn't;

Gabriel, like any human man, was powerless against the erotic power of any faerie queen.

'I will make the bargain.' Sylvia's voice was low. 'He was… he is one of my coven. He is my responsibility.'

'Sylvia! No!' Faye stared, uncomprehending, at the High Priestess. She tried to move towards her, but a flick of Lyr's hand rendered her immobile. She tried to speak, but he'd taken her words.

'I see that one of you has common sense. Perhaps this is not Faye's choice after all.' Lyr smiled, pleasurable intrigue on his features, turning to Sylvia. Bathed in the golden luminescence that surrounded him, the High Priestess looked as if she'd been set on fire.

Faye stared wildly at Mallory, frozen like the rest, and watched, powerless, as Sylvia trod noiselessly across the circle and came to stand in front of her. Mallory's kohl-rimmed eyes were half closed; her long black coat billowed from her tiny frame like a flag, portending death.

'I'm in charge here,' Sylvia repeated. 'This is my responsibility. A High Priestess summons the powers; she does what is right for her coven.'

Faye tried to shout, to say anything, to warn Sylvia, but she was mute. *No, please, don't,* she willed Sylvia to resist Lyr. But the faerie king's power was too great; he'd persuaded Sylvia already.

'And this one?' Lyr ran his fingers through Mallory's blonde fringe. 'She is not also one of your charges?'

'She is not…' Faye could see that it pained Sylvia to say it, but she continued, 'She is not an initiate. I have not sworn to protect her, and she has not sworn to be a full member of the coven,'

Faye's heart sank. Could Sylvia be so heartless? But no: this wasn't malice. It never was. The faerie kings and queens could manipulate humans into doing whatever they wanted. They had done it to Faye, before she'd gained some power to resist them.

'She will be perfectly safe.' Lyr stood behind Sylvia, reaching out to trace his finger over Mallory's cheek. 'Such a pretty one. She will bear a son.'

'How do you know?' Sylvia spoke as if she was in a trance. Faye's heart sank deeper.

'I know,' Lyr replied, smiling.

'Is there no other way?' Sylvia's voice was eerily calm.

'There is not,' he said, quietly.

'Take her. But I want Gabriel back. Now!' Sylvia cried out.

'As you wish, Priestess.' Lyr smiled, and touched Mallory's forehead; she unfroze, but her expression was still vacant. Lyr took her by the hand. As he did so, a black pathway appeared through the forest where there hadn't been one before: Faye knew instinctively it was the road to Falias.

'Daughter, if you seek the wisdom of plants to rid yourself of your affliction – seek out my sister, the Faerie Queen Moronoe,'

As Lyr and Mallory disappeared, Faye felt herself able to move and talk again. The rest of the coven unfroze and looked around them in expressions of confusion. Some of them stumbled and fell. Faye knelt at the centre of the circle as branches, twigs and leaves rained down from above her, released from her fury, and hugged the inert body of Gabriel Black, who lay unconscious in her arms.

Chapter 41

Faye sat on the side of Gabriel's single bed and held the mug of herbal tea to his lips.

'Drink up. It's good for you,' she instructed.

'What is it?' Gabriel sat bolstered by pillows, too weak to hold himself up.

'Valerian for the pain. Turmeric, Yarrow, St John's Wort.' Faye tipped up the cup gently so he could drink without having to lean forward. 'Penny gave it to me.'

The coven had carried Gabriel's body out of the oak grove and Manu had called for an ambulance on his mobile phone. Ruby had noticed Mallory was gone. *Did she go home?* Ruby had asked, like a child awoken from a dream. Sylvia had said, *I'll explain. But not now.* Ruby and the others had exchanged glances, but no-one had said anything.

Sylvia and Penny had helped Faye get Gabriel into a cab after he'd been checked over by the medics in the van; it looked like just another inebriated end to a night out to most passing by on the street, Faye supposed, as she'd stood around the ambulance with the rest of them. Manu had his arm around Victoria's shoulders; Simon crossed his arms over his chest, his expression stony.

There was nothing apparently wrong with Gabriel except severe exhaustion, the ambulance worker said, pushing a strand of red hair from her tired eyes. Someone should keep an eye on him for a day or two. Faye could tell from her expression that she assumed the lot of them had been partying for a few days up in the woods, and Gabriel was the worse for wear. None of them explained otherwise; they would hardly be believed.

Their glances at her were wary as they stood in the street, after the ambulance had gone. Did they understand anything of what had happened? Had they seen it? Faye thought not. Faye wondered what the High Priestess would tell them. How she'd explain Mallory being taken. *I had no choice. It was Gabriel for Mallory, and she isn't one of us.* How callous that sounded, under the streetlights. How unreal.

No-one said it, but Faye could hear it nonetheless; all their thoughts were the same. *You have caused nothing but chaos since you came. You're not one of us.* They feared her. They thought that she could banish and return people to faerie on a whim. They didn't yet know what Sylvia had done. What she was willing to do for them. What she'd do to anyone who wasn't one of her chosen ones.

Faye wanted to tell them there and then what had happened: that she'd screamed at Sylvia not to do it. That Sylvia was as much a pawn in the games that the faerie kings and queens played with humans as anyone else. But it was too much. There were too many of them, and she could hardly breathe from the grief over Aisha that still crushed her chest. Yet, now, there was also a blinding, cutting relief that Gabriel was still alive.

Faye had taken him home. Sylvia had lain her hand on Faye's arm after they had got him into the cab. *I'll make it right*, she'd said, desperation in her eyes. Faye had nodded. What else could she do?

Gabriel lay back and closed his eyes.

'Can you talk about it?' Faye returned the half-full mug to the bedside table and kept her eyes on it, away from his. It hadn't been her fault, his time in Murias, but she felt responsible nonetheless. It was too recent, too raw, this nursing of someone that had been lost in faerie. She told herself that Gabriel had wanted to go, unlike Rav. But it made no difference either way when you saw how close to death humans came in the faerie realm. She remembered Aisha's face under the ice-glass ballroom floor, and closed her eyes in horror.

'Yes,' he breathed. His voice was cracked, as if he'd forgotten how to speak.

'What happened? Did you... go willingly? Or did you get taken with me? By accident?' Guilt weighed Faye's heart. She couldn't bear it that she'd endangered another friend.

'I wanted to go.' Gabriel coughed, and she waited for him to catch his breath. 'I planned to go. When Finn came, I jumped into the wave with you. When I woke up, I was in her bed. I didn't want to leave, either.' He lay back on the pillows and closed his eyes again. 'I told you. What life did I have, here? Whole days go past and I don't see a soul in that bookshop. I don't have anyone special in my life.' His eyes met hers and she saw the pain in them. Faye looked away, not knowing what to say.

'You would have died there,' she said quietly. 'Sylvia... saved your life.' She didn't explain how; it was a bargain that should never have been made.

'I didn't want it saved!' Gabriel's voice cracked again, the shout lost in his throat, but Faye felt his anger, nonetheless. 'I wanted her. Glitonea. I still want her.' He tried to sit up, but his muscles were wasted, and wouldn't let him. 'I'll go back. When I'm strong enough. She's calling to me.'

Horror spread its fingers over Faye's skin as she recognised the dull shine of a possessed soul in Gabriel's formerly bright eyes. Was this how she'd been with Finn? Had she been this lost, this willing to sacrifice her humanity to the power of faerie?

'You can't go back. You won't survive there,.' Faye repeated. 'You'll die. Aisha died. I saw her.' Her voice broke.

A tear rolled down Gabriel's cheek. 'She loves me, Faye. And her love is… so powerful. Like the ocean. She took me to the deepest places in myself, Faye. You must know how that feels. To want and be wanted so intensely. To be devoured, over and over again. There's no point being alive if I can't have that.'

He cried, letting the tears wrack his weak body, unable to stop them. Faye held him, knowing that he was as addicted to Glitonea as she had been to Finn; knowing that he'd go back to her if given the slightest opportunity.

'I'm so sorry,' she repeated, over and over again as she held him. 'Gabriel, I'm so sorry.'

And as she held him, she thought of Mallory, and her stomach twisted. Lyr had promised that Mallory would be safe, but he couldn't be trusted any more than Finn or Glitonea.

Gabriel's desperation was one she knew all too well: it was the lust of the human for faerie, and of the almost-dead for life. Gabriel's darkness resonated with her own shadow: they had both known the desolation of having been loved so intensely that they would die to remain in the dream – if a dream was what it was – and had felt the deep despair in waking. It was as though, for a moment, she saw herself and Gabriel standing on opposing sides of a flat, black lake, as glassy and perfect as the obsidian wand she carried in her pocket. And in her vision, they were reaching for each other, both alone in their sorrow and desperate to be held.

Yet, though there was sorrow there for both of them, there was also kinship, now, in a way that there hadn't been before.

'Gabriel,' she said softly, feeling the weight of his confusion and sorrow break like a wall in an earthquake. She held him to her as he sobbed desperately. 'I'm here. I… I understand. What you feel. I know.'

Faye closed her eyes, and the vision of the black lake reappeared. Yet, even though Gabriel was in her arms, he remained standing at one edge of the water, now looking away from her. And she knew that no matter how loudly she called him, he wouldn't wade across to her. Not yet.

'What did you… what was the bargain? To get me back?' he asked, against her shoulder.

Faye sat back and put her head in her hands.

'Lyr took Mallory. I tried to stop it, but he had control of me. It was Sylvia who agreed to it.'

'Mallory?' Gabriel's hands were on his knees, now: a posture that implied he was keeping himself upright with a force of will. Despair ordered his body like a slumped puppet; he had no strength for the demanding weight of the human world which pulled him down. Faye knew that he craved the flowing moments of Murias, even though it was while under their spell that he'd been so horribly tortured.

'She's a… friend… of Rav's. She's in Falias with Lyr.' Faye felt dizziness overcome her and shook her head to clear it.

'Falias?'

'Yes.'

'With Lyr,' Gabriel repeated, dully. She wondered how much he was really taking in: he was dazed, confused. Half of him was still lost; he might never be whole again.

Faye nodded.

'I'm sorry. I…' She didn't know what to say.

Gabriel said nothing, staring blankly at his knees. He had lapsed into a kind of waking fugue; she spoke to him, nudged him, called his name, but he was gone again, blank and absent from the human world in everything but his already-starved body. How long had Glitonea kept him there, in faerie time? How long had he suffered at her hands, and how long had the pressure of Murias impacted his body?

She settled him back on the pillows and sat back in the chair by his bed. It seemed fitting to Faye that she should be with Gabriel, in his dark night of the soul, watching over him while his spirit tried to free itself from Murias.

The light from the bedside lamp was dim, but she didn't put the overhead light on for fear of disturbing whatever rest Gabriel could get. Instead, she sat in the near-darkness and thought about Mallory.

It might already be too late for her; if Mallory returned, would she be like Gabriel? Would she be mired as deep in the despair of leaving the faerie realm? Or was she, even now, calling out to return to the human world, frightened and alone? She couldn't stop thinking about Aisha, and every time she did, the grief crushed her.

She closed her eyes. Over and over again she weighed up every offer, every possible way, but every time, she came up against a faerie king or queen that sought only to manipulate her. Lyr was no different.

But she also needed something for herself, and she was frightened of the kind of help she might need. Because it had been two months without a period, and she was sick, still, every day, long past the point where she should have recovered from being in the faerie realm.

For the first time, Faye placed her hand on her flat stomach and dared to imagine that she might be pregnant. Worse: that the bargains she'd struck with Glitonea might have to be fulfilled.

Chapter 42

She wasn't aware of falling asleep in the chair, but she suddenly found herself standing in a golden-green forest. Sunlight dappled the yellow, red and green leaves: all the colours were slightly too bright to be real, as if rendered by a child. Silver birch stood alongside ash and oak, and a row of the prickly hawthorns with their red berries lined a pathway through the trees.

Faye walked slowly along the path, feeling the pull of faerie in her blood; she smelt the tang of lemon and the savoury tinge of wild oregano in the air. The green light welcomed her in, and the wild power of the cold, black earth seemed to soak through her boots. It was December, but in the dream – or was it a dream? – there was no distinct season. The earth was cold and damp, but the sun was warm; the leaves on the trees could have been spring shoots or autumn colours. The grief she carried for Aisha was still there, but being in faerie muted it somehow, like a drug.

To her right flowed the same merry stream she'd visited with Lyr on their way into Falias: the bridge in the shape of a woman's body was still there, as beautifully carved as it had been before. She crossed it, and stood before the tall black gate. The Queendom of Moronoe, High Queen of the Realm of Earth.

Faye remembered Lyr's expression as he'd talked about his sister; it was dismissive, distant. Clearly there wasn't a great love between them as brother and sister, or even as co-rulers of Falias. Finn and Glitonea didn't keep themselves separate in Murias: both resided in the castle and ruled from it. Faye wondered what had happened to mean that Lyr and Moronoe were so estranged that they had split a realm between them.

Something about that black door fascinated her. She touched it lightly with her fingers and it swung open without her needing to do anything more.

The last time she'd visited this place, roots and vines wrapped themselves around her feet and ankles, and she could go no further. *Stop, traveller. Only one pure in her desire may enter the Queendom of Moronoe, Mistress of Earthly Delights* a chorus of voices sang out: it was the same phrase as before. *Have knowledge of where you tread. Know thyself and admit thy deepest desires.*

Beyond the gate, the forest was more densely packed, and moonlight rather than the warm sun filtered between the gaps between thick-trunked yews, dense with their dark green needles and poisonous red berries. Faye could see their exposed roots under the black soil that glowed with jewels: amber, citrine, jet and emerald. The air that drifted out of the gate smelt of copper, and it reminded her of her monthly blood. *Know thyself.*

Faye took a deep breath and put one foot inside the gateway; the jewelled black earth beyond accepted her weight, and no vines sought to trap her. Carefully, she stepped between the dense yews, and though there was no black lake, the ground itself reminded her of the vision she'd had of standing opposite Gabriel, lost and seeking refuge from the faerie realms.

Perhaps the recognition of her shadow was something to recommend her to the faerie queen here

Come to terms with your desire, Faye, the same voice sang, as she walked further and further into the jewelled yew forest. *Accept that*

desire does not have walls, or rules, or niceties. Desire does not arrive packed safely in a box and wait to be looked at. It rips itself from the box, from the womb, it is born bloody and with teeth, and it feeds.

Faye walked deep into the faerie forest, where the trees became a labyrinth and led her down long, sinuous paths that twisted and bent under the moonlight. Faye walked and walked until time had lost all meaning, and as she walked, moving images like film appeared on the leafy branches of the trees that she followed. As she walked past, an unfolding record of her lovemaking with Finn and with Rav were played out for her in lurid colour and detail.

At first, Faye turned her head away, repulsed both by seeing her own body and the expressions on her face that captured moments of lust and ecstasy. She broke into a run, tripping on her own feet or on stray fallen branches or vines on the ground, desperate to escape the vision. *If this is a dream, I want to wake up!* she thought, but she didn't find herself back in her bed. But, when she was breathless and her heart was hammering, she was forced to stop and watch.

And, as she watched, remembering, she came to a new peace. Her body was more beautiful than she'd imagined. She saw arousal and passion in the images, but she also saw tenderness on Rav's face, and on Finn's. What they did was all for pleasure. Was any of it so wrong? Perhaps she was the only one that had ever thought it was. Faye had categorised faerie as the shadow because of the sexual boundaries she'd crossed when she was there. She'd thought shadow was wrong, and light was good. But in the tree labyrinth with the milky glow that filtered through the shadowy pines, Faye pondered whether light and shadow were all part of one spectrum of being.

She could have been walking for an hour or a day; she'd no idea of how long she'd been in the trees, but unlike the fear she'd experienced in the labyrinth leading to Murias, she felt only calm. And as if they had been waiting for her to reach acceptance with what she'd seen, the trees opened onto a clearing.

Chapter 43

Queen Moronoe crouched with her back to Faye on a throne made from rock, held together by moss and covered in ivy. She was completely naked, and her impossibly wide, stout thighs suffocated the head of what appeared to be a human man. He lay on a kind of reclined green velvet chair, on his back, with his head buried in the faerie queen's large, rounded bottom. The queen's thighs rippled with pleasure as she moaned loudly, grinding her whole bottom half onto his face; he was also naked, and Faye looked away in embarrassment as she noticed the man's erection. His head and face was completely obscured by the mountainous behind, and Faye wondered if he could breathe at all.

Moronoe's throne room – Faye guessed this was what this was – resided in a hollowed-out cave where insects scurried up the walls and roots poked out of the black earth. The coppery smell of earth and blood was stronger here, but combined with the freshness of a lemony resinous smoke that rose from a number of crude earth pots with holes at the top.

Sex was thick in the air; the cave-like room was womblike and dark, and the whole place seemed to have a heartbeat of lust uniting it.

It was a different allure to Murias, but Faye could feel it entering her senses, nonetheless. It seemed that all the faerie realms had this sexual element: they were the primal places of elemental power, after all, and nothing was more primal than the life force of nature, forever seeking to perpetuate itself, to grow and spread.

Faye called out to the faerie queen, who had dismounted her prone human lover.

'My queen! I would speak with you.' Faye bowed her head before the vast presence of Moronoe, who, despite being naked, gave her such an imperious look that Faye felt mortified by her own presence in the room.

'Who is it that interrupts my pleasure?' the queen boomed. Her breasts were the largest Faye had ever seen, supported by voluptuous rolls of fat; her arms were thick with muscle and dimpled flesh like her thighs, and her stomach was wide and curvaceous. There was simply so *much* of her; her power, Faye knew, would be great, like all the faerie queens. But there was something in her simple physical presence that screamed power, like a mountain. Where Glitonea seemed to merge with her surroundings, Moronoe pulled everything in the room to her. Moronoe represented every pleasure that the body could ever possibly experience. Her largeness was testament to the strength and vitality that emanated from her, like a battery of life.

'Faye Morgan. I'm… I'm your brother Lyr's daughter.' Faye bowed her head again.

The queen regarded her for a moment and let out a sigh.

'Fine. My robe!' she shouted, and a faerie servant, rather like the gnomes Faye remembered from Murias, emerged from the shadows, handing Moronoe a ruby-red gown of some kind. The queen nodded to a door at the far end of the room. 'In there,' she ordered, pulling the robe around her.

Chapter 44

Moronoe had the same dark beauty as her brother Lyr, but her black hair was braided and dreadlocked, partly piled on her head and partly threaded with ribbons, reaching the floor. The robe that she drew casually around her body was a deep wine-coloured red velvet, though different to the gowns that Faye had become accustomed to in Murias; Moronoe's ample breasts bulged from the front opening and her arms strained at the velvet fabric. Instead of the delicate leather boots and shoes Faye had worn in the water kingdom, Moronoe's feet were bare and covered in smudges of mud and dust. She settled herself into another throne, though this one was much grander, made of gold and studded with natural crystals, which sat at one end of a much smaller room. The same roots grew into the room from the earth walls, but they were alone, and there was no other furniture apart from a golden table next to the throne on which there was a large bowl of fruit and a cup of wine. If she was in a dream, it wasn't an ordinary one. Yet Faye knew that her body sat, slumped, in the chair next to Gabriel's bed.

Faye bowed her head again.

'Blessings to you, my queen. I come—'

Moronoe interrupted her, biting at a pomegranate from the fruit bowl, spitting the thick pith onto the floor and licking the fruit's sticky juice from her palm. 'I know why you're here. I summoned you. I know who you are. Approach the throne.'

That would explain it. Faye approached her aunt carefully.

'You summoned me? Am I... in a dream?' she asked.

'After a fashion,' the queen replied. 'Closer.' She narrowed her eyes. 'Hm. You don't have our colouring. A shame.'

'I'm... I'm sorry, my queen.'

'Aunt. I am your aunt. And I am also a queen, though not *your* queen. Be correct in your expression,' Moronoe chided.

'I'm sorry, I... Aunt,' Faye stammered, taken off guard.

'No matter. You are blood and that is enough.'

'Why did you summon me here?' Faye was wary; her journey through the trees had been pleasant enough, but she knew that she should fear Moronoe as much as any of the other faerie kings and queens.

Moronoe leaned forward and studied Faye's face.

'You are with child, niece. But you cannot have the baby. It will be too dangerous.' The fairy queen sat back in her throne. 'It isn't too late. A little tea and your problem will not be a problem any more.'

'No, I... I don't want that.' Faye's hands shielded her belly protectively. 'I mean... I don't need it.'

'Many come to me for it,' her aunt sighed and clicked her fingers at the rabbit goblin. 'Hermione will fetch it.'

Faye's stomach lurched as if in reply to Moronoe's offhand statement. *No, no, no* her inner voice pleaded. *This isn't happening.*

'How can you be sure?' Faye whispered. *A little problem*, Moronoe's words echoed in her mind. *Just a little tea, and the problem goes away.*

'Because I am the Faerie Queen Moronoe, the ruler of the element of Earth. All bodies are made of earth. I am sovereign ruler of all material life – human, animal and plant – and I govern the eternal flow of birth, life and death. I am the womb of the world and also its grave. Trust me that I know when seeds of new life grow in one such as you.' The queen held out her arms towards Faye who watched as a vine twisted along Moronoe's arm. Grapes bulged from the stems and swelled to ripeness; as Faye watched, enthralled, the deep purple fruit split open and then shrivelled. The vine retracted as if it had never been and Moronoe shrugged.

'You should know as well as anyone that the circle of life follows its path, death and life, life and death,' she said. 'I know you lost your friend in Murias. Do you understand now the power that the faerie realms hold?' she demanded.

Faye took in a deep breath, feeling her stomach twist in grief. Yes, she knew. She could never forget Aisha.

'Glitonea started to teach me. About the magic of water—' Faye ventured.

'Glitonea is not your blood. The High Queen of Murias should not be instructing my niece in the ways of power!' Moronoe shouted, and Faye stepped back in alarm as the roots in the walls shrivelled and the flowers on the table next to Moronoe shed their petals. 'You went to her, and she asked that of you that should never be asked. She asked you for a child. You must know that if you gave her the child that is inside you, Murias would gain a terrible weapon against us. Against your own kind.'

'I wouldn't give her my baby. Ever,' Faye retorted. 'I made the bargain, but I had no choice.'

'There is always a choice, niece. You just mean that you disliked the options.'

'Whatever.' Faye wasn't in the mood to be lectured, and for a moment she forgot who she was standing in front of; she'd reverted into a defensive mood, like when Grandmother used to tell her off. Her mother Moddie never had done much lecturing; she wanted to be more like a sister to Faye. *I became a mother too young*, she'd been prone to saying. *I love you more than the world, but I missed out on being young when I had you.*

If I'm pregnant, what will it do to my life? Faye wondered. *And whose baby is it? Rav or Finn?*

'Do not sass me, Faye Morgan,' Moronoe snapped. 'You are thinking of your own mother. She was Lyr's lover, and she fell pregnant by him. She was young, yes. Younger than you are now.'

'I… I don't know if I'm ready. To be a mother,' Faye mumbled.

'No-one is ever ready. It is in your fate to have a child: that, I can see. But it is your choice as to when and how.'

'How do you…' Faye started to ask, but Moronoe raised an eyebrow, and Faye didn't finish the question. It seemed irrelevant. Instead, she asked '*If* I'm pregnant—'

'You are with child. I assure you of that.' Moronoe nodded her head.

'Whose is it, then? Rav or Finn?'

Moronoe narrowed her eyes; Faye felt as though she was being stared through, that Moronoe could see her bones, sinews; nothing was hidden from her.

'I do not see any fae in this baby apart from that which you bring to it. He will look like his father, who is dark haired. If he is born. Which cannot happen.'

Rav. She was pregnant with Rav's baby. Faye suddenly felt the need to sit down. In her bones, she knew Moronoe was right; she was pregnant; the sickness hadn't been entirely due to the effects of Murias. She'd felt different; her whole body felt softer, stranger. *Rav's baby.*

Faye genuinely had no idea whether that was better or worse than the baby being Finn's. She felt a wave of relief that she wouldn't have to explain herself to Rav that it wasn't his – but that relief was immediately shadowed by the realisation that she and Rav were no longer together.

But this is different. This will change everything between us. For the better, perhaps she thought. And then, another thought came: *Do I want it to?*

And what about Finn? Faye was ashamed of the thought that followed, but nonetheless it came: *will he still want me?*

'If you have the baby, Glitonea will want it. You made the bargain with her. And, in fact, I imagine that you getting pregnant in the first place is her doing. She wants what is owed to her and she will stop at nothing to get it.'

'But she won't be able to just steal a baby away from me!' Faye protested, but she could hear the weakness in her own voice. 'And how… what would she do? How could she make me pregnant?'

'Your grandmother told you the stories of the fae. Of them taking babies from their cribs in broad daylight. If you have the baby, she will take it. And have no doubt that she will have cast a fertility charm on you. Murias is famous for such things.'

'What about Finn? What will he do?' Faye couldn't meet the faerie queen's stare in response, but she needed to know. He would be angry. What would he do if he found out that his lover was pregnant by her human lover?

'You already know what he will do. Rage at you. Hurt you, perhaps. Finn Beatha is tempestuous and foolhardy. He lives by desire, and desire only.' Moronoe rolled her eyes. 'The faerie kings are so emotional. They overreact. They conduct wars, they hold dramatic grudges and then change their minds. The queens are, for the most part, far more rational.' The faerie queen sighed.

'He may try and harm you in jealousy. Or he will try to harm your human lover again. He is predictable in his unpredictability. However, you are under my protection now, and as such, he cannot harm you or the child. However…' she mused for a moment. 'If Finn found out that his sister had helped you to conceive another man's child, I have no doubt that it would cause some friction between them.' She smiled then, like a fat, satisfied cat.

'And that Glitonea is responsible for your escape with the human in the first place. Interesting.' Moronoe was watching her shrewdly; from time to time as they talked, an animal would emerge from one of the many holes and burrows in the wall and curl up on the queen's lap, or nestle in the folds of her capacious gown. She stroked them absently as she talked.

The rabbit-creature, Hermione, set a rough stone cup in front of Faye. In it, a clear liquid steamed; Faye picked up the cup and frowned at the dried herbs that floated in the water.

'I am your aunt. I called you here because I want to protect you.' Moronoe picked up a squirrel by the scruff of the neck and set it carefully on the dirt floor, where it found the crumbs of food she'd dropped and began feasting on them. 'Drink, and all will return to the way it was.' The faerie queen watched the squirrel, smiling as if it were her child.

'But this is Rav's and my baby. Doesn't he get some say in the matter?' Faye appealed to the faerie queen, who glared at her in response, her mien changing suddenly, from indulgent mother to terrible queen.

'Does he deserve to know? He has not treated you honourably! It is your body that will bear the child. Grow it. Feed it and nurture it.

And you will care for the child when it is born. His opinion is moot!' Moronoe cried; for a brief moment, the ground under her shook.

'I… it seems right that I should at least tell him,' Faye stammered.

'No!' Moronoe shouted, and her voice was the grinding of rock on rock. 'It would be one thing if you had intended the child together, if you had brought it forth in love and with plans for the future. But this *Rav*, whose opinion you hold in such high regard…' Moronoe made a dismissive noise, and reached for a black mirror in an ornate gold frame that lay propped against her throne. She passed her hand over it and tilted it so that Faye could see. 'This is the truth. Though I understand that my brother has taken the girl now, so the way is clear for you to reunite with the human, should you wish to. *After* your problem is dealt with, of course.'

Reluctantly, Faye looked in the glass.

Mallory and Rav lay entwined in Rav's bed, sleeping. Mallory's arm was draped over Rav's chest, and moonlight slanted through the curtains, bathing them in its blue-white glow. Faye closed her eyes and pushed the mirror away. He had denied it, and he'd lied. It didn't matter now, but it still hurt.

'Moon tea. Pennyroyal, rue and blue cohosh. You will bleed for a few days and have sickness, but Glitonea's control over you will be gone. Drink.' Moronoe's voice was firm, and Faye felt a kind of fugue come over her, a little like when she was with Finn. She felt herself lift the cup to her lips. The stone was cold against her mouth. 'It's better this way, niece. You will have a baby in the years to come, another child, free of obligation to the faerie realm. But not this one.' Moronoe's voice spun a charm around her. Faye felt terribly tired.

'Drink it up; there's a good girl.' Moronoe's voice was soft and persuasive and Faye tipped the cup towards her lips.

Chapter 45

Faye dropped the cup onto the dirt floor; the liquid spilled out into a puddle, and the cup rolled away. The steam was pungent and it had awoken her from her daze.

'I don't want it.' Faye shook herself, horrified that she'd almost drunk it without really wanting to. 'It's not for me.'

'Then you are a fool,' Moronoe retorted. 'If you have that child, Glitonea will take it from you. Better that you end it now and save your grief, and the fate of the child.'

'There will be another way. There must be!' Faye cried. 'Surely Lyr wouldn't stand by and—' but Moronoe laughed cruelly, interrupting her.

'Lyr is the father of countless bastards that he has no interest in protecting. Don't expect him to help you.'

'But… there must be something I can do. Please, my queen. Help me.'

The faerie queen stared at Faye with a grim expression.

'Drink the tea,' she repeated.

Faye thought, furiously. 'What if I go home, back to Abercolme? I won't tell anyone about the baby.' The faerie queen kept an unbroken eye contact with Faye, frowning.

'Finn and Glitonea will know where you are, regardless. You cannot hide from them.' She shook her head. 'Better you end it now.'

'I won't do that.' Faye met Moronoe's gaze levelly. 'I can't avoid them knowing where I am, and I can't stop them knowing that I'm pregnant. But if Glitonea wants the baby, then she knows I have to carry it to term. That I have to be healthy, and I have to stay in the ordinary world to be well, right? It would be too risky to transport me into Murias, wouldn't it? At least for long periods of time?'

Moronoe nodded. 'Your human body needs human food, water, the nourishment of the human world. She knows this as well as I.'

'All right. So, she'll watch me, but she'll think I'm honouring the bargain.'

'And then what? When it's born?' Moronoe demanded. 'She will not change her mind. She will take the child. Are you willing to give it up?'

'No.' Faye shook her head. 'But you can help me. Hide us here. Glitonea can't come here, can she?'

The faerie queen gave Faye a calculating look.

'No, you would be safe here. But you would have to re-enter the human world at some point. You are only half-faerie, and your human body needs to be in its element.'

'What about the baby?' Faye was desperate, but she had to find a way to protect it. She'd no more drink the moon tea than cut her own throat. She could see that it would be a logical option, but Faye just couldn't do it. 'Could you keep it here? Until it was... I don't know. Old enough to not be of interest to Glitonea any more? I mean, how old would that even be? When will she stop being interested in the child?'

'You *could* bear the child with the help of the fae midwives,' Moronoe mused. 'You would not suffer, for they are skilled in the childbearing arts. And when the child is born, I could keep him here. He would be protected in my realm.'

Faye looked around her, at the rough walls of dirt and roots.

'But for how long?' She hated the thought of trusting Moronoe, but it was the only solution she could think of. At least here, the baby would be protected.

'It is possible that I could teach him magic, when he is old enough,' Moronoe suggested. 'It might be enough to deter her. Or, she may only want a baby. A child may not suit her purposes, in which case, we need only keep him here until he is four or five of your human years.'

'But don't you know for sure?' Faye demanded. 'This is my child we're talking about! I'm considering giving him up to be looked after in your realm. I need to know it's going to be safe.'

Moronoe glared at her.

'How can I know what is in Glitonea's mind? I can guess, with reasonable clarity. But she is one power, I am another,' the faerie queen thundered. 'Let us not forget that it is you that is asking me for a favour here, niece. Perhaps a little more gratefulness might be in order.'

Faye took in a deep breath.

'I am grateful for your help. But you have to understand that I'm trying to find some kind of workable solution to…' she shook her head. 'To an unthinkable problem. All right?'

But what does Moronoe really get out of helping me? Faye watched the faerie queen with a critical eye. Was she really so committed to protecting Faye? There was no reason why she should. Granted, she'd also indicated that she liked the idea that the baby might drive a wedge between Finn and Glitonea. However, Faye imaged Moronoe had other ways of doing that if she wanted to.

'Humans are so emotional.' Moronoe rolled her eyes. 'Fine, fine. I understand.'

She'd learnt that there were ways of subverting the will of the faeries, though it wasn't easy, and there were always consequences.

'Wait. If the baby's human, then it can't stay here. It will kill him. Or her.' The surreal nature of what she was talking about with Moronoe struck Faye. *Surely she couldn't be considering leaving her child in the faerie realm?*

'He will be partly fae, taking that from you. And if I have him from a newborn, he will adjust. That is why the fae like to take human babies. They can live in our realms more easily if they grow within it than if they arrive from another realm. Then, it is too much of a shock. If they are here from the beginning, they are reared on faerie milk, which gives them what they need to survive here.' Moronoe patted her large, rounded breast. 'I will suckle him myself.'

'Won't Lyr protect me against Glitonea? Can't he do anything? He is my father, after all.' Faye was desperate for any ray of hope that meant she didn't have to leave her baby in Falias to be brought up in Moronoe's court.

'Lyr.' Moronoe spat on the ground. 'My brother is no help to anyone. We are no longer speaking, so I cannot ask his help even if I wanted to, which I do not.' She tossed her head proudly.

'Why not?' Lyr had mentioned he and his sister were estranged, but he hadn't explained why.

'Because I am a queen, and I do not need his rulership or approval; I am head of my own Queendom. I need not submit to the Kingdom of Falias to have power.' She snorted. 'I also disapprove of the way he uses human women, like a harem. Faerie kings and queens have always had human lovers, for pleasure, but Lyr seems to be obsessed with fathering as many half-fae children as he can. There is no need for it.'

Faye was surprised.

'I wouldn't have… expected you to care so much. About the women,' she replied carefully.

'I have no sympathy for them, individually. They *choose* to become enamoured of him.' Moronoe shook her head angrily. Faye thought it was prudent not to mention that the average woman would have no protection against the seductive power of a faerie king – she hadn't, and she was half-faerie. 'But the principle angers me. I am the protectress of reproduction, of the seed of life in nature. It is a sacred process; a human woman is the creatrix of her world. There is a balance to these things that he ignores. In the old days, it was one human child a year given to the fae. Not a hundred, born because Lyr of Falias can't control himself.'

Moronoe's tone was brisk now. 'Also, I disapprove of this war, and my brother dislikes being disapproved of.' The faerie queen smiled grimly; Faye shivered at the thought of being the object of Moronoe's disapproval.

'What is the war actually about?' Faye asked. 'Finn said it was for territory… a disagreement over boundaries between your lands.'

'That is correct, but it is not about boundaries between the elemental realms. The kings, and one of the queens, Thetis, Queen of the Kingdom of Fire, are warring over the control of the Crystal Castle.' Moronoe looked to the roof in disdain. 'I refuse to be involved. It is a war of stupid against stupider; no-one can control the Crystal Castle except Morgana Le Fay.'

'Lyr told me that.'

Moronoe raised her eyebrow.

'I doubt that he told you the whole truth. All faerie realms have their own magic,' Moronoe continued. 'But Morgana is the great Queen of us all, and her magic is unsurpassed. She takes her power from the Moon; she is the Moon, in a manner of speaking. These fools battle over harnessing the Moon in a net and making it do their bidding. It cannot be done.'

'Surely they know that. Why are they even trying?' Faye frowned.

Moronoe sighed. 'Because they believe an ancient prophecy.'

'What prophecy? Do you believe it?' Faye asked.

'Fate is fate. I cannot change it. If it is to happen, it will happen. No point going to war over it.' Moronoe picked up what looked like a sweet pastry from a plate on the table and tore half of it off with her sharp white teeth. 'I have enough to do, governing the realm of earth, without playing at war. Morgana can take care of herself, and anyway,' she chewed the pastry with a smile of contentment, 'they have no doubt misinterpreted the prophecy. She knows that, as well as I do.'

'What do you mean?'

'It will be what it will be.' Moronoe pushed the other half of the pastry into her mouth and licked her voluptuous lips with her tongue. 'It is not for you to worry over now. Now, you must go back to the human world. Your body grows weaker here and you need your strength for what is to come.'

Faye looked around her, at the roots pushing through the earth walls and the glass and stone lamps, flickering with strange coloured light. Would she really end up hiding her baby here from Finn and Glitonea? It seemed unthinkable. Perhaps this had been a dream. Perhaps she wasn't pregnant. Her heart leapt with the possibility.

Moronoe unhooked a jet black necklace interspersed with citrine and amber crystals from her own neck, and held it out to Faye. Each bead was a cube about an inch square; it was a heavy piece that weighed on her neck when she held it against her own throat.

'Take this. Wear it all the time, as protection. And when you need me, call out and I will hear you, wherever you are.' Moronoe helped Faye with the clasp; her touch was gentle. 'Now. Go home, and think about what we have said.'

There's another way. There must be, Faye thought as she closed her eyes and felt the strangeness of transitioning between the fae and the human realm overtake her senses. *But I will go home.* She felt it, sure and right and clear in her gut. Abercolme was where she needed to be and that was where she'd go. Perhaps when she was there, it would become clear as to what she'd do next. She hoped so.

Chapter 46

Annie stood behind her on the steps that led up to Rav's front door as she looked for the key in her bag. Passers-by and shoppers walked past, going about their business.

'Are ye sure he isnae in?' Annie whispered, though it was the middle of the day, a week after Faye had returned from Moronoe's queendom. As usual, she had taken a few days to recuperate, assuring Annie and Susie that it was normal, that the sickness was a part of her withdrawal from faerie and that it would pass soon. She hated lying to her best friend, but she had to. She knew Annie, and she wouldn't be able to resist the urge to berate Rav for splitting up with Faye when she was pregnant. Annie's protective instinct for Faye was as old as their friendship.

'As sure as I can be. This is usually an office day,' Faye replied, turning the key in the lock. 'Anyway, I'm not going to be long.'

She didn't have much to get, which was, in a way, symptomatic of her and Rav's communal uncertainty about the relationship. Annie followed her into the shared hallway, carrying two large holdalls; Faye pulled an empty suitcase behind her, up the stairs to Rav's flat.

She opened the door to the flat, and her heart lurched.

Rav was sitting on the sofa with his back to her, working on his laptop.

'That was quick, I thought you were—' the words died on his lips as he turned around and saw Faye. 'Oh. It's you.' A shadow crossed his features.

'I came to get my stuff.' Faye concentrated on keeping the tremor out of her voice. 'I won't be long.'

Without waiting for a reply she went into the bedroom with Annie following, and started pulling clothes out of the wardrobe and the drawers.

'Ye all right, sweetheart?' Annie whispered. 'I'll do this for ye. Go an' sit in the car, I'll be ten minutes.'

'No, it's okay.' Faye opened the drawer she'd kept her t-shirts and tops in 'It won't take…' she trailed off. None of her clothes were in the drawer. Instead, expensively-distressed black and grey vests and t-shirts, the kind that she'd seen Mallory wear, were folded neatly under each other. Annie looked over her shoulder.

'They're not yours,' she confirmed, and stormed into the living room, where Faye heard her shout *Where the fuck's all her stuff?* at Rav.

Faye sat on the bed, fighting the tears that were too insistent to be kept away. What had happened to her? Her whole life felt completely out of control. She had loved Rav. And now she was pregnant with his child and couldn't tell him.

How long had Mallory's clothes been here? And was she here, or was she still in Falias somewhere with Lyr?

Annie thundered back into the bedroom, carrying two full black bin bags.

'I found yer stuff, sweetheart. Bagged up like trash. Fuckin' mean-spirited bastid. Come on, sweetheart. We're outta here. Ye dinnae need to be around him one minute longer, aye.'

Faye shook her head, feeling the tears leaking down her cheeks; the knot that was in her chest felt like it would choke her.

'Annie, I can't,' she sobbed, plunging her head into her hands as she cried. 'I…I…' but she couldn't tell Annie, not even her best friend, that Rav's child was inside her. She knew that if she did, Annie would storm back into the living room and tell him, and she couldn't. He couldn't know.

'Aw, come on, darlin'. He's no' worth one of your tears.' Annie held her tightly and stroked her hair. 'Let's go home, eh.'

Faye nodded, trying to pull herself together. She'd already booked her train ticket to Edinburgh, though she hadn't told her friend yet. In a couple of days she'd be back in Abercolme, where she'd reopen the shop for a few months. She'd find a way to keep the baby: if she could just go back home, be in her rightful place, then the magic of the Morgans would help her. She knew it, in her bones.

Faye followed Annie back out to the living room, where Rav was still sitting on the sofa. *He hasn't even moved. Not got up to see me, talk to me. Nothing* she thought, anger replacing her tears. *That's how much he ever cared about me.*

'Don't worry, I'm out of your hair now,' Faye said, Annie's arm around her shoulders. 'You can get on with things with Mallory.'

'For fuck's sake, Faye. I'm not with Mallory,' Rav muttered. 'You're obsessed with her. You need help.'

'Don't lie!' Annie yelled.

He stood up, putting his computer to one side.

'It was *you* that cheated on me, Faye. With your faerie king, or one of your witch friends. Oh, don't worry. Mallory told me all about him. The one with the shop? I guess it's nice for you to find someone who speaks the same weird language as you,' he spat, angrily.

'What? Gabriel? We never…' Faye argued, but Rav spoke over her.

'You don't see it, do you? You're so lost in your… magic, your shop, all that stuff your mum and your grandmother taught you, you can't see what's real. *I* was real, Faye. *I* loved you. We could have had a future together, but I could never get to you. It's like you're behind this wall of water. I can't see you clearly, everything's… it's all an illusion. And no matter how hard I shout, you can't hear me.'

Despair overwhelmed Faye. She wanted to tell him so badly: that she was carrying his child. The words sat in her throat like a frog, but she couldn't say them. They would cost her too much.

'I'm sorry,' she whispered. 'I'm sorry for what happened to you. You have no idea how sorry.' She wiped a tear from the side of her eye, and felt the strength of Annie's arm; felt the love of their long friendship filling her. She was sad, but she was also worth more than this. And she was sorry for many things, but she was never going to apologise for who she was.

'I was born a witch, Rav; I was raised a witch; my family, the Morgans, are a family of witches. We've always had this power, and I've spent my whole life being afraid of whatever it is that makes us different. My great-grandmothers, my ancestors: some of them were killed for who they were. Some of them were tortured. So, if you can't see me properly, maybe it's because I was afraid to be seen.'

He didn't reply; Faye knew in that moment that she'd never change his mind. *I know you're not the one for me,* she thought. *I always knew.*

'Come on, darlin'. Let's go.' Annie opened the front door and held out her hand for Faye's. Rav nodded at her, but stayed silent.

In the moment before she walked out of the flat, Faye's eyes alighted on a picture frame. In it, there was a photo of her and Rav; he'd taken it whilst they laid in her bed, back in Abercolme. Before they had come to London, in that bubble of sweetness, when they had holed up in her flat above the shop and done nothing but slept and ate and made love. They had known very little of each other then; though it was months ago, it felt like an age had passed.

In front of the framed photo, a new one had been wedged into the gap where the frame met the glass. The small black and white picture was blurry, but the outline of the foetus was obvious.

Faye's eyes met Rav's, and the tears at what she couldn't say came roaring out of her; the sorrow that she couldn't contain. Annie pulled her through the door and down the stairs; she heard Rav shouting after her, *it's not mine, it's not mine, I'm just looking after her, she had nowhere else to go,* but she couldn't focus, couldn't respond. If that was Mallory's baby, then she must already have been pregnant before going to Falias with Lyr. Or, Lyr had kept Mallory there for as long as he needed her, and sent her back pregnant – time did move differently in the faerie realms. Could it be that she was back, pregnant by Lyr, already?

It was possible. But it was also possible that Mallory's baby wasn't a half-faerie baby at all and someone else's. Someone much closer to home.

As Annie gunned the engine, Faye closed her eyes and reached for the necklace that Moronoe had given her. The cube-shaped jet and citrine beads were cold in her hand.

Chapter 47

The shop was exactly as Faye left it, apart from the thick dust that had accumulated on the shelves while she was away. Faye sank into one of the easy chairs by the old hearth with a deep sigh: five hours on the train from London, followed by a taxi to Abercolme, was a long time travelling. She reached down and rubbed her ankles, which were swollen. She had had morning sickness, though she hadn't realised what it was, and now other things were starting to bother her; she supposed that it would all get worse before it got better.

Faye stared around at the shop, at the pictures on the wall that were so familiar she didn't usually see them: the *Support Your Local Witches* sign that Moddie had hand-drawn and hung behind the counter; the photo of Grandmother in an old gilt frame. The comfort of being home emanated from the thick walls of the old house like heat, wrapping her back up again in its protection. She was home. But the shop also reminded her painfully of Aisha, who had worked there.

She looked at her phone; there were several missed calls from Rav, and a text message. *I'm sorry for the way it all happened.* She deleted the message immediately.

Though she'd refused Moronoe's moon tea, on the train up to Edinburgh Faye had given motherhood a lot of thought, watching a young family in the seats opposite. A mother, about her age, was keeping two little ones occupied – a toddler boy, who wanted to walk up and down the train carriage continually, and an older girl of about five, who sat quietly, colouring in a book with fierce concentration. Faye watched the mother's face move from bright to tired, through patience to irritation over and over again as she walked with the toddler, talked quietly to the girl about her pictures; as they played a game over lunch, and as the toddler snuggled into her for a sleep.

Could I do that? Faye wondered, as the mother caught her eye and smiled. *Do I have that in me, that patience?* She didn't know. It was another kind of power, another kind of strength, to do everything for others, all the time. She guessed that the mother might have a day job too. *Did she have a partner to help with it all?* Faye wondered. If Faye had the baby, she'd be alone. And, if Moronoe was right, the baby would be in danger if she tried to raise it in Abercolme. She'd have to risk that, or hand it over to a faerie queen. Or, some other option that she hadn't yet thought of.

Faye wandered to the kitchenette and found a box of peppermint tea bags in the cupboard. She filled and boiled the kettle; the water and electric was still on; she'd paid all the bills when she was away. Some part of her had known that London was temporary, even if she hadn't wanted to admit it to herself.

She leaned against the kitchen worktop and looked back out into the shop, thinking suddenly about Finn Beatha. It felt like such a long time since he'd first walked into the shop and changed her life completely. She felt a sudden urge to go to Black Sands Beach and feel the wet sand between her toes; it had always been her special place.

She drank her tea and pocketed an energy bar from a box in the cupboard, pulling her coat around her. Abercolme in January was cold and the wind and rain had no mercy, but she went nonetheless. It was hers; she was at home in its icy winds and under its dark skies.

The village was quiet; Faye nodded to a few people she knew, though not well; now that she'd been seen, the rumours would start. *Faye Morgan's back, aye, not with that boyfriend though, wonder what happened there.* And before long the gossip would take into account that she was pregnant. *An' with a bairn too, with no dad.* They'd shake their heads. *All ye expect from a Morgan, aye.*

Perhaps Faye was being unfair. The village opinion of her had certainly changed after Midsummer, when she'd helped the survivors at the concert. But people had short memories.

The beach was dark, but Faye knew her way. The tide was halfway in, and the waves were choppy, blown by the winter wind. Despite the cold, she took off her shoes and socks and rolled up her jeans. She could still just about get into them – before long she'd have to start wearing those pregnancy jeans she'd seen in shops.

The ice-cold water slashed at her ankles as she waded in further, keeping in front of the point where the pebbly sand dropped off in a sudden ledge a few feet out. Her jeans weren't rolled up far enough, and the water soaked them on the second wave, but she didn't care. It was so good to be back in her home element; to feel the freshness of the air and taste the salt on her lips. She closed her eyes and breathed the sea in as she'd done countless times.

For the first time in months, Faye relaxed. Sorrow rose up in her throat, and she let it: she let the tears come and the wail tear itself from her. Spectral, it echoed over the beach, thrust back to the land by the force of the wind on the tide. She wept for Aisha, who she hadn't been able to save. For Rav, who she'd met almost on this spot. *I need help*, she screamed into the night. *I can't raise this baby alone. I don't know what to do. Please, help me.*

The wind screamed back at her; it pulled at her hair, whipping her long plait across her face like a slap. The water pushed at her feet, trying her balance. Faye dropped to her knees, despair filling her. *I can't do this. I can't do this.*

There was a hand on her shoulder, and Faye cried out, stumbling to her feet.

Gabriel Black caught her, and she clutched in desperation at him, burying her head in his chest.

'Hush, hush,' he whispered as Faye sobbed. With a sudden drop in wind, the tide calmed, and they stood together, ankle-deep in the freezing water. 'Faye. All will be well, I promise,' he breathed. They held on to each other under the moonlight: two suffering souls that desperately needed a friend.

Chapter 48

When she opened the door to the shop to enter the house, he reached up for the hagstone charm that hung by the door. Grandmother had made the charm before she was born, threading pebbles with natural holes in them onto a thick string and chanting a spell of protection over it. It was old lore that if you looked through the hole in a hagstone, you could see the faeries that were usually invisible to human eyes; it exposed spells and rendered them useless.

'Morgan magic?' Gabriel smiled wanly. When Faye turned on the shop lights, she saw how gaunt he was; he'd hardly improved since she'd last seen him a couple of weeks ago. Faye nodded, not remarking on his grey pallor or the dark circles under his eyes.

'It's a protection. Against the fae,' she replied. 'Come in and get warm. I'll light the hearth.' The bottom of her jeans were still wet where the sea had splashed them; she was chilled to the bone.

'Can it protect me from nightmares?' Gabriel shuffled in behind her and folded himself carefully into the chair by the fireplace. Faye knelt, arranging kindling, and sat back on her heels as it caught, waiting to add the dry wood stacked in a basket next to the hearth. He closed his eyes as the firelight started flickering over their faces. Faye regarded him cautiously.

'I don't think so.' She wouldn't lie to him: the nightmares would be with him a long time. Yet Faye didn't ask whether Gabriel's terror was the memory of his torture, or the masochistic loss of his torturer Glitonea: she knew it could be either. Still, she was glad of the charm. At the beach, she'd felt watched, and she knew Glitonea and Moronoe's eyes would be on her every moment until she'd had the baby.

'Why did you come?'

Gabriel sighed, his eyes still closed.

'I needed to get away from London, Sylvia, the coven. All of it. You always spoke so lovingly of Abercolme. Clean air, cold sea, wide horizons.' He opened his eyes and stared into the fire that crackled, now that Faye had added two logs. 'I didn't have anywhere else to go.'

'What about Fortune's?' Faye sat in the chair opposite him.

'Penny will look after it until I get back. I trust her.'

'Oh.'

Neither of them said anything more for a moment. *What about Sylvia, has she told you what she did? Has she told you she offered Mallory to Lyr? Or has she told you all it was me?* Faye wanted to ask him, but she could see him slipping away, his eyelids fluttering as exhaustion took hold.

'I'll make up the spare room for you,' she murmured, as her own eyes closed. She'd just close her eyes for minute, she thought. But they were both so exhausted that they slept in the old, sagging chairs, until the early hours when Faye woke up cold, the fire having gone out.

Chapter 49

It was odd, having Gabriel there, but Faye realised that she was grateful for the company.

Faye reopened the shop, closing a little earlier than she used to, to make sure she didn't get tired. She talked to her customers about all the little familiar things – candles, incense, spellbooks. She read their cards and recommended places to visit to tourists – stone circles, natural springs, holy wells. She pottered in her herb garden, and slowly the spring came and the days started to stretch again. Faye made a little altar for Aisha in the shop; it was the least she could do and, somehow, it made her feel a little better. She put a photo of Aisha in a silver frame on the mantelpiece and burned a candle in front of it, arranging crystals and fresh flowers on either side. She would never be able to make it right, but she could remember.

She wrote to Annie, telling her about her pregnancy, but swearing her to secrecy. Annie wrote and called, at first incensed she hadn't known about the baby, but gradually accepting the reasons why. Faye wrote honestly about Gabriel: the night terrors, the sleepwalking and the sorrow he held inside him, like a blunt knife that dug into his heart, but one that he wasn't ready to part with yet. There were good days, too, when Gabriel returned, whistling, from a day walking the coastal path with seashells in his pockets and the spring sun in his eyes.

Gradually, he began putting on weight, and sometimes he helped her in the shop, charming the customers with an occasional flash of the old Gabriel. Yet Faye knew that the faerie road lay on Black Sands Beach and, one day, she suspected that the temptation would prove too much for him. She couldn't keep him from it: he was a grown man. Faye just hoped that the strength that Abercolme was slowly returning to him would be enough to make him resist. Faerie was never far away for either of them, and both Faye and Gabriel knew how to find it if they wanted to.

The power of Murias is too dark for Gabriel, Faye wrote to Annie. *His soul seeks the dark, but it's not strong enough to bear the weight of faerie. I'm afraid for him, but there's nothing I can do. He has to learn to live with it. So do I.*

Faye would always feel responsible for taking Gabriel into Murias, though it had been an accident on her part, and intentional on his. At the same time, she understood what he felt better than anyone. The shadows of faerie were half of who she was, and she desired them; no, she needed them to survive. She regretted Gabriel following her, but she could do nothing for him now except listen, and understand. At the same time, it was a relief to have someone with her. She was seeing a midwife for all the ordinary check-ups, and the villagers popped in now and again to check she was all right. Despite his suffering, having Gabriel there made Faye feel less alone, and caring for him distracted her from the cloud that grew steadily closer: how she'd protect her baby from Glitonea when the time came.

By contrast, Faye had hardly left the shop for months. When they needed food, she ordered it online from a supermarket three villages away and had it delivered. She worked in the shop and spent the evenings with Gabriel playing old board games when he was feeling up to it, or alone, reading in bed, when he wasn't. She wanted nothing taxing; all she wanted was to be home, and wait for the baby. She knew that the queens watched her, and she was uneasy.

*

One night Faye lay staring at the ceiling of her room. She was just a few weeks ahead of her due date and dread had started to seep into the corners of her daily life. She'd heard very little from Rav recently – the phone calls and texts had dissipated reasonably quickly when she didn't reply. The fear that sat at the edge of her awareness, like a toad, waiting, wasn't about Rav.

Moronoe had reassured her that with her protection, Finn and Glitonea could do nothing to her child, but only if Faye gave her the baby to raise in her part of Falias. There was no guarantee of safety, or that Faye would ever get her child back, but she'd failed to think of any other option. She'd considered running away, to another country, but the fae operated in a reality outside of human space and time. Where she was wouldn't matter to them: they would always find her. She'd also, briefly, considered having the baby adopted, but her heart screamed *no*. No, she wouldn't give the baby away. It was hers. And who was to say that Glitonea wouldn't just take the baby away if it was adopted by someone else, anyway?

Finally, she'd gone to what she'd always had: magic. She might not be a faerie queen, but she was a witch, and that meant something.

First, Faye had consulted Grandmother's grimoire for protection spells, and particularly protection against faeries. The hagstone charm was effective for keeping the fae outside one's house, but Faye also made four protection bottles – filling old whisky bottles with offcuts of thread and ribbon and cloth from her spell-making, closing the tops with wax and placing them around the house; she even buried one in the garden.

The closely-packed thread and ribbon would, the book said, distract the lower faerie beings, and act as a faerie catcher. She also sprinkled salt around the boundary of the shop, outside in the garden as well as around the doors, and hung a small perfume bottle on a necklace, filled with bay leaf, rue and rosemary in water, as protection for herself. Grandmother's grimoire, whilst helpful on summoning the faerie kings and queens, was less helpful in protecting oneself against them. *Perhaps that was always our family's problem,* Faye thought.

She was reading the book Gabriel had given her: *Faeries in Their Elements*, by Reverend R W Smith. It was a fascinating story of a Scottish reverend who had been abducted into the faerie realm and returned to tell the tale. Faye flipped through it, scanning for anything useful. If the reverend had managed to escape, then perhaps there was something here. She frowned as she came across something that might have been written in Grandmother's grimoire: the reverend had, after his abduction, always kept a powder of burnt bay leaves, garlic skins and ground clove with him in a small bag, ready to sprinkle on the ground or to dispel *malign faerie spirits,* alongside a short chant:

Break the spell, truth to tell,
Faeries, heed my magic spell!
Dark thy magic, dark thy throne,
I banish thee from hearth and home,
I banish thee from body, mind,
Heart and organs, shadow-kind,
Dark thy magic, dark thy throne,
I bid you leave my heart alone
Break the spell, truth to tell,
Faeries, heed my magic spell!

Faye repeated the chant a few times, unsure whether it would really work or not. As she lay there, her phone screen lit up: it was a text from Annie.

How are you? I'm worried about you.

I'm fine, Faye replied quickly. *Don't worry. The midwife is keeping a close eye on me, and so are the old wives in the village.* She added a smiley face at the end and pressed send, guilty that she was lying to her best friend. She wasn't okay, but she didn't want to worry Annie. Annie knew now that she was pregnant, but not what Moronoe's offer was.

Annie replied with a sad emoji face, and Faye put her phone back on her bedside table, guilt gnawing at her. She'd expected something, some entreaty, a visit or message from one of the queens, both of whom thought they were the child's rightful guardian. Or, at least a dream; Faye had communed with Finn in dream many times. But Faye's dreams had been quiet and strangely unremarkable.

Yet something waited at the edge of things; something was coming, like a cloud over the sea. Faye could feel it; *it's the baby,* she told herself. *That's all. All mothers probably feel like this before the baby comes. You're just nervous. It's a life-changing experience.*

Yet, she wondered whether the baby's arrival should have felt so ominous. Shouldn't she be happy; excited for him to arrive? She was happy. She was looking forward to being a mother. But if it wasn't the baby that was making her feel this way, what was it?

Chapter 50

She dreamt of Finn Beatha.

In the dream, Finn stood before her on the beach. Even though she knew him well – every dip and rise of his perfectly sculpted body, what his smooth honey-brown skin smelt like, how it tasted – it was as though she was seeing him for the first time. He wore the kilt he'd worn onstage when she'd gone to see his band, Dal Riada, play at a bar in Edinburgh with Aisha. Yet, even in the dream, the memory of Aisha made her step back from the faerie king; he had as good as murdered her. Faye had to resist him. He was dangerous.

'I have nothing to say to you!' she shouted. 'Leave me alone!'

'*Sidhe-leth*. Please.' Finn stepped slowly towards her, his hands open and raised up in a submissive gesture. 'I know you are with child. My child. You cannot ignore me.'

Faye felt an uncontrolled hilarity threaten to take her over; it wasn't amusement, but shock that pushed the laugh out of her mouth. She felt consciousness tug at her, as if it rejected what Finn had said.

'Your child? Are you mad?' She heard her own voice: it was high-pitched, not like herself.

Finn reached out to touch her belly.

'You know it is,' he said, softly.

She pushed his hand away. 'Don't you dare touch me. This is Rav's baby.'

'It is mine,' Finn insisted.

'How do you know?' He was barefoot and wore a soft black t-shirt on top of the kilt; his dirty blonde hair had grown a little, and touched his shoulders. Why he'd chosen to wear human clothes to see her instead of his faerie robes, she wasn't sure: perhaps to make her forget what he was. She had to keep it straight, in her mind, who Finn really was. Faye made herself recall his sudden temper, his selfish pout, like a child denied a toy. He is a faerie king, she reminded herself. He has no human morality; he takes what he wants, uses it and discards it. Uses people.

'I know,' he replied, reaching for her. 'Faye. You know it too.'

'It's Rav's baby,' she insisted. 'Moronoe told me.'

'You believe a faerie queen over me. Why?'

'Because she has no reason to lie. Because she is my aunt,' Faye argued back, hotly. 'Because she has never betrayed me and murdered my friends.'

'The fact she is your aunt is nothing to do with anything. She is the High Queen of Falias, and I am at war with her realm. She will have offered to take the baby, yes? Told you that she must have it, otherwise great evil will befall you and the child? Am I right?' He searched her expression; Faye turned her face away. 'Yes. I am.' He nodded.

'She didn't lie,' Faye insisted, doggedly, but she realised Finn was right in questioning whether she should trust Moronoe over anyone else. 'She said she has nothing to do with the war. She is not speaking to Lyr because of it. Her... her palace is not even connected to his,' Faye stammered, searching for something that would explain why she believed Moronoe.

Finn sighed. 'She played on your weaknesses. She knows you have a desire to belong to something, now that your mother and grandmother are gone. She made you believe you had some kind of family bond with her. And she also knew that your relationship with the human – who I tried to protect you from, but you insisted on learning the hard way what manner of man he was – was one fraught with tension. If she could make you believe your baby was his, you would be more likely to give it up, given his treatment of you.'

'You're saying that Lyr and Moronoe have plotted all along to take this baby. Because it's yours.'

'Yes.' Finn reached for her hand. 'She is a powerful queen. Murias has had some victories in the war, and Falias has been looking for a way to destabilise my advantage over the Crystal Castle. Moronoe may have used her magic to help your pregnancy in the first place. That, I do not know. But I do know that if she has my child in her kingdom, she can use it against me.'

'You talk about your children as if they are weapons. All of you. This scheming, it's so….' Faye exhaled, exhausted. 'I don't know what to believe. If the baby's yours, why didn't you tell me before?'

'Moronoe and Glitonea constructed a web of magic around you, Faye... I didn't know until you called out in this moment. I am sorry.'

Though it was a dream, Faye still felt Finn's familiar magic coursing through their linked hands.

'How can I believe you?' she whispered 'How can I believe anything?'

'You don't have to believe me, Faye.' Finn drew her to him softly, and kissed her cheek. 'But you are the mother of my child now.'

She woke with a start, still feeling Finn's hand in hers. Regardless of what she thought of Finn, she couldn't deny that the link was still strong between them.

If the baby was Finn's, then it thrust her even deeper into the faerie world: Faye had no idea how she'd be able to navigate the road ahead of her.

But at the same time, if it was Finn's baby, then it gave her more power over him than she had ever had.

Faye watched the dawn filter in through her light coloured curtains, and felt the baby kick for the first time. She rested her hand thoughtfully on her belly, not knowing what to feel.

Chapter 51

Faye woke up early, confused by the wetness she lay in until she realised that her water had broken. Carefully, she hauled herself out of bed and went to the bathroom, trying to clean herself up; the stretchy jersey nightdress she'd started wearing at night was soaked through. She peeled it off and ran the shower, climbing carefully into the bath and out again to wash herself as best she could.

Gabriel wasn't there. It wasn't unusual – often he'd be gone in the early morning, walking the shore, but today she needed him. Faye resisted feeling abandoned and instead, she called the midwife, who asked if her contractions had started – they hadn't, as far as Faye could tell – and said that she'd be out to check on Faye in an hour or so. *In the meantime, just take it easy and let me know if anything changes*, the midwife said cheerily at the end of the phone. *Have a cup of tea and put your feet up.*

It was July, and the height of a heatwave. Soon it would be Lughnasadh, the old Celtic festival of the first harvest; when she was a child, Grandmother had taught her how to make corn dollies with wheat fresh from the fields around Abercolme. It was a symbolic gesture; saving the ripe corn to use in winter.

Faye stood at her bedroom window, naked, looking out on the garden below. Life was in bloom everywhere. She was part of nature, and, in her late pregnancy, she'd come to understand much more instinctively the symbolism of the ripe corn goddesses of the old ways that Moddie had told her about. She was as ripe with life as the apple tree below: it was so heavy with fruit that they dropped off onto the lawn and wooden decking below with loud thumps; sometimes it woke her in the night.

With one hand on her belly, she thought of all the things she looked forward to sharing with her child: telling him the stories that Grandmother told her; making corn dollies, foraging for plants at the seashore.

Yet, already, the sun was relentlessly hot. The roses were parched and the fresh herbs were browning at the edges of their delicate leaves, even though she'd been watering them faithfully. Nature wasn't kind, or moral. It was an eternal cycle of life and death: it drew no distinctions between hunger and glut.

Apprehension made her step away from the window, though she couldn't explain why. She got dressed and made her way carefully down the stairs; she'd need to let the midwife in the shop door.

Downstairs, she made a cup of peppermint tea in the kitchenette; there were still no contractions; she wondered when they would start. Rather than sitting, she opened the shop door and stood in the early morning sun to drink her tea.

Gabriel, I need you – she spoke his name into the air. *The baby is coming. Please, I need you here.* He had promised to be with her, and he wasn't here. She picked up her phone and called his number, and heard his ringtone from the soft chair in front of the fireplace. He'd left it behind.

Her own phone rang again almost instantly. It was the midwife, saying that her car wouldn't start – she'd be with Faye as soon as she could. Were there any contractions yet? Faye told her there weren't, and asked whether that was usual. *Yes, that's quite usual, don't worry*, the midwife said. *Let me know if they start. I'll be there as soon as I can.*

Faye finished her tea and made some toast, but she was restive. She decided to walk down to the beach; walking was supposed to induce labour, wasn't it? She missed it; she'd hardly been there in the past months. She ignored the fact that she was already in labour, technically; that the contractions could come at any time, and the midwife had told her to put her feet up. And if she walked down to the beach, she'd probably find Gabriel.

She felt like a duck, waddling down to the beach. She took the quieter road that went around the village rather than through it – she didn't really want to see anyone, and have them ask about the baby.

As she walked away from the shop, something shifted; it was like a cloud moved over the blazing sun overhead and shielded her eyes from a glare that she'd been squinting in all this time – only, it was inside her head rather than outside. Faye stopped dead, the beach visible in front of her.

A sudden clenching sensation made her hold her back; she took a deep breath, and it passed. She waited for another, but nothing came, and so she resumed walking slowly to the beach. She supposed it was a contraction; it wasn't too far to get home from where she was if she needed to turn around.

The sand at the edge of the deserted beach was dry; the grasses that grew at the sandy boundary had turned to straw in the heatwave. Scotland without rain for this long was almost unheard of; the people of Abercolme were suffering. Faye had been telling customers for weeks to stay out of the sun, to drink plenty of water to avoid heatstroke and dehydration. She'd also sold out of calendula cream for the sunburn that striped the villagers' milky Celtic skin. She hadn't visited the beach because she was afraid of being near the faerie road; at least now, she'd come armed with protection. The bay, rue and rosemary charm hung around her neck, and she'd put pouches of the reverend's suggested powder of burnt bay leaves, garlic skins and ground clove in all her coat pockets. Last, she still had the black obsidian crystal Lyr had given her as protection, tucked into her bra. It had worked when she was in Murias, so perhaps it would keep her safe from the faerie queens in some way.

She slipped off her sandals, letting the tide cool her hot feet.

Faye took a few more steps into the sea; she didn't care that it wet the hem of her dress. She shaded her eyes from the sun as it glinted on the water, glittering like jewels.

Another contraction came, and she instinctively crouched down as the dull squeezing ache came and went. As it faded, the tide swept away, back to the sea, leaving her feet exposed in the wet sand. Next to her foot sat a hagstone; a medium-sized pebble with a hole all the way through the middle.

She picked it up; it sat comfortably in her hand.

'Gabriel?' Faye cried out, looking around for her friend, but there was still no sign of him, and her voice was consumed by a wind that blew it back to her. She felt another contraction coming, and realised their frequency was increasing. She'd left her phone back at the house; she cursed herself for her stupidity.

'Gabriel!' she shouted before the pain could hit her; she breathed into it, the way the midwife had taught her. She wanted to sit down. Gradually, the feeling abated again, but it left her legs weak. *I need to sit down,* she thought.

Clouds appeared on the horizon; Faye was sure they hadn't been there a moment ago. On the horizon, lightning flashed, and the wind that had pushed at her the moment before grew in power, raising the waves around her knees. She turned and staggered out of the water. The villagers had been saying a storm was coming for days, and the atmosphere had that hot closeness, the stillness before thunder rolled in.

Sure enough, in the same second that she thought it, there was a rumble of atmospheric pressure in the distance, off the shore. *Home. I need to go home*, she thought. Her body was insistent, and she needed to listen to it. *I was stupid to come here. Why did I come at all?*

The pressure in the air made her ears pop. The clouds had rolled in towards land faster than she thought they could, and lightning forked down into the sea from the charcoal-grey clouds that formed above her head. Faye took a deep breath as an intense contraction came, making her fall to her knees and groan in pain as the storm gathered above her.

But when she looked up, it wasn't Gabriel she saw in front of her, but Glitonea, the High Queen of Murias, who faced Moronoe, the High Queen of Falias, on Faye's opposite side, and both regarded her with the glittering, cold stares of beings that weren't human; of queens that always got what they wanted.

Chapter 52

Faye cried out, trying to get to her feet. 'Please. The baby's coming.' Her first instinct was to ask for help, but she realised her error instantly: she'd receive no compassion from either faerie queen.

'I will help you, *sidhe-leth*.' Glitonea's eyes never left Moronoe's, and the tone of her voice was icy. 'Yet I hoped you would call on me before now, when it is almost too late. Tell the Queen of Falias that she may leave us. She has no business here.'

Faye managed to get to her feet, and backed away from the tide that was sweeping in; at the edge, it carried branches, bottles, rusted cans and other wrack, which it never usually did – the shore of Abercolme was a clean one, as a rule. Yet suddenly, the sea seemed to be attacking the shore with anything it could find. Glitonea stood in the tide, and Moronoe on the sand. Both queens were taller than humans, and Moronoe's heft and girth was at odds with a kind of translucence that emanated from the faerie queen of water. Lightning crackled between them, and the day had darkened to a kind of twilight.

'Niece. I asked you to call on me when the baby was coming, and you have not. Will you ask me now to take you to my realm, where I will help your labour, and protect the child from this vulture?' Moronoe boomed over the storm. 'You do not have long before the baby comes. Take my hand and all will be well.'

'No,' Faye cried out, clutching her belly as another contraction came. This time, the pain left her breathless. 'Please. Leave me alone. I won't give you the baby. Either of you,' she panted. She reached for the obsidian crystal she always carried inside her bra and held it aloft, as if to fend them off.

Glitonea laughed; her eyes glowed under the cowled blue hood of her robe, and flicked her hand: the crystal flew from Faye's grip and landed on the sand several metres away.

'You have already given him to me. We have struck a bargain. I do not need any further permission,' she said, reaching out her hand. 'All I have to do is touch you, and he will be mine. Do not worry, *sidhe-leth*. You will not be harmed. You will be free to make as many more babies as you like with your human lovers, after this. But this one is mine.' Glitonea's tone was dismissive.

'There is no way that I'm letting you take my child!' Faye screamed. 'I banish you! Both of you! Back to the realms from which you came!' The contractions were coming fast now, and her mind was focused on the pain. *Breathe through it, breathe through the pain*, she told herself, her hands clutching at the wet sand in panic. She knew, with a sudden flash of inspiration, that she'd have to give birth here, on the beach. There was no time to get away now.

Faye held up the hagstone to her right eye and looked through it at Glitonea.

'Break the spell; truth to tell!' she cried out, and Glitonea took a step backwards; Faye repeated it with Moronoe. She pulled her strength together as hard as she could and recited the faerie protection spell from the book Gabriel had given her: *Faeries in Their Elements*, by Reverend R W Smith, reaching into her pocket and opening the felt bag. Faye sprinkled its contents around herself in a circle, as wide as she could make it.

Break the spell, truth to tell,
Faeries, heed my magic spell!
Dark thy magic, dark thy throne,
I banish thee from hearth and home,
I banish thee from body, mind,
Heart and organs, shadow-kind,
Dark thy magic, dark thy throne,
I bid you leave my heart alone
Break the spell, truth to tell,
Faeries, heed my magic spell!

She grunted with the effort and returned to her hands and knees, panting hard.

'Stupid girl! Do you think your folk charms can stop me?' Glitonea crowed, and reached forward for Faye's belly with her long, blue-white fingers. But as the herb powder touched the sand, it raised a wall of shadow around Faye. Glitonea's black fingernails grazed it, and she pulled her hand back as if in pain. 'What is this sorcery?' she raged, and threw herself at the shadow wall, but it threw her back like an electric fence.

'Faye. Look at me.' Moronoe's hands were outstretched; Faye so wanted to fall into them; wanted the support that they promised. Of the two queens, Moronoe was at least her kin in some kind of distant way; what if Finn had been lying when he said that Moronoe wanted her child for her own reasons? Faye had believed her when she said she wasn't involved in Lyr's war against Murias and the other faerie realms, but that didn't necessarily mean she could be trusted. 'Faye. Undo this charm. We only want to help you. You are our kin, Faye. Dear child. There is no need for this,' she cooed, her voice honey, but Faye resisted.

'No.' Faye panted, grateful for the protection of her own spell, though she was unsure how long it would last. She looked up, meeting Glitonea's furious gaze. 'Is it Finn's baby? Tell me the truth. For once.' Faye grimaced as another contraction came, searing and intense.

'What kind of whore doesn't know whose child she carries?' Glitonea laughed cruelly; the thunder rumbled and cracked directly above them. 'You do not deserve this child if you do not even know that. Give it to me and I will make sure it is raised in our royal house. And, you, fat bitch: get out of my way. You know as well as I do that when a mortal makes a bargain, you have no right to stand in my way to claim it.' Glitonea shoved Moronoe out of her way and began circling the shadow boundary. 'Your spell will only hold so long, Faye. And when it breaks, I will take the baby. You might as well give it to me gently as have me force you,' she threatened, snarling.

Faye, on her hands and knees, felt the desire to push with the next contraction. She had no choice; the baby was coming, and wouldn't wait. Her perception reduced itself to a kind of tunnel of pain in which there was nothing apart from the searing, tearing pain in her abdomen and the breath that heaved in her chest. Faye rested her forehead on the sand and tasted it in her mouth. Dimly, at the edge of her perception, she heard Gabriel's voice. She looked up, racked with pain, and saw him running across the headland towards the beach.

No, keep away. Run away! Faye wanted to cry out, but she had no strength left.

'Faye. Say the word and I will take you to Falias. I will ensure you are cared for, and the child is safe,' Moronoe called out. 'Just say yes, and this ordeal will be over. You do not have to fulfil a bargain such as the one the Queen of Murias proposed.' Her voice was gentle and motherly, but Faye ignored her. She felt the last, biggest contraction hit her and she screamed with the pain. She felt the baby between her thighs and reached back with her hand for it; there was nothing to protect it from the elements. *Help me, anyone, anything, please,* she prayed, rolling onto her back.

The sky went black, and everything became completely silent.

Chapter 53

Morgana Le Fay, Mistress of Magick and Queen of the Castle of the Moon, towered over Black Sands Beach like a statue carved into the headland, or an ancient effigy, risen from a land long-forgotten under the waves.

There was a sudden hush, and everything stopped: the wind, the waves, the thunder. Everything found a moment of stillness, and in that stillness, the sun shone a bright, wide beam of light onto the beach.

Faye, on her knees, feeling the baby come, was only dimly aware of it: all her attention was focused on the pain, and the overwhelming desire to push. The pain was a dark red sea, and every breath brought her to the surface for a brief second of respite before sinking back into its churning depths. There was nothing but her body and the child that seemed desperate and yet unable to get free of it: like a fish in a net, grasping and bucking, terrified of the air that awaited it, and the loss of the comfort of water.

Morgana Le Fay, the Faerie Queen of the Crystal Castle, the place where all faerie magic ended and began, held up her left hand. Her skin was black and scaled like a snake or a kelpie, and she had no fingernails. She wore a silver robe with a hood that lay on her shoulders; the outer edges of her were indistinct, shadowy; but her gaze was as though moonlight projected through slits cut in a black mask.

At her command, the two faerie queens, Moronoe and Glitonea, froze in stillness like the storm they had created. Without speaking, Morgana swept Faye into her arms and disappeared into the moonlight.

*

Faye awoke to the sound of quiet singing. She tried to sit up, but couldn't; immobility forced her head back against the soft pillows that held her in a reclining position. Her eyes adjusted to the pinkish light.

She lay in a wide, white bed in the centre of the seven-pointed Crystal Castle of the Moon. It was exactly as she remembered from before: made of a pink, glowing crystal, the walls reached up into towers, and the floor under her featured a seven pointed star that mimicked the shape of the castle in black crystal of some kind – jet, perhaps, or obsidian, like Lyr's crystal. Apart from her bed, there was nothing and no-one else there. The singing, which sounded like someone was nearby, appeared to be coming from the castle itself.

Remembering the beach – that she'd been on her hands and knees, giving birth as the two faerie queens argued over her baby – her hands went instinctively to her belly. Something was wrong. The baby. Where was the baby? She could feel nothing at all from her breastbone downwards: no pain, no movement from the child. Her belly was slightly deflated, though it was nowhere near flat.

'Where am I? Where's my baby?!' Faye screamed, terror giving her strength; despite her paralysis, she pushed herself up on her arms and looked around her. 'Please! Where have you taken my baby?!'

Her voice echoed back at her from the crystalline walls; there was no answer.

Faye started to cry. Despite everything, the child had been taken from her. She knew this was the realm of Morgana Le Fay, and was regarded as the centre of all magic in the faerie realms. What did that mean for her and the child? Did it mean that Glitonea had won, and brought them here? Or Moronoe? It seemed unlikely that it was Faye's aunt; surely Moronoe would have taken her to her own queendom. So, she must be here at the behest of Glitonea. Which meant that she would never see her child again…

There was a sudden movement in the air, and Morgana Le Fay appeared next to the bed. Faye took a deep breath at the faerie queen's presence; they had met before, once, and Faye had forgotten what an intense experience it was, being in the same space as the Mistress of Magic.

Morgana's appearance had changed; now, as she laid a hand on Faye's brow, she appeared as a maiden – young, milk-skinned, with waist length white hair; she wore a silver crescent moon circlet on her forehead and a white garment that suggested an old fashioned nurse, with a long apron over a longer, full-skirted dress. She held a bundle in her arms.

Faye's eyes widened, and reached for it. It felt as though her heart was exploding with a warm desperation.

'My baby! Give him to me. Is it a boy? Or a girl? Please, Morgana. Please,' she begged, alight with an electric blue panic that surged from her womb and clutched her heart in its cold grip. It was more than worry, more than anxiety: she *needed* to hold her child, like she needed to breathe and eat and drink. It was her body that told her; the baby was part of her. It needed to return to her.

Morgana smiled as a thin cry reverberated into the crystal chamber.

'You can do better than that, little one.' She held him aloft, above her head, and shook him gently. Faye flinched, reaching out for him. The baby cried, louder now. The faerie queen cocked her head, listening to the baby wail, and lowered the bundle so that she could study it dispassionately. 'It is a boy,' she added.

'Please. Give me my child.' Faye tried to move, but was still motionless from the chest down.

Morgana smiled and brought the baby back down and, as Faye watched, unhooked her apron and unbuttoned the white dress underneath.

'All in good time, *sidhe-leth*,' she said, and held the bundle to her naked breast.

'No! He isn't yours. Please, Morgana. Please, give him to me!' Faye cried, the blue electricity spiking and cutting into her aura. She felt as if she was being slowly torn in two.

The faerie queen turned up the white sheet in which the baby was wrapped, so that Faye couldn't see his face. Faye watched with the possessive horror of a new mother as her son suckled at the faerie queen's milk.

'Yes. Drink, child,' Morgana murmured, turning away from Faye. Faye felt a tear roll down her cheek.

'Why can't I move? What have you done to me?' she screamed at Morgana, but the faerie queen kept her back turned.

'We have given you the gift of a painless delivery,' she replied, levelly. 'Many human women beg for it when their time comes. You should be grateful. The paralysis will wear off soon.'

'You can't... keep him from me,' Faye panted, trying to pull herself up the bed and failing. *A boy. The baby was a boy, like Finn had predicted. Did that mean it was Finn's?*

'Do not be sad, Faye Morgan,' the faerie queen said. 'Now I have given him the milk of the faerie realm, he has my magick in him as well as yours. This will be a son of the realms as none has been before. He is the one that songs have been sung of, *sidhe-leth*.'

'Why? Why did you bring me here?' Faye appealed, holding her hands out for her baby. 'And where is Finn? If this is his child, why isn't he here?'

Morgana held out a glass of water; Faye took it with her spare hand and drank thirstily.

'I did not say that the baby was his,' Morgana answered coolly, as Faye tipped the glass up to get the last of the water.

'Is it his? Finn?' Faye demanded, but the faerie queen smiled and shook her finger playfully in Faye's face.

'You will see soon enough,' she chided. Frustration and fear tore at Faye again; she felt as though she was going mad. Morgana was torturing her by not letting her have the baby. She was holding her hostage, but why?

'Who won? Of the two queens? Glitonea? Did you take me for her?' Faye handed the glass back to the queen: it disappeared in her hands as if it had never existed.

'Neither of them. I brought you here. You must remember I am impartial. I am not part of their petty rivalries, and my magic surpasses all magic.' Morgana laid the baby in a cradle made of plaited green reeds a few feet away from the bed; from where she lay, Faye couldn't see into it. Her heart and stomach lurched with grief. Every second that the baby wasn't with her, she felt him pulling away from her; renouncing his humanity and becoming more and more faerie. If she could only reach him and feed him from her breast, he would be hers. She ached for him.

'Why? Why not let whichever of them have me?' Faye was crying, and couldn't stop. Morgana sat down on the side of the bed and placed a cool cloth on her brow. Faye could smell lavender and something else; another, more musky herbal smell.

'Try to be calm, Faye. I intervened because Finn Beatha asked me to watch over you and the child.' Morgana's tone was soothing, but Faye railed against it. She'd be soothed when she had her baby, and not before.

'Finn?' she took some deep breaths to try and regain her composure.

Morgana looked grave. 'It is best that you recover and look after the child. You are safe here.'

'Where is Finn?' Faye kept her voice low so as not to wake the baby, but she was desperate, and the baby stirred, half-woken by the urgency in her voice. 'Why won't you tell me if he is the baby's father? Is he?' She had to know.

'He has been captured in battle. In the kingdom of Gorias, the faerie realm of Air,' Morgana replied.

'What?' Faye cried; the baby stirred again, and she lowered her voice. 'Captured? How?'

'The legions of Falias. Lyr's son, Luathas, took him in battle. He is alive, held prisoner there.' Morgana sighed. 'The battle has grown intense. All sides wish to control my castle.'

'But none of them can. You're more powerful than all of them,' Faye whispered. 'Please. My baby…' she held out her arms. 'Please let me hold him,' the desperation was turning now; Faye felt a wall of despair coming for her. *What if she never got to hold her child?*

'In good time. Finn Beatha did you a good deed, Faye Morgan. I was surprised, but it seems he has… feelings for you. Perhaps. But more importantly, there is a prophecy that some of them have interpreted – they think there is a way for me to be overthrown.' Morgana smiled, untroubled. 'Finn Beatha believes in this prophecy. He believes that your child will be the one to take my castle.'

'But that doesn't make sense. If he thinks that, why did he ask you to protect us? And why would you protect the child that will one day destroy you? Don't you believe the prophecy?' Faye hugged her arms in an attempt at comfort, but the grief for the child just a few feet away was overpowering. 'Please. Please, Morgana. My baby. Please give him to me,' she begged again, but the queen of the Crystal Castle of the Moon ignored Faye, and wrapped her long hands in each other.

'I believe it. How it transpires, I cannot predict. I play my part in the weaving and unravelling of life. I am of the Moon, and the Moon is changeable. It waxes and wanes. Your son has drunk of my power. That may mean that he will challenge me, one day, for power. Or it may mean that my milk has protected me from him. We will see. But I chose to take control of the prophecy of my ending. I chose not to let it be decided by Moronoe or Glitonea.'

'Can I see him? Finn?'

'He is in Gorias.'

'Does that mean yes or no?'

'It means that is where he is.'

Faye felt as though Morgana's every answer was a stream of mystery and obstruction.

'You're not telling me anything. And what do I do next, anyway? Stay here forever?'

'You cannot stay here for long. But I can protect you in the human world.' A soft sensation of pins and needles had started in Faye's toes, and she wiggled one set carefully. Her body was starting to awaken. Morgana couldn't keep her from her baby much longer.

Morgana turned the cold cloth on the forehead over. 'Every one of the faerie realms seeks this child. I will protect you both until he becomes old enough to walk into his power.'

'How?' Faye stared at the woven reed cradle. How could anyone so small and helpless hold such power over the entire faerie realm?

'How is not your concern,' Morgana sighed.

'And Finn? Will he… will he come back?' Faye's emotions were a jumble. Part of her was elated that Finn had been captured. He had caused Aisha's death and the deaths of other humans. Finn was amoral, dangerous, selfish. But a deep, instinctive part of her grieved for him. Even if he wasn't the father. He had been her lover, and – indirectly – he had saved her child on the beach.

'It is unclear,' Morgana said as a wave of tiredness overtook Faye. She felt her eyes closing, and Morgana's gentle touch lifting the cloth away. 'But I have never known Finn Beatha to lose his grip on the things he wants. He wants you, and he will want your child.'

The faerie queen stood up and went to the crib. Faye watched her fearfully, dread rising in her gut as Morgana bent over and reached her black, scaly long-fingered hands into it.

'Please don't hurt him.' Faye felt the tears come again; she was helpless. She still couldn't move.

'I would not hurt him,' Morgana said, reprovingly, as she laid the swaddled baby in Faye's outstretched arms at last. 'I will protect him, and you.'

'Oh, thank goodness.' Faye held the baby to her, and relief flooded her still-paralysed body.

'He will need a name before long,' Morgana warned. 'It is unlucky to be without a name, especially in the faerie realms.'

Chapter 54

It was the baby's name day, and Faye had taken him for a walk in the sling she'd finally worked out how to use, hoping to get him to have a nap before everyone arrived for the garden party she and Gabriel had planned for the afternoon. Gabriel had ushered her out of the shop before turning the "Open" sign to "Closed"; he was setting up the buffet and putting up the decorations while she was gone.

As Faye walked through the village, people stopped her to coo over the baby and ask how he was getting on, or how she was feeling – some even asked after Gabriel, who was becoming quite the celebrity in Abercolme. Having baby Alasdair had apparently changed Faye in the eyes of the Abercolme villagers: from suspicious witch to acceptable mother. Faye realised in speaking to some of her neighbours – some, that she hadn't exchanged words with for years – that she'd suddenly been admitted into a club she'd never known existed: as a parent, she now had something in common with every other parent on the planet.

Gabriel would never be totally free from the grip of Murias. Faye had no idea how he had managed to evade Glitonea's grasp at the beach that day, but she suspected Morgana had a hand in protecting him. Some of his old sparkle had returned. He had started talking about returning to London and to Fortune's, but he wasn't in a hurry: he pretended that he was staying for Faye, to help her with the baby, which may have been partly true – Gabriel was surprisingly good with Alasdair and could often get him to sleep when Faye couldn't. The Abercolme air had brought colour back to Gabriel's cheeks, and he was beginning to sleep better. Whole weeks passed when there were no nightmares at all. He had offered to be gone for the name day, suggesting that no-one wanted a recovering addict at a party, but Faye had told him off. He was family now.

Annie's busy filming schedule at *Coven of Love* had an autumn break, and she and Susie were coming to stay; Faye had also invited Ruby and some of her friends from the village: Muriel from the bakery was bringing a huge cake she'd made Alasdair, and the minister had offered to do the naming ceremony, much to Faye's surprise and insistence that it wasn't a christening. But Faye thought it would be nice to have everyone together in the old Morgan house. It would feel like the house had a family again, and Faye needed family. So did Alasdair.

The autumn sun glowed golden orange on Faye's auburn curls as she walked; she shielded Alasdair's face from it with her hand, but relished its warmth on her shoulders. Following one of the small roads that led to the beach, she walked under the yellow, gold and russet leaves that fell from the trees like autumn confetti.

After passing out in the Crystal Castle, Faye had awoken in her own bed with Alasdair lying on her chest. Both of them had been bathed, dressed and cared for; Faye was completely healed from the birth, and felt strong and clear-headed. Alasdair seemed none the worse for being delivered on a beach, and fed happily when she breastfed him.

There was no other message or sign from Morgana other than Faye and the baby were well, and nothing bad had happened to them. However she was protecting Faye and Alasdair from the faerie queens, Morgana's magic seemed to be working. There was no hint of threat or danger anywhere; Faye had no dreams, sudden visions or communications that suggested Glitonea or Moronoe could reach her. Faye was so busy, and so preoccupied with Alasdair, that she had little time to worry about it. For the moment, as long as they were safe, that was enough.

Black Sands Beach spread out in front of Faye; the horizon shone gold with the afternoon sun. There was no-one else there, as ever. Faye walked to the tide, kicked off her sandals, and stood in the cold water. It seemed a different place to the beach where the queens had warred over her; where she'd crouched and prayed for help, knocked over by pain. But it *was* the same place, and Faye bent her head respectfully to the water and the sand. These lines between the elements were the places of magic, and she'd never forget their power.

Alasdair squawked a little; he would only go off to sleep with constant movement and often grew impatient when she stood still, so Faye walked along the tideline, stopping short of the house that was once Rav's. She was surprised to see a SOLD sign outside it. Her thoughts turned to him, and the sonogram picture she'd seen at his flat. Mallory was pregnant, but was it Rav's baby, or Lyr's? And if it was Lyr's child, would it spend its life in Falias, being trained to be Luathas's expendable double, or would Lyr have another fate planned for it?

Faye hoped, for Mallory's sake, that the baby was Rav's. They could have a normal life together, in that case, and the baby could grow up a normal child. Faye might have disliked Mallory, but she knew the pain of having your baby stolen by the fae – even if, in her case, it had only seemed that way for a short while – and she wouldn't wish it on anyone. She realised that she wished them well. Perhaps they could be happy together.

Faye turned away from that side of the beach and strode through the rocks just before the point where grass met sand, humming a lullaby to

Alasdair. *Please sleep, little one*, she crooned to him. *Sleep, my darling.* Alasdair's eyes started to flutter closed.

Thank goodness, she thought, retracing her steps along the beach. If she kept going for another forty minutes or so, that would be enough to get the baby through another couple of hours of a party. She couldn't wait to see Annie and Ruby, and she knew it would be good for Gabriel too.

It wasn't often that she allowed herself to think of Finn – she felt, somehow, that it was dangerous, reaching out to him with her mind – but she couldn't avoid it, being on the beach. It would always be a place synonymous with him.

Her and Finn's connection was so strong that he'd been able to visit her in dreams and appear to her in the human world, but now, as she thought of him, she felt a curious nothingness, a slackness at the end of the line. *Where are you?* she thought, fiercely, but there was no reply.

Faye closed her eyes, continuing to walk, holding her sandals in one hand, feeling the wet sand between her toes. She didn't want Finn, but she wanted some kind of closure from him. That he wouldn't bother her, but, most importantly, that he would leave Alasdair alone. She believed in Morgana's protection, but nothing had so far protected her from Finn Beatha.

Finn? Speak to me she appealed again in her mind, and a sudden vision came to her.

Finn Beatha sat in a dark cell, shadows masking the ethereal beauty of his face. His knees were steepled, and he hugged himself in the dark.

Faye opened her eyes, startled; her sudden stop jarred Alasdair, who fretted for a few moments until she had begun walking again, and returned to sleep. Faye had never seen Finn look so small, so miserable; he had never been anything but tall, imperious, beautiful;

he was a faerie king, a powerful being. She semi-closed her eyes again to try to return to the vision, but it had gone, and she had to keep her eyes open to walk, otherwise Alasdair would wake up.

He was imprisoned in Gorias. He was suffering, and being kept against his will.

He deserves everything he gets for murdering Aisha, Faye thought, balling her fists up with the anger and grief of her friend's death. *And the others. See how you like it*, she raged. Something had happened in the war he was fighting, and he was losing. She didn't care which side won or lost: all Faye cared about now was keeping Alasdair safe. *They may think he's the child of a prophecy, and they can fight each other for him for a thousand years, but they will never have my child* she vowed, her heart full of such fierce love for Alasdair that it felt as if it would consume her. If Finn had to suffer to keep Alasdair from harm – or, even if Finn's imprisonment had no effect on anything – so be it. In fact, as long as Alasdair was protected, Faye didn't care about the faerie realms at all. Her own half-fae nature was nothing compared to being his mother.

After she had walked home the long way, letting Alasdair sleep, she returned home to find that Annie, Ruby and Susie had all arrived, and there was no opportunity to tell anyone about her vision. Even if she had had the chance, she realised she wouldn't say anything: this was Alasdair's day, and she wouldn't ruin it by talking about Finn. Everyone was in the back garden, drinking champagne; Susie handed her a glass.

'We started without you.' She kissed Faye on the cheek. 'It's so good to see you, Faye. And this must be Alasdair!' She held out her finger and the baby grasped it and held it firmly.

'You too!' Faye gazed around at the garden. Gabriel had been busy: the trees were draped in bunting and white paper garlands, a trestle table bulged with food and drink and music played in the background.

Annie enveloped Faye and Alasdair in a bear hug until the baby squealed, and she reluctantly let go.

'Aye, he's a bonny wee thing!' she exclaimed, tickling Alasdair under the chin. Recovered from his squashing, he gummed a smile at Annie. 'An' what a smile, eh?' She beamed at him, and cast a concerned eye over Faye. 'Ye alright, sweetheart? How's he treatin' ye, the wee bairn?'

'I'm fine, I'm fine!' Faye felt tears in her eyes and wiped them away. They were happy tears; she'd missed Annie so much. 'It's so good to see you.'

'Stop it, ye'll make me start,' Annie chided.

'Gabriel's been a huge help.' Faye smiled at Ruby and Gabriel hugging; they'd clearly missed each other.

'He's looking a lot better.' Susie nodded. 'You were kind to let him stay. It's clearly done him the world of good.'

'Honestly, it's as good for me as him. I think if he hadn't appeared on the beach that day, I dunno… I don't think I'd have coped alone.' Faye kissed Alasdair's head as he fussed a little. 'Gabriel was in a real state when he got here. But he seems to have turned a corner.'

'Aye, well, the air's good up here.' Annie looked away, pretending to study the buffet.

'What?' Faye found Annie so easy to read after all these years; something was up.

'Oh, nothin'. Just…' Annie sighed. 'Ah dunno, Faye. I've been away twice when ye needed me. It isnae right, that's all.'

Susie hugged Annie.

'Come on, babe, we've talked about this,' she said, kindly. 'Faye's a grown up.'

'I am,' Faye agreed. 'It's okay, Annie. You've waited so long to get a job like *Coven of Love*. You've got a life in London. We'll still see each other.' She held Annie's hand, squeezing it. She would never tell Annie how much she missed her; that, selfishly, she would love it if Annie came back to Abercolme. She wouldn't tell her, because she loved Annie, and when you loved people, you did what was best for them.

There was a pile of presents on the end of the table nearest to her, and Faye's eye was suddenly drawn to a strange little woven basket sitting on top. Instinctively, she let go of Annie's hand and picked it up; Susie was refilling Annie's glass.

Cradling Alasdair with one hand, Faye put the box down on the table so that she could lift the lid with her other hand.

Inside, there was a note.

Blessings on his naming day to my grandson. A baby without a name is forever in danger, the note read; it was written in a spiky, unusual script, in a dark brown ink on thick parchment. *My grandson.* Faye stared at the words in shock.

There was only one person this could be from.

Under the note, a small necklace of black tourmaline beads sat amongst red, gold and yellow autumnal leaves. *Lyr.*

The air caught in Faye's throat; panic overwhelmed her.

Faye caught Gabriel's eye across the garden. He read her expression and hurried over.

'What is it?'

She showed him the note, unable to speak, cradling Alasdair closer to her.

Gabriel picked the box up and took it inside the house without a word. Faye tried to rearrange her face into a happy expression as her friends laughed and chatted; she drained her glass of champagne. Alasdair seemed unaffected by her tension and gurgled at her; she kissed his cheeks, and felt some of her poise returning.

Gabriel returned in a few moments, his hands empty.

'Where did you put it?' she asked quietly. The fact that Lyr – or one of his fae minions – had been here, in her house, put her on edge.

'It's all right. It's just a gift,' he murmured, rearranging some bowls of salad.

'But it means… he can get to us. That they can all get to us.' Faye's heart fluttered like a bird against Alasdair's soft weight.

'I don't think so. Or, whatever protection it is, perhaps it's not so much that they can't get to you. It's just protection from anything harmful. A gift isn't harmful,' Gabriel reassured her.

'How do you know?' she whispered, hugging the baby to her.

'I don't. But what else can we do? Hope, that's all.' Gabriel smiled at Muriel as she set a huge white-iced celebration cake down on the trestle table. On it, she had iced *Welcome, Alasdair Morgan*. Faye was glad he had a name, and that they were making it plain to whoever was watching. Lyr's message was right: a baby without a name was in danger from the faerie realm, and that was something she was determined Alasdair would never be.

She swallowed down her apprehension. If Lyr's gift was genuine, then she had nothing to fear. If it was some kind of threat, Morgana would hear about it. And Faye would renew the magical protections around the house until she, Gabriel and Alasdair were safe inside a crystal castle of their own. Nobody would ever threaten her or her baby again.

The minister cleared his throat.

'Shall we begin?' he asked, smiling, and the adults stood in a rough semicircle around Faye: Alasdair gurgled happily in her arms, reaching up to the leaves that fell from the trees around them like a slow magic.

Faye nodded and folded the soft white blanket away from her son's cheek.

He had his father's eyes.

THE END

A Letter from Anna

Thank you so much for reading *Queen of Sea and Stars*. I hope you enjoyed it as much as I liked writing it. If you'd like to keep up-to-date with all of my latest releases, you can sign up at the following link. Your email address will never be shared, and you can unsubscribe at any time.

www.bookouture.com/anna-mckerrow

I came up with the idea for this book and the one before it, *Daughter of Light and Shadows*, when I was visiting family in Scotland. For this book, Scottish Faye comes to London, a city I have lived in for many years, and it was a delight to describe some of my many favourite places – Regent's Park and its romantic rose garden, Bloomsbury with its antique bookshops and mysterious history, and even the British Museum, one of my most favourite places to visit. Faye Morgan's homely magical shop *Mistress of Magic* has always belonged to her family, and in *Queen of Sea and Stars*, Faye finds a friend in another magic shop owner, Gabriel Black, who runs another type of magic shop entirely.

I am fascinated with Scottish faerie lore and when I write about it, I feel as though I'm a little bit "away with the faeries" myself. I'm also a little bit obsessed with magical shops, and that might be why I invented another two – *Fortune's* and *Star Herbs* – in this book.

If you have time, I'd love it if you were able to write a review of *Queen of Sea and Stars*. Feedback is really useful and also makes a huge difference in helping new readers discover one of my books for the first time.

Alternatively, if you'd like to contact me personally, you can reach me via my website, Facebook page, Twitter or Instagram. I love hearing from readers, and always reply.

Again, thank you so much for deciding to spend some time reading *Queen of Sea and Stars*. I'm looking forward to sharing my next book with you very soon.

With all best wishes,
Anna

www.annamckerrow.com

annamckerrowauthor

@AnnaMckerrow

@annamckerrow